THE SCARLET STILETTO

30 YEARS OF MYSTERY, MURDER AND MALICE

EDITED BY LINDY CAMERON

Clan Destine
PRESS

First published by Clan Destine Press in 2023

Clan Destine Press
PO Box 121, Bittern
Victoria, 3918 Australia

National Library of Australia Cataloguing-In-Publication data:

Editor: Cameron, Lindy

TITLE: The Scarlet Stiletto: 30 Years of Mystery, Murder & Malice

ISBN: 978-1-922904-62-1 (paperback)
ISBN: 978-1-922904-63-8 (eBook)

Cover Design by © Jill Cooper
Design & Typesetting by Clan Destine Press

Clan Destine
P R E S S

www.clandestinepress.net

Sisters in Crime Australia
dedicates this anthology to the writers of all
4332 stories entered – over three decades – in the annual
Scarlet Stiletto women's
crime and mystery short story competition.

Contents

In the Beginning

"What if we ran a short story competition?"

It was 1994 and the Sisters in Crime convenors were sitting round a table somewhere in St Kilda having lunch and plotting their next move. What we didn't know then, but do now, was that the next move would result in a competition that would run for over thirty years, attract 4,332 entries, launch the writing careers of a whole battalion of now famous crime writing women, and result in the collection of winning short stories you now hold in your hand.

'But what shall we call it?'

Almost more than merchandise and stationery, the Sisters love a good slogan or a good brand. In terms of a slogan, 'It's criminal what a girl's gotta do for a good read' was emblazoned on our highly collectible tee shirts. In terms of a brand, while we knew the Crime Writers Association in the UK had their Dagger Awards, what we wanted had to be something sharper, more lethal, more - dare we say it - more feminine/ist.

I can't remember who called it first, probably the supreme mistress of the double entendre, Lindy Cameron who is also the editor of this volume, but what we came up with was (customary drum roll please) The Scarlet Stiletto Award.

This immediately gave us the inspiration for the best crime trophy in the world – a red high-heeled shoe with its lethal steel heel plunged into a perspex mount. It was a perfect fit. The op shops of St Kilda were immediately raided for every red high-heeled shoe we could find, the Sisters being more inclined towards a comfy pair of flats than a murderous pair of tortuous heels.

In the first few years the awards, with prize money attached, went only to first, second and third prize stories, but many writers received Special Commendation certificates. Because we wanted to 'get them while they were young' the Best Young Writer award – for girls under 19 – was soon introduced. Gradually other categories were added to the competition and prize money pool: Malice Domestic, Best Film Idea, Cross Genre, History with Mystery, the Body in the Library, Most Satisfying Retribution.

The only criteria: the writer must be a woman, the main protagonist must be female, and the story must – obviously – be a crime or mystery story.

As someone who was closely involved in the judging process from the start, I can testify to the professionalism with which this was accomplished. Although it was, of course, another good reason to get together and have a party. Being a Sister has always been about having fun, even if our ultimate goal was to promote women's crime writing and create more opportunities for this to flourish. So we went away together for annual 'judging weekends' full of reading, laughing and arguing fueled by 'lashings of ginger beer', or something similar.

No names were attached to the stories. As a judge you were handed an anonymised bundle of typewritten pages that were read 'blind' to produce a long list that was hotly debated. Each judge had a first-round co-reader. It was, therefore, always an exciting moment when the 'reveal' occurred and we discovered just who our winner writers were.

When the same person won it twice in the first two years (and we are looking at our first winner here, Cate Kennedy, who would go on to have a short story published in *The New Yorker* no less), we instituted a new rule. Winning a pair of Scarlet Stilettos obliged the author to become a judge. So far this has happened an astonishing five times. The Sisters evidently have an eye for new talent.

Over the last thirty years our winners have included librarians, editors, teachers, union officials, journalists, public servants, psychologists, investigators, hairdressers, exercise instructors, medical autopsy specialists, doctors, pharmacists, cattery managers, mothers, retirees, and, very occasionally, former police officers and full-time writers – all of whom have drawn on their vast and varied experience to give us a range of short stories that narrate a crime from the point of view of an extraordinary diversity of characters from all walks of life.

This precious volume contains all 30 of the winning stories that are so different in their approach that it is evident that there is no 'right' way to write a winning Scarlet Stiletto story. Indeed, what the unpredictability of these stories suggest is that the more unconventional and original your take on the genre might be, the more likely you are to succeed. For example, there is even a crime story in verse and one from the point of view of a ghost.

Sometimes there were trends, like the year when a large number of stories seemed to be about women 'disappearing' their partners, a trend not reflected in the crime statistics we hasten to add. Another observation is the fact that not many of the winning stories featured conventional private detectives or investigators. But the Scarlet Stiletto writers *were* doing 'domestic noir', featuring women dealing with crime in the course of their daily lives, long before it became a subgenre of published crime fiction.

Reading through this collection, you will find stories that will make you laugh and make you weep. There are stories that are funny, heart-rending, terrifying and breathtaking in their beauty. You will meet women of all ages from all walks of life. You will be entertained, surprised and often moved. Perhaps even moved to enter your own short story in the next Scarlet Stiletto competition if you have not already done so.

So here it is. Thirty years of The Scarlet Stiletto in one volume. Read it, marvel, enjoy and be inspired. There's always another crime story to be told.

Senior Professor Sue Turnbull
Sisters in Crime Ambassador

1994

EVERYTHING $2 ON THE RACK

Cate Kennedy

WHY IS IT THAT IN THE FIRST SCENE OF PRIVATE EYE FILMS THE GUMSHOE gets visited by a breathless, ditzy blonde woman worried about her disappeared husband? Nobody like that ever came into my office. My stock-in-trade was more like the specimen in front of me now – male, mid-forties, thinning, paunching and practically wilting with tedium. He may as well have had "middle-management public servant" tattooed across his head. He sipped prissily at weak, white tea, sweetened with his own saccharine that he kept specially in his pocket.

I could feel a headache coming on.

'My wife's left me,' he said, 'and I want you to find her and find out why.'

I can tell you why now and save you the money, I felt like saying, but stayed quiet. I needed the work.

'Please go on, Mr Michaels.'

'I think she may have joined some weird cult.' His pale eyes blinked, his tone was solemn.

I needed a Disprin badly. 'With respect, Mr Michaels, that seems a little far-fetched.'

'You don't know Carol. She was always reading books about astrology and past lives. She had these ideas about the anti-aging process. We had to drink grass juice!'

The thought of wanting to prolong your time with this guy was a depressing one. He sat looking at me accusingly, as the coach-bolt was being tightened across my head.

'That doesn't really qualify as cult behaviour. Was there…anyone she was seeing?'

Always a delicate question, this one, when dealing with the rejected spouse; because nine times out of ten, there was.

'You mean an affair?'

'Well someone she may have wanted to…' The words 'escape with' hovered dangerously close; I changed them in the nick of time to, 'leave with.'

I was expecting a stinging retort to the contrary, but instead he slumped his round shoulders and looked defeated.

'There could have been,' he said helplessly. 'I hardly knew what was going on in Carol's head most of the time. If it wasn't belly dancing it was chant and be happy. She was talking about going to Nepal a few days before she left.'

It struck me that, even if a little eccentric, Carol Michaels was a good deal more interesting than her husband.

'I tried,' he was saying. 'She was dead keen on aquarobics all this spring, and she wanted to cash in some of my super to build a heated pool, so we started that. She had an appointment with the fellow to look over some pavers, trying to decide what colour we should landscape with around the pool area, then she up and left.'

I was beginning to like Carol Michaels more and more. I took a few notes, trying to shield my headache from the early summer glare outside.

'Did she take her passport?'

'I have no idea. I certainly can't find it anywhere. Mostly of her clothes are gone, and her make-up and what have you. She's got a sister in North Queensland she's thick as thieves with. Shirley's into this yoga and beansprouts business as well. Came down last year and they both went off to hear Shirley MacLaine talking about dolphin energy or something.'

'I'm actually more interested in the boyfriend angle,' I said, writing CD – my code for Complete Dill – in my notebook next to his name. 'Did she work with anyone likely, or was there a neighbour or friend?' I could imagine his wife, any woman, pulling the pin on this guy and shooting through; but with whom? Her aquarobics instructor? Was she at this moment reaching enlightenment in a Nepalese monastery with the guy from the health food shop?

'If it was anyone, it'd be the bloke from the nursery up the road,' said Bryan Michaels firmly, surprising me.

'Why do you feel that?' I pressed patiently, underlining the CD and putting a star next to it.

'She had him around all the time. They're always gossiping over catalogues and aromatherapy and what have you,' he sighed gustily. 'She's been consulting him about the meadow of native grasses she wants to turn the front lawn into.'

Suddenly, as I rooted in the desk drawer for a soluble aspirin, I felt a flash of pity for him. He couldn't help being a dullish, um – I consulted his details (oh my god, spare me) – pharmaceuticals salesman. Okay, so peddling new brands of casting plaster to dentists and trying to get enthused about thermometers could turn someone dull. Perhaps Carol Michaels was a flighty, fad-obsessed woman who'd just got it into her head to take off with the chap from the nursery. Maybe her husband was the long-suffering one.

'What's this guy's name; the nursery man?'

'Er, Haynes, Francis Haynes.' He gave me the address and I took copies of Carol's birth certificate, licence number and medical history, which he'd brought with him in a tidy file.

'I'll check whether your wife has used her passport or booked airline tickets somewhere. And I'll find out if this Haynes is missing too. Okay?' I smiled as winningly as I could under the circumstances.

He nodded rapidly, running his finger nervously under his collar. 'Getting very warm, isn't it?' he said, in a sudden attempt at small talk. 'Soon be summer.'

A thought struck me. 'Did your wife take summer or winter clothes, Mr Michaels?'

'Winter, sort of. Some sweaters and a coat, you know the kind of thing. Er, some slacks, a few long-sleeved shirts. Mostly she's taken to wearing those Indian-style clothes, cheesecloth baggy things – they're all gone too.'

I studied the photo he'd given me – a blurry shot of a woman at a barbecue, her plate piled high with tabouli. She looked distracted; her short hair blew in her face. She could have been anyone. She looked like a librarian, or the lady at your lead-lighting class. Her shirt was green-striped, with a long pointy collar, circa 1970s, and big red buttons.

'I'd like to see some more photographs, if I may; this one doesn't tell me much.'

'Yes, I'm not much of a photographer. I have an album at home. Would you like me to bring it in?'

'No. How about I drop by and see them tomorrow? Right now I'm going home to sit in a cold bathtub for a while.' I smiled wanly. The late afternoon sun was pouring through the window; we were both shiny with sweat, and my headache was still pounding at my temples.

Mr Michaels stood and nodded. 'I just want you to find her and ask what's going on,' he said.

'I'll make it my business,' I replied, rising to shake his hand.

The next morning was just as hot, as I drove slowly to his house – a bigger anonymous suburban number than I had imagined – and flanked on either side by dwellings based around the same generic plan. A huge hole had been torn into the back lawn, like tooth from a gum. I glanced down into it then made my way around the idle earth-moving machinery to the outdoor furniture set where my client sat, his hand on a photo album.

'Well, that's her pool,' said Bryan Michaels with a humourless smile.

'I never realised they made such a mess.'

'They have to dig down a fair way. Look at the rest of the lawn – it's ruined. And there's going to be another great truck here this afternoon when they come to pour the concrete.'

Again I felt a tweak of sympathy for the man left paying the bill for his wife's dream project.

'It might all be a misunderstanding, Mr Michaels,' I offered lamely. 'Your wife might just need some, um, space.'

'That sounds exactly like her,' he said bitterly.

'Let's look at your photos then, shall we?'

Here was Carol Michaels over a period of years. Bryan was right – her tastes in clothing had veered towards the floaty and ethnic of late; but she'd obviously always had individual tastes: a camel coat with a fur collar and kelly-green trousers, a pair of spotty bathers and a big straw hat. In each photo she smiled determinedly into the camera with mild blue eyes. It was hard to say whether she was shrewd or credulous, happy or sad. She had the kind of face that could slip into a crowd and not be noticed by airline stewards, hotel staff or the person at the corner shop. Tracking her down might be more difficult than I'd thought.

Up in her room, her wardrobe was pretty well cleared out, as well all the drawers. No jewellery left, no incriminating letters declaring ardent love for someone other than her husband, no notepads with hotel reservations conveniently outlined. I returned to Mr Michaels and the photos.

'Thanks for letting me see these, Mr Michaels. I'll take a couple for reference, if that's okay?'

'Certainly and now, if you'll excuse me, I have to deal with the tradesmen about the pebble-dash.'

I left and headed down to the local nursery, a patch of greenery in an industrial zone of hardware shops, car detailers and discount tyre marts. I wandered into the greenhouse area and gazed at some shrubs for a while, feeling guilty about my own garden or, rather, my eight square feet of decking.

'Can I help you at all?' A tall, extremely handsome young man was standing behind me, a spray pump in his hand.

'I'm looking for something that thrives on neglect.'

'Hmm, you'd better get a cactus. Although people don't realise how much water a cactus actually needs.'

'Well I can certainly simulate a desert environment,' I smiled. 'Actually I'm looking for a Francis Haynes, does he work here?'

'He certainly does; we run the place together.'

'Oh good. He's not on his summer holidays by any chance?'

'We never take holidays around here,' the guy laughed, heading for the greenhouse door. 'Hang on, I'll give him a yell.'

Francis Haynes, when he joined us a moment later, was the second most perfect specimen of manhood I'd seen. And both on the same day! I wondered if the heat was getting to me.

'What can I do for you?' he asked, taking off his sunglasses and wiping his forehead.

I told him my name and business. 'I'm wondering if you know a Mrs Carol Michaels?'

'Sure I do. Nice lady with a drip-dry husband. She comes in here often. We're helping her design a rockery landscape garden.'

'She seems to have left for parts unknown with person or persons unknown,' I said.

He raised his eyebrows. 'How intriguing. Good for her.'

'Her husband had a feeling she might have left with you.'

Francis looked at his business partner then they both looked at me, their mouths twitching. I'm slow – it took me about five seconds; and then we all burst out laughing.

When I took my leave with a cactus 10 minutes later, we were the best of friends.

So absolutely no leads there, I thought with a sense of frustration. Maybe I'd phone the sister in Queensland and see if Carol had gone there, or at the very least confided in her.

I'd just put the cactus in the car and was wondering if there was a café in walking or short driving distance, when I spotted the opportunity shop. Op-shops are my weakness. There's something about coming out with a bag full of stuff you've just bought for a couple of bucks that just lifts the spirits. I looked at my watch, decided I had a few minutes to spare and ducked inside.

Humming to myself I wandered up the aisle of $1 BARGAINS! and past the WOMEN'S WINTER TOPS to the rack that said ANTIQUE CLOTHES AND FANCY DRESS. Op-shops always have a rack like this – it's where they put unusual stuff. Once, in a small country op-shop in New South Wales, I found a fabulous red ball gown made in 1952... but I digress.

Something made me stop and focus on the $2 rack. Looking back, I marvel at the random set of circumstances that allowed me to fluke my best-ever find; and how close I'd come to resisting temptation and walking away to find some lunch.

I slowly reached out my hand for the coat-hanger, as a cold wave yawned up and turned over in my stomach, because there was the shirt, the green-striped '70s number with the pointy collar and red buttons. And a little further back on the rack was a camel-hair coat with a fur collar.

It was only later that I considered there could have been a different logical explanation for this. Carol Michaels could easily have cleaned out her own wardrobe on the way to her new life; she could have turfed all this old stuff into the op-shop bin on her way to the airport. I don't know why this sensible, perfectly feasible scenario didn't occur to me at once.

But I just knew, somehow, that that wasn't so. I knew, without a second thought, that all Carol's clothes would be here somewhere; along with her suitcase and make-up and the poor woman's stockings and underwear. I knew, because I felt tears of pity filling my eyes as I stood there holding her shirt with the childish buttons.

Fluking it – not a very professional investigative method I know, but there you are. And how can you say to a police detective you know and respect, 'Look, I just know she's dead because I'm already grieving for her.' Sometimes a person just has to take their stomach's word for something; and that's all there is to it.

I arrived back at my client's house a few minutes before the police.

I skirted a neat pile of pink and dove-grey pavers and caught the attention of the guy backing the concrete mixer up to the edge of that huge, dark, wet hole. When I flashed my ID he turned off the engine, leaving the mixer turning, and climbed out.

Bryan Michaels emerged from the house looking polite and helpful – wearing the professional face that no doubt helped him sell a lot of pharmaceuticals.

'I'm sorry,' I said loudly to the driver, 'but you won't be pouring any concrete here for a while.'

I watched Bryan Michael's face twist and sag.

'You ruthless bastard,' I said, hearing the doors slamming on the squad cars in the drive.

1995

Habit

Cate Kennedy

I'VE NEVER BEEN MUCH GOOD AT READING THE FINE PRINT ON CARDS, AND least of all after a 28 hour flight. But now that I was actually carrying three kilos of cocaine, I read the Customs declaration form with, you might say, a whole new vested interest. Any illegal or contraband goods? Well, you'd have to be pretty jetlagged to fall into that trap, wouldn't you? "Tick no". Any weaponry? Any exotic flora or fauna?

'They must think we're idiots,' says the person next to me, an insufferable bore in black leather pants that have squeaked ever since we left Singapore.

Well, no, they don't think we're idiots. It's the only way to nail us if we're carrying anything, otherwise we can plead ignorance of the law. I don't tell him this, of course. It would be open provocation to continue talking to me, and the last thing I want is another instalment of his failed marriage. I seem to be inviting confession and disclosure, and I wonder why: people have been doing it to me since boarding the first plane in Bogotá. My silence seems only to encourage them.

I am also steeling myself for the three questions, the three biggies they hit you with as your suitcase hits the examination table. 'Is this your luggage?' 'Did you pack it yourself?' 'Are you aware of its contents?'

Then they pull open the zip and all bets are off; you're cactus. Foolish couriers, in these intolerably stressful circumstances, take a couple of tranqs to settle their nerves for this ordeal. Personally I can't think of anything that would give me away more than pinhole pupils and a Mogadon stupor.

I suppose I should say a few words about the cocaine.

'An illegal drug, certainly, but a word in my defence, Your Honour.' I have, I suppose, a habit – if you can call three snorts a habit – because they instilled in me a craving for the drug that surpasses mere physical hankering. Three years ago I tried some street coke and the hit was just enough, through the Glucodin and speed percentage which seared into my nasal cavities, to make me make a vow to myself. I decided that, if I ever had the chance, I would try the real thing: the purest, whitest, Colombian cocaine available to the casual buyer.

As I said, that was a few years ago now, at a party where most people were on the nod around the room with alcohol and dope. With narcotic drugs, in fact. Ridiculously, cocaine is also classified as a narcotic drug, and that evening illustrated for me that misnomer, the vast gulf between cocaine's effects and alcohol's effects.

Me and a few friends mashed the grass down in the back yard with our dancing. I went straight from the party to work and put in a good day. When I got home and pondered on my energy, rapier-like memory retention and sparkling intellect, I made the decision that, if one day I had nothing to lose, I'd make the trip myself and take the risk, to buy enough coke to last me the distance.

And it's not long to go now, that distance. I have a trusted doctor, Dr Mick I-won't-tell-you-his-last-name, who'll keep me out of jail, if it comes to that, on humanitarian grounds. He'll show the court the x-rays, the images of "the shadow" and its advance, and the judge's heart will be wrung with sympathy. At least, that's what I'm banking on. A year – 18 months or whatever it is – I want to spend it full of energy and memory and sparkle, not dry-retching into a bucket after pointless chemotherapy.

So, here I am on the plane, inviting intimate disclosures from the squeaker, with my pen hovering over the box that could seal my fate: Have you anything to declare?

Well, yes, as a matter of fact, I have. I declare that if I get out if this airport intact, undiscovered, I will put one bag of cocaine aside and savour the rest slowly, sit up at night feeling awake and powerful and not sick, and write letters to everyone I need to, to be opened at the party at which my Will will be read out.

My Will, for what it's worth. My spotless record as a youth worker has left me with no assets outside a VCR so ancient that no-one can repair it and no-one in their right mind would steal, a flat full of furniture that may as well go straight back down to St Vinnies, and a collection of books that friends will find are mostly theirs, anyway. Not even a car. I sold the car, to pay for the airline ticket to South America. So, sue me. And as for the cocaine, I cashed in my super. Hell, you may as well spend it while you've got it; you can't take it with you. No, indeed.

I've read up a lot about cocaine. A wonder drug, mistreated cruelly. More sinned against than sinning. More maligned than malignant. A perfect anaesthetic and, many exponents say, completely non-habit-forming. I will give that theory a run for its money, and get back to you. If there's an addiction to be had, I volunteer to be the one to take it on. I go now bravely where no-one has gone before, fully cognisant.

In fact, in all respects, without parallel, it seems to me, it is non-addictive except as a painkiller. No, heroin must take that crown. Hence the third bag. The Exchange Bag.

Many years ago there was a preparation available in hospices for terminally ill patients called Brompton's Mixture, which alleviated both the pain and the terror of dying and it was composed – you can look this up if you like – of cocaine and heroin. Brompton's Cocktail. Brompton's Elixir. The gods must quaff this stuff in Heaven. I'm not ashamed to say it was this information, about the painkilling, which played a big part in my decision. I've taken enough paracetamol to make my kidneys unfit for organ donation, even if anyone was stupid enough to want to take them.

'I'm not looking forward to the pain side of things,' I told Doctor Mick.

'There's always morphine,' he said, and I imagined myself, in a bed hard and crisp as a white envelope, tubes up my nose and arms, souped to the eyeballs on morphine and trying to tell my friends what I thought of them. Not a good look. Not at all. I want to be jolly and on my feet and full of the kind of wit that people will repeat at my wake. I'm only 32, God help me. I want to mash the grass down with my dancing, and one day fall as gracefully as a leaf. Once you decide to take a risk with a clear head and full knowledge of all possible consequences, you're filled with calm.

'I don't want any of these drugs,' I had told Doctor Mick with a firm resolve, gesturing to his happy little chart of radiotherapy and chemotherapy treatments. 'You've said yourself that it's too far gone'.

'Well, I shouldn't have said that,' he replied, in a miracles-can-happen voice.

'I'll choose my own drugs,' I'd said, for at that point the Colombian option had occurred to me.

'Well, you let me know if there's anything I can do for you,' he'd replied sombrely. And I'd looked over at him, suddenly remembering doctors were allowed to sign passport applications.

The thing is, I still feel reasonably okay. On a sunny day, when you're about to start a descent through angel clouds to land back in your home town, it's just too hard to comprehend. I have an image of this thing on my X-rays, and it's low and it's dark. And so I will combat it, with high and with white.

Narcotrafico. My magic crystals. The no-smoking lights go on and I tune back into the guy next to me, who's setting off a volley of new squeaks as he settles into his seatbelt.

'I don't suppose you've ever smoked,' he's saying to me.

'No, never.' I allow myself a small smile. 'We-e-e-ll…maybe a few puffs at school once, when we were all trying to be daring.'

He smiles and nods as I go back to my declaration, and tick that yes, I do have something to declare.

Then I fold up my table, get out my passport, and it's in the hands of the gods.

Jesus, Mary and Joseph. A perverse decision on my part, a memory of my Irish grandfather's favourite oath. A handful of coins each at the stall. All three looking grave, as if understanding what was going down. Jesus, like his dad, holding a carpenter's tool against his flowing cloak. I wonder if, had they made him make his own cross, would he have chiselled and mortised the joints? Now, that would be dying with dignity.

We descend, land and taxi into the unloading zone. I'm hot in my blue dress; it's sticking to my back. It's a wash and wear synthetic and I'm going to bundle it up and throw it in the garbage first thing when I get home. When I get home. I close my eyes and call up a vision of the kitchen, the smell of the lino, the chug of my ancient fridge. If all goes well, I can be there in a couple of hours. Just through Customs, a short trip through the airport, past security, and into the taxi rank. I imagine pulling away in a cab, away from the airport and home free.

The thing to do now is forget about the cocaine, pretend I really am an innocent person. I keep my face demure as I watch the luggage turning on the silver conveyers. My case is an absolutely nondescript black. A luggage label is tied carefully to the handle in Spanish and English. Inside there are two changes of clothes, my toiletries and towel, a spare pair of shoes and three kilos of cocaine. Wonderful, splendid cocaine, meltingly pure and snowy. My superannuation fund brochure had outlined many exciting ways to spend your payment, but up your nose was not one of them.

I pick up the case. I carry it carefully to the Customs declaration points and stand in a queue at the first gateway. I find that if I keep my mind on home and refuse to think about where I am, I can keep my heart rate down. Meditation, taken under sufferance at Dr Mick's urging, is proving to be an unexpected bonus. I meditate on the Customs Officer's hands as he takes my passport and declaration and notes things down, ticks boxes, glances into my face to check the likeness in the photo. His pen hesitates.

'Something to declare?'

'Yes.'

'Go to number Seven at the end there. Thank you.'

Thank YOU. Gates one to six, green lights, are choked with people, children, luggage trolleys, and bags. They will be hours. Number seven, a red light, has two people standing in it, both holding yellow plastic bags of duty free and whatever else they think is declarable. As I move into place behind them the first one sorts out his query about camera lenses and moves off. Through this gateway is the escalator, then the forecourt, then the self-opening doors to International Arrivals, then onto the windy pavement of the airport and the taxis. God, God. Hold it together.

'I bought these lily bulbs in the airport in Hawaii,' the punter in front of me is saying, 'and the girl said they're vacuum sealed and OK to take through without quarantine.'

'I'm afraid there's always someone who'll tell you that,' says the man in the uniform shortly. My heart rate, despite me, goes up a few notches. A closed face, an unhappy mouth, a stickler for the rules and in a bad mood to boot. 'They're illegal to import.'

'What do I have to do? Have them sprayed?'

'No, I'm afraid you have to surrender them to Customs to dispose of.'

Down into the big chute they go. The passenger looks glum, but he's also through declarations in record time. I wonder if it was a deliberate ploy. His bags are searched in a rudimentary fashion.

Cocaine is also surrendered to Customs upon detection, and destroyed. Breaks your heart to think of it. All that brain-sharpening, energy-giving, nausea-suppressing potential chucked away. I make my brain go somewhere else, focused anywhere rather than on the case in front of me. It has been my experience working with juvenile offenders that when they have stolen something their eyes keeping swerving back to where they have hidden it. If it is secreted on their person they can't seem to stop their hands going to the place. I look away but there suddenly seems remarkably few places to look. My turn. Five minutes and I'm out. Five minutes. Jesus, Mary and Joseph.

'Good morning. Something to declare?'

A deep breath. Hold body still, hold head still. Head-waggers are liars. 'Yes, I think so.'

I reach over and snap open my own suitcase, and dig down the side. 'I thought I'd better check, better to be safe than sorry.'

I find the bottle and bring it out. He looks at it, noticing the seal, the liquid inside. He doesn't look surprised. Oh God, has this been tried before?

'It's holy water, you see. From the font at the Sisters of Mercy mission in Popayan.'

He checks my passport stamps. 'That's where you've just come from?'

'Yes, for the Semana Santa. I promised I'd try to get some for an ill friend. Does it have to be confiscated?'

He pauses, rubs his chin. 'Look, I'm afraid so. That water could contain all kinds of bacteria.'

'I just thought...since it was sealed...' I trail off. 'That's all right, I don't want to get you into trouble. I suppose the idea of water having healing properties seems quite ridiculous to you.'

He looks up briefly and gives me a quick, tired grin. 'Not at all. I'm a Catholic. Or was.' He reaches over and opens the suitcase. 'Is this your luggage?'

'Yes.'

'Did you pack it yourself?'

'I did, yes.'

'Are you aware of its contents?'

'Yes'.

He moves my clothes aside and takes out the three newspaper-wrapped packages. As he unrolls one I have a sense of standing looking at this scene as if through a long lens, the edges grey and prickling. When this happened when I was a child, it meant I was about to faint. Blue and white plaster appears, the face simpering with goodness. He raises his eyebrows enquiringly.

'It's a statuette of Our Lady, from the sisters at the convent,' I say.

He holds it in his hand. I concentrate on the bottom of the statue for a moment, down by the foot where she's crushing the snake, down where the minutest crack can be seen in the plaster. It's smooth but not machine smooth, not solid-cast. No, it's been smoothed by hand, sitting on the floor of Emilia's kitchen with plaster mixed up in an old tin. Me having an attack of nerves and gabbling about taking it back, forgetting the whole thing, pissing off home. Emilia's low and sombre voice as she crouched there: I took this risk for you, yeah? Now you take risk for yourself. It will work, you trust me. It will work.

I can't drag my eyes away from that rough spot of plaster. Maybe it's an uncontrollable reflex after all. I look at the newspaper. The hands start wrapping the statue up again with quite careful deliberation, and he goes to unwrap the other two. Then hesitates. Oh Jesus, oh God, I promise that with whatever time I have left I'll sing nothing but glory and praise to the short gift of my life, just please don't let him look too closely. I look at the coloured stamps on my passport, the ridiculous photo that Dr Mick had signed after a similar long silence of fervent prayer on my part, and professional hesitation on his.

The Customs guy smooths the newspaper and packs the statues carefully back in the case.

'I'm afraid I have to confiscate the water,' he says, his face grave.

I lower my eyes. 'Well, don't feel badly. I should have known you'd have to.'

He leans closer to me – God, another person about to betray an intimate confidence.

'You know what we sometimes do,' he says in a low voice. 'If the person's a really devout Catholic, say, and they've just made a lifetime trip to Lourdes, and the bottle's unsealed, then I say I just need to take the holy water into the quarantine office for a moment. Then I tip it into the disposal bin, and fill up the vial with ordinary water out of the tap, and take it back out to them. And they're as happy as Larry.'

He smiles again and I smile back, finding it easy now to look straight back into his eyes. 'Thank you for telling me that story,' I answer, 'because it doesn't matter a bit, you know, whether it comes from Lourdes or the tap. It's the faith that matters, the faith that heals. That's how you're blessed.'

He snaps my suitcase shut for me and turns it towards me, stamps my passport and hands it back.

'I'll let you get on your way then, Sister,' he says. 'Best of luck for the future.'

'Thanks,' I say, moving away towards the escalator and the doors out. There's a future out there all right, and once I get this outfit off I'm not going to miss one sweet open-mouthed breath of it. I am as light as a cloud as I walk towards the doors. I am as free as air. I am blessed.

1996

Luisa

Christina Lee

I LOST TOUCH WITH LOUISE AFTER WE LEFT SCHOOL. YES, I KNOW I SHOULD call her Luisa, but I still think of her as Louise. No, I never asked about the new name. It didn't seem polite, like bringing up some awfully embarrassing thing that someone did when they were 12. Anyway, she did Arts at Sydney Uni and I was going out to Lidcombe every day for the physio course, and we just never saw each other. When I met her again she was Luisa.

It was at Jacquie and Belinda's party. I'd actually met Jacquie as a patient. Lateral ligament, left ankle, quite a nasty sprain. It's a classic netball injury but in her case it was line dancing. I'd never even heard of line dancing then, can you believe it? Well, I'd led a pretty sheltered life. The physio course was pretty demanding, and then when you graduated it was all shift work and long hours and you tended only to socialise with other physios. That's how I met Mark, of course. Physios are very nice people but I suppose Jacquie would say we're a bit straight. Certainly, we seemed to live in a different world from her and Belinda.

I don't usually socialise with patients, but Jacquie was lovely and it turned out that she and her friend Belinda lived just around the corner. And the ankle had healed up beautifully, so she wasn't an ongoing case or anything. Besides, most of a physio's patients are about ninety. People tend to think we spend our days treating football players for groin injuries and massaging Olympic swimmers, and so on, but in fact it's mostly strokes, rheumatoid arthritis, and post-surgical. So Jacquie made a nice change. She used to giggle if it hurt and tell me funny stories about her job and her flatmate, and so on. Which certainly made a change.

So I said yes, we'd love to come, although I was a bit doubtful about how Mark would take it, going to a party with a bunch of people we didn't know. But in the end he had a marvellous time; even though, well, I know I should have twigged after all the stories Jacquie had told me about Belinda this and Belinda that and the things they did together, trekking in Nepal and backpacking in Europe, and all the rest of it.

But as I said, I do lead a fairly conventional life and it really wasn't until we got to the party and they were standing there arm-in-arm that I realised.

I mean, it's not like I'd never met a gay person or anything. Now I come to think of it, I'm sure a couple of the girls in my year were lesbians. But you didn't talk about that sort of thing, so I suppose it never occurred to me. I don't really see why it should be such a big thing; I mean, you're there to do a job and what you do in your own time is your own business, isn't it?

Anyway, Mark took it all in his stride. He kissed them both on the hand and turned on the smile and in about two seconds they were running around finding him a glass of champagne and taking his new distressed leather jacket off to the coat heap in the bedroom and introducing him to people left, right and centre.

I turned around, and there was Louise. Of course, she'd changed a lot. When we were at school she had long bunches of fat white ringlets and lots of pimples. Now she was very tanned and athletic-looking, and she had a sophisticated cropped haircut and one of those short slim little dresses that just yelled at you that here was a girl who grew up on the North Shore and whose daddy gave her a monthly clothing allowance.

'Jane,' she said to me. 'What a surprise. Have you got a drink?'

So she got me a drink and we caught up on what had happened to us. For me, of course, it was pretty simple; physio, six months working in London, back here to marry Mark and a job at the Prince of Wales. For her, as you might have expected, there was rather more to tell, and I must confess that I never really did get the whole story straight. The arts degree, yes, but all the sailing in the Med with Jean Paul and skiing at Val d'Isere with Claudio and the study exchange in Padua and the part-time job in Seville; it all got a bit complicated.

Anyway, she said she was a freelance writer, which confirmed my suspicion that her daddy was paying her an allowance, and she lived in the flat next door and knew Jacquie and Belinda from a publishing party. Most of the people at this party were in publishing or writing, because Jacquie is an editor at a big publishing house and Belinda tutors in creative writing, so of course most of their friends are writers and such.

Well, after we'd got all that sorted out, she looked over my shoulder and asked me to introduce her to Mark because she was really looking forward to talking to someone who wasn't a friend of Dorothy's for a change. I didn't know Dorothy, either, and I was going to say so. But Louise was the sort of woman who, when she said "someone", you knew that other women didn't count.

So I took her over to Mark and she held out her hand and said, 'Hi, I'm Luisa.' That was the first I heard of this Luisa business, and I was going to ask, but just then Jacquie came bouncing up and dragged me off to look at the knee of a friend who'd fallen off his high heels. And the friend's knee turned out to be perfectly all right, he just wanted a photo of himself in drag having his leg massaged. So we had a lot of champagne, and he and his friend kept taking photos of people doing outrageous things, which made them do even more outrageous things, and the next time I looked at my watch it was half past one and we had to go.

Mark was still talking to Louise, and he kept saying how wonderful it was that she and I had met up again after so long and we would have to keep in touch, and the friend with the knee took a photo of me hugging Louise and another of Mark and Jacquie drinking champagne out of each other's glasses. It wasn't at all the sort of party we usually go to.

Well, I dropped over to Jacquie and Belinda's a couple of days later with some flowers to say thank you, and Louise was there, sitting at the kitchen table drinking peppermint tea, and I wound up staying talking for hours. After that it just became a habit. I had an early shift most Wednesdays and Mark was hardly ever at home; he had a private sports physio business as well as the hospital job, so there was nothing much to hurry home for.

I would buy a few Hungarian cakes and then go to Jacquie and Belinda's. We'd have tea and cakes, and then they'd sit at the kitchen table writing or talking and I'd cook and then we'd all eat. Luisa wasn't there all that often after the first time, and usually she didn't stay long if she was. She said she was very busy on a writing project, but Jacquie said that she had been saying that ever since she moved in next door and as far as she knew Luisa had never published anything.

They talked a lot about books. Belinda wrote short stories and reviews and magazine articles, and she always had stacks of creative writing exercises to mark and, of course, both of them read all the time. It was very different from our place; we had a lot of books, too, but they were mostly anatomy textbooks and things like that.

One week, Belinda asked me if I'd read a story she had just had published in a short-story magazine. She'd never shown me anything she'd written before and I was quite flattered to be asked. So I sat there and tried to concentrate while she pottered around the kitchen making curry.

It was about a physiotherapist called Madeleine who falls in love with a patient, who's a woman, but the woman's got this great boyfriend and isn't interested. At the end, the boyfriend turns out to be the physio's ex-husband. So this woman she's become so keen on is the same person as the bitch who stole her husband.

It sounds rather ordinary like that, but it was a lovely story. The physio realises that she's been feeling sorry for herself, and she's been blaming the new girlfriend for her own misery, without even knowing her. And she realises it's time she got on with her own life.

The disturbing thing, though, was that it was about me. Well, not about me; I mean nothing like that has ever happened to me, but it was me, all the same.

When I'd finished, Belinda turned around from the stove and said, 'What do you think?'

I must have looked a bit shocked, because she said, 'Oh, no, I've upset you, haven't I?'

I said, 'It's me, isn't it?'

She said, 'Umm...in a way.'

And I said, 'But I'm not like that. I haven't got a thing about an old boyfriend and...' and I stopped, because I was going to say I wouldn't fall in love with a woman, but I couldn't think of a way to say that to Belinda without sounding rude.

She poured me a drink and said, 'But that's what writing's all about. You start with something real and you think, what if this happened, or that happened, and it turns into something else. You were telling me once about touching people who were very unattractive and how you coped with it. So I started thinking about how a physio would cope with having to touch someone she found very attractive, and it grew from there.'

I was a bit puzzled. I understood what she meant, all right, but I wasn't too sure about it. I suppose I'd never thought about where writers got their ideas from. But, of course, what else could they possibly do; they take incidents from other people's lives and turn them into something else. But when you read something, you don't think about the friend or whoever started the whole thing, and how maybe how they felt about it.

It did feel a bit uncomfortable, but I couldn't really see what she had done wrong. Anyway, just then Jacquie came in and we wound up having a really interesting talk about writers and how they steal events out of their friends' lives or things they read in the paper or conversations they overhear on the train.

'That's what creative writing is all about,' said Jacquie, pouring us all another drink. 'Taking things that you hear about and turning them into something different, something that expresses a new truth.' She talked like that sometimes.

I still wasn't too sure about it all, but when I told Mark later that night, he couldn't see what the problem was.

'She wrote a story about a physio. You're not the only physio in the world. What's the big deal?' he said. 'She met you, it made her think about physios, she wrote a story. She's a writer.' And he turned over and went to sleep.

Put like that, it sounded pretty reasonable. But it wasn't just a story about physios, it was a story about me. Once I got over the initial shock, though, I decided it was quite flattering. I mean, how many other people have had stories written about them? So the next week I took her a bunch of orchids. To say thank you, or sorry, or something.

And so life went on. Mark was working long hours, and I found myself looking forward more and more to seeing Jacquie and Belinda each Wednesday. Sometimes we'd go out together on a Saturday, too, to big raucous pubs or little jazz clubs. Luisa came along every now and then, but not all that often. I had a feeling that she saw us as a fall-back option, for nights when she didn't have a date with some man.

Anyway, it was all very settled. Like family, really. So when I came in to the flat one afternoon with my bag of sticky cakes and found the two of them just sitting there, in this awful, oppressive silence, with no books on the table and no drinks or snacks or newspapers or any of the usual clutter, I got this heart-in-my-mouth feeling and stopped in the doorway. At first I thought that somebody must have died, except that they were both looking angry rather than sad, so then I wondered if they had had a fight.

Jacquie looked up and I could see that she was making a big effort to pretend that everything was okay and that she was just about to offer to put the kettle on or something. But if they were upset about something, then as a friend I should ask about it, so I put my bag down and asked what was wrong.

Belinda sort of groaned and ran her hand over her face as if she had to do that to stop herself hitting something, and Jacquie went over and picked up a book that was lying on the floor. That was odd in itself, because they were very careful about books. They certainly never left them on the floor. And there was something about the way this one was lying that gave the distinct impression that it had been thrown.

'What do you think of this?' she asked in a grim sort of voice.

It was a paperback with a sort of mediaeval-looking woodcut of four women dancing together on the cover, done in purple and green and with the two colours printed crookedly, so it was like seeing double. Pretty Maids All in a Row, it said, by Luisa Mayfield. And underneath, in smaller writing, "The book that lifts the lid on lesbian Sydney".

'Luisa's book,' I said, stupidly. 'She's finished it.'

I looked at the two of them, who glared back at me.

'But...' I persisted, dropping my eyes to the book again. The blurb on the back described it as a rollicking lesbian love story set in the pubs, clubs and back lanes of Paddinghurst. There was a black-and-white photo of Luisa sitting in a cafe wearing a grunge cardigan and smoking, which I had never seen her do, and underneath it said "a witty, fast-paced tour de force".

I looked back at the two of them. I didn't know what to say. I suppose I'd expected them to be pleased that Luisa had got her novel published, they were always pleased when their other friends had things published, but obviously there was something terribly wrong.

'Oh, Jane,' said Belinda. 'For heaven's sake. I know you're naive but you're not stupid. Can't you see how insulting it is? That girl is not a lesbian, she's got absolutely no understanding of what's important. How dare she write a book about it?'

'But,' I said, and then stopped, because I didn't know what to say next. Fortunately I had a bottle of wine in my bag, so I pulled it out, opened it, and poured us all a glass. We all drank and I thought they'd both calmed down. Jacquie certainly seemed happier; she got a bowl of olives and feta cheese out of the fridge and things started to feel almost normal again.

'Stupid girl,' she said in a dismissive sort of way, and I had the feeling that whatever it was about, was over. Boy, was I wrong.

'Explain it to me,' I persisted. They usually liked me asking dumb questions. 'Why shouldn't she write about lesbians? I mean, can't people write about whatever they like?'

Well, that was entirely the wrong thing to say. Or perhaps the right thing, I don't know. Belinda was still absolutely hopping mad, and I really set her off. The arrogation of the subjective experiences of an oppressed societal group by a member of the oppressors, a woman who spent her entire life chasing men while ridiculing other women, exploiting her few female friendships, using a false voice to give the wider public a distorted view of Luisa Mayfield and a distorted view of lesbian life.

'And the thing that really hurts,' added Jacquie, who had got steamed up again while she was listening to Belinda, 'is that there she is, right next door, and did she ever talk to us about it? Did she ever discuss her ideas with us? Did she ever tell us her plans? Did she even have the decency to show us a copy? Oh, no. This just turned up on my desk at work. In the recent-publications-from-rival-publishers heap. That's the first I knew that our precious Luisa was actually putting pen to paper instead of just talking about it.'

A few months ago I would have been really intimidated by the amount of anger that was flying around in that kitchen, but they were always telling me that society tried to control women by making them afraid of negative

31

emotions and that one had to have the courage to face anger and learn to deal with it. So I gritted my teeth and kept right on going.

'Well,' I said. 'I can see you're both terribly upset.' Jacquie had told me that acknowledging another's negative feelings was often a good way of neutralising them, so I thought I'd give that a go too. 'And, I know you wouldn't be upset without good reason. But I don't understand. Isn't this what a writer does, taking what she sees and turning it into a story?'

'There's taking and then there's taking,' said Belinda. 'The thing is, lesbians, genuine lesbians, have fought for the right to have our voice heard. And now, here she is, never had to fight for anything in her life, calmly taking that voice and using it, not in solidarity, but to exploit an oppressed group of women, to use us to further her so-called career as a so-called writer.'

Well. It was one of those nights when we drank and talked until two in the morning. I could sort of see what Belinda was getting at, although I still wasn't sure how it was different from her writing about a physio when she wasn't one. Although, of course, physios have never had to pretend to be something else, or been insulted in public. Belinda talked a lot about what it was like, how hard it was, how her parents didn't understand and that some of her oldest friends wouldn't bring their children to visit. I must say I had no idea; I mean, why would anyone care about what other people do at home in private?

Anyway, we wound up deciding that Luisa could do whatever she wanted, why should we care, and I slept the night on the couch. When I got home at about eight the next morning, Mark was hopping mad. He said he'd been really, really worried about me, and how was he to know where I'd been, and he'd been that close to calling the police. So I told him all about it. I suppose it was bad timing more than anything – he must have been really worried and upset and obviously he can't have slept properly – because he called them a couple of stupid bitches and said he thought they were just jealous that Luisa had written something good enough to get published. Then he grabbed his distressed leather jacket and said he'd be home late, and pushed off.

Well, that wasn't much help, but it had been a bit stupid of me not to call and let him know where I was, so of course he would have been worried. But I had to get to work, too, so there was no time to think about sorting things out with Mark till later.

And then later that day I heard the news on the radio in the hospital cafeteria. I don't usually bother too much about the news, but the name Luisa Mayfield caught my attention while I was having lunch.

Louise had won a prize: the Voices of Diversity Award for New Literature.

Well. At least I had some idea what to expect when I got round to Belinda and Jacquie's this time, but even so it was a bit of a shock. Luisa had dropped in to see them; she wanted to borrow Jacquie's Reclaim The Night T-shirt for a television interview, and Belinda had screamed at her, and Luisa had screamed right back, and now Belinda was sobbing quietly in a corner and Jacquie was planning some horrid revenge.

I didn't stay long. I don't think I could ever get to like that sort of atmosphere, whatever Belinda says about how liberating it is; and anyway, I wanted to be home when Mark got in. Only he didn't get in until midnight, which meant I wound up seeing Luisa on the television. She was wearing a pink triangle t-shirt, and the interviewer was gushing about her wonderful book and the film rights and the overseas rights. Luisa didn't get a chance to say much but she was looking pretty pleased with herself.

The next few days I seemed to see Luisa everywhere I looked. The bookshop next to the bus stop had a huge window display of her books, with big photos of her and blow-ups of the cover, and there were articles in the newspapers about her novel, which everyone said was daring and fresh and exciting. I started wondering whether I ought to buy a copy, since it did sound rather good.

I hadn't seen much of Jacquie and Belinda because I was trying to get things back on a better footing with Mark. He really couldn't see what Jacquie and Belinda were so upset about. He just kept saying that Luisa could write about lesbians if she wanted to; it was only a novel after all. He actually had a copy of the book, though neither of us read it. It was hidden away in his underwear drawer, which I thought was pretty odd, but I supposed that it was just his way of avoiding even more conflict. And it did seem silly for us to be fighting over something that Luisa had done.

The next thing I knew, there was this huge feature article in the Sydney Morning Herald. "Will the Real Luisa Mayfield Please Stand Up. Written by Belinda". It was brilliant. All those things she'd said to me about betrayal and dishonesty and bad faith and so on, all turned into this really good argument about how outrageous it was and how nobody should buy the book because it exploited lesbians.

I read the article in the cafeteria at lunchtime, and I went straight over that night to the flat and told Belinda how good it was. She gave me a hug and said, 'I'm glad you're back on our side,' which I wasn't too sure how to take, but I hugged her back and she cracked some champagne. Quite like old times.

Anyway, as you know, things really heated up after that. Louise just disappeared. The papers said she had gone to the Blue Mountains but of course I found out later that she was still around.

But lots of other people jumped in to the argument. The people who had decided on the prize said that they didn't care whether she was a lesbian or not; they couldn't see that it changed the quality of the book, and they thought it was a good book. And a group called the Sydney Attack Lesbians said that this just showed that the judges were a bunch of doddery old heterosexual fools and that lesbian writing should be read only by lesbians. And some other people said that a novel is fiction; Luisa had the right to write fiction about people who were different from herself if she wanted, and at least it wasn't a boring, thinly disguised autobiography like most first novels.

And a couple of academics wrote articles saying that it was exactly the same issue as with B. Wongar, only since I'd never heard of B. Wongar, it didn't really shed much light on the situation for me. And, sales of Louise's book kept going up. They brought out a new edition with "The most controversial book of the decade" across the front. I kept dropping in at Belinda and Jacquie's flat, which had become a sort of a nucleus for the anti-Luisa camp, and then going home to Mark, who kept saying that there was no such thing as bad publicity and that Luisa should dedicate her next book to Belinda, with thanks for all her help, and that Belinda was taking the whole thing far too personally. The book was being read by lots of people who didn't know Belinda from a bar of soap and didn't care whether Luisa was a lesbian or not, so what was she worried about? I was pretty confused.

In the meantime, I actually read it, and I must say it was really good. Very funny, with lots of action. I didn't tell Jacquie or Belinda that. But of course that wasn't what they were upset about, anyway.

Well, after a bit, things started to die down. Novels aren't the most exciting thing in the world, and there was an election coming up and more stuff about police corruption, and it all sort of quietened down. Luisa's publisher sold the US rights to Pretty Maids All in a Row for some enormous amount of money but nobody except Luisa really cared.

Belinda still used to make comments about Luisa, but more out of habit than anything else. She was editing a book of poems to come out during the Mardi Gras and that was taking up a lot of her time. Jacquie was busy, too. And I was worried about Mark, who hardly ever seemed to be home these days, and who always seemed really tired. I wanted him to ease off on the extra work but he said he was really starting to get somewhere with the sports physio and he didn't have time to ease off. He didn't seem happy, and I had this feeling that our marriage was going through a bad patch, so I was trying as hard as I could to be there as much as possible.

But tonight he was out, so I was cutting onions for a curry in Jacquie and Belinda's kitchen when Belinda walked in and handed me this magazine. There was a photo of Louise on the cover and the blurb said, "Luisa Mayfield tells: My secret lesbian lover".

I couldn't believe my eyes.

It was me.

There were two pictures. One was at that party where we'd met again, and there I was, looking pretty drunk, actually, with Luisa giving me a big hug, and some man dressed in feathers in the background. It was the other that really shocked me, though, because it was a photo of me at the beach, lying on my front with my bikini straps all undone and sort of laughing up at the camera. You could see about a mile of cleavage and I was looking awfully relaxed and happy. Of course, the implication was that I was looking at Luisa, only of course I hadn't been, I'd been looking at Mark.

I just saw red. How dare she? I didn't know what was worse, coming around and stealing my photos, or telling these terrible lies about me. I didn't even put the onion knife down, I just walked straight across the landing to her flat.

It's exactly the same as Jacquie and Belinda's flat, only mirror image. You walk straight in and turn left and there you are in the kitchen. She wasn't in the kitchen and I was so upset that for a moment I didn't even stop to wonder what Mark's distressed leather jacket was doing hanging over that chair; it was such a familiar jacket, and the kitchen was so familiar, that it seemed perfectly natural. In fact, it wasn't until I went down the passage and into the bedroom that I realised. A lot of things. Suddenly. Why Mark was always so tired, why he was out so late, why Luisa used to nip off as soon as I turned up anywhere, how she had got my photo for that filthy magazine article.

And now I've got blood all over my work clothes.

1997

FLOATING IN A LIVE CIRCUIT

Siobhan Mullany

DOTTY SAT IN THE CAR, CONTEMPLATING HER UNDERWEAR. WAS IT SUITABLE TO die in? She wanted to go the toilet.

The car was a live but floating circuit. Dotty knew the game. She could earth it, and die, by getting out. The car, now shorted out, rolled to a stop neatly inside the garage. The garage door slid down behind her. The plan was as good as he'd predicted.

The spark that flashed off the bonnet was confirmation that Dave carried out his plans. He killed people. He was finally going to kill her and no one would know. She would die of a heart attack caused by the electric shock. The beauty of the scheme was that she had an irregular heartbeat, documented by her doctor. The shock would leave no trace. Dave would turn off the power and put the wiring back in place. The ambulance would be called to treat her, sadly too late, for a heart attack. Dave would have won. Simple.

Dotty looked through the doorway into the kitchen. Dave sat just inside. His square body planted in a hard-backed chair, elbow leaning on the bench, feigning casual ease, his tension betrayed by the drumming of his fingernails on the bench-top. He loved this.

'You mad bastard,' Dotty yelled as she wound down the window. 'Do you really want to kill me? Do you want me to die?'

Dave raised one eyebrow, the usual sign of a dare. 'Up to you, Babe.'

That was right, according to Dave's rules. If she could get herself out, she would win. If not, it was Dave's victory. She would be dead and it would look like an accident. The conclusion of the game, either way.

Dotty reviewed the state of play. The electrical wire must have been hanging from the garage ceiling when she drove up. The spark signalled the car was live. Dave hadn't been sure it would work but the rubber tyres and his removal of the earth wire obviously prevented her being electrocuted, for now.

If she put a foot on the ground, the current would travel by the shortest route to earth. Her body would be that route. She couldn't back out of the garage, the car touching the roller door would bring her out of the floating circuit, to earth, to death. The car wouldn't start, anyway. That was something Dave hadn't figured, that the car would short out.

The urge to go to the toilet was overwhelming.

'Hey, Hon, how about you let me go to the toilet and then we start again?' Dotty called.

'No way, Babe,' Dave smiled.

There was no one like him. Polite, helping her along the way, enjoying the process and quite prepared to kill her. The smile was genuine. This was fun, for him.

'Give it a bit of thought. Remember what we discussed? It's quite straightforward. Don't spoil this for me,' Dave said sulkily.

No one quite like him. Here he was trying to kill her and he was sulking. How could she be such a bitch as to ruin his fun?

Dotty was his comforter. She could cheer him up, calm him down. As he got more insecure, as the world closed in on him, she was the only one that could be trusted. Most of the time she could be trusted; sometimes he had to reassure himself. Sometimes he had to follow her around to make sure she wasn't doing any secret deals with the enemy. He would have no one without her. Dotty loved having that power over her exceptionally intelligent man.

The game had been their fun. The game of planning the perfect murder, victim dead and perpetrator beyond detection. Dave's marvellously devious mind was always excited by new plans. He met the challenges of Dotty's imaginary complications during dinners. She'd laughed when he ran into the bedroom trying to articulate the latest solution through the toothpaste in his mouth. They'd gulped down breakfast before swapping that dream-induced ironic touch over a cup of tea. Dave had a rule that nothing could be said about the game before breakfast was eaten.

Dave, the lover of rules, maker of new rules, expanded the rules gradually. Victims must be real people. Previous methods and victims could not be mentioned. The victims started adding up: world leaders, sporting identities, television stars. Later, the personalising and narrowing of the victims started: neighbours, friends and relatives. All victims, all banned from mention.

The only victims left were each other. A development in the game, a new rule by Dave, kept it going. Each would have the other as the victim. But the victim would be saved if he or she could work out a way to escape the scheme. Dave, the new-age man, was empowering the victim. Dave, the competitive man, knew the victim didn't stand a chance.

'Clue, Babe. Conductors,' Dave called helpfully. Dotty was obviously boring him by just sitting in the car.

Dotty's heel started gently tapping, a metronome for her thoughts. Electric currents travel through conductors; metal was best. People can be conductors but remain unhurt if they stay within the current. She was sitting within a current. She had to get out of the car without becoming the current's conduit to earth.

The car had metallic paint. That was something Dave had worried about. Would the car conduct the charge? He had rung the car company and asked them about the metallic content of their paint. He concluded that it would. He had also worried about the tyres. Would steel radials conduct? The whole effect was ruined if the car stopped before the garage door went down. You never know what the neighbours might see. There was no point to the game if you got caught. Obviously, Dotty thought, the metal content and the tyres were adequate for the job.

She could jump. She could open the door and leap out. If the car door shut on her or she couldn't make a clean leap, it wouldn't work. At her height, Dotty didn't like her chances of a jump to freedom. The car seat was fairly low to the ground. She would have done better in a four wheel drive or a prime mover. For her size, a cherry picker would have been perfect.

Her foot was beating a frustrated tattoo. Anger didn't help. Dotty tried to suppress the rising heat of rage. If she ever got out of this car, she would kill Dave. She could feel herself brutally hacking him to pieces, stabbing again and again. She didn't care if they caught her. She didn't care if she went to prison forever. She was angry at the waste of time, love, energy, the future.

'I'll kill you, Dave, you fucking bastard,' Dotty muttered.

'What was that, Babe? Didn't quite hear you,' Dave taunted. 'You want another incentive? Remember Taylor?'

Dotty remembered. Taylor had been her work enemy. He'd made her life miserable. She'd become so angry with him she could barely function. Dave had wanted to help, to protect her. She loved him for it.

He'd got her to play the game using Taylor as the victim. Dave started hanging around her office. Research, he said. Her workmates commented on Dave's constant presence. She couldn't tell them the reason. Dave developed a plan and devised the most elegant torture for Taylor before death. The finishing touches, destroying the evidence, were Dotty's own. It had given Dotty a rush of excitement, a sense of power. She made sure they got away scot-free.

She left work just after that. Dave convinced her she didn't need to work. He needed her. With the world working against him, he needed her on call to reassure him. She was the only one who could calm him, make him feel safe. The only one who understood the need for the game and the emotional release of a successful kill.

A workmate had rung after Dotty quit. Laughing, he'd said someone had suggested that she and Taylor had run off together. No one had seen Taylor since her last day. She mentioned the call to Dave. He said nothing. Dotty felt odd, a sneaking fear, a secret pleasure? She didn't know. Their lovemaking that night had a desperate fury, a grasping, urgent frenzy.

If she got out of this, it would be the ultimate victory, an adrenalin rush like no other. Dave knew it, too. She could almost feel the force of his lips on hers. The full length of his body against her. The heat travelling to her every pore. Wrestling like two children fiercely protecting a secret tenet of their lives. Afterwards, his weight like a concrete slab on top of her, contracting her breath. He was a cave protecting her from the storms of the world.

That was the reason she stayed, Dotty thought. They protected and nurtured each other. Her world, with him, was floating above that of mere mortals. The game stretched her mind. Dave let her, insisted she could, go further than she would have dared. The thrill of finding a solution, seeing Dave's eyes light up when she thought of a scheme, was magic.

This morning she had threatened their magical world. Was this just a threat, a warning, not to scare him again? A way of showing her the awful fear he felt most days? Or did he now hate her enough to kill her?

She had to do something. Slowly, Dotty removed her hands from the steering wheel. Nothing happened. Stretching each finger, she eased the stiffness. She placed one leg over the console onto the passenger's seat. The turning of her body increased the pressure on her bladder. She could let it go. Who cared? If she lived, she could clean it up. If she died, that would be the least of her worries.

Potential differences. There was something worrying about potential differences. Maybe some parts of the car had different potentials. Urine might change the potentials. She'd be killed by wetting herself. Dotty laughed. What a way to go, pissing herself to death.

'That's the spirit, Babe,' Dave's fingernails stopped drumming. Now the excitement was beginning.

'Fuck you, Dave. I'm going to get out of this,' Dotty screamed at him.

'Always thought you would, Babe.' Dave gave her the thumbs-up.

Dave's encouragement sparked her determination. She had to think. Electricity could jump. Dotty would have to get rid of all the metal on herself. She started by taking off her ring, earrings, hairclip, watch. Dave watched, interested. She twisted in the seat as she unhooked the waist and slid down the zipper of her skirt. Dave sat up straighter in his chair. She slid the skirt down and threw it onto the passenger seat. Dotty arched her back, slid her hands up to her bra and unhooked it.

'Get it off! Get it off!' Dave started to chant, banging his fist in time on the bench-top.

Dotty wriggled the bra straps over her shoulders. Under her shirt she pulled a strap over her hand and felt the elastic snap into her side. She reached up through the sleeve of her shirt and pulled the bra out.

Dave was now clapping in time to his own chant. Dotty balled the bra and threw it out the window. It landed short of Dave. She would love to see him forget himself enough to go and pick it up.

Dotty checked her remaining clothes. The shoes had metal eyelets but they also had rubber soles. Tough call. Her shirt was cotton with plastic buttons. The only other things she had on were her underpants and panty hose. The underpants, far from glamorous, were a good, sensible cotton; even the elastic was cotton-covered. The pantyhose worried her. They gave off static electricity at the drop of a hat. Now she was being paranoid. Still, why take chances? She slipped off her shoes and rolled the panty hose down her legs.

'I'll be right with you, Dave,' Dotty mouthed a kiss as she threw the panty hose at him. 'Just you wait right there.'

It hardly needed to be said. He wasn't coming near her. Maybe a few years ago he might have been tempted.

The changes to the chemistry of their relationship had crept up on Dotty. Dave's anxieties increased. There were big and small conspiracies aimed at him and her. The game had been their trustworthy safety net, their currency of communication. To ease anxiety, the perpetrators of the torment would be the victims of their game, like Taylor. The demise of the victims would bring them back to laughter, to a shared scheme. Other topics of conversation dwindled and were nearly forgotten.

Dotty spent her time verbally avoiding death. A tiny part of her became afraid that, if he won, she would die. He would put his idea into action. It was just a small seed of doubt. Dotty had told herself she was getting as paranoid as Dave. She decided it had to end; she couldn't live with the doubt, the fear growing. This morning she'd told Dave she wasn't playing anymore.

'I'm taking my little red wagon and going home,' she'd said. What she meant by home, she didn't know. The friends had dropped off. They had been banned from mention for years. She didn't know if they were alive or dead. She couldn't stand her relatives saying, 'I told you so.'

'Go. You'll be back,' Dave said with certainty. 'You can't bear to leave anything unfinished. Not to win.'

He was right. Here she was, back at the house. Dave knew her well, but not as well as he thought. She had tried to contact some of her old friends. None of them were at their old address. They were not listed in the telephone book. She almost rang her mother but Dotty couldn't bear it if she was gone, too. It crossed Dotty's mind that Dave had been doing more than playing a game. She told herself not to be silly. Her mother would never move, but she couldn't test it.

She knew Dave. She came back to prove that her niggling fear was just her imagination. She couldn't have lived with a man for five years and not know that about him. She came back to prove to herself that her feelings for him were well placed. To show everyone who said he was weird that they were wrong. To show them all that she had made the right choice.

Dotty tried to think logically as she put her shoes on over her bare feet. What she needed was something big and insulated. The spare tyre, a big lump of rubber.

She crawled into the back seat. Her fingers clawed the seat catches. She laid the seats out and lifted the cover to the spare tyre. Dotty stared at it. She had forgotten that the metal wheel was part of the spare. She could still use it. As long as just the rubber touched the ground it would give her the extra room to get out of the car without touching its surface.

Dotty scrutinised the doors. The back doors were out, angle too narrow. The front doors were better. The driver's side was out because of the steering wheel. The passenger's side may be okay. The hatch-back was a maybe. It had the advantage of being nearer the spare. She could lift the hatch, ease the tyre to the floor and roll it away from the car. Perfect, except there wasn't enough room with the garage door shut.

The front passenger door was the best option. Dotty needed to get the spare into the front seat. Then she had to get out without touching the floor and the car at the same time. If the wheel fell over and the metal touched the floor before she had cleared the car, she was gone. Not a good option. The chances might improve if the tyre didn't have the metal rim inside it. Dotty dug out the tools from the gap under the spare tyre: a jack and a bolt tightener. Not particularly useful.

Dotty nearly cried with frustration. She stole a look at Dave. The smug bugger was enjoying the view of her bum between the seats. All she wanted to do was hit out, to smash something; Dave's head preferably, but anything would do. She grabbed the bolt tightener and smashed into the soft upholstery of the seat back. She could see Dave through the windscreen, smiling at her frustration.

The windscreen. A nice big sheet of glass. A non-conductor. If she could push it onto the bonnet, she could easily jump away from the car.

Dotty twisted round to face the front. She squatted on the passenger seat inspecting the windscreen joins. She gave it a push, which produced no effect at all. The glove box would have the manual. Hopefully, a nice set of instructions on how to push out a windscreen. Dotty opened the glove box. Neat as a pin, bloody Dave, tidying up before the big event. He had, of course, removed the manual. He couldn't make it too easy. Dotty looked across at Dave. His grin reflected the satisfaction of thorough planning.

Fury rose like bile. Dotty grabbed the bolt tightener and smashed the windscreen. It cracked. She smashed again and again. It cracked, then split and finally shattered. Dotty kept bashing the bolt tightener against it. She became an automaton, determined to smash every last shred of glass out of the windscreen. Glass flew everywhere. She was covered in it. Blood seeped from small cuts to her face, arms and legs. A piece flew towards her eye. It hit her glasses.

That stopped her. The glasses, metal frames, she had forgotten her glasses. She couldn't see a bloody thing without them. Well, she could see something: blurred outlines. She could see enough to know where the car ended. They would have to go, but not yet.

Dotty used her discarded skirt to brush the glass off the dash. Sweeping the skirt in front of her, she crawled up to the dash and out onto the bonnet. She was out of the car. She took off her glasses. All she had to do now was jump. She couldn't do it.

'Come on, Dave. You can see I can make it. Turn off the power and we can get some dinner,' Dotty said. She was too tired to yell.

'Scared, Babe? Just because you can't see? Afraid of the bogeyman in the blur?' Dave knew her fear of moving without her glasses.

'Look at me,' Dotty thought as she spoke. 'This whole game was up once I did anything other than get out of the car. How are you going to explain these cuts? How are you going to let them think I had a simple heart attack when the car is smashed? Didn't think of that did you, smart arse?'

'Now, now. No need for language.' Dave didn't seem worried.

Dotty wondered what else he had planned. Maybe he just didn't care. He might hate her enough to just want her dead. His calm infuriated her. To calm herself, she took deep breaths.

'That's the way, Babe,' Dave encouraged her. 'I know you can do it.'

Dotty tried to ignore him. She cleared her mind of all thought. Slowly she straightened and stood, balancing against the disorientation brought on by blurred vision. One last breath and she leapt.

She landed with a crunch. The pain in her ankle proved she was still alive. Relief and pain overcame her. Suddenly all she wanted to do was to curl up and go to sleep right there. She could deal with everything else after she had a sleep.

'Well done, Babe.' Dave was looking down at her.

'Just go away. I won, so leave me alone.'

'You haven't won, Babe,' Dave said softly.

'I'm here, aren't I? So I won. Or have you changed the rules again?' Dotty didn't care at this stage.

'Just perfecting the system, Babe. Ironing out the rough edges before the main game.'

1998

THURSDAY NIGHT AT THE OPERA

Christina Lee

BEING THE ONLY LEFT-HANDED, BLACK, DISABLED LESBIAN IN THE NEW South Wales Police Force isn't nearly as funny as a lot of people seem to think.

At least, the people I work with now just go right ahead and joke about it. The worst thing about my previous job was the way everyone used to go out of their way to make sure that I got the message that they were going out of their way to make sure I didn't feel stigmatised in any way. And, I wasn't even disabled back then!

No, okay, the worst thing about my previous job was how everyone went on and on about abused kids and nobody ever did anything about it. That's why I'm where I am now. Okay, the paperwork is just as bad as it was in the Department of Community Services, but I do get to arrest the occasional villain, which is kind of nice.

Of course "society" is still to blame and, okay, I know the poor old perpetrators have tragic stories to tell: abuse and broken homes and dyslexia and attention deficit disorder and bed-wetting and glue-sniffing and nose-picking and dizzy spells. But the point is – and I think there is something of a tendency to overlook this in these interesting times – that these guys are choosing to deal with life's challenges by committing violent acts against small, defenceless children. And there comes a time in a girl's life when what she really wants to do is drag one of these guys down to the police station by his hair and get her not-quite-so-disabled, oestrogen-challenged mates to belt the shit out of him.

I sleep well at night.

The main problem with the job is that there's a bit much to do. I'm on every inter-sectoral committee and promotions review and special reporting group that comes our way, and there are days when I think that if the Police Force wants to give the impression to the wider community that it's full to the brim with hard-working, dedicated career women, then it should employ a few more of them and not work poor old Sergeant

Rima Ruakuri to death. It's not like I get time off from my normal duties or anything for all this bullshit, and I'll give you three guesses where I'm stationed.

Lane Cove? Leafy, law-abiding Lane Cove? Nope.

Gulargambone? Nothing for a million miles in any direction but peace and quiet and DUIs? Nope, again.

Kings Cross, maybe? Crime, grime, drugs and thugs? You got it! I guess the committee thought I'd blend right in here.

'Ruakuri?' they probably said. 'The one that got shot in the leg? The black lezzo? Send her to Kings Cross. Nobody's going to notice her there.'

Well, it's true. I do seem to blend right in. You have to be nine-feet tall with a couple of extra limbs to stand out from the crowd around here. But I kind of like it; the passing trade tend to be a bit of a pain but the regular clients aren't that much different from what you'd find in Community Services except that nobody expects you to turn them into the Brady Bunch.

It's quite relaxing, actually. Senior Sergeant Donnelly takes the view that as long as we do our best to stop the street girls and the boys on The Wall from getting themselves murdered, keep the dealers and the junkies out of the main thoroughfares, and periodically round up anyone who looks under about twelve and doesn't seem to have a home to go to, that's about all anyone could realistically expect.

I get to know some of the regular workers quite well, especially the parlour girls. They seem to last a bit longer than the street kids, but they're still in and out of the station often enough, and I've been known to get quite upset when one of them gets sliced up or makes an irrevocable error in her choice of pharmaceuticals. They're much friendlier now I'm a police-person than they were when I worked for good old Community Services. I guess they know I have no intention of taking their babies away or trying to make them see that virtue is its own reward.

So… it could be worse. And here I am. It's a quiet Wednesday night; well, as quiet as it ever gets around here. There's a 14-year-old called Shonelle having the screaming meemies in one of the cells, something of a regular occurrence just lately. I make a note to explain to a couple of the managers that we are not a free detox centre and, if they don't want us hanging around their clubs on a regular basis checking on whether or not their staff are old enough to be legal, then they'd better exercise a bit more quality control in what they give them to stay happy. There's a madwoman at the counter demanding over and over again that we take her home to Daisy; there's a couple of drunks who've spewed up everything they ever ate in their entire lives and are wishing there was some way they could just be switched off until it was all over; and a couple of boys waiting for their dad to turn up with a lawyer.

I'm also trying to draft a report for my latest committee. As the most junior member – and, of course, the only woman – I tend to be the one who gets to do the drafts. And a source of great joy it is, too.

This one is on snuff movies, and the party line is that it's all a load of bollocks. See, every time a young person goes missing, which happens about eight times a week in the fair State of New South Wales, large numbers of concerned citizens are convinced that they've been abducted, raped and horribly murdered on video for the titillation of the perverted few. But Assistant Commissioner Hooper – the head of this committee that I'm on – keeps saying that nobody on the committee has ever seen a snuff movie, nobody has ever met anyone who is willing to say they've seen a snuff movie, and those people ought to know. Besides, he says, where are all the bodies? Bodies are notorious for their habit of turning up inconveniently, just when you think it's safe, no matter how carefully dismembered, weighed down, treated with acid, or coated with shark bait.

Now, we know that; but we also know that nobody ever found Christopher Flannery. Or Azaria Chamberlain. Or Juanita Neilsen. Or the Beaumont children.

Assistant Commissioner Hooper isn't stupid; and besides, I remember once going to an in-service on crime and other nasty stuff back when I was a District Officer for Community Services and he was the speaker, and I distinctly remember him saying that if you could imagine it, there was somebody out there doing it.

That was years ago. Something seems to have happened to Hooper, but a girl with any sense of self-preservation is not going to ask what. It's a whitewash and, well, normally I'd think, fine; makes a change from hysterical accusations and seeing who can come up with the name of the most unlikely public figure.

But I have to say I've got a funny feeling about this one. I've made a list of everyone who's been reported missing in the past three months and then sorted them into those who turned up okay, those that turned up hacked to death by their nearest and dearest, those whom we know have pushed off to New Zealand on false passports, and so forth. There are about six names left over. All girls. All disappeared from our patch.

On Thursdays.

Well, how likely is that? We're into evidence-based practice these days and I think about presenting this evidence at the next committee meeting, but I know it's a waste of time. They never set up commissions such as this unless they've already decided what the outcome will be, and I know perfectly well that I'd need a signed confession witnessed by JC himself before Hooper would bother to look at it. There's no point in antagonising important people like him, especially when they also sit on the police promotions board and your hearing happens to be scheduled for some time next week, and I can imagine how Assistant Commissioner Hooper will react to the suggestion that someone around here is making a habit of picking up a do-it-yourself stiff with their Thursday night's grocery shopping.

So, I'm trying to say as little as possible as politely as possible, while all around me drunks, thieves, tarts, muggers and Senior Sergeant Mick Donnelly are clamouring for my attention.

It's Mick that finally gets through.

'Stiff in a back alley, Rima,' he says cheerily. 'Get down there.'

'Why me?' I ask.

'She's a pro,' replies Mick. 'You're good at that sort of thing.'

'You mean, pros mean sex, I'm a lezzo, lezzos mean sex, so I can sort her out. Is that it?'

'Near enough,' says Mick. 'Off you go.'

Shit. Sometimes I think I was put on this earth in order to explain to people that lesbians don't spend their entire lives having sex. Mick's okay; he feels approximately the same way as I do about men who abuse women and who think if they're prostitutes, it really doesn't count. But, like most blokes, he can't get past the fairly minor point that, at least when things are going well, I go out with other women.

Things aren't going well at the moment.

Anyway, off I go and, sure enough, there's a dead prostitute in a back alley. I don't know her, which usually wouldn't mean much because those street girls have a pretty short shelf life and the Recording Angel himself would have trouble keeping up with who's doing what to whom behind which garbage bin in the big city on a hot summer's evening.

But this one's not your usual teenager with a Gosford bus pass in her back pocket, either. This stiff looks nearer 40 than 14 and I'm a bit surprised I don't recognise her. Up from St Kilda on a job exchange, perhaps? She's got about a dozen scars on each wrist, running across, not down, which is enough in itself to set a suspicious policeperson to wondering. At her age she ought to know what she's doing. But anyway, she's crawling with track marks; it looks like a fairly straightforward OD, so I call the boys with the van and have a look around. She can't have been here long because she's still warm and besides, her bag's still here. I scrabble through it for ID.

There's a packet of tampons, a packet of cigarettes, a packet of condoms, and a packet of Panadol Forte. There's a purse with $21.75, a couple of wadded-up tissues, a syringe, a bottle of silver nail polish, a ticket to tomorrow night's performance of Nabucco at the Opera House, and a one-year diary in a black plastic cover.

I look at these last two items and I am frankly puzzled. For one thing, here we've got someone who's come out without a front door key, suggesting to the thinker that she very probably hasn't got a front door to call her own, and she's carrying a $75 ticket to the world's dreariest opera. And this diary; well, how far ahead does a person need to plan if she's a prostitute whose hobbies are injecting smack and attempting suicide?

The guys are taking their own sweet time so I flick through her diary. There's not much there, just a few names. Nicki. Shantal. Brandi. I've seen those names before, I think, as the boys screech to a halt in the truck. I look at the current week-to-an-opening page and I notice the name Shonelle. It's on Thursday. I flick back again and I notice that Nicki, Shantal and Brandi were on Thursdays, too.

The boys are distracted, taking a few perfunctory photographs and trying to keep the citizenry at arm's length, so I drop the diary and the ticket in my shirt pocket and limp off up the alley to the squad car.

Back at the station, I sink an orange juice and a felafel sandwich, a last remnant of my old Community Services persona, thinking (as I always do) that I really must try to get a taste for Diet Coke and hamburgers if I'm ever going to blend in properly, and then I deal with a couple more drunks, a citizen who's been mugged, and a partridge in a pear tree. Then it's back to the desk. Just as I thought. Nicki, Shantal and Brandi are all names on my missing-teenagers list, and the dates in the diary match the last dates that anyone whom we could lay our hands on is prepared to admit having seen them alive. I wonder how many Shonelles there are in Kings Cross and then I limp down to the cells for a bit of community policing.

Sure enough, Shonelle's got an appointment tomorrow with some woman whose name she doesn't know, who wants to introduce her to some bloke whose name she doesn't know, either. What she does know is that he's after someone who'll do something rather special and can be discreet about it.

Well, "something special" could be anything from golden showers to nude wrestling in baked beans, but somehow I've got a gut feel about this one.

I think it through and decide that I definitely do not want to be the sole repository of this information if there is anything more than the faintest chance that it is in some way connected with dead bodies. I've seen too many movies in which the glamorous heroine decides not to tell her boss about the gang of murderous jewel thieves before setting out to right wrongs single-handedly, and I know that the chances of Al Pacino turning up at the crucial moment to rescue me would have to be on the slim side. I decide the best thing is to take precautions.

I ring Assistant Commissioner Hooper and say I seem to have something of a new angle on this snuff-movie business, and can I have a spot of backup for a bit of a poke round, see if I can turn up something a bit more definite? Predictably, he tells me that I've let my imagination run away with me, that prostitutes and junkies are notorious for their lack of respect for the rules of evidence, and that there is such a thing as getting too close to one's job. He's on the point of saying "going native" when he remembers to whom he's talking to and manages to turn it into a rather nasty sounding cough.

But I must be on to something, because next day I get a signed letter saying I'm being promoted to Senior Sergeant and transferred to Gulargambone, effective immediately.

That might have been that, if it hadn't been for good old Mick. Say what you like about blokes, they do have their uses, and when I put my side of the story to him, he turned out to be unexpectedly quick on the uptake.

The only thing I regret, really, is that I wasn't there when Mick walked into the Opera House thirty seconds before the lights went down. I would have loved to see Assistant Commissioner Hooper's face as Mick took the empty seat beside him.

1999

VERMIN

Janis Spehr

THE FIRST TIME WE DONE IT, WE DONE IT FOR A JOKE. IT WAS CRAIGIE'S IDEA. We went down to the dunny in the park one night and waited until one of 'em came along. Simmo and me held him while Craigie put the boots in and when we left him he was curled up on the ground, moanin' like a woman. Craigie stood over him and spat. Fuck you, faggot, he says. Be a while before ya come lookin for another bum chum. Then we got out of there. Fast. We seen him a few days later in the bookshop where he worked, all Yes, madam and No, madam in his fucken yellow vest. One of his eyes was as purple as a baboon's arse. We fucken cacked ourselves.

It got to be a bit of a habit until Grand Final night. We drunk a shitload of cans on the way to the match and then tried to sneak some through the gate, but it was a no go; the poofta takin' the tickets looked in our bags. Ya gunna drink 'em y'self, ya fucken spastic cunt? Simmo yelled over his shoulder. Piss off, fat boy, the bloke on the gate says and Simmo turns around ready to go him but then we see Brett McKenna and the boys come out of the club rooms wearin' the old blue and red. Go, Brett! Go, mate! we yelled. Come on the mighty Gulls! And big Brett, he did'n let us down, soarin' above the rest like a hawk, like an eagle then, and diving so fast.

It was all Brett all the way, and the other side never had a fucken hope. It was over by three-quarter time and, when the final siren sounded, people started streamin' onto the ground. Some of the fellas had big Brett on their shoulders and were singin' the club song. You're a legend! You're a legend! Simmo kept yellin', and even Craigie was grinnin' fit to beat the band. Me, I just had me hands out, tryin' to touch him. I would have done anything for him then.

After the players went into the club rooms, we hung around pervin' at chicks. A blonde piece with really big norks went past. Hey, tits! calls Simmo, pointin' at his dick. How about it? Piss off, you pack of morons! she says, really pissed off, and Simmo runs up behind her and grabs her arse. We fucken cacked ourselves.

We got sicka hangin' around so after a while we piled into Craigie's panel van and hit the Royal. My shout! I tell 'em and head for the bar. Wayne Preston, the half full-forward for the Gulls, is there. Great game, mate! I say, but the cunt just looks straight through me. Fuck him. We start drinkin' and keep drinkin', getting really shitfaced and, just before closing time, Craigie says, Let's go and find a faggot. We all start poundin' the table. Find a faggot!

Out the front of the pub there're cars revin' and people yellin' – fucken spastic! – but when we get to the park it's as quiet as a fucken grave. We creep up to the dunny and wait and pretty soon we hear footsteps. Craigie steps out of the shadows. He and the poofta just look at each other then the poof says, You lookin for something, mate? and there's the sound of him unzippin' his fly. Yeah, this, says Craigie and then it's on for young and old. Die, faggot! Die! yells Simmo.

He was strong – who would have thought a fag would be so strong – he fought like a fucken tiger and even when Craigie kicked his teeth in he didn't cry or moan. That'll teach the cunt a lesson and we hung a wheelie and took off outta there. He was all right when we left; just lyin' there in a puddle of blood.

The next mornin' the whole town's gotta hangover and I just stuff around feedin' the dogs and watchin' telly. I don't think nothin' about it til Simmo rings me first thing Monday. Troy, Troy, have ya seen the paper, mate? 'Course I hadn't seen the friggin' paper, but I go out for it 'cause he sounds cactus; he sounds really fucken scared, and there on the front page is the headline: "Footy Hero Slain in Mystery Killing", and underneath in fucken black and white: Brett McKenna dead at the hand of person or persons unknown.

'This is it?' Gina gazed uneasily out the window.

'This is it, babe.' On the left-hand side, behind the dense banks of scrub that lined the road, the sea rolled in a sullen blue mass and looked nothing like a postcard. A few salt-stunted trees bravely defied the wind, their tops flattened out by years of exposure to storms and squalls. I shivered. Graeme had said the place could be desolate but I hadn't expected it to be this bleak.

'Keep an eye out for the motel,' I told Gina as we came to the sign bearing the name of the town and, underneath, the number of friendly people who welcomed us. We drove along the main street, where harried-looking shoppers to-and-froed, heads bent down into the wind. A few people turned to stare at the Sharkmobile.

'There it is,' said Gina, pointing to a sign that flashed "Four Seasons" in pink neon against the dark grey clouds, but the first and last letters were on their way out and blinked only intermittently. Our "season" looked as though it was winter.

'Mrs Weatherall?' asked the young woman at the reception desk.

'Ms,' I replied, curtly.

'Miss,' she said, beaming benignly. 'Please sign here.' I signed, took the key and went outside to the car as my mobile rang.

'Lauri Weatherall.'

'It's Graeme, Lauri.'

I repressed a sigh. I was already regretting the impulse that had caused me to agree to his request at 5am yesterday morning. I'd been half asleep when he'd rung, with Gina, warm and smelling of roses, curled up next to me. I was weak. I hadn't had breakfast. I said, 'Yes.'

'Let's meet at Café Pelican. It's not far from where you're staying and it's the only place in this dump where you can get soy milk lattes.'

Soy milk lattes, soy milk lattes, who gave a shit about soy milk lattes? But I said, yeah, sure, see you in fifteen. Gina had the bags out of the car and was standing in front of the door numbered 9.

'Gotta dash, darl'. I'll see you later,' I said, after I'd parked the car and opened the door. On the way out I glanced longingly at the Sharkmobile but thought I'd do the right thing and walk. I couldn't see any pelicans but a few seagulls foraged on the nature strips, pale yellow eyes alert for suitable refuse. The café was a cheery, hippy looking place with a wooden replica of its namesake in the window and wooden tables and chairs painted in primary colours. Graeme cut a natty but slightly incongruous figure in a paisley vest, plain shirt and dark tie. We kissed and exchanged greetings and ordered.

'So, tell me about this dead footballer.'

It took me a while to get the whole story. He was scared and, even though the café was almost deserted, he kept looking around and lowering his voice, but eventually it all came out. A "family man" dead and found where he shouldn't be, a spate of violent bashings, and people frightened and intimidated. As he spoke, his hands clenched and unclenched and a dull flush mounted in his cheeks. I looked at him closely.

'It happened to you, didn't it?'

He nodded miserably. 'The police said they'd look into it but I didn't hear from them again. You're my last hope, Lauri. I don't want anyone else to be killed.'

'How well did you know Brett McKenna?'

Graeme moved restlessly in his chair. 'Everybody "knew" Brett McKenna. When you're a small-town footy hero, you're like God. But there were rumours. Word gets around among the queers in a place as small as this.'

I bet it did. I wondered if Brett McKenna had realised just how vulnerable he had been. I drummed my fingers on the table and thought about my commitments back in the Big Smoke. I thought about grief and guilt.

'Alright,' I said. 'I'll do it.'

I took a cheque from him and left some coins on the table. A gust of wind caught at my clothes as I stepped from Café Pelican. Across the street, an old derro swigged from a bottle in a brown paper bag. What a great place to be gay, I thought, where Saturday night entertainment probably meant Tabaret and Neil Diamond tribute bands and where men grew up to marry their best friend's sister. I shuddered and high-tailed it back to the motel where Gina had filled the spa bath, picked a rose from one of the ailing bushes outside the reception office, and floated petals on the water. I sank beneath it with relief. She'd done some research of her own.

'This is the place where the dolphins play.'

'Excuse me?' I nuzzled her neck.

'The dolphins. They come here to mate in the spring.'

I made diving movements with one of my hands. She giggled, took the hand, put it between her legs and moaned just as my mobile — which was sitting on the tiles near the bath — sounded. She groaned — a completely different sound — when I answered it, but there was no one there. Must have been a wrong number, so I went back to playing dolphins.

Next morning I made a call to the local police station and asked for the senior officer. I was told Sergeant Winston had an RDO and could anyone else help?

'What's Sergeant Winston's first name?'

'It's Wally. Hey, hang on...' but I'd already hung up.

"Winston, W" was listed in the phone book at an out-of-town address. I put the keys in the Sharkmobile and drove Gina and her credit cards a couple of blocks to the town centre — she was brought up a Catholic but her real religion was shopping — then consulted a map of the district.

As I took the road out of town, my mobile rang but again there was no one there when I answered.

Wally Winston was a big man with a beer gut and very pale blue eyes. When I drove up he was standing in his front yard polishing a big white truck. I could see his face in the gleaming chrome metal.

He took my proffered hand reluctantly and frowned when he saw my PI's licence.

'You're a long way from home.'

'I've been employed by someone local.' I tried for a pleasant smile.

'Oh, yeah? Well, you know what they say…' He smiled and the effect wasn't pleasant at all. 'You're a local only if you've been here thirty years.'

There didn't seem to be any reply to that so I pressed on with my real business. When I mentioned the bashings, he looked non-committal.

'We investigated those. We couldn't find anything to substantiate the allegations.

'The allegations? One man was in hospital for three days!'

'We know why they go there.' He leant against the side of his truck. 'They've only got themselves to blame.'

I thought about Graeme, lonely and closeted in a small conservative community and Brett McKenna, who had died because he lived a lie.

'Everyone has a right to justice.' The words came out sounding more pompous than I intended.

He looked at me and his eyes were very cold. 'They're just vermin. Disease-carrying vermin.'

As I drove down the driveway I glanced in the rear-view mirror. I'm a fit, very strong woman, but when I saw him standing there, hands on hips, watching me, I got a cold feeling at the base of my spine. My mobile went off again and this time I heard breathing.

I asked, 'Who is this?' but there was just the faint, shallow breathing. I threw the phone down and contemplated my next move. Clearly I was not going to get any further with the police. It was time to visit "the wife".

On Tuesday mornin', me'n Simmo took the dogs to the beach. They love it down there. We put 'em in Simmo's old station wagon and drove out of town to this quiet spot where we can run 'em up and down the sand with no idiots gettin' in the road. I put their muzzles on because greyhounds are nervous animals and I did'n want 'em hurtin' each other. Thimble, the grey one, started actin' up and I put my hand on her head and said, Steady girl. The waves were crashin' quietly and the sun had come up like a big fried egg as I got down one end of the beach and back. Bullseye flies down the beach like a black arrow and I think how great dogs are because dogs aren't like people; dogs don't disappoint ya, dogs never let ya down.

When we finished we put 'em back in the car then leant against it and had a smoke. What we gunna do? Simmo asks, and I know he's not talkin'

about the dogs. I take a deep drag of me smoke. No one saw us do nothin',
I say, at last. We should just try not t'think about it, but I know that's easier
said than done.

All through the week I have dreams about blood and slime and
on Sunday night the phone rings and it's Craigie sayin' some real
butch type's been snoopin' around, askin' questions and makin' a
real fucken nuisance of herself. A real bulldyke, but when he starts
tellin' me what she looks like, I say, Yeah, yeah, 'cause I've seen her
drivin' round in her big fucken tank of a car; drivin' round with the
top down and her girlfriend sittin' up beside her like king dick – not
that she'd have one, ha ha! She wasn't bad lookin' in a dark, woggy
sort of way; the girlfriend's got long, wavy dark hair and norks out
to here. I never seen any lezzos before except in porn mags; two
sheilas goin' at each other, real 'flash the gash' stuff. We could teach
her a lesson, Craigie says, and I say, Hey, steady on, 'cause I know
what Craigie's like; he can be a real mean bastard. His father use
t'beat him with chains, and when his mum left home, she did'n take
Craigie with her. We gotta keep a low profile, I tell 'im, and t'change
the subject, I ask How do ya reckon lezzos do it? Probably use
falsies, he says. Great big fucken rubber ones they buy at sex shops,
and we fucken cack ourselves.

Chez McKenna was a large split-level brick veneer with a neat and
tidy garden. The windows were shuttered with apricot-coloured Kosta
blinds, which no doubt matched the interior. Karin McKenna was a
slim, small-featured blonde wearing jeans and a crisp white shirt –
everything clean and neat and nice. She was probably about 30 but
today she looked older than her years. I'd rung and told her I was a
reporter from a footy magazine – Marks and Matches – and wanted to
do a profile on Brett that emphasised the community-building aspects
of sport. She showed me into a lounge room with apricot-coloured
walls and paler carpet. A blonde girl and boy smiled from framed
photographs on the coffee table.

'Nice kids,' I said, after I'd given my condolences.

'Sherrine and Jordan,' she said and for a moment her face relaxed. It
was a good opening for an "interview" and I took advantage. I learned
that she and Brett had been high school sweethearts – her brother Gary
was Brett's best mate – and that they'd married young. She told me – it
was one of those weird ironies of life – that Brett had had offers from
big city clubs but had decided to stay in the town because he and Karin
thought it was a good place to bring up kids. Brett's job as a sales rep

for a large agricultural fertiliser company had flexible hours and allowed plenty of time for training. They'd been happy.

'You didn't resent the time footy took him away from the family?'

She smiled. 'How could I, when it meant so much to him?'

I turned back to the photos. One showed Brett, blokey and handsome, wearing a football jumper. Who would have guessed he'd gone to public toilets to have sex with other men? Karin saw me looking and for a moment her face blazed with anger. Not just anger: it was the look of a woman betrayed. She'd known about his life but she could never tell anyone, not even herself. I thanked her, said I would send her a copy of the finished article and went outside to a day where the sun had finally decided to shine.

Two young boys stood inspecting the Sharkmobile. One was stroking a tail fin. 'Cool car,' he said, by way of greeting.

'Thanks.' As I opened the door I noticed someone up the street, watching me. An old guy, bundled in clothes against the sun, with a shuffling walk and ginger hair.

'Who's that old bloke?' I asked, pointing.

'That's just old Lou. Lou Chutney,' said one of the kids.

'Lou Chutney?'

'Yeah,' said the other. 'That's not his real name,' he added.

'I've seen him before.'

'He hangs around,' snickered the first. 'Usually in the pub or the park.'

'He's an alchie,' volunteered the second, cupping his hand and raising it to his mouth.

'He used to be a teacher,' said the first one. 'But then he started drinking. Big time.' He mimicked his friend's gesture. Now I remembered I'd seen the old man outside the café the day I'd arrived. So he liked to wander around. I gave a mental shrug.

'Thanks, fellas.'

'Check ya.' The first one raised his hand magisterially as he and his mate moved off. Lou Chutney had disappeared. I stood by the car, dazed by the unexpected warmth and trying to order my thoughts. I had run up against a wall of silence and no one was going to help me. What next? A languid cappuccino with my darling appealed but I needed to clear my head: a solitary walk was required. The beach was on the other side of the caravan park just a few streets away. I would get the car on the way back. This walking was getting to be a bad habit, I thought, as I set off.

The caravan park had the usual kiosk and phone box as well as a few people making the most of the sun. A section of natural vegetation had been left at the rear of the park; you reached the sand and water by means of track that cut through the scrub. As I started down the track my mobile rang. There was the same rapid, shallow breathing, then a faint voice.

'We have to meet.'

'Why?'

'I know things.'

'Where?'

'Just keep walking. I'll meet you on the beach.' The caller hung up. The sun went behind a cloud and I suddenly realised how quiet it was. A twig snapping made me start and, although I couldn't see anyone when I looked about, I quickened my pace towards the dull thud of the waves. There was another sound, closer this time and the hair on the back of my neck rose. I've learned never to distrust these primeval reactions; I was certain I was being followed. I stopped and turned.

'Who's there?' There was only silence. Fragments of sunlight reached me through a black lattice of branches as I broke into a jog. Had Wally Winston disliked me enough to want to hurt me? The caller must have rung from the caravan park: perhaps I was being set up by an unknown psychopath. Or a murderer. There was the sound of someone crashing through scrub and I ran. The waves were louder now but so were the footsteps behind me. An arm went round my throat and I saw red before my eyes as I tried to struggle free. A voice shouted something and then the world fell on me.

I woke up in a hospital bed, with a little ginger-haired man sitting next to it.

I get the phone call and it's the dyke sayin', Meet me in the aquarium. What the fuck? I nearly decide not to show but want t'see what she knows so I go down to the beach to the big fucken pile of rocks where the aquarium is. It's underground, real fucken dark and creepy. There's water in puddles on the floor and a drip, drip, drip that's the only sound. I check out the fish while I wait, little stripy black and yella ones, big old crays, and an octopus crawlin' around on the bottom of its tank. I knock on the glass and when it waves an arm at me I wave back. In the biggest tank there's this shark. It's only a little shark but you can see its real mean teeth and its real mean eyes, cold as the sea in winter. I stand there watchin' it swim around and around but I don't want t'go any closer.

I'm getting bored, getting ready to go, then I feel someone behind me and when I turn around, there she is. Watchin'. G'day, I'm… Yeah, I know who you are, she says, real snotty, like. Bitch. There's glass at the top of the aquarium to let in the light and it makes weird stripes on the stone floor like the stripes on the fucken fish while she looks at me from behind her dark glasses and doesn't say nothin'.

Why d'ya pick this place? I say at last. To look at the fish, and she gives me this weird fucken little smile and starts ravin' on about her car; how it's a shark, it's her Sharkmobile, and she likes cruisin' in it. I think about that good-lookin' chick of hers and say somethin' about the back seat havin a lotta room, and she laughs and says, Yeah, it does. We talk about fucken buzz and she says, Yeah, it would be.

We talk a bit more and I'm startin' to think she's alright for a lezzo, then right outta the fucken blue she asks me about Brett McKenna. Did I know 'im? Did I know anythin' about the murder, and where was I that night? I play it real dumb and say, I was at the pub with everyone else till closin' time, then I went home.

That's not what I've heard, she says, and I give her a big shit-eating grin and say she musta heard wrong. She just looks at me from behind the shades and doesn't say nothin', while the shark swims around and around, bumpin' its nose against the glass. She looks at it real thoughtful and mutters something about predators and victims.

Can I go now, miss? I ask, cheeky as though I'm talkin' to Miss Johnson, the old bag who use t'give me the cuts in primary school, and she just gives me this vacant sorta nod, not lookin' at me, as though she's got something on her mind. Hey, Troy! she calls after me as I head towards the steps. A man always kills the thing he loves and she gives this weird fucken funny little laugh and I get outta there. Fast.

'How did you get my mobile number?' I asked and he smiled slyly and said I wasn't the only detective. He was probably younger than he looked; years of alcohol and living rough had taken their toll. He was well spoken, with the refined English-type accent that I'd associate with old-style ABC newsreaders. I wondered what had brought him this low. His eyes were bloodshot and his hands shook but he seemed sober as he told me what he'd seen the night Brett McKenna died. The moon had come out briefly. He'd got a good look at one face.

'Would you testify?'

'Yes. People shouldn't suffer like that.' His face opened for a moment and I caught a glimpse of some old unhealed wound. My mouth framed a question, then I decided against it.

'Thanks for rescuing me.'

'Think nothing of it.' His face twisted with a brief smile. He'd followed me from Karin McKenna's and, when he'd seen I was heading for the beach, made a call from the phone box and followed me into the bush.

If it hadn't been for his presence I'd have ended up with far more than a bump on the head and bruising. He hadn't been close enough to identify my attacker but when he'd shouted at him, the man had fled. After Lou Chutney left I sat in bed thinking about the choices we make and how people can live their lives in silence until it destroys them.

Gina collected me the next day. It wasn't hard to track down Troy Harris and, as soon as I saw him, I knew all about the poor sad little sonofabitch. Born in a backwater of genetically impoverished stock, his dad had pissed off early, leaving mum to do it all alone. This, combined with impatient teachers, inadequate education and declining job prospects in rural areas had all made Troy a bored, stupid young man with poor self-esteem. Lou Chutney had seen three men attack Brett McKenna because Troy wouldn't have done it alone. Troy was like one of Hitler's innumerable henchmen who were "just following orders". No, there'd have been a leader, someone born cruel or made cruel by the world.

I had to let Troy go at the aquarium, but after he'd gone I stood there leaning against the shark's tank, listening to the relentless drip, drip, drip of the water and looking at the table covered in tacky little dolphin souvenirs – dolphin pencil sharpeners, dolphin fridge magnets, dolphins that doubled as both… I had doubts about Lou Chutney making a statement. Even if he didn't change his mind, the word of a semi-itinerant alcoholic was unlikely to carry much weight with unsympathetic cops. I climbed up the stairs and trudged back to the Sharkmobile. The sun was going down, throwing harsh gold light onto the waves as it sank beneath them. I put the top down on the Sharkmobile and drove back to the motel with the breeze in my hair, thinking that there was only one thing for it. It would have to be the boy, and I'd have to break him.

Last night I had the weirdest fucken dream. I'm in the water deep down in the sea and it's real bright blue, fulla light and beautiful. I'm swimmin' around, lookin' at the light shinin' down through the water, swimmin' and swimmin', but then there're clouds, shadows, above. I look up and all I can see is these big, pale bellies, blockin' out the light. I can't see nothin' else but then there's blood, great big streams of blood, swirlin' all through the water and I see that the big pale things are sharks come after the blood. It's Brett's blood; there're his arms and legs turnin' over like some great big fucken sacrifice. The sharks come nearer and nearer, nosin' through the water and I can see their big fucken teeth and suddenly, I know it's not Brett they're after, it's me. It's punishment for what I done.

Ya see, I knew it was Brett standin' there that night: me mum's always said I've got eyes like a hawk and just for a second the moon came out from behind the clouds and I seen him. I shoulda stopped it. I coulda stopped it, somehow stepped in fronta Craigie and made out we was doin' it for a joke. Hey, Brett, how's it goin', mate? Fancy abit o'me arse? and we coulda all hadda laugh and gone home. But, once Craigie started kickin' him, I had to join in and, once I started, I couldn' stop.

So, it's my fault he's dead. In the dream the sharks are closin' in, and the water's boilin' with blood. Bits of hand and arm float past me like some sicko horror movie. Brett's eyes, 100ks up, look at me like they did the night he died. I woke up sweatin' and screamin', then lay there lookin' out the little winda of me bedroom, thinkin' about the dogs and who's gunna take care of 'em, 'cause that lezzo's onto me. She's out there cruisin' in her big fucken Sharkmobile and she's come to get me.

2000

Dead Woman in the Water

Janis Spehr

I WOKE UP SCREAMING: A DEAD WOMAN'S BODY WAS IN THE WATER. HER eyes stared vacantly at the sky and her hair floated about her like dark seaweed. All around me, other people screamed and my mother turned my face into her belly while the floor rocked under my feet. I switched on the light and lay sweating in bed, waiting for my heartbeat to subside. Gradually it slowed, my stomach stopped churning and the terrible image receded, but it was a long time before I slept again.

'Hard night?' Kevin frowned as I entered the office next morning.

I flapped a non-committal hand and sat down. There's just the two of us, apart from a woman who comes in part-time to do the social pages, and when there's just the two of you, you have to get on so it was just as well I liked him. He was a local boy and not bad looking in an Irish, slightly-going-to-seed kind of way.

When I began at the Star I half-expected the occasional snide comment or even a casual hand on the bum but he'd been alright. If he knew about my history, he didn't let on. Now he regarded me quizzically and put down the morning's Star.

'That girl who was found washed up at Stanthorpe's Bay the day before yesterday. The police have released her name.'

'Oh, yeah?'

'She's Melissa Dalton, nineteen years old, a kind of freelance pro. She used to advertise in our illustrious journal.' He circled something in the Star's "Personals" section and pushed it across the desk:

Introducing

gorgeous Tiffany

petite busty blonde

for caring and discreet service

There was a mobile number listed underneath. There were a whole column of these kinds of "leggy brunettes", "curvaceous redheads", even the occasional "exotic Asian", all selling the same thing, and yesterday I wouldn't have given them a second glance, but that was yesterday.

'I've been on the phone to the pathologist,' Kevin said. 'The autopsy's done. Apparently her bloodstream was full of cocaine.'

'Well, drug use isn't unusual in her line of work.'

'No. On the surface it looks as though it was suicide – life getting her down, a drug habit – but I want you to get onto it. See if you can find out a bit of background. Family details, stuff like that.'

I stared at gorgeous Tiffany's advertisement. Another dead woman in the water. It would make a change from reporting the prize-winning dahlias at the local agricultural show or tallying up the footy scores after the weekend. The Sleepy Hollow Times, I usually told my friends from the city when they asked me the paper's name. I did cover pretty much everything from sheep dog trials to debutante balls, so a dead woman in the water was major news, indeed.

'Start with the family.' Kevin turned back to his computer screen. 'I think they live out in the bush somewhere.'

Out in the bush. It was all "out in the bush" as far as I was concerned, but then, I spent my formative years on the North Richmond Housing Estate. I got out the phone book, rang three Daltons at out-of-town addresses, getting polite denials on each attempt. On my fourth try a woman answered then abruptly hung up when I identified myself. I figured this had to be Melissa Dalton's mother so I set off. As I drove out of town, the sun, which had been shining brightly all morning, momentarily went under a cloud, turning the sparkly blue water captured in my rear-vision mirror to a bleak grey. A few fishing boats moved along the horizon. I shivered. Some people love the ocean; I'm not one of them. When I'd got my marching orders from the Big Paper I'd hoped they'd send me somewhere inland, but I hadn't had any choice about that.

Thirty kilometres later I turned off the highway then down another road that eventually narrowed to a gravel track. There were only a couple of houses; Melissa Dalton had grown up in the small cream fibro one. Several car bodies in various states of disrepair sat in the front yard and the trailer part of a semi-trailer was parked along one side of the house. I searched my mind for the appropriate piece of Australian lexicon. "Battlers". The Daltons were battlers.

The woman who opened the door to my knock looked as though she'd been battling all her life. She had a frazzled perm and the prematurely aged skin I'd seen on so many Australian country women. She looked a bit surprised to see me, but I'd got used to that around here.

'I'm Vee Nguyen, from the Star.' I held up my card. The only people who have ever called me Veronica are my parents and the nuns at school.

'Go away.' She started to close the door but I got my foot there first.

'Look Mrs Dalton, I know you're grieving, I know you've suffered a terrible loss...'

'You don't know anything about it!'

'...But don't you really want to know what happened to your daughter? There are rumours of suicide – would Melissa have killed herself?'

She hesitated. Her face was haggard from sleeplessness and she had the look of holding in too much emotion. I assumed my most compassionate expression.

'You better come in,' she said reluctantly.

There was a big old wooden table in the centre of the kitchen, spread with a sheet of flowered plastic.

'D'you want a cup of tea?'

'Thanks Mrs. Dalton.'

'Call me Val.'

She boiled the kettle, set the two mugs on the table and slumped into a chair. Suddenly she started talking in a flat monotone, a far-off expression on her face.

'Melissa was a bright kid but always in trouble, wouldn't listen to anyone. Ivan was always away driving trucks and I was left with the kids. She left school and worked in a supermarket for a while but the money wasn't enough. She started doing telephone sex – just for a joke, really. She said it was safe and clean...' Val Dalton's voice broke; I nodded sympathetically.

'When she started...seeing men...I tried to talk her out of it. I cried, I got angry, but nothing I said would change Melissa's mind. She just laughed and said they were stupid to part with that much money for something that lasted three minutes.'

'Is that when she started doing drugs?'

'No! Melissa didn't take drugs!'

'What about the cocaine?'

'I don't know!' Val Dalton almost shouted. 'But Melissa didn't take drugs – I would have known!

Oh, yeah. If my mother knew everything I'd ever done her hair would be snow white, not its current steel grey.

'She lived in town but she kept some of her things in her old room,' Val said, rising suddenly. 'She wasn't a bad kid, just easily influenced.'

The room was small and painted pink. Stick-on pictures of rabbits covered the cupboard doors.

'She had some nice clothes,' Val said.

She had some very nice clothes, I noted, before the doors were quickly shut. Versace. Armani. Expensive wear for a country call girl.

'Here's her photo.' A rounded, slightly chubby face stared from a chrome frame. The frame was cheap, the face pretty but unexceptional, with blonde hair smudged dark at the roots. A bluish-green dolphin curved across the swell of her left breast and buried its snout in her cleavage.

'Here's another.' A younger, thinner, dark-haired Melissa stood on a beach with three boys. All four held surfboards and smiled. They looked as though they were enjoying themselves. I repressed a shudder at the thought of all that water around me.

'Very nice.' I gave Val back the photos, asked her a few more general questions, then thanked her and left. On the way to my car two teenage boys, who had been fiddling with one of the old wrecks outside, gaped at me and sniggered. I flicked them the finger and drove off.

That night I dreamed about the woman in the water again. Nothing remarkable about that because I'd been having that dream for as long as I could remember. It was something I carried with me – like an ulcer or an ache – but I'd never had it two nights running. The cold sea slapped against her dead flesh and the waves rolled her over and over until she sank from sight. I lay sleepless and sweating at 3am and thought about Melissa floating in the dark and hostile ocean. Something didn't add up. The autopsy had shown that Melissa hadn't had sex recently, which seemed to rule out a client turning nasty. The cocaine in her bloodstream had been almost pure, which was unusual. On my way to work, irritable and bleary-eyed, I rang Val Dalton.

'The three boys in the photo, the surfies. Who are they?'

She thought for a moment. 'Dazza, Wayne and Chook,' she said finally.

Chook. How I love these charmingly whimsical Aussie nicknames. I'd never met a Chook although I did know several boys born in the Year of the Tiger.

'Where can I find them?'

'As far as I know they're still surfing,' she said and hung up. Damn! Never mind. Kololoroit only had two beaches – the surfie beach and the family beach. Dazza, Wayne and Chook shouldn't be too hard to track down. All this would have to wait, though, because this morning I had to interview the mayor.

'Nguyen, eh?' said the big, florid-faced man heartily after his secretary ushered me into his office. 'I was in 'Nam myself.'

'So was I,' I replied, smiling. Like it takes a genius to work out that Nguyen is the Vietnamese equivalent of Smith.

He gave a burst of laughter and gestured towards a chair. 'What can I do for you, Vee?'

'I'd like your perspective on this development project the council is proposing, the large scale building of luxury waterfront apartments.'

'Look, it's a fantastic opportunity for Kololoroit, Vee.' He gestured expansively again. I got the feeling Peter McCulloch liked to think of himself as an expansive sort of bloke. I watched him as he sat behind his big, well-ordered desk, with the big wall planner behind him neatly marked. One corner of the desk held a photo of a handsome, slightly hard-faced woman. I noted the absence of children.

'...And, of course, besides creating jobs in the construction sector, it'll bring a lot of tourist dollars into the town.'

'What about the opposition from various community groups? Aren't there concerns about what the development will do to the habitats of various marine life?'

'You mean the greenies who're worried about the porpoises, ratbags led by that stirrer, Rod Shannon?'

'Well, you can understand their concern.'

He looked at me for a moment. 'The council will commission a full environmental impact study when the development project goes ahead.'

By whom, I wondered, but I left it at that for the moment. I asked a few more questions about his hopes for the project then wrapped up the interview. As I stood up to leave I noticed some small, whitish-gold stones sitting on the corner of his desk.

'Hoping to strike it rich?'

He looked at the pieces of quartz and gave a slightly embarrassed laugh. 'I was up north attending an official function last week in the centre of the gold rush district. I used to go fossicking there with my father when I was a kid. Brought those back for old times' sake.'

He escorted me to the door and put his hand on my shoulder. I felt his slight but unmistakable ripple of sexual interest.

'You take it easy now, Vee,' he said.

I was in my car on my way back to the office when my mobile rang. Bloody Kevin, I thought, but it was another male voice.

'Is that Vee?' it asked nervously.

'Yes.'

'Vee the journalist?'

'Yes. Who is this?'

'Dazza. You wanted to talk to me about Lissa.'

'That was quick work, finding me.'

'Yeah, well, word gets 'round.'

Oh, it certainly does. I arranged to meet him on the beach where Melissa's body had been found, swung the car in the opposite direction and contemplated how quickly word can get around. Ten months ago I'd been an A-grade reporter on a major metropolitan daily. I was hot. I was so hot I'd managed to uncover a paedophile ring. I'd watched and followed, researched, then had done some more watching and following. I'd gone close enough to take photos of some of the men I'd believed were involved. One of them was the newspaper owner's son. I'd gone to my editor with the photos. He'd spread them out on his desk then looked at me.

'If you try to make a story out of this, I'll fire you.'

I was stunned. I'd counted on his support.

'You can't do that,' I said at last.

'Yes, I can.'

'No, you can't!'

We stared at each other for a moment and he looked away first.

'This is the wealthiest, most powerful family in the country,' he said.

'Who just happen to own this paper and pay your $100,000 salary and provide your company car and all the other perks that go with your job.'

He picked up a pencil from his desk and turned it over and over in his hands.

'If you don't drop this, I'll drop you.'

'You gutless prick!' I stormed out of his office, so angry that I had to go for a walk to calm down, which was stupid, stupid because by the time I got back my desk had been mysteriously rifled and the photos and the file about the paedophile ring had disappeared. I stormed, I ranted, I accused, but because I'd told no one else about the photos, I couldn't prove I'd ever had them. Anyway, it was too hot for me to stay in the city. Eight weeks later I was working on the Kololoroit Star.

I sat on the beach and waited until the three black specks far out on the ocean paddled in. The bleached blond from Val Dalton's photo stuck his hand out.

'I'm Dazza.' Chook was short and chunky with a square, acne-scarred face. Wayne was lean, dark and taciturn-looking.

'Good weather for it.' I gestured towards the water. 'Thanks for seeing me.'

Dazza shrugged. 'Val said you were all right. What do you want to know?'

What did I want to know? It suddenly seemed pointless being here. All I had were a couple of half-arsed ideas and a feeling in my gut.

'I don't know...' I floundered about. 'Why did Melissa like surfing?'

'She liked the freedom,' Chook said. 'She used to say that riding a great wave was like flying.'

'She used to go surfing at night,' Wayne said.

'At night!' I remembered my dream – it's always night in the dream – and shuddered. 'Wasn't that dangerous?'

'Lissa was wild.' Dazza glanced across the ocean as though searching for something – or someone. 'She was a wild chick. You couldn't tell her anything. In warm weather she'd go out on her board and sometimes she'd be naked. She used to say it was like being bathed in starlight.'

Shit. It sounded bizarre, but then so does bungy-jumping and plenty of people do that. I pressed on.

'What else did she do?'

'When she wasn't working, you mean?' Wayne glanced at me sharply. 'She liked raging, she liked a few drinks, she liked reading.'

'Reading?' Not an activity I'd envisaged her spending much time on.

'She acted like a bimbo when it suited her, but she wasn't dumb,' said Chook. 'She liked to read poetry and that.'

Oh, yeah, and Elle McPherson's a brain surgeon.

'No, true story.' He caught my expression. 'The last night we saw her we lit a fire on the beach and sat around having a few bongs. Lissa was ravin' on about some old Pommy guy, William Blake, about how important he was...'

'So she did use drugs?'

'Not hard stuff.' Dazza frowned. 'Not cocaine.'

'But someone might have talked her into–'

'I reckon we would have known if she'd started on it.' Wayne voice held a note of finality.

I felt I was getting nowhere. 'You were her friends. Isn't there anyone else she was close to?'

Dazza gave another of his shrugs. 'She used to hang out at PAG.'

We live in a world of acronyms and it's impossible to know them all.

'Porpoise Action Group,' said Chook. 'The people who are against that beach development. Lissa was a bit of a greenie.'

I remembered the tattoo on her breast; not a dolphin, after all.

'Check out Rod Shannon.' Dazza fixed his eyes on the waves again and started moving off. 'Lissa used to talk to him.'

This was the second time Rod Shannon's name had come up today. I thanked them and made my way across the sand, past the place where

Melissa Dalton had died. There was a piece of crime scene tape sticking out of the sand, surrounded by some pretty shells and pebbles. I picked a few up and stuffed them in my pocket as my mobile rang.

'Vee, where are you, for Christ's sake? You were meant to be interviewing Valmai Turner about the CWA embroidery exhibition an hour ago.'

I figured Valmai could wait, gave Kevin some bullshit excuse and followed the directions Dazza had given me. The wind had freshened slightly; out on the water a number of fishing boats plied their trade. The PAG office was located, along with a number of other community groups, in a ramshackle weatherboard building not far from the beach. Rod Shannon was about thirty, with dark hair and a good-looking face marred by a rather sneering expression.

'Yeah, Lissa used to come in here. She made that.' He indicated a silk screen poster of leaping porpoises. The colours were crude but the poster had a certain vitality.

'It's a pity she couldn't have put her talents to better use.'

'Ah, well,' he grinned. 'Things weren't going well on the farm so she came into town to hawk the fork.'

What a charmer. What a prince. I gritted my teeth and persevered but he couldn't tell me much except that Melissa had helped out with some PAG activities. I glanced around the room. Leaflets and posters proclaimed various environmental concerns and there were also a number of organisational charts and diagrams.

'Is that the date the PAG meetings are held?' I asked, pointing.

'What?' He followed my gaze then glanced at me sharply. 'Oh, yeah, yeah...we have them every month.'

'You have them the night of each new moon. Is that something symbolic?'

'Eh? Oh, yeah, yeah.'

'I see. And you do a bit of surfing?' A sleek, tri-finned board stood propped in a corner.

'Yeah,' he laughed. 'Although it's been gathering dust. Things are so hectic – with everything that arsehole McCulloch's trying to do – I haven't had the time.'

'Did you ever go surfing with Melissa?'

'No.' He gave me another surprised look. 'Did she surf?'

I left his office feeling annoyed and perplexed. Why had he denied knowing about Melissa's favourite pastime? His evasiveness only strengthened my desire to find out about her death. Something stank around here and it wasn't just the seaweed drying in the sun.

That night I had the dream again but, unlike all the other times, the woman held up her arms and seemed to beckon me forward. The wind whipped her long black hair around her but when I got close, her features dissolved and the water pulled her from my grasp. I startled out of my sleep, sweating; the clock read 4:10. I went into the kitchen, made myself a cup of herbal tea and tried to put all the puzzle pieces together. They all had something to do with the ocean – and with surfing. Perhaps a long walk by the sea was the place to work all this out. I started feeling drowsy; a woman's face appeared briefly behind my eyelids as I dozed off, but I couldn't tell who she was.

The sea was jade-green and flat as a dinner plate. Huge limpid clouds stretched out across the sky, looking like the lost continents on antiquarian maps and, at the horizon, a smudged cobalt line delineated ocean from air. The wind would be at work out there, pushing the water up or flattening it down and, miles below, currents of warm water collided with currents of cold water to create the tension which broke the ocean's skin and came rolling in as tier after tier of white-cresting foam. The waves carried secrets, the unwanted cargo of ships and lives, which were tossed up on the beach or buried beneath the shifting dunes. Years might go past before a heavy storm stripped back the sand to reveal shards of rusted metal or the smooth-polished wood of ships' ribs.

There were stories in the district of women walking on the beach last century, lifting dragging skirts as they waded towards the flotsam and jetsam of wrecks, but today there was only the sun shining benignly and a cormorant dipping its neck for food. It almost looked pleasant. I felt the breeze blow away the tension clustered in my temples and at the base of my skull as I walked but I still couldn't see the answer to the puzzle. A dead prostitute who read William Blake; greenies who held their meetings on the night of the new moon: all these things rolled around my mind like the stones and shells rolling about on the sand. I stood looking out to the ocean's dark secret places and at the boats on the horizon. The boats on the horizon. Suddenly, as I gazed at the boats, all the pieces clicked into place and I knew why Melissa Dalton had died.

I was hungry so I went to the Chinese restaurant, which is Kololoroit's only "ethnic" eatery. I've nothing against the Chinese although my father always speaks about them guardedly: 'They've been in my country for 1000 years and we've been friends for 100'. Excellent noodles. After I'd eaten I went back to the office, braved Kevin's wrath and made some phone calls. I had a trap to set.

He was waiting for me on the beach that night, with the water still as black ice and the stars gleaming coldly above.

'You dropped this.' I held up the small piece of quartz. 'I found it down here yesterday.'

Peter McCulloch was no longer dressed in a suit or his mayoral robes. He wore jeans, a windcheater and an expression of extreme dislike.

'I used to go with girls like you in 'Nam, you slant-eyed cunt. One of you miserable whores gave me gonorrhoea, which I passed onto my wife when I came home. It made her infertile. We couldn't have kids.'

'You don't like women much, do you?' I said. 'Is that why you killed Melissa?'

'The greedy little bitch wouldn't have kept her mouth shut! She kept asking for more and more money.'

I remembered the Italian designer clothes. 'She found out about the cocaine smuggling, didn't she? She was out surfing one night and she saw Rod Shannon bringing it in. It was very convenient to have the development project acting as a smokescreen so the two of you could carry on your little business undetected.'

He gave a short laugh. 'You're more than a nice pair of tits, Vee. How did you work it out?"

'Your wall planners. They had identical dates circled. It was stupid and arrogant of you both to have them displayed. When I asked Rod Shannon about his he got flustered and told me the circled dates were PAG meetings, but when I checked with another member of the group, I was told a different story. And the stuff about the new moon – which I thought was hippie tangential bullshit – made it just that much easier for him to go out on his board and collect the drugs. But he didn't count on Melissa's starlight safari. That's why he told me he didn't know she surfed.'

'You'll never prove it,' Peter McCulloch grinned.

'Oh, I already have. The fixation Melissa had with William Blake. When I checked with the harbour authority, I found there's only one boat whose visits coincided with those dates – the Tyger. The captain got taken into custody this afternoon and I believe he's singing like the proverbial canary. You're in deep shit, McCulloch.'

'And you're going to be in deep water, bitch,' he said, advancing across the sand. I hadn't been thinking. I'd let myself get between him and the ocean.

'It's going to be so easy to hold you under for a few minutes.'

'This is stupid!' But I knew whatever I said wouldn't help. I recognised an ego out of control, a maniac whose plans had gone wrong. I screamed as his hands closed around my throat. I struggled but he was stronger. As he pushed me down, I had a brief vision of a woman staring lifelessly up at me. I couldn't breathe. Things started to go black and I felt the water close over my head.

I couldn't swim, of course. I'd had hysterics when they put me in the pool in primary school, so I was glad I'd strategically posted Kevin – and his best mate, the local copper – behind the dunes. I didn't like relying on men so much but they proved more useful than a pair of water wings. When they pulled me from the sea I was cold and choking. Kevin put his coat around me then took me home while the cop took Peter McCulloch somewhere else.

'You sure you'll be all right?' Kevin asked anxiously.

'Yes,' I replied and, strangely, after I'd eaten and had a shower, I was.

It was as though being forced into the ocean had removed some old and heavy weight. That night I slept deeply and dreamlessly and in the morning I phoned my mother.

'Mum,' I asked, 'what really happened on the boat out to Australia?'

There was a long silence on the other end.

'If you really want to know that,' she said at last, 'you'll have to come home.'

So I drove home through the green rolling plains until I reached that peculiar no man's land of warehouses and oil refineries outside the western suburbs, where nothing grows, nothing survives, except a few scrubby trees sucking at the grime. When I got to my parents' neat brick bungalow in Footscray, my mother told me.

It had been a long voyage from Vietnam, three nights and two days with no food and very little water. On the morning of the third day the boat had been attacked by Thai pirates. They'd swarmed on board, killing some of the men; then they'd started on the women. My mother had been heavily pregnant with my younger brother. That's why they'd spared her. Others weren't so lucky.

'There was one girl,' my mother said. 'She was only about nineteen. She had a young baby. She was raped three times before she jumped overboard. I tried to stop you watching but that's what you saw, that young girl drowning. You were only three. I hoped you wouldn't remember.'

Tears rolled down her face as she spoke, and I knew she'd never talked to anyone about this.

'I tried to stop you watching, but...' We held each other and cried.

'Yes,' I said, when I could speak. 'I've always liked to know what's going on.'

Two months later I stood on the sand where I had almost died and watched the big gold disc of the rising sun gild the water. It hadn't yet warmed the air but I had my wetsuit on; I had my almost-new board under my arm. I'd been learning for a month and was already improving. 'You're a natural, girl,' Dazza had said recently. I'm not a very religious person but as I paddled out to meet the first wave I said a prayer for Melissa and hoped she'd be happy to see me there, because when you overcome your deepest fear, a whole new world can open up to you.

I didn't know whether I'd be staying in Kololoroit. I'd already had two job offers from larger papers. Perhaps I'd choose the one that had a beach nearby. Anyway, after all that had happened there didn't seem to be much enthusiasm for the development project going ahead. As I felt the surge of the water beneath me and stood to embrace its power I saw, far across the ocean, the grey arcs of porpoises leaping and rising, leaping and rising, against the waves.

2001

BIRTHING THE DEMONS

Josephine Pennicott

"For the hand that rocks the cradle
is the hand that rules the world."

William Ross Wallace, *What Rules the World*

"We're still blaming mothers."

Joyce Flint (Jeffrey Dahmer's mother)

THERE IS NO ESCAPE.

When you realise that fact, there is a small measure of acceptance. A slight, cooling breeze of relief.

No escape. No escape. No escape.

Tears can flow then. Anger can escape at different times, but at least these states are preferable to the early shock. The numbing denial.

No escape. Even the night is not a friend. Odd little memories come creeping, whispering malevolently into your ear, waking you up, screaming.

I'm as much a prisoner as he is.

Jim refuses to discuss it with me, as he has refused to discuss so many things over the years, but I know that the same demons embrace him in the night. I've heard the agonised sobbing into the pillow in the early hours before dawn.

Last night I walked into a room. It felt like a room from my childhood, but it was not familiar to me. Fresh flowers were in the vase, there was a fire in the grate. The hearth…there was something on the hearth, cold, dark and wet. An icy, wet communication spurts in my veins. I know, I know what the horrible thing is. Her. Bits of her. Skull and hair and brains and blood, all over my nice clean hearth. Then I wake up with a rush and I begin to cry quietly. But not quietly enough, for Jim hears.

'Leave it, Evie,' he says wearily.

I spend the rest of the night listening to the sounds of traffic gradually increase, cats fighting on the roof next door, a light shower of rain around 4am. Then light, gradually breaking.

No escape.

I lie there, trying not to cry, trying not to think, to remember her. Him. Her. Her. Him.

I wait for dawn.

It is hard to believe that one act can alter so many people's lives; that your routine can change so quickly overnight. And how, after that one act, all the old rules of the game have been replaced, but nobody has told you what the new ones are. Yesterday, I walked into the butcher's on High Street, thinking that Jim might like a nice roast. I couldn't remember the last time I had cooked him a proper meal. There was once a time that I wouldn't have gotten away with that. If a clean cloth wasn't on the table, butter in the butter dish, fresh bread rolls and a cooked meal with four veg, he would have been complaining. Now he doesn't seem to notice or care. We sit with trays on our knees in front of the TV, eating scrambled egg, fish fingers, finger food.

In the butcher's, the conversation ceased as soon as I entered. Enid McKillop and Rita Davies were there. I went to school with Rita. They said hello. Their faces had that half-interested, half-embarrassed look, and they hurried out together, clutching their bundles of white-papered meat, as if I was a bad smell.

I cooked the lamb and vegetables. They were too soggy, and we ate on trays in front of the TV. Once, I looked over at Jim, and he was sitting there, quietly crying.

That night I stood in the darkened sunroom, looking out the window at the house across the street. Shadows surrounded it. The "For Sale" sign, dim in the moonlight, mocked me with the change to come. I watched the shadows move silently around the house for hours, remembering another distant night, when those shadows had come to life and entered that house...

I asked the house for answers, for I had long given up on asking God. I could feel the lamb sitting heavily in my stomach. I would have to take some Normacol before I went to bed tonight. Steam from my breath frosted the glass, and for a wild moment I thought I saw Joy sitting on her floral outdoor sofa, a pile of glossy magazines beside her. She would often cut out little recipes for me that she imagined we would like to try.

'Here's an easy recipe for Thai coconut soup, Evie. Do you think that they will carry the ingredients for it down at Warrens?'

'Bloody interfering old busybody,' Jim never failed to complain. 'Probably only hoping for a free feed at our house.'

But I enjoyed the little ritual, that small attention. My parents had long retired to the warmth of a Queensland retirement village, and Joy's little clippings had made me feel nurtured.

Our son Leslie had never taken to her. 'She's a snob,' he'd say if I tried to encourage him to do chores for her. 'She has evil eyes,' he would add.

A part of me knew what he meant. Joy did have unusual eyes. Vivid blue, hardly the eyes of an old woman approaching her 84th birthday. Perhaps there had always been some ominous warning in those young girl's eyes that I had failed to see. Then a darker thought. A memory I had once – for I had been there – but had blocked out. What did those eyes look like when they found her? Were they open or closed?

It had been the flies that had warned me. A great swarming mass of them. I could hear them as I stood behind the screen door. 'Joy?'

Jim had been furious at me for not listening to him, for ignoring his commands to stay home and not cross the street to see if Joy was all right. I hadn't seen her for days. Jim sulked in front of one of his wildlife specials; gorillas in the wild, or chimps; some kind of monkeys, anyway.

Leslie had screamed at me when I voiced my concerns out aloud. 'Leave it, Evie!' he said. 'Don't go interfering and encouraging the old bitch. You do too much for her now!' He hadn't forgiven me for telling Joy that he would mow her lawns and do some handiwork around the house. He'd been sulking for weeks over that one. Jim and Leslie were like two peas in a pod at times. It was depressing.

It had been the flies on that hot, summery day. I could hear them buzzing as I wondered what to do.

'Joy? I've made you some caramel slice,' I called, trying to balance the slice and the weekly magazines I had finished with. The door behind the screen was ajar. Without thinking, I pushed it open and stepped into the cool hallway I had been in a thousand times before. There was a faint smell. Something rotten. Oh, God. I had been preparing myself for this for years. I had always known when I befriended Joy there would come a day when I would visit her to find her lifeless body in the bath, or in bed.

'Joy?' The flies buzzed angrily back at me. I could hear the loud, annoying tick of Joy's antique grandfather clock. I walked into the small lounge room, placing the plate of caramel slice down carefully on the table. God, the place was such a mess. Drawers were pulled out, a broken glass lay on the fire hearth. I pulled my cotton T-shirt up over my nose. I knew, but I had to see. The rotten smell intensified as I approached the bedroom.

I had often sat, looking at the television, eyes fastened on the pages of a book, trying to trace meaning and reason in my mind. If I hadn't nagged him to help out next door. If I hadn't befriended Joy. If I hadn't sent him to the local high school. If I had taken more attention of the reports from his primary school of behavioural problems, of his fights with other children.

If he had not made friends with Jude Ward and Timothy Bailey...

IF.

The word had seared into my brain. IF I had bought him more pets. IF I had fed him less meat. IF I had been able to have another child. IF we had never hit him to discipline him. IF we had hit him harder when he was caught shoplifting. IF I had monitored his television viewing, his Internet access. But, there was one IF that I inevitably returned to, a one-way nightmare ending in a dirty truth...

IF I had never given birth to him. IF I had never conceived him.

The pregnancy had been far from easy. I vomited constantly, head always over a toilet bowl. That was how I remembered most of my pregnancy. The smell, and the off-white colour of the porcelain. Even back then it was as if my body had somehow known and tried to eject the dangerous seed it nurtured. Then there were the nightmares. I would wake screaming, bathed in sweat, the sheets soaked, with Jim trying to calm me. My hands would be on my stomach, my body stretched flat and rigid and tremors rippling through my body. Mine was never the glowing, radiant pregnancy I had dreamed of. My body had seemed alien to me. Death filled my head with fear, and death had lingered in my nostrils and in my mouth. I became convinced I was going to die in childbirth. I often dreamt a black seed was sprouting within me, filling my body with dark hairy roots, with dark octopus tentacles. Then there were the dreams I felt too ashamed to discuss with well-meaning friends, who smiled benignly and gave me coloured booties and stuffed animals. I knew my dreams were not normal. If only I had said something.

IF, IF, IF, IF.

The birth was agony. A baptism of pain. I had longed for death, for oblivion. I hated everyone for concealing the pain of delivery from me, and when they had cut the cord I felt only relief that the thing inside me was free. Jim cried over the fact that it was a boy, but I had remained weirdly detached. Between shit and piss we are born. My grandmother liked to cackle that phrase before my mother had her committed to the

nursing hospital. It used to hurt and anger my mother when she said it, but now I knew what she meant.

Over time, I gradually recovered from the crippling depression that had filled me when Leslie was born. My initial rejection of him was replaced by an intense love that rippled through every facet of my life. His first steps, his first tooth, his first Christmas. These were all symbolic milestones to be treasured. Time now contained a depth it had always lacked. I longed for another child, quickly forgetting the pain of birth; but Jim already had two grown up children from a previous marriage and baulked at the idea. If we had had more children, would things have been different?

IF, IF, IF, IF.

There had been no signs. That was another detail I had tormented myself with. He had always seemed happy enough. I knew he worried about his weight and had been depressed over Bill and Cynthia's daughter rejecting him. But, most teenage boys went through things like that, didn't they? I found it difficult to recall my youth, but I was sure I had copped my fair share of rejection. I knew he could be antisocial and didn't make friends easily, but I just put that down to shyness. I could be like that myself. That was why Joy's friendship was so important to me. Had been important to me. Then there were the times he had sat staring into space for hours on end, vacant-faced like a zombie, his mind seemingly void of thoughts.

Jim blamed Leslie's friends for what happened, but I wasn't convinced. 'They need a bullet between the eyes,' he said once, his voice low and intense, hands shaking. From what I had been able to gather from the different policemen who spoke to me over the weeks, all three boys were equally responsible, and each had taken their turn in mutilating the body. But there had been no signs! I had read in the newspaper a list of symptoms that we were meant to see: bedwetting, fire-starting, cruelty to animals. There had been nothing. Nothing. Well, nothing that had stood out, so I felt cheated of even those small signs from God that might have helped me.

Lavender and roses. That was the overriding impression when I closed my eyes and thought of Joy. The sweet fragrances of Crabtree and Evelyn. For sure, it would have been Crabtree and Evelyn that she liked to anoint herself with, I thought. Not just any old supermarket floral talc or spray like I'd put in my shopping trolley. No, Joy was about quality. I wasn't used to luxuries – there'd never been enough money for too many extras when I grew up – but there was no mistaking the sheer quality of Joy's possessions. The fine bone china crockery, the simpering china figurines, the gold fountain pen that she wrote her shopping list with, in flowing copperplate script.

I could see Joy now, in her smart brown slacks and her cream silk blouse, immaculately pressed. She'd peer through her tortoiseshell glasses, carefully considering each item on her list, then open the wooden camphor chest from Thailand where she kept her large green purse and count out her money for me to take to the shops for her.

I loved to visit that house. Its mellow, measured tones spoke of other, exciting lifetimes; of people who thought nothing of eating out in restaurants, of reading books by Proust and Jane Austen, which had bindings of red leather. Around the house there were large black-and-white photographs of Joy and James when they had been young and glowing with health. On safari in Africa, outside the Eiffel tower. These places were as remote to me as the Moon. Joy looked like a young Jane Russell with her shoulder-length, dark crimped hair and her bright lipstick; and James was a fair-haired Clark Gable. But time was cruel. James had died years ago of bowel cancer, and now Joy...

Joy, or what remained of her, had been carried from her home by faceless paramedics. As the covered stretcher disappeared into a vehicle I floated in a tranquillized haze, where pain lurked like the neighbours twitching behind their curtains.

Joy wasn't a local. She had moved to the quiet little seaside community of Oricheno on the central coast from Sydney. Many of the locals had thought her too uppity for the town, and watched with resentful eyes when she would make her way up our street with the tortoiseshell walking stick she had bought in Italy. They had used that walking stick to...

I had to fight to control the mental picture that I knew would follow.

I was local, but it was me that the locals had turned on like a pack of rabid dogs. Just a few days after it happened I went to the shop for some milk. The stares, the comments, the people whom I had known all my life crossing the street to avoid me! Then Jilly Edwards – she always was a dirty slag – stepped up to me and spat at me in front of everyone.

'You're responsible!' she hissed. 'You gave birth to that creep!' She pushed me suddenly and I stumbled into the gutter.

'Leave her alone!' a man's voice called, and slowly the spectators drifted away to gossip about it behind closed doors. Jilly waddled into the schoolyard and I watched her fat bottom disappearing whilst I attempted to pick myself up. A part of me wanted to go after her and engage in a screaming match in front of the whole town, but it was useless. I was defeated and I knew it. For I agreed with her. I felt responsible. I was the one who bore him. Between shit and piss we are born. I could feel my grandmother cackling triumphantly over me.

I went to visit him only once. Jim drove me there, but refused to come in. Instead he sat in the car, listening to talkback radio and munching his way through packets of Quick-Eze. He was so wired up, smoke could have drifted from his body; he looked ready to combust before my eyes. I had been afraid to insist that he accompany me inside; afraid that he would erupt into a tirade of abuse, or strike out at me. Although, when I really think about it, anything would have been preferable than his withdrawal, his half-smothered sobs in the privacy of night.

I was wearing a cotton floral dress I had bought at Katies years ago on a rare trip to Sydney. I felt underdressed and frumpy as I approached the prison – or correction centre – whatever they called it.

I could feel Jim's eyes on my back, like twin rays of hate. 'What's happened to us?' I wanted to turn and call. 'Once we were young and in love. You left your wife and kids for me. We dreamt of travel, and we made love in the afternoon on the sofa. How could it have all gone so quickly? When did we age?'

But I knew the answer. It had all gone when Leslie was born. Slowly, irrevocably, like a miniature vampire living amongst us and feeding daily, surreptitiously on our youth, love, lust and hope.

There were forms to sign, and I was searched. Other friends and relatives were going through the same degrading procedure. A young, skinny blonde girl sat chain-smoking outside. Chinese symbols were tattooed on her fragile arms. A pram sat next to her, which she shook violently, screaming into it in a futile attempt to stop the incessant crying from inside. She could have passed for fourteen. A young man was mopping the floor. I avoided his eyes, fearing that he was one of the inmates. The foyer smelt of lemon disinfectant, and there were Australian bush scenes on the walls.

I was shocked when he first appeared from behind a door at the rear of the room and approached the glass where the visitors sat. He looked so different. Older, fatter. I felt tears come to my eyes at his transformation.

He sat down and avoided my eyes. 'You shouldn't have come.'

I began to cry, feeling that the pain would splinter me into a thousand pieces. Guards looked on with boredom; they must have seen it all a thousand times before. The skinny girl was about three chairs down from me, holding the baby up to the glass. The screaming continued and the child was now red in the face.

'Where's the old man?' Leslie muttered. The words came filled with contempt.

'He couldn't face it. He hasn't been well, Les. All the worry about you. And his work laid him off.'

My son, the stranger, looked at me directly. Did I glimpse a momentary pain in his expression? 'He's in the car outside,' he sneered.

'Are you eating well?' I asked. He leaned forward, ignoring the inane question.

'Go home, Evie,' he said. 'I don't want you here.'

'Why, Leslie?' I cried from a terrible place within me. 'What made you do it? Were you drunk? Did those friends of yours make you do it? Was it something I did? It's not you, Leslie! God, you gave to World Vision! You hated fights and scenes. Something happened to you! Please talk to me! Make me understand!'

He laughed. 'You would never understand Evie,' he said. 'You would never understand. I did it because she was there, and we could. It just got out of control.'

'What did I do wrong?' I asked again. I desperately needed an answer. He looked at me with disdain.

'Everything, Evie,' he said. 'Everything. I wish I had never been born.'

In my mind, I walk across the road and Joy is waiting for me. She is smiling as she opens the front door, pushing her hair back from her forehead. Her young woman's eyes are genuinely delighted to see me. The sounds of Bach waft from the house, and I hold my arms out to her and embrace her. I smell her hair which smells of lemon shampoo and I feel her warm skin and her bones. She is alive and she is filled with the sunshine that has disappeared from my life.

In darker dreams, I approach my sleeping child's cradle. I tenderly place a white pillow over his peaceful little face, and hold it tightly. I take the evil that even now is smouldering inside him. IF. IF. IF. IF.

The truth is so much harder to think about. Leslie had been grudgingly doing odd jobs at Joy's for a month or so. Mostly it was the heavier tasks that were too much for her. Sometimes it was a little job inside, adjusting a mirror, cleaning a chimney. He had come to know the house, her possessions, where she kept her money. He had waited, shown a patience and slyness that I would not have guessed him capable of. The police found emails he sent to Jude and Timothy, detailed plans of what they called Operation Gaa Gaa. They had entered the house silently while Jim and I slept oblivious over the road. Then for the next few hours they had given rise to every perversion they carried within them.

They had woken her. I can only imagine her terror when she opened those bright eyes to see the three boys looking down upon her. They had shown her no mercy as they bound her to the bed, taunting her the entire time. They tortured her. Jim and I had almost frozen with horror in the court when we heard what they had done to her body. They had taken their turns raping her, cheering each other on and calling obscenities as they rode her. They kept her alive for hours, smearing her face with their semen, destroying her valued items in front of her, breaking her fingers one by one and using her as a human ashtray for their cigarettes. When they had finished with their Dionysian madness, Timothy cut her throat. Then they dismembered her body, placing her parts in assorted corners around the room like a grotesque broken doll.

I found her head first, that day I walked into her fly-covered room. It sat by itself, obscenely disconnected, in its own world of blood and gore. At first I thought the shock of that discovery would kill me.

But worse was yet to come.

It is not easy being the mother of a demon. At times I imagine even Jim is looking at me with suspicion in his eyes, believing that at some crucial point I must have failed him to create this evil. But, somehow Jim has been excused by the townspeople; it's my blood they bay for.

I think of mothers across history; Hitler's mother, Judas's mother, Saddam Hussein's mother. I feel for them, mourn for their innocence lost. We have to bear the shame, the blame. We have to be the object of outrage and venom spat by people who were once friends. I remember reading an article by the mother of one of the juvenile killers of James Bulger, that little boy in England. She said that everywhere she went she felt as if she had killer engraved into her forehead.

We are mothers who are mourning death, destruction and chaos, like a grotesque Pieta statue. We have been judged guilty by societies who fear the contagion of demons. We are the rotten trees that have sprouted rotten fruit. I feel like whispering to mothers as I pass them in the street: Take care, take care, take care. Do not think you are indestructible, that it can never happen to you. Take care, for unknown shadows deep within your silent soul might one day shift without warning and echo in another.

The house across the street continues to haunt me. I long to move and start a new life under a new name, but Jim won't hear of it. 'We'll take that bloody house with us,' he says with red-rimmed eyes. I sense accusation in his glance. He had always opposed me befriending Joy, had always been critical of Leslie working at Joy's. I was convinced that I represented failure in his life. Kathy, his first wife, had raised his two other children. One became a doctor, the other a teacher. Kathy hadn't harboured a killer in her womb, a monster destined to become the talk of Australia. The fruit doesn't fall too far from the tree. There had been some madness in my family. My mother's mother and her brother had both killed themselves. Was there some dark artery running through our family tree that Leslie had emerged from? Was my son the innocent victim of destructive silent demons lurking in our genetic closet?

One day a new family would move in over the road, and I dreaded the day. Their children would play in Joy's garden and their pets would chase her ghost from the house. I wanted to allow myself to somehow believe she was still inside the house, looking at her beautiful photographs, gardening, clipping out recipes for me, smiling peacefully in her refined, genteel world.

Last visit. Last memory of him. Sitting there, fidgeting awkwardly across from me. There are sleep buds in the corners of his eyes, his hands are pudgy and there are cuts over them. I hate to think of what his hands have done. I am crying openly now into a tissue, a million memories flooding through me. The stranger sitting opposite me is my history. I have cherished all his birthdays, his early drawings, read him books, scolded him over his smutty magazines, taken him to the doctor, bandaged his knees, and yelled at him for a thousand little misdeeds. I know the smell of his sweat, the look of his dirty underwear. I nervously related the facts of life to him. I comforted him when he woke up screaming from nightmares. 'Stop it, Evie,' he says. 'Just go. You're just upsetting yourself.'

'Why?' I plead again. 'What did I do wrong? Or was it something else? Did something else trigger you?'

'It just happened,' he says again. His eyes are wary, not wanting to have to relive that night. 'There doesn't always have to be a reason, does there? You're as bad as the fucking shrinks.' His eyes flicker with a trace of buried emotion. Is it remorse? Mirth? Anguish? I will never know.

He leaves me quickly, without looking back.

I return to Jim, my feet swollen and aching in shoes that I never normally wear. I can feel a blister beginning to form on my heel and I welcome any pain that will distract me, punish me. I must deserve some punishment to have reared this monster from my flesh and blood.

'Ready then?' Jim says. I can sense his curiosity, his anger. He will not ask. I will not tell. I watch the city streets, the strangers at traffic lights, all a blur. I can smell rain in the air. A headache is building within my temples. We are halfway home when the storm breaks and we are treated to a sudden lightning display over Berries Hill. We journey like familiar strangers, in silence.

PECKING ORDER

Roxxy Bent

THIS IS NOT A COOL STORY FOR VEGETARIANS. I MYSELF WAS A VEGETARIAN for a short time. However, even though I will never eat meat again (and here I include fish), a horrific action I took disqualifies me from the pure status of vegetarian. I've given myself a 10-year sentence for my crime. I'll be 25 by the time I can declare myself a bona fide vegetarian. Do I have regrets? Was it worth it? Would I do it again? Yes, yes, and yes again.

I read that after a traumatic event, it's advisable to tell the story to sympathetic ears at least eight times. As this is not a story I can tell to my friends, not least because of my recently acquired stutter, I am hoping that the act of writing it down will do the same job.

This tale of great changes begins, typically you might think, on a Monday. Monday mornings had always been a wrench for Mum and me. All weekend we'd be outside doing countless, interesting projects on our two-acre block, then reach Monday morning and it'd be, 'Oh, no! Back to reality!' I loved being with Mum, doing projects, gardening. Until a year and a half ago, that is. Until then I thought Mum and I were both blissfully happy, busy little bees. But apparently, according to Trevor, I was wrong.

A year and a half ago, Trevor arrived on the scene, became Mum's live-in partner (notice I don't volunteer the term "step-dad") and then the world I knew, and everything I thought was important to me, changed.

Although it was a project – Project Chooks – which led to the murderous act that would ultimately put a stop to the world Trevor had forced upon us, I believe it was only a vehicle. I would have found some other way to rock our so-called family's boat. I had to. It needed it.

The idea for Project Chooks came at the tail end of the first weekend Mum and I had spent together since Trevor moved in eighteen months ago. We'd had such a good time. We'd made this awesome sandpit for my half-sister, Caitlin, who's very cute, only sixteen months old and staggering around on her two pins.

Maybe you'll have gathered by now that Caitlin is the reason why

Trevor moved in with us. Mum got pregnant when she had a one-night stand with Trevor after her end-of-year work party. One minute there's just us, next there's Trevor, and a few months later, Caitlin, too! Mum was unbelievably happy to be pregnant. I didn't fully grasp the fact that our radically altered living situation was permanent. When I did, I went into shock.

Back to the Monday. It was a tad more stressy than usual because, as well as Mum and me getting ready for work and school respectively, Caitlin was banging on the door and screaming, 'Out! Out!' to get to her sand pit.

'Caitlin, bubs,' comforted Mum as she rushed by to answer yet another phone call.

Trevor, not about to be torn from his paper a second before "clocking on" (that's Trevor-Speak for when we leave and his time looking after Caitlin begins), groaned and huffed.

'This Monday morning mayhem! You should prepare for work on a Sunday.'

Trevor's perfected this pained voice. It's like it's a personal insult to him that Mum's rushing around getting ready to go out and earn the money to keep him in the style to which, since he moved in with us, he's become accustomed. You wouldn't believe the unit he inhabited before he moved in with us. Sad. Very sad.

Mum works in Equal Opportunities. When she got pregnant with Caitlin, she took a lower position so she wouldn't have to do so much overtime (still not as lowly as Trevor's when he worked there). But in a media crisis, the department still treats her like the boss.

On the way back from the phone, Mum kissed Trevor's cheek.

'Another crisis averted by Sarah-Solve-Everything. We'll be heading for the car any second now, darl'. Ready, Reb?'

I wasn't but I could take a hint.

'Sarah!' said Trevor flapping his newspaper. 'That metallic, coffee-breath smell! Either clean your teeth or keep your distance.'

I'd been wondering how long it would be before Mum's supposed Equal Opportunities principles would kick in. She lectures me on equality between sexes, races, abilities. But on the personal front, she really lets herself down.

Trevor's at his worst when Mum's about to leave for work, which makes me wonder how he really feels about being a stay-at-home dad. He's into this "man with a pram", politically correct position. He raves on about it to anyone and everyone who'll listen.

'My life has become very particular, very domestic,' he goes. 'I've designed a small, precious life for my daughter and me. My life has reduced, like a good sauce.'

I've been tempted, at more than one of the twenty occasions I've heard him spill this bilge before, to point out that, seeing as he didn't have a life before, it's no great sacrifice.

But my stutter, which started just before Mum gave birth to Caitlin, means I no longer say what I'm thinking. It's been an interesting transition. A year or so ago I was a person not afraid to voice her opinions. But that's all changed. At first, I was lost. Now I've made use of my affliction. I've become introspective, a keen observer and have taken up shooting video.

What I like most is editing. I've got a cool computer programme that lets me manipulate and juxtapose the images. Editing is like the debates I used to love having with Mum. Arranging the images and words is like organising my thoughts for a good argument.

Mum disapproves of my new computer lifestyle: 'It's not healthy.' I showed her what I was doing and she was impressed plus it kept her off my back for a while.

When Trevor first moved in he said, 'I think it only fair that you accommodate my domestic arrangements. I have to drink an entire pot of tea before I interact with another human being.'

'That's all very well when you're living the bachelor life,' laughed Mum.

Caitlin, like most kids, rises early and demands attention as soon as she wakes. Trevor protested about his peace being disturbed every morning for a year. After Caitlin's first birthday, Mum must have had enough. She said, 'Trevor. If you want time alone, stay up late.'

But, like the true dinosaur he is, Trevor was unable to adapt. When he does stay up late he goes on next morning about what a sacrifice family life is. To make up for all the compromises he's made, he stays in bed until well after midday on weekends.

Back at "mayhem Monday", Trevor was spluttering out of the window at the rain. 'You should have put a roof over the sandpit!'

'It's got a t-t-t-tarp,' I said.

'Now you want to start another p-p-p-project!' sneered Trevor, imitating my stutter for the millionth time.

He'd been waiting to get a dig in about Project Chooks ever since we'd been raving about it last night. I'd had such a good weekend working outside with Mum. I was over the moon when she suggested doing something else with me. But she hadn't asked Trevor what he thought and he was furious.

Mum grabbed Caitlin for a goodbye smooch and we all trouped out to the car. Our departure was accompanied by Trevor bleating on.

'Chooks! Impractical, labour intensive, expensive! We need thorough research, a budget…'

'Research?' Mum interrupted. 'Right,' Mum turned over the engine.

Trevor winced as usual. 'Sarah! Listen to the engine!'

'Reb, let's go to the library on our way home tonight.'

'Tonight?'

'Bye-bye, my poppet. Kiss for Mummy.'

'Library? But…what about dinner?' said Trevor, desperately.

'You have a turn at cooking.' Mum closed her car door.

Trevor, horrified, knocked on my window at her. 'But what will I make?' he asked.

'Check the fridge. Be inventive. If not, go shopping.'

'But you've got the car.'

'Walk to the deli.'

'But…' Trevor's panic was beginning to upset Caitlin. Personally I hadn't had this much fun for ages. '…I'm looking after Caitlin.'

Trevor was so caught up he neglected to give the full daily lecture which goes something like: 'Warm the car, Sarah. Ninety-eight per cent of engine damage occurs within the first five minutes of it starting'.

As Mum drew away I had to stuff my hand in my mouth to stop my giggles. That is, until I realised she was laughing, too.

At the end of our street, just before we rounded the corner, I turned and took a last look at Trevor holding onto Caitlin at the end of our drive. It was then I got a goose-bumpy feeling. Project Chooks was momentous. It would change everything. Finally, we had reached a fork. I had this profound feeling that Mum wasn't going to have to keep taking everything Trevor slung anymore. I was right.

Mum was seven months pregnant when Trevor moved in. A week after that I had cause to come home from school unexpectedly. I won't go into detail, but suffice to say it's not that bad every month. Thank goodness.

I arrived home to find a little red sports car was parked in our driveway.

I was in the bathroom getting a bottle of painkillers from the medicine cabinet when I heard Trevor's voice. 'Oh! Oh! Yes! Yes! YES!'

Then I heard a female's voice that wasn't Mum's yelling, 'Oh God! Oh God! Oh GOD!'

I froze. Seconds later, Trevor, naked, flung open the bathroom door and headed for the toilet.

'What the…? Rebecca? Hi.'

I was like a kangaroo trapped in headlights.

'Trev? I have to go! Trev!' sang out the woman.

I ran to my bedroom, slammed the door.

I peeped out and saw an older woman of about thirty pulling on red shoes.

Then Trevor was at my door. I tried to close it but he had his foot wedged.

'You breathe a word,' he hissed, 'and I'll make your life a living, breathing, hell. Got it?'

The woman came up behind him.

'Trevvie, kissy. See ya soon, big boy?'

'You betcha.'

I watched through a crack in the door as they pashed and groped.

I kept the knowledge to myself for a week, but one night I couldn't bear Trevor going on at Mum.

'Jesus, Sarah. Who are you eating for? A couple of elephants?'

Mum put her fork down and her eyes filled with tears.

'It's salad!' I said. Then I couldn't help myself. 'Mum...Mum...I-I-I came home from school last Wednesday...'

Trevor kicked me hard under the table, but I didn't care.

'Wednesday?' Trevor said. 'I was out Wednesday.'

'I found Trevor and...what's her name?'

'Who?' asked Trevor as if I was mad.

'They were in your bedroom, Mum.'

'For chrissakes, Rebecca! Sarah?'

'It's true, Mum.'

'Who was where?' asked Mum.

'You're surely not going to believe...' Trevor looked rattled.

'She drives a red car, wears red shoes,' I continued.

'In your fantasies!' Trevor exploded.

'And they were on your bed.'

'I'm out of here.' Trevor got up. 'You wanna bring up another kid on your own, Sarah? Be depressed for years? You believe this lying little...'

'Depressed?' I looked at Mum.

'You want this child to have a Daddy?' Trevor continued.

'This situation is really hard for you, Reb, but...' said Mum.

I couldn't believe it! Mum thought I was making it up.

'I've never ever lied to you, Mum.' I started for Trevor. 'You arsehole.'

'Arsehole! Sarah? I don't have to stay.'

'Rebecca, take back the..."arsehole".'

'I wish I could. To the hovel he came from.'

'You know what I mean! Apologise!'

'Never.'

'Go to your room, Rebecca. Now!'

That night I woke up to find Trevor's hand over my mouth.

'I warned you.'

I tried to bite him. He put his other hand under the covers.

'You keep your mouth shut. Say, " Yes, Trevor". Rebecca. Say it!'

He was hurting me so much I had no choice.

Next morning I was fitting a huge bolt to my bedroom door when the phone rang. Trevor answered it and brought it to me. It was my friend Jazmyn and she was ropable. Apparently Trevor had just answered the phone by saying, 'Jazmyn? You're the one Rebecca refers to as "fatty".'

Mum wanted to know what I was doing with the lock.

'A young woman needs her privacy,' said Trevor, quick as. 'As do we. Come here, sexy.' Eyeing me, he gave Mum a huge pash.

About a month later, and a week before Mum gave birth, she was ready to leave for her final check-up. Trevor was still in his pyjamas.

'What do you mean you're not coming?' Mum was saying.

'Exactly that. You overbearing bovine.' Trevor poured himself another cup of tea.

'Don't call me that!' Mum said.

'You remind me of my mother!'

'I'll come with you, Mum.'

We had to sit in the driveway for ages, Mum was crying so much.

Just as I suspected, the little red car was there when I came home at lunchtime. The sound effects were the same, too.

That night I told Mum. Trevor did the same act – total disbelief – as before, only more so.

'She's jealous, Sarah. I'm about to be a father. I've got my woman! What more could I want?'

He put his arm around Mum. She couldn't see, but he grinned at me like the full liar he is. Then he got serious.

'Make a choice, Sarah.' he said. 'It's me and the baby. Or...Rebecca.'

'How about you go and stay with Auntie Charlene, Reb?'

'N-n-n-o!' I couldn't believe she would send me away!

'Until I've had the baby?'

'Before she goes, I want an apology.' said Trevor, loving every moment of it.

'M-M-Mu...'

'Now she's pretending to stutter.'

'I'm n-n-n-n...' I couldn't stop the stuttering, nor the crying. Mum looked confused. Torn.

'Sarah. My sweet Sarah.' Trevor got on his knees, slid his hand up Mum's skirt. You could see Mum wanting to believe him.

Doesn't take too much guessing as to the night my stutter began.

After Caitlin was born, life was radically different at our house. That I loved Caitlin more than I hated Trevor saved me. Mum stayed at home for the first three months after Caitlin was born so Trevor wouldn't have seen anything of Maria and the little red car. But it started up again as soon as Mum went back to work. I kept quiet out of fear, I'm ashamed to say.

Back to the week where this whole family affair starts to heat up, the week of Project Chooks. That Monday afternoon after school, Mum and I had serious fun at the library. We weren't there long; Mum was desperate to see Caitlin. We got fish'n'chips on the way home. She made me stay in the car just in case Trevor had set a new record and had a meal on the table.

That night me, Mum and an ecstatic Caitlin poured over the chicken books we'd got from the library. I'd no idea how beautiful and varied chickens were.

'A G-g-g-golden Seabright.'

'Sir John Seabright bred intensively for 30 years,' Mum read. 'Imagine that. Your life's work.'

'W-w-w-wings like lace.'

'Come and look, Trevor,' Mum called. 'Stop sulking.'

'Domestic animals, Sarah, are a financial burden.'

'Trevor! How did we manage without you?'

Very well, I thought.

By Wednesday night that week, we had the chicken breed we wanted, the hen house designed, and Mum was working on her chicken connections. We had the new gay liaison officer at Mum's work lined up to come and help build on the weekend. Me, Mum and Caitlin were very excited, but Trevor was still vehemently opposed. He'd refused to join in discussions or be part of the preparations.

After dinner, Trevor went to bed before Caitlin had her bath. Later I heard Mum knocking at the spare room door for a goodnight kiss, but he refused to let her in.

I passed Mum on the way to the bathroom. It was obvious she'd been crying.

'Are you okay, Mum?' I asked.

'Fine. Night-night, darling.'

'I love you, Mum,' I told her. I know she loves me, despite what Trevor says.

We were late home on the Thursday night of the week of Project Chooks. Mum had had a rough day. If Trevor had taken the time, he would have noticed her shoulders were up by her ears.

But he was ready with one of his lists and started reading it before she even put down her briefcase. He'd done this before in the face of a project, and Mum had always listened to him.

'One,' he read. 'You want three birds, that's $75. It's at least $300 for a basic chook shed set-up. Five dollars per month per bird for wheat, that's $180 per annum. That's $555. We spend $5 per week on eggs, that's $260 per annum.'

'Stop right there,' said Mum.

'This took me all day, Sarah,' he protested. 'At least have the decency to listen.'

'I don't give a shit about your list, Trevor. We're building a hen house this weekend.'

'You don't have the skills,' Trevor scoffed.

'Rebecca's not staring at a computer screen! We're having chooks. End of story.'

Mum called Gordon, the chicken contact, as soon as she took off her coat and set up a time to go a pick up three Rhode Island Reds. The breed is reputed to be one of the best layers and are fairly docile.

Trevor didn't speak for the rest of that night.

Before Trevor, I used to love Friday nights. Mum and I would get a takeaway and discuss our plans for the weekend. When I got home from school that week it was just like old times. Mum and I pored over our list and agreed to get an early night in anticipation of the work ahead.

Building the chook shed goes down as my most divine learning curve. Alan from Mum's work was unbelievably good-looking, plus he had great tools. Mum hung out with Caitlin nearby, encouraging us.

Trevor emerged midway through Saturday afternoon. You could see he was amazed by how much we'd done.

But all he said was to Mum about Alan, 'He's not gay. They can't build things like that.'

'He's far too good-looking to be straight,' Mum fired back.

Next day, just before noon, we put the finishing touches to "The Chook Palace", as Mum called it. We put shell grit in bowls, newspaper and straw in the nesting boxes, sawdust on the floor, and water and wheat in special new containers.

That evening we settled our three, fluffy red hens. They were so busy. Much more fun than I'd thought they'd be. Caitlin learned the hard way how to give a chicken a cuddle and when she refused to leave at dinner time we ate in the chook pen!

Trevor prowled outside, scowling. 'They're just chickens.'

'Why not let us enjoy our simple pleasures, Trevor?' I'd never heard Mum be cold to him before.

Trevor stalked into the house. Then paced up and down looking out of the bedroom window with his arms crossed.

The next Wednesday I came home from school early because of my intermittent monthly problem. All I wanted was to take a tablet and lie down in the dark. But the little red engine was there in the driveway and the grunting was in full swing.

'Yes, yes, YES!' That was Trevor.

'Oh God! Oh God! OH GOD!'

The female's voice, I assumed it was still Maria, reached an ear-splitting volume. Caitlin started to cry. I struggled out of bed and barrelled into Trevor outside Caitlin's room just as Caitlin stopped crying.

Trevor pushed me up against the wall. Luckily Maria appeared, pulling on her skirt. 'I came to see the little red rooster, not listen to some kid screaming.'

I dashed into my room, bolted the door and leant against it, panting. A few seconds later there was a tap.

'R-r-r-rebecca. You say anything and you're t-t-t-t-toast.'

I don't know how, but I went out like a light. I awoke to aromatic cooking smells and laughter. It was a few seconds before I registered the afternoon's events.

In the family room, Mum was bouncing Caitlin on her knee. She looked radiant. Trevor was wearing an apron, cooking and sipping red wine.

'What's the occasion, Trev?' Mum asked.

Infidelity, I thought.

'Reb, Trevor says you had to come home from school early?'

'Is that all he said?' I asked.

'No. He apologised.'

'What for?' I looked at Trevor.

'For being a total pain about our chooks.'

Eyeing me, Trevor slipped down close to Mum and stroked her stockinged knee.

'Now. What about this surprise?' giggled Mum.

'Follow me.'

Trevor was at our chook shed, arms wide as if he owned it. 'There,' said Trevor. Strutting, cock-sure, shiny, was the hugest rooster. Then, right in front of us, he pinned down a hen despite her frantic resistance, did his job, plumped his plumage, strutted and crowed.

Outside the pen, Trevor echoed his movements.

'Go, Rodney!' he screamed. Caitlin started to cry.

I marched into the hen house and picked up the victim. What happened next was a flurry of feathers, squawking, screaming as Rodney flew at me, talons first. I was scratched deeply on my arm. I'd dropped the hen and put my hands up to protect my face. Otherwise I'm sure he would have got me in the eye.

'Reb,' Mum rushed to my side. 'Are you hurt?'

I felt warm, wet blood on my sleeve, but held my arm close to my body. I didn't want her to see.

'I'm f-f-fine,' I said.

I walked back to the house.

'Trev's making lamb korma,' called Mum. 'He even rang me at work to find out what your favourite dinner is.'

I stared as hatefully as I could at Trevor. He narrowed his eyes, warning me.

'I'm a v-v-v-v-vegetarian.'

'As of when?' asked Mum.

'I c-c-c-couldn't kill a ch-ch-chicken,' I said. 'It's h-h-h-hypocritical to eat m-m-meat if you can't.'

'Fair enough,' agreed Trevor.

'But,' said Mum, 'start tomorrow, Reb. Come on.'

'Mum,' I so wanted to tell her everything. 'I'm going back to bed.'

'Sweetie! You're still feeling poorly?' said Mum. 'I'll bring you a hottie.'

'I'll take it' said Trevor. 'You relax.' He patted Mum's bottom then did another mock cockerel strut.

Of course, I locked my door and didn't answer. 'R-r-r-rebecca,' he whispered, 'z-z-zip your l-l-lip. Or else.'

That night there was a session of 'Yes! YES, JESUS!' from next door. Nothing to match the decibels of that afternoon. But when I heard Mum sobbing, it was clear they'd made up. I'd asked her about the sobbing. It was ecstasy, apparently. She even said she hoped I'd feel like that one day!

After it had gone quiet, I still couldn't sleep. The gash on my arm throbbed like crazy. At about 2am I decided to get a pain killer. Half-way down the stairs I was stopped by Trevor's voice. He was pacing, speaking into the phone.

'Maria, she means nothing. Nothing. I'll see you tomorrow.'

I fled back to my room. I had to put a stop to this situation. Eventually I came up with my plan. If all went well, the lies and deceit would be over by the end of the weekend.

Early next morning, Mum was in full corporate gear, feeding Caitlin, with Trevor drinking tea and reading the paper.

'Are you still going to Auntie Ch-Ch-Ch,' I started.

'Charlene's!' said Trevor, exasperated.

'On S-s-s-aturday?'

'Yes,' said Mum.

'Do you mind if I don't c-c-come? I have this idea to make you two a m-m-multimedia feast of the senses. I w-w-wanna do something for you and Trev. Show I accept Trev's part of our l-l-lives.'

'Rebecca! That is so sweet!' Mum was amazed.

Trevor was less convinced.

'S-s-seriously, T-T-Trev. I wanna show you I care.'

It seems unbelievable, but he bought it! He actually crowed. 'Cock-a-doodle-doooooo!'

Mum laughed, overjoyed at what she thought was us getting on at last.

I almost came unstuck that night. He was lying in wait for me on the landing and pushed me into my bedroom. My heart thumped right up in my throat.

'Leave your room unlocked tonight, okay? You can show me how much you care.'

He was starting to do gross things with my neck, pushing me towards the bed. I had to think really quickly.

'I've got my m-m-monthly! Sorry, Trev. Rain check?'

He strutted then, like Rodney, mouthing a silent cock-a-doodle-doo. I made out I was laughing.

After he left, it took me ages to stop shaking.

Next day I dashed home from school, set everything up and hid, heart thumping, waiting for the little red car to arrive.

It all went to plan. There was the usual chorus of, 'Yes! Oh God!' and the headboard thumping.

That night Mum knocked on my door to tell me not to stay up all night, but to get everything ready, I'd need that time and more.

The next morning Mum, Trevor and Caitlin were in the car, ready to go.

'P-p-promise you'll be gone for the whole day?' I asked.

Reassured, I set to. Later, I had only just finished setting up the TV screen in front of the table where we'd be eating, when they arrived home.

Mum, carrying the sleeping Caitlin, admired the white cloth, flowers, candles.

'Darling! This is beautiful,' said Mum.

'C-c-c-cool,' agreed Trevor.

They got changed and I served the first course; chicken noodle soup.

'So much for v-v-vegetarianism,' slurped Trevor.

'Trev!'

'He can t-t-t-tease.' I smiled.

'Me and R-R-Reb. have got an understanding, haven't we?' he said, winking.

For the next course I brought out a massive silver, oval dish. A humongous roast bird with all the trimmings, steamed. I pressed "play" on the video as Mum and Trevor admired the meal.

'Look! Our chookies!' said Mum about the video.

The video is of the chook pen, the three hens and Rodney. I'm there, waving at the camera.

'And Rodney! Cock-a-doodle-do!' crows Trevor.

'How did you do that?' asks Mum.

'The c-c-c-camera's on a tripod.' I shrug. 'I just pressed the record button.'

Trevor rips into a leg, juices dripping down his beard and chin.

'Excellent. So fresh!'

On the video, Rodney pins down a hen.

'That's my Rod! Doing his bit for blokes.'

'I fiddled the speed up, sort of Marx Brothers ma-ma-manic screwball music,' I tell them.

'What's that?' Mum asks, peering.

A grainy, fleshy picture gradually sharpens into focus.

But the mysterious image is short-lived. We are back with Rodney, flapping on top of a hen.

In the candle light, confusion flickers over Mum's face. Trevor is too intent on his second massive leg to register much.

On the video, I'm waving to the camera and running into the chook pen.

I check they are watching the video and duck under the table. I make out I'd dropped something, while actually I am chaining Trevor's legs to the table.

I pop up in time to see more Rodney and his mating antics on the video screen, then another, more obvious this time, fleshy picture. A clear, split-second of buttocks bouncing.

'Rebecca?' queries Mum. 'What…?'

But before I can answer, we've cut back to me chasing Rodney the rooster using kick-boxing and karate moves.

Trevor and Mum are quiet now as they watch me catch Rodney, hang him by his feet upside down and pull his neck until it breaks. The sound of crunching bones, a.k.a. Kung Fu movies, accompanies. It's brilliantly ghoulish.

'It's way harder than the manual said,' I say.

Mum lowers her forkful of chicken, Trevor his leg.

The human grunting from the video is loud. We're in Mum's bedroom and a male bottom is going up and down like the clappers. A woman's legs, the feet encased in red, high-heeled shoes, are gripped hard around the man's back.

'I've doubled the length here… It was over so quickly,' I say.

From three angles (I had cameras hidden on each bedside table and one behind on the dressing table) the video cuts between close ups of Trevor's and Maria's faces, plus (of course) the bottom.

'Drawing it out adds impact.'

'Rebecca!' Mum is stricken.

'Turn the fuck'n thing off! Off!' Trevor screams. He gets up, but then falls, tripped by his chains. 'You bitch!'

On screen I'm slowly lowering Rodney into a vat of bubbling water. 'That softens the f-f-feathers for easier plucking. Again, way more d-difficult in reality,' I comment.

The music from the movie Misery runs over the top here. The final image is me, smiling into the camera, as if butter wouldn't melt in my mouth.

As I said, not a cool story for vegetarians.

Slasher's Return

Also won the Police Procedural Award

Jacqui Horwood

It's 11 o'clock in the morning and I am empress of all I survey. True, what I'm surveying doesn't amount to much. A large rectangular room, its walls covered by layers and layers of faded and fading posters. A pool table jammed into one corner and a broken jukebox collecting dust in the other. A spray of battle-weary wooden tables and shabby plastic chairs litter a threadbare carpet of an indeterminable colour and pattern. Dirty windows line two walls. It's sunny outside but you wouldn't know it from in here. Still, the pub is well known, having been voted the grungiest pub in Melbourne. No mean feat, I have to tell you.

I wipe the bar clean with a wet cloth and cast an eye down one end where Percy and Gil are silently enjoying their third beers of the day. Their glasses are three-quarters empty, so I pour two more.

'Ta, love.'

I've been here for eight months. And it's been my one, constant link to human beings. My handful of shifts keeps me sane.

Occasionally, on busy nights, I look around the room and see a face I remember from my former life. I marvel at how well I remember the person's details. Their life story.

A few times I've noticed someone studying me with a frown. I know they are trying to place me somewhere. I don't worry that they'll remember. It's unlikely that the last time they saw me I was wearing a tight t-shirt and a pair of faded black jeans, pouring drinks in the grungiest pub in Melbourne.

Things have changed since my meltdown. My life, my friends, my ambitions. Many of my former work colleagues have disappeared. Superstitious. Scared that my demons may tap them on the shoulder. Scared, too, by vulnerability.

The door to the public bar swishes open. A solid man in a shabby grey suit saunters in. He steps out of the shadows and a neon shower lights his face, catching the hooded dark eyes and large blotched nose. Catching me unawares. I take an involuntarily step backwards and scan around me for a quick exit. Three big steps and the man is leaning over the bar. His beefy hands are like baseball mitts and they splay out across the Formica in front of me. I glimpse his knuckles to confirm my suspicions. A patchwork of faded blue tattoos covers his skin. Crucifixes, spiders' webs, people's names. A living history. It's him. I lift my face and look him straight in the eyes.

'What would you like?' I ask, although I already know the answer.

'Scotch and Coke.'

The man shifts his bulk onto a barstool and waits as I pour his drink. I place the glass on the coaster in front of him and take his money. It's him.

The shift manager, Joe, taps me on the shoulder. 'Smoko, Lizzie. I'll take over.'

I nod and walk away, leaving Joe with the man.

I grab my handbag and stumble outside, shading my eyes and squinting into the bright sunlight. I usually go behind the pub into the smelly back lane for a smoke, but today I sit on a park bench on the main street. From there, I can watch the door to the public bar. I light up a cigarette and pull out my mobile phone.

The man in the pub, sitting there with his scotch and Coke and no conscience, is a drug dealer. Big time manufacturer and trafficker of methamphetamine. Close cohort of bikies and crims. Not known to the public. Not interested in becoming a legend like other crims in Melbourne. Quiet, unobtrusive. And a murderer.

His name is Byron Penrose. Byron! Of all the names for a criminal! His friends lack the education to appreciate the irony and call him Slasher. There's a story attached to the nickname, but it's unpleasant, just as you'd imagine.

I tap my left foot on the concrete beneath me and think. Debate with myself and fiddle with the mobile. Finally I punch in a number as familiar to me as my own name.

'Brett Johnson.'

'Johnno, it's Lizzie. Guess who just walked into the pub?'

'Who?' he asks.

'Slasher Penrose.'

There's a barely perceptible intake of breath and a pause.

'Are you sure?'

There is a cautious note in his voice and I grimace.

'Johnno, I've been depressed, not delusional.'

He sighs. 'I'm not doubting you.'

I flick ash from my cigarette and watch as it tumble-turns in the breeze.

'Okay, Lizzie. I'm on my way.'

The line goes dead. I stub my cigarette onto the concrete below and head back to the pub.

Percy and Gil are waiting expectantly with empty glasses. Slasher is nowhere to be seen. In between me leaving the park bench and walking back to the bar, he has gone.

Johnno and Mick swing through the front door. Mick with slicked-back dark hair like a seal and Johnno with short dark-blond hair. Dark suits and dark sunglasses. Johnno catches my eye. He tilts his head towards one end of the bar, away from Percy and Gil.

'Where is he?' he asks.

'Gone now,' I say.

Mick cocks an eyebrow at Johnno. 'Are you sure it was him?' asks Johnno.

I fold my arms tightly across my chest, sensing that a nervous breakdown has now labelled me as being flaky. Mick is unable to meet my eyes.

'Yes, I'm sure.'

Johnno picks up on my body language. 'We're not doubting you, Lizzie. We just need to be sure you're right.'

A dry cough interrupts us. We look down the bar and Percy is facing us.

'The lady copper's right. He was here.'

'Who was?' asks Mick.

'Slasher Penrose.'

I smile at Percy. 'You've just earned yourself a freebie, Perce.'

Johnno shrugs. 'Well, I guess we'll start checking out all his old haunts.'

Mick put on his blank copper's face. He says, 'I'll believe it when I see it.'

Like he can't believe the word of two drunks and one nervous wreck. Johnno turns to me as he leaves. 'Stay in touch, Lizzie.'

After they are gone, I pour Percy and Gil two pots.

'You called me lady copper, Perce. How'd you know?'

Percy and Gil dissolve into phlegmy laughter. They sit in front of me cackling like emphysemic hens. Percy's laughter subsides and he says, 'Once a copper, always a copper.'

True enough.

Hours later, I finish my shift and go home to an empty flat. I'm living with my mother, a woman in her sixties with the social life I had in my twenties. Tonight is bingo night.

In the shower I wash away the ever-present smell of stale beer and post mix Coke. I stand in the middle of the torrent of hot water and my body trembles. Slasher Penrose. Where had that bastard been?

When I first learned of Slasher Penrose, I'd just started a six-month secondment with the Drug Squad. Our major project was getting enough evidence to bring him down.

I turn off the shower but linger in the damp warmth and semi-darkness. If it wasn't so uncomfortable I would curl up and lie on the tiles.

It all seemed so straightforward. One of our undercover operatives was to meet with Slasher in a warehouse in Fitzroy and pay for a kilogram of methamphetamine. Johnno and I placed listening devices in the warehouse and wired our operative for sound. Everything was set for the bust.

Slasher was waiting in the warehouse and we were waiting nearby to make the arrest.

I wrap myself in a towel and pad from the bathroom to my bedroom. Throw back the doona and jump in my bed. Damp and naked. Scared and lonely.

In the middle of our set-up wandered a 16-year-old girl, innocently making her weekly secret rendezvous with a boy her parents hated. She crawled through a camouflaged hole into the warehouse. A hole none of us knew about. Crawled through the hole and straight into Slasher. He reacted by pulling out a gun and shooting her. He ran and disappeared into the laneways of Fitzroy before we could react.

We were left with a mess. There was no evidence that Slasher had been in the warehouse. He hadn't spoken so our tapes were useless. We hadn't taken photos of him arriving and our undercover cop hadn't seen him. Slasher was nowhere to be found. All his family and friends swore black and blue that he hadn't been around for days. That they thought he had been interstate.

From there on in, my life began to unravel.

I drag myself off my bed and pull on my flannel pyjamas. My mirror mocks me. Who's the fairest of them all? Not me. Not right now. Pale skin and dull eyes. Hair that hangs like a tattered curtain past my shoulders.

There was an internal investigation into our disastrous operation. My husband chose that moment to leave me a blunt goodbye note. One morning in the shower I started crying and couldn't stop. The Force agreed to give me a year's leave without pay.

So here I am: 37 years of age, living with my mum, working part time in a pub. In three weeks' time, my year's leave without pay will be over and I'll have to decide my future. Stay in blue, or move on. Right now I can't even decide what to have for dinner.

On my days off, I like to sit in other people's pubs. I am sitting in possibly the second grungiest pub in Melbourne. There are two old drunks at the bar and the barmaid is studying the room like she is empress of all she surveys. A couple of old timers are sitting at a nearby table, huddled over the form guide. A battered transistor radio sits between them, squawking like a parrot. I occupy my time by doing the crossword in one of the daily newspapers.

Halfway through the crossword, the door swings open. I look up. It's Slasher. What is going on? For the past week , half of Victoria Police had been unable to find neither hide nor hair of this man and I seem to have a Slasher magnet on me. He is not alone. My legs twitch, ready to turn and run, and I can feel my heart flip into a calypso beat. I grip my pen until my knuckles gleam white and will myself to stay put.

Slasher and his companion sit at the table close to mine. Slasher sits with his back to me. The other man goes to the bar and asks for two scotch and Cokes. As he walks back, I give him a surreptitious glance from under my eyelashes. He is in his mid-thirties and has the bloated features of a man who has enjoyed the high life. He's not bad-looking; I can tell he was once handsome. Now he hides his thickening waist underneath a baggy floral shirt. He seems familiar. I go through my mental files and can't find a match. I definitely know him from the past.

Slasher and the younger man talk with their heads together. Their voices low and urgent. I fix my eyes on the crossword and nibble the end of my pen, while my ears strain to pick up crumbs of the conversation. I pretend to scribble letters into the empty boxes. It is difficult to hear anything but I catch a few words. Nothing that makes any sense. My head aches from trying to listen and trying to remember from where I know the other man.

An old timer has a win and whoops with pleasure. He proclaims that all drinks are on the house. Last of the big spenders.

Slasher and his friend finish their drinks and seem to come to an agreement. They stand and head for the door. A glint of metal catches my eye and I notice a gold object dangling from the belt of the younger man. I recognise it as an old membership medallion from a nightclub that was popular in the late nineties. A light bulb goes off and I realise who the younger man is. And, coupled with the handful of words I picked up from their conversation, I have an idea of what is going on.

The younger man is Mark O'Toole. Back in '97, he used to be a regular feature in the doorway of a number of King Street nightclubs. There was always rumour and innuendo that, apart from providing security, he was involved in criminal activity but because he was always on the periphery of the action, the police ignored him to chase the bigger fish. I'd heard ages ago that Mark now was a part owner in a couple of clubs in Melbourne. A leap from the periphery to the nucleus.

I sit back in my chair and ask myself what I think a methamphetamine dealer and a nightclub owner would be up to. I answer myself.

Fake Ecstasy.

It hadn't taken the methamphetamine manufacturers in Victoria long to cash in on the popularity of Ecstasy. Since the late nineties, the market had been flooded with fakes made with methamphetamine and a mixture of other powdered substances like paracetamol and seasickness tablets. It appears that Slasher is now busy staking a claim in the business.

After Slasher has gone, I pull out my mobile phone and creep off to the toilets. In one of the grimy cubicles, I ring Johnno. I sigh as I listen to his voicemail message.

'I'm at the Pier Hotel. Slasher was just here. He had someone else with him. Remember Mark O'Toole? No prizes for guessing what they're up to. Anyway, I heard a couple of things. They're meeting tonight at 10pm. Unfortunately, all I heard about the meeting place was that it's a car park behind a shed. Give me a call when you can.'

I come home to an empty flat. Mum is at ballroom dancing. I heat up a piece of two-day-old barbeque chicken pizza in the microwave, before flopping onto the couch. My head throbs. I peek at my wrist watch. The nightly news will be starting in 10 minutes. I reach for the remote control and switch on the television. Light and colour flicker before my tired eyes. Loud voices exhort me to buy, buy, buy.

The news starts, although I barely register what's going on. Something about local politicians brawling over taxes. News, déjà vu. The faces change but the script is always the same. The news finishes with the usual good news story. Smiling faces and positive chat. An exhibition of some sort at the Melbourne Exhibition Centre. The camera pans along the rectangular grey building with its sloping roof. A pinprick of interest wakes me from my stupor. The Exhibition Centre was commissioned by the previous State Government, by the previous Premier, Jeff Kennett. At the time it copped the nickname "Jeff's Shed" and it has stuck.

I go out to my car and bring back the Melways road map. The patchwork of black and blue lines shows me that there is a car park behind the Exhibition Centre, close to the Yarra River. The Exhibition Centre is also not far away from the nightclub district in King Street. I smile in amusement to note that the car park is also across the river from Victoria Police headquarters. I close the Melways and lean back on the couch. So, do I take this seriously? I imagine the tone of Johnno's voice after telling him my hunch. Definitely not worth the humiliation. I have two options.

I can ignore my hunch and settle in for the evening. Or I can do what I'm trained to do.

For the next hour, I trace figure eights around the furniture. Turning things over and over. Tossing a mental coin. Best two of three. Get a hold of yourself, I say, finally. Just go down there and have a look. Much to gain and nothing to lose. I change out of my sweat-stained T-shirt and into a black long-sleeved top. I put on sturdy work boots and tie my hair back. I have no gun so I arm myself with my mobile phone and a shaky attitude.

At nine o'clock, I leave a note for Mum on the kitchen bench. Don't wait up. Out chasing drug dealers.

I start the car and drive off without waiting for the engine to warm up. If I give myself too much time to think now, I'll just go back inside.

The Monday night streets of Melbourne are quiet and full of loitering taxis. I park the car in Whiteman Street, close to where the St Kilda and Port Melbourne trams turn off Clarendon Street. Over the road, the casino burns as bright as ever. The Exhibition Centre, however, is empty and dark. Nothing to exhibit. Nothing to attract attention.

I walk around the back of the Centre, through the shadows and the back car park. Past additional exhibition spaces to the main car park. To where I think Slasher's meeting will take place.

The car park is expansive and very open, with little foliage to soften its edges. Ten or so cars are dotted about in random parking spaces. I look around for somewhere to hide and come up empty. There are a couple of unoccupied yellow tollbooths but they are too far away from likely meeting spots. On the far side of the car park, running parallel to the Yarra River, is a long line of grey and white buildings. They are business spaces, mainly for event and catering companies. I notice that each business has covered steps leading up to their front doors. Maybe I can wedge myself somewhere behind those stairs. The car park is fairly well lit but in one corner, close to the grey and white buildings, there are patches of darkness caused by broken lights. Not a bad place for a clandestine meeting.

A quick examination reveals the space under one set of stairs is covered by worn palings in need of repair and a fresh coat of paint. I wiggle a couple of palings loose and squeeze myself into the space under the steps. It's 9.45 and I am squatting amongst spider webs, used condoms and God knows what else. Empress of all I survey. I peer between the timber slats and have a view of most of the car park.

A set of headlights illuminates the car park and I hear the dull rumble of a big, old car. Sure enough, a Ford Fairlane sidles up close to where I am hiding. The driver pauses for a moment before rolling the car into a parking spot. The door cracks open and the interior light catches Slasher's face. My eyes widen in disbelief. My hunch has paid off. Slasher lights up a cigarette and leans against the bonnet of his car. Arms crossed, he waits.

I edge back from my viewing position and pull out my mobile phone. I dial Johnno's number with trembling fingers. Again, I get his voice mail. Irritated, I whisper a terse message, telling him where I am and urging him to get himself down here.

Slasher sits on the bonnet, smoking and waiting. Ten slow minutes meander past and I am developing a cramp in my left calf. I have forgotten just how boring surveillance can be.

A navy blue Commodore slips in alongside Slasher's car. Mark O'Toole parks and emerges from the car, a briefcase in his hand. He nods to Slasher and sits beside him on the Fairlane's bonnet. They exchange a few words and lapse into silence. I frown and wonder if they are waiting for someone else. A few more minutes lumber past. Another car appears and parks beside the Commodore. The driver gets out and I hold my breath as I wait to see who it is. I gasp and tumble backwards, landing in the dirt and dust with a thud. It's Mick. He opens the boot of his car and pulls out a large leather suitcase. What the hell is going on?

From where I sit, I can still see the action. I watch, trying to interpret what I'm seeing. I wonder if Mick is undercover but he is dressed as he normally would be as a detective. There is no attempt to behave like anyone other than who he is. Maybe he is trying to get them to think he is a copper gone bad? The more I watch, the more I am confused. And frightened. Mick is over there being Mick. I remember him not being able to meet my eyes and shake my head in disbelief.

Another thought settles uncomfortably in the pit of my stomach. How much of this does Johnno know about? When we were working together, working as partners, Johnno and I told each other everything. And what wasn't shared, we'd find out about anyway. I don't want to believe he is involved. But his unanswered mobile phone nags at me. He knows where I am and what I've seen. I have to get out of here. I don't want to find out where Johnno's heart truly lies.

The three men head my way. I back into a corner, trying to disappear into the black. Hoping one of them doesn't look between the cracks of the steps. They thump over my head like a stampede of cattle and open the door. Fear now drives me, picking at my skin like vultures. I shove aside the wooden palings and throw myself out into the car park. I start to run.

'Hey, what do you think you're doing?'

I turn in fright. Mick stands at the top of the steps, unlit cigarette in one hand and a look of complete surprise on his face.

'Shit,' he says when he realises who I am. He pulls out a gun and shouts to Slasher and O'Toole. I duck between the cars, desperately searching for the quickest way to escape. Crouching near the driver's door of O'Toole's car, I notice that he has left his keys in the ignition.

Keeping low, I open the door and crawl into the car. The window above me shatters and I yelp. Glass confetti covers my head and shoulders, and grinds into the backs of my legs as I sit on the driver's seat. Fingers wet with sweat, I start the engine. Bullets crack the bonnet and roof of the car. Mick clatters down the steps, yelling and waving his gun. I slam the car into reverse and hit the accelerator. I reverse and keep reversing, keeping my head down and hoping I won't back into anything. I peer over the dashboard. The three men are diving into Mick's car. I do a backwards u-turn and put the car into drive…and drive headlong at two police cars, lights flashing and sirens screaming. They swerve around me and skid to a halt. Behind them is an unmarked police car, Johnno at the helm.

'Over there, over there,' I shout, pointing to Mick's car, which by now is heading in the opposite direction. The police cars race away in a cloud of dust.

Johnno jumps out of his car. 'You okay?' he asks.

I catch my breath and, to my surprise, smile. I feel good. Really good. I smile again. 'That was a rush.'

Johnno gives me a hug.

I ask him, 'Did you know about Mick?'

He nods, 'Yeah, we did. I was busy installing listening devices in his house when I got your voice message.'

I grimace, 'Speed things up, did I?'

Johnno laughs and puts his arm around me, leading me to his car. 'You've saved me a lot of boring hours of surveillance.'

Don't I know it.

It is 11 o'clock in the morning and I am Empress of all I survey. A squad room full of noisy detectives and a desk loaded with files. Someone else will have to pull Percy and Gil's next beer.

2004

BROUGHT TO BOOK

Liz Filleul

WHEN SIMMO TOLD US SHE'D BEEN BURGLED AND THAT HER PRECIOUS collection of girls' school stories had been stolen, my heart sank. Not entirely out of sympathy, I must confess. Of course I understood her grief – what fellow collector wouldn't? – but my first reaction was to think: 'Oh, no! Now I can't tell them about my books.'

The books I'd been so looking forward to showing off were in my bag, placed carefully beside me on Gin's battered red armchair. One was a hardback copy of The Chalet School in Exile by Elinor M. Brent-Dyer. It would have cost more than $50 to purchase via Abebooks.com or eBay, but I'd found it for $2 at a local garage sale two weeks ago. The second was a paperback by Harriet Martyn called Jenny and the New Headmistress, which I'd successfully bid for on eBay. The cost had been ludicrous for a 1985 paperback, but since I'd spent nearly 20 years searching for a copy, I figured it was worth it.

Up till recently, I'd believed I was the only thirty-something woman in the world who, in times of trouble, turned to the well-thumbed pages of the Chalet School or Malory Towers the way most people flew to the bottle or the fridge. Only last winter, when I'd been made redundant from my job as a university librarian, I'd spent many a cold, dreary day curled up on the sofa in front of the wood heater, absorbed in an endless round of difficult new girls, practical jokes, lacrosse matches and midnight feasts. And it was during that – thankfully brief – period of unemployment that I'd made two surprising discoveries, courtesy of the internet.

One was that many of the books I'd been collecting since childhood were actually quite rare and valuable. I told my husband and my parents about the prices they were commanding, and suddenly they started regarding my school story collection as an acceptable investment rather than a disturbing sign of arrested development.

The second was that internet forums devoted to girls' school story authors and their books were both abundant and active. For the first time, I found other fans to discuss my childhood favourites with. And it was through these online forums that I'd encountered a group of local women who met up in real life to discuss school stories and book collecting – AFOGS (standing for Adult Fans of Girls' Stories and pronounced "Afogs"). AFOGS comprised 10 women aged from 25 to 60, who lived in and around Melbourne, and who met at one another's houses on Friday evenings on a bi-monthly basis. I'd been a member for just under a year.

Tonight we were meeting at Gin's chaotic flat in Prahran. Gin was 35, just three years younger than I; small and slight, with short blonde hair. Up till a couple of years ago, she had been a small-part actor; these days she translated Spanish plays into English and produced them on the Melbourne stage. As well as a talent for acting and languages, Gin had an incredible knack for finding the rarest and most valuable of children's books for next to nothing. She'd once found a pristine first edition of Elsie J. Oxenham's Girls of the Hamlet Club – worth more than $1200 on eBay or Abebooks.com – for 50 cents in an op shop while on holiday in Queensland. Rarely a meeting went by without Gin turning up with a showbag of amazing finds. Whereas, until I found Exile, I'd netted precisely nothing at my weekly garage sale and trash and treasure hunts. Which was why I'd so much looked forward to showing it – and Jenny – off.

But now I couldn't. It simply wasn't appropriate with Simmo close to tears over the loss of her collection.

'You mean they took every single book?' Gin said. She sounded half-disbelieving, and I couldn't blame her. Who ever heard of burglars breaking into your house and nicking books?

'Every single one,' Simmo sighed. She was an accountant, in her mid-fifties, tall and large with short, red-dyed, spiky hair and huge, red-rimmed glasses. All the AFOGS members had impressive collections of girls' school stories, but Simmo's had been far and away the best. You name the author, and she'd owned all their books, all first editions, all with immaculate dust jackets. She'd completed her collection of New Zealand writer Clare Mallory's school stories only a week or so before the previous meeting, having forked out $150 for Merry Marches On on eBay.

'Was anything else taken?' I asked.

'Of course. The DVD player, the computer, the camera, jewellery…the usual things. Those things didn't bother me, other than the inconvenience. Everything's insured. But, the books are impossible to replace, some of them literally impossible…'

This was true, I thought, recalling how Jenny and the New Headmistress had appeared on eBay only once in the past 12 months and never on Abebooks.com in the same period of time. Simmo would struggle to replace some of the books she'd had. Then there were the memories associated with them – she'd read her first Abbey book coming out on the boat from England with her ten-pound-passage parents, a farewell gift from the grandmother she'd never seen again. How could insurance replace that? We spent the rest of the meeting disconsolately slugging dry white wine and nibbling peanuts and cheese and crackers, murmuring appropriate comments while Simmo told us that the police had barely been able to conceal their smirks when she'd informed them that her collection of school stories was among the stolen goods.

'I suppose they'll turn up at a trash and treasure somewhere, earning somebody a quick buck,' Jude said. She was in her late forties, with greying hair, and was almost as short and slight as Gin. We all envied Jude for being able to legitimately claim that her avid reading of school stories was "research" because she was a university lecturer in children's literature and its history, and regularly penned feminist perspectives of the girls' boarding school story for academic journals.

'That's what the police said,' replied Simmo. 'If that's what's happened, they'll be a lucky haul for some collector at the market.'

'I'll look out for them at the trash and treasures I go to,' promised Gin.

We broke up shortly after that, after arranging that in two months' time we'd meet at my place. I'd show them Exile and Jenny then, I thought, grabbing my bag and saying goodbye. By then, Simmo would be over the shock and would probably have gone some way towards replacing her collection.

I hurried to the corner of Gin's ill-lit street, and stomped up and down like a stood-up teenager while I waited for my husband Peter to pick me up on his way from the football.

He finally arrived, fifteen minutes after our prearranged time. 'How was the game?' I asked, as I jumped into the passenger seat and pulled on my seatbelt.

'Terrible. We were terrible,' he said. By "we" he meant Hawthorn, his team, which, judging by his dejected expression, had lost yet again. 'How was the meeting?' he asked me as he drove off.

'Terrible,' I echoed. 'Simona has been burgled, and all her books have been taken.'

'Oh, well,' Peter replied, carelessly. 'That's what you get for living in Footscray.'

We stopped at the supermarket on the way home, and it was well after eleven when we finally arrived back at our own house miles away from the city in the Dandenong Ranges. Peter grabbed a couple of shopping bags and bounded off into the house, while I trailed slowly after him, juggling shopping and books. When I reached the top of the short flight of wooden steps that led up to our deck, Peter was standing on the doorstep, looking shocked.

'Lucy,' he said, 'we've been burgled.'

The widescreen TV, DVD player and stereo had gone. So too had Peter's digital camera and some of my jewellery. And every single one of our books.

Now I knew how Simmo felt, I realised, as I wandered miserably around the house, staring at the empty bookshelves in disbelief. The big bookcase in the study that housed all my children's books now held nothing. The two large wine-rack-cum-bookshelves in the living room were now devoid of my "grown-up" fiction and Peter's collection of sports books as well as the wine. Even our recipe books had been taken from the kitchen. The only books I now possessed were the two I'd taken to Gin's.

The police came, looked around, took statements, examined the side window that the burglars had smashed to break in, then went off to ask our neighbours if they'd seen anything, which was unlikely given our house was shrouded by trees. We promised to compile a list of what had been stolen and take it down to the station within 24 hours. I told them about Simmo's burglary, hoping that they'd recognise the similarities between the break-ins even though Simmo lived on the other side of the city.

Over the next few days we made out a list for the police, filled in the insurance forms, talked incessantly to friends and relatives about what had happened. At work, my mind constantly wandered. I wanted to do something, anything, to get my books back. Whoever broke in to our house had taken the books for a reason, I surmised, presumably because they were valuable, or at least some of them were.

Maybe they'd taken them to a second-hand bookshop, rather than a trash and treasure, hoping to get a good price? At lunchtime, I grabbed the Yellow Pages and started ringing antiquarian bookshops on my mobile, asking if anyone had come in over the weekend with boxes of books, including a hundred or so school stories... After five futile calls, I gave up. There were too many booksellers in the Yellow Pages alone. And I knew from internet surfing that there were plenty more whose businesses were solely online and not listed in the telephone directory. It would take forever to contact every bookshop in Melbourne, and I didn't have the patience.

After a couple of weeks, our insurance money came through, and we started to replace the goods we'd lost. Somehow, though, I couldn't bring myself to begin replacing my book collection. They'd taken so many years to amass, and many of them were so hard to find. I had just come offline one night, half-heartedly searching for Chalets on Abebooks.com, when the phone rang. Peter came into the study to say it was for me.

It was Gin. To tell me she'd been burgled. And that all her books had gone.

It was Saturday evening and Simmo, Gin and I were sitting in our living room, relishing the warmth from the wood heater, and guzzling Pringles and a ten-year-old bottle of red.

'It must be someone who knows us, Lucy,' declared Gin. 'Someone who knows our movements, knows that Simmo and you and Peter go to work every day from Monday to Friday, knows that I go out to the theatre for three hours every afternoon.'

'Someone who knows we all have books that are valuable,' added Simmo.

'I'm not convinced of that,' I objected. 'Oh, I admit the target seems to have been the books. But why take every book, not just the valuable ones?'

'No time to sort them out,' Simmo said decisively.

I refilled our glasses. 'Just saying you're right, Simmo, and that whoever took our books knows us and our collections, then who do you think it might be? The only people we all know are the AFOGS lot and it can't be any of them.'

'I agree there,' said Simmo. 'I've known most of them for years. None of them are dishonest.'

'There are the forums,' Gin pointed out. 'We all go to forums, and you never know who's lurking there.'

'But we don't use our full names on the forums, let alone give out our addresses,' I argued. 'And the only list we're all on is the Girls Own list. Other than that, we're on different forums.'

'True enough,' sighed Gin.

'Did you lose all of your books, Gin?' Simmo asked. 'Or did you have a couple tucked away somewhere, like Lucy here?'

'All of them,' Gin said gloomily. 'And to make matters worse, I'd finally completed my set of Chalets. I figured I'd had so much luck finding books for next to nothing that I could afford to fork out a few dollars for Prefects at the Chalet School. So I bid for it on eBay and got it. I'd only had it about a week when I was burgled.'

'You know,' said Simmo slowly, 'that could be the connection.'

'What's that?' I asked.

'eBay. When we were burgled we'd all recently bought books from eBay. The person I bought Merry Marches On from was in Melbourne, in Eltham. What about you two?'

'The woman I bought Jenny off lived in Eltham,' I confirmed. 'I remember that because Peter's parents are in Warrandyte, and I thought about asking if I could pick it up from her and combine the trip with visiting them. But then Pat and Dan announced they were heading to Queensland for the winter, so I had it posted here instead.'

'I can't remember whether she was in Eltham, but she was in Melbourne, and her eBay name was Joy something. Joy with some numbers after it,' said Gin.

'That's right – same with my seller,' Simmo said eagerly.

We trooped into the study, where Peter had tucked himself away for the evening, and interrupted his computer game to fire up the Internet. We all checked our eBay accounts. Sure enough, we'd all purchased books between three and five days before our respective burglaries from an eBayer called Joy93, who lived in Eltham. All three of us had paid by making direct deposits to her account. She had posted our books to our addresses, so she knew exactly where we lived.

'This woman would realise that people usually buy old children's books to add to their own collections,' said Simmo. 'So if she sells to someone in Melbourne, she burgles the place, gets back the book she sold and lots of others besides – presumably to sell them all again on eBay. Very neat.'

'We should tell the police this,' I said. I wondered how long Joy93 held on to the books before deeming it safe to sell them on eBay. My books might still be in her house, in a box somewhere, waiting to be auctioned.

'And what use would that be?' Simmo scoffed. 'It's circumstantial evidence. They'd go round, and if she had books in her house that we said we'd lost, she'd say she'd found them at garage sales, at trash and treasures, in op shops, second-hand bookshops. We can't prove the books are ours – unless one of you wrote your name in them? I certainly didn't.'

We both shook our heads.

'So what do we do?' Gin asked. 'We can't just ignore this. The police need to know, even if they can't prove anything. A visit from them might at least prevent her from burgling the next poor sod.'

'I've got an idea,' said Simmo.

Blame it on the three bottles of wine we eventually ended up demolishing. Or on the girls' own tales of derring-do we had all spent at least three quarters of our lives devouring. Whatever the reason, the fact was that nine days later I found myself driving to my in-laws' empty house, with two sets of their house keys in my jacket pocket and a box of books on the back seat. Unknown to my in-laws, and to Peter, I was about to use their home to set up a sting.

When Simmo had first told us her idea, she suggested we use her family's beach house in Sorrento. But then I'd remembered Pat and Dan's house, the fact they were in Queensland until the end of August, and that it was so conveniently located in Warrandyte, a mere twenty minutes from Joy93's apparent location in Eltham. Peter, ensconced in the study, hadn't heard a word of our plans. And I'd figured it was best it stayed that way.

Our plan had gone into action within two days of its boozy hatching. Simmo had persuaded Jude to join us, and to move into my in-laws' place for a few days, posing as Pat Dixon. I'd signed Pat Dixon up on Yahoo and eBay and, under that name, had bid on Elsie J. Oxenham's Rachel in the Abbey, auctioned by Joy93. 'Put in an $800 bid,' Simmo advised. 'It won't go for anywhere near that much, and it'll mean you'll be sure of getting it. And I'll reimburse you – I need that book anyway.'

Five days later, Rachel was ours for $250. I emailed Joy93 from Pat Dixon's Yahoo account and asked if it was OK to send carefully concealed cash as payment. She agreed, and sent me her P.O. Box address in Eltham. I posted the money and confirmed the address where the book was to be sent. That was the Friday. I alerted the other three, and we agreed that Jude should establish herself at my in-laws' place on Monday, when the book would most likely be delivered.

Pat and Dan lived in a quiet, five-house court in Warrandyte, a pretty, bush-flanked township that lay deceptively close to bustling, built-up central Melbourne. I arrived at their double-storey weatherboard at a quarter to eight, parked inside the double garage and let myself into the house. It had been empty since Mother's Day weekend, and felt chilly and smelt musty. I switched on the heating, and opened the half-closed curtains. I was in the kitchen filling the kettle when Jude arrived, parking her car out on the drive. Then Simmo and Gin appeared at the back door, having parked up at the nearby state park car park and taken a short track to the house through the bush.

'This house is lovely on the outside,' Gin said. 'But inside...' We all followed her gaze through to the living room, taking in the shabby old sofas and table, a prehistoric-looking television and video, and off-white walls enlivened only by the occasional family wedding photograph.

'I know,' I agreed. 'Colourless and characterless – rather like my in-laws.'

They giggled.

'No books,' Jude remarked.

'They're not readers,' I answered. 'There aren't any bookcases here. We'll have to put the books in the display cabinet.' I nodded towards the cabinet, which held more family photographs and various hideous trinkets. 'I'll box all that stuff up.'

Simmo wandered around the house, and returned downstairs after inspecting the master bedroom and ensuite. 'They don't have much worth nicking,' she said.

'I know. That's why I thought this house would be good,' I said, passing around cups of tea. 'No DVD player, no computer. Pat doesn't wear much jewellery and what she has she's taken with her to Queensland. So all the burglar will take will be the books, and Pat and Dan won't lose anything should everything not work out.'

'Of course it'll work out,' Simmo said. 'Let's make a start on the books, shall we? Jude will need to go off to work soon.'

We'd deliberately chosen the university holidays to bid on Joy93's auction, so that Jude could join us. Simmo and I had both taken leave from work, and Gin planned to join us only during the mornings, and head off to the theatre as normal in the afternoon. Our plan was for Jude to leave the house for three hours every morning, so that any watching burglar would think she had a part-time job, and use that timeframe to break in. In reality, she would head for one of the cafés in Warrandyte's main street, where she planned to catch up on some essay-marking. Since we needed to operate in pairs, Gin would join Jude separately in the café every morning. Simmo and I would watch for the arrival of anyone suspicious from Dan and Pat's bedroom.

So, now we set to work on the books. We had all spent the past couple of weekends hitting garage sales and trash and treasures with a vengeance, and had accumulated as many worthless hardbacks as we could find. Between them, Jude and Simmo had photocopied mountains of dust jackets of valuable children's books. This morning we covered all the worthless books with the spurious dust jackets, and opened every book at page 93 – in honour of Joy herself – and pencilled the name P. Dixon somewhere on the page. Then we arranged the books in the display case.

'They look rather nice,' Jude remarked admiringly.

'Shame they're not real, otherwise Pat and Dan would be in-laws worth having,' I joked.

At 9.30 Jude headed off to the café. Ten minutes later, Gin headed off via the bush track to join her. Simmo and I settled down upstairs, taking it in turns to watch from the window. At 11.30 the post arrived. Jude brought it in when she got back at 12.30. We cooed over Rachel in the Abbey, then I tucked it into my bag ready to take home that night. Simmo was going to stay overnight at my in-laws' with Jude. We didn't expect the burglar to strike then – so far they had come during the day, when they knew the house was empty – but it was better to take precautions, just in case.

The following morning, Simmo and I saw a man in his early 20s, sporting a pony-tail, jeans and a black T-shirt, saunter down the drive. He knocked at the door a couple of times, wandered around the house, then headed back up into the court.

'That'll be him,' Simmo said.

'He doesn't look the book type to me,' I replied. 'More like your average burglar.'

'You mean like the ones in *The Bill*?' Simmo scoffed.

Now that someone had checked out the house, we all started to feel more apprehensive. I worried that the burglar would be frustrated by the lack of nickable goods at Dan and Pat's, and maybe damage the house in some way. When no-one showed up the following morning, I felt relieved. Maybe the man had seen there was nothing worth stealing when he walked around the house, and wouldn't come back.

But the following morning, at around 10.30, a white van turned into the drive. The pony-tailed man we'd seen previously jumped out of the driver's side. His companion was also young and male, but with short dark hair. As they knocked on the door, then wandered around the side of the house, Simmo quickly texted Jude, giving her the cue to park at the end of the court. She'd just about finished when we heard the shattering of glass.

Simmo scurried behind the ensuite shower screen while I slipped into the built-in wardrobe. We had already replaced the light-globe with a dud, to ensure it was so dark no-one could be seen.

From my hiding place, I could hear muffled thumping sounds from downstairs and prayed that nothing was being damaged. Then I heard footsteps on the stairs. Someone came into the bedroom, poked in a couple of drawers. The wardrobe door opened.

I stiffened. I could feel my heart thudding and hoped the burglar wouldn't hear it.

A hand flicked at the light switch, two, three times.

The burglar swore, turned away and clattered back downstairs. Phew. I breathed out.

'Nothing up here either, mate,' I heard him call out. 'All we'll get out of this job is whatever she gives us for taking the books.'

"She" presumably being Joy93, I thought.

'Let's get going then,' said the other burglar.

I crept out of the wardrobe. Simmo was already standing beside the window, her hand on her mobile. 'Just texting Jude with the rego,' she murmured. 'They're loading a couple of boxes into the van.'

As the van veered out of the drive, we ran downstairs and I unlocked the internal door to the garage. As I drove out, Simmo's mobile beeped. It was a text message from Gin.

'Research-Warrandyte Road,' Simmo read.

Then we were indeed heading to Eltham, I thought. As I drove through the house-dotted, drought-browned bush, I remembered the smashed window at the side of Dan and Pat's house. I'd go back later, I thought, organise a glazier. Eltham wasn't far, we wouldn't be away long. A text message from Gin told us to head for Eltham at the end of Research-Warrandyte Road; another one a few minutes later said the van had parked opposite Eltham's train station, outside an antique store called Olden Days.

As I drove into Eltham's busy main shopping strip, Simmo kept a look out for Olden Days. 'There it is!' she shouted, pointing to a large, yellow-painted, weatherboard shop with a notice advertising "Fine Antiques" on one window, "Old Books" on the other. I snagged a parking space just up the road. Gin was already walking towards us.

'Okay,' Simmo said, 'you and Gin go in. Text me if you think I can call the police.'

I jumped out of the car and joined Gin.

'Good chase?' I asked.

'Easy,' answered Gin. 'Jude always drives like a maniac, anyway, so trying to keep up with those two cowboys wasn't a problem for her.'

As I opened the door to Olden Days, a bell clanged, noting our arrival. Gin and I entered a large, rectangular room crammed with furniture – ornate tables, grand writing desks, enormous bookcases. To the right of the doorway was a desk. Our burglars stood in front of it, our boxes of books at their feet. Behind the desk was a woman who appeared to be in her early sixties, with short grey hair. Above the desk was a sign bearing the proprietor's name: Mrs Joan Adamson. On the far wall to the right of the desk were two imposing bookcases. A sign above them said, "Old Books".

While Gin feigned interest in a davenport near Joan Adamson's desk, I sauntered over to the books. I found the children's shelves quickly: the bookcase contained Chalets, Abbeys, Dimsies, Biggles – you name the rare children's book, she had it.

I rejoined Gin in time to see Joan Adamson hand the pony-tailed man a wad of notes.

'Thanks very much,' she said. 'I'll be in touch.'

The two men nodded at her, and left the shop. I texted Simmo to let her know that our fake rare books were safely inside the shop, so there was no need to follow the van. Then I wandered over to the desk, smiled at Joan Adamson, and bent down over the two cardboard boxes.

'There are some great titles here!' I exclaimed. 'Look, Gin! Abbeys, Chalets, Antonia Forest…'

'I haven't priced all these yet,' Joan Adamson told me. 'They've only just come in. A couple of lads brought them in. Their grandmother died; they found the books in her attic.'

'If only I had a grandmother who left things like that in her attic,' Gin said. She picked up a couple of the books. 'Oh, look, Lucy! This looks like a first edition Chalet. And here's a Clare Mallory; they're so hard to find…' She put them back in the box and picked up a couple more. 'Oh, goodness!' she exclaimed, browsing through it. 'This isn't a Chalet at all! Look!' She held the book out to the shop owner.

Joan Adamson took the book from her, opened it and frowned. She came around to our side of the desk and started hunting through the boxes, picking up each book, checking its contents, then dropping it onto the floor.

'Looks like you've been conned,' Gin said.

'Those bloody stupid…' Joan Adamson began.

The door clanged open. Two uniformed police officers entered the store.

'Mrs Joan Adamson?' asked one officer. 'We've had a complaint from a Mrs Judith Larcombe. She says you've taken a box of books from a house where she's been staying. Apparently they're easily identifiable.' He picked up one of the books from the boxes, and opened it. 'She says they all have the name P. Dixon written in pencil on page 93.'

When Jude spoke to the police a couple of days later, they told her that they'd managed to trace the van and that the two men had admitted breaking into houses to steal books for Joan Adamson, plus anything else they wanted to dispose of for themselves. Once she'd been dobbed in, Joan Adamson admitted organising the burglaries. When books had been brought to her, she'd dumped anything of no value, and had sold the rarer and collectable ones in the store and online. And, of course, she sold some of them on eBay, often being lucky enough to have the winning bidder live within burgling distance of Eltham. The police also told Jude that arrangements would be made with burglary victims to see if they could prove that any of her current stock belonged to them.

That news came later, though. In the wake of her arrest, Simmo, Jude, Gin and I headed triumphantly back to Warrandyte, where we went to the pub in the main street and ordered a bottle of champagne.

We were well into our second glass and Simmo was describing how she'd spotted the police passing by just after I'd texted her, when my mobile rang

It was Peter. He sounded panicky.

'Lucy,' he said. 'I'm at mum and dad's place, waiting for the police. I was driving past for work, and thought I'd go round to the house to check it was okay. And the side window's been broken. It looks like they've been burgled!'

DUST DEVILS

Also won the Malice Domestic Award

Julie Waight

EXTRAORDINARY THINGS HAPPEN ALL THE TIME. CYNDI KNOWS THIS TO BE true because she watches Maury Povich, Oprah and Jerry Springer.

Her house is a mundane suburban weatherboard, dirtier than most. Cyndi is not fond of cleaning. Tonight, the six o'clock news appears decidedly hazy through concentrated layers of dust on the television screen. As Cyndi sits on the couch, Danny struts between her and the television, holding the Electrolux vacuum cleaner.

'What do you do all day?' he says, brandishing the nozzle in the air.

Cyndi notices a carpet thread hanging from the end, a long dirty piece that wriggles about like an erratic worm.

'Why don't you clean?'

Cyndi frowns. She thinks to tell him that Oprah had a host of burn victims as guests this afternoon and that Jerry Springer's show had centred on paternity tests, but it doesn't seem appropriate.

'I went to the supermarket,' she says.

'Look at the dust devils,' Danny says, wide-eyed and vacuum-cleaner-encumbered.

'Dust devils?' Cyndi can't imagine what he means. 'Don't you mean dust bunnies?'

'Nothing so harmless,' he says. 'Not when you're a chronic asthmatic.' Danny wheezes the last two words to add credence to his asthma chronicability. And he's wearing his satisfied expression, the one where the side of his mouth curls at the corner.

'You can't expect me to do it,' he sighs in pretence of great weariness and breathlessness. 'Work all day to come home and work some more.'

The white hose thumps the Electrolux's side. The hose is as thick as a boa constrictor.

'You're high maintenance,' Danny says. 'High maintenance.'

Cyndi supposes she is.

'And lazy,' he adds, as if this new information is a sudden epiphany.

'I'm not lazy,' Cyndi says, looking at her hands. Her nails are chewed to the quick. Raw cuticles dangle and bleed at haphazard intervals. She might be high maintenance, but not lazy. Cyndi gets up to change channels on the television; Danny doesn't. Lazy people use remote controls.

The house surrounds them in dusty repose. Cushions squashed into uncushion-like shapes on the couch, crookedly hung curtains in the blotchy windows, and spider webs droop heavily from the ceiling. Cyndi had meant to disengage the webs last Tuesday; Tuesday came and went, but the spider webs didn't.

But dust devils? Who's heard of such a thing? Danny is making it up.

Cyndi stops staring at the ceiling because Danny is staring at her.

'What is wrong with you?' he says. The satisfied expression has slipped from his face.

'Nothing,' she says, chewing at her index finger and tasting blood. 'Lots of people don't like cleaning, you know.' She points the bleeding finger in his general direction.

Danny scowls. This expression makes the left corner of his mouth dip further than the right. It isn't an attractive look and she's meant to tell him this, but like removing the spider webs, she hasn't got around to it.

'Like it or not, people still clean.'

My mother used to whistle while she worked, Cyndi thinks.

Her mother had whistled, except for a brief period after her father had knocked out three of her teeth. Her mother had said that they were only false teeth and that it didn't matter.

Cleaning had been her mother's passion. Less likely to be beaten if you were scrubbing the floor, or had your head in the oven.

At least Danny doesn't hit her. It's a small concession, but a worthwhile one.

Cyndi's mother is in a nursing home now. The last time Cyndi visited was after the home's coordinator complained that Cyndi's mother had wrestled a cleaner to the floor for ownership of a Chux Superwipe and a bottle of cloudy ammonia.

Danny begins to stride about the living room, dragging the Electrolux behind him. One of the wheels squeaks. It's her mother's vacuum cleaner, a family heirloom.

'You know my condition,' Danny says. 'You know how I suffer.'

How can he think she doesn't know when he reminds her daily? She considers telling him about yesterday's episode of Maury titled My husband had sex with my brother, but decides against it.

'You need help,' Danny states.

It would be nice to have someone come in and clean, Cyndi thinks. They could certainly afford it. But she realises that isn't what Danny is talking about.

'Pardon?' Cyndi says.

'I said, this therapist comes highly recommended.' He drops the Electrolux nozzle to the floor and reaches into his pocket. For a moment, the hose slithers on the carpet then lies still. Danny hates to repeat himself. Cyndi waits for him to say just that.

'Why don't you listen to me? You know how I hate to repeat myself.'

Frisbee-like, he throws a business card at Cyndi. Its corner jabs the base of her throat. She swats at the spot and when she looks, her fingertip bears a smudge of blood.

He has made her bleed for the first time.

That night Cyndi dreams she's on Jerry Springer.

She sits on stage in a red leather chair. Without surprise, Cyndi sees that the audience is articles of furniture and fixtures from her house. Lying across an entire row is the couch and, next to it, the coffee table. In the row above are the lamp, a set of crockery with white flowers on the plates, the clock from the kitchen, and her and Danny's wedding photo. The television is perched in the front row and somewhere there will be the remote control.

Their bookcase leans into the aisle, dusty encyclopaedias fall out. Jerry steps over these on his way to the stage.

It isn't until Jerry reaches the stage that Cyndi glances to her right. Her mother sits in another red chair, wearing her favourite pink blouse, black slacks and of course her floral apron and rubber gloves. Her mother smiles and claps; the rubber gloves make the sound hollow and squishy.

On Cyndi's left are three empty chairs. She wonders which guests will be joining them, then she looks again and sees that the chairs are occupied – by dust devils.

Threads of fear twist in Cyndi's stomach. Danny didn't make it up after all. Here they are, not dust bunnies, no; nothing so harmless. They're darker and dirtier than dust bunnies and not fluffy at all, but share their appearance with that of overused steel wool.

One has ears, or are they horns? Another has a piece of old cheese for a head. The last has a spongy middle of mould, the sort you find on vegetables left too long in the fridge.

Jerry nods, smiles and turns to face the homely audience. He opens his mouth but it's her mother's scream that Cyndi hears.

'Look out!'

Heart thumping, Cyndi watches her mother leap from the chair. Somehow she's acquired a broom; perhaps she wrestled it from a stagehand.

'Filth!' she screeches. 'Get out of the way! I've got to clean.'

Jerry moves incredibly fast. He is, Cyndi supposes, a professional at handling volatile guests. With the assistance of some extremely clean cameramen, Cyndi's mother is dragged from the stage. In the scuffle, a rubber glove falls to the floor. Cyndi sees her mother's hand, as white and wrinkled as a dead fish, flap on Jerry's shoulder.

Left in the company of the dust devils, Cyndi nervously grips the arms of her red chair.

'Don't be afraid,' the dust devil with the mouldy middle says. 'You are our friend.'

'Yes,' agrees the dust devil with the cheese head. 'You leave us in peace.'

The audience clatters, ticks, and flashes. More books tumble into the aisle. The television tunes into a station with applause.

True, thinks Cyndi, her fear subsiding. She certainly has no reason to be considered an enemy to anything composed of dust, dirt, or even the black goop that accumulates in the plastic base of her kitchen tidy. Doesn't she leave sleeping dust devils lie? By God, she does.

When the dust devil with horns speaks, (Cyndi can now see that the horns are crumbled corn chips) it sounds like Yoda from *Star Wars*.

'Help you, we will.'

Cyndi isn't fond of the character, Yoda. She can't understand how something so all-knowing and wise fails to grasp the English language.

'A friend in need, you are. Yes.'

Books fall. The lamp flashes. The wedding photograph slips between seats and disappears. The television tunes into another station and there's Darth Vader, sounding like he suffers from an acute case of asthma.

The dust devils say other things, but Cyndi can't make out their words. The awful gasping, wheezing sound coming from the television gets louder. Cyndi realises that it's Danny panting in the bed beside her and thinks how strange to comprehend something like that from inside a dream.

Danny leaves for work the following morning and doesn't kiss her goodbye. He hardly kisses her at all any more, but they still have sex regularly. This puzzles Cyndi and she considers writing to Jerry Springer to request a show based on dwindling kisses and invariable sex.

The card Danny assaulted her with yesterday sits by the phone. She stares at it as if it may come alive and attack her of its own will. She senses it is dangerous.

Danny expects her to call. He'll ask if she has when he gets home. Does she want to sit with a stranger and discuss her personal life? No. Will the stranger gaze at her chewed nails and write something on a notepad? Probably. Will it be decided that she needs some sort of experimental drug or treatment? Anything is possible. Extraordinary things happen all the time.

Cyndi hurries to the bathroom to inspect herself in the mirror. The face that gazes back is plump and unattractive. Her hair needs cutting. Fear lies beneath her eyes in the form of dark smears. She can't possibly go out looking like this. Her gnawed fingertips painfully grip the basin. Something brushes against her hand.

Cyndi yanks her hand away and glares at the grubby basin. The three dust devils from her dream are assembled by the drain, like fat spiders trapped by the slippery surface.

'You don't need therapy,' Mouldy Middle says.

'You have to take control,' Cheese Head adds.

The horned dust devil wears pieces of Cyndi's hair from the drain. 'Fine, you are.'

Cyndi isn't convinced. 'Danny thinks I should speak to someone. He thinks—'

'He is unkind,' Cheese Head says.

'He's never hit me.'

'Bosses you, he does.'

Mouldy Middle agrees. 'And he talks down to you, like, like—'

'Dirt,' Cyndi finishes. She hopes she hasn't offended them, speaking of dirt like it's something bad. They don't appear offended.

'If you want to speak to someone, why not your mother?' says Mouldy Middle.

'My mother?'

The thought wraps around her brain like hair in a drain.

The Treeside Hostel is a pleasant enough place, yet Cyndi doesn't like coming here. She suffers an uneasy feeling in her stomach. She knows what the feeling is, but avoids using its given name.

Her mother spent her life poised between Cyndi and her father's fists. Being put in a home is hardly a reward for heroism.

Cyndi wishes she could look after her mother, but Danny won't allow it. She knows this to be true, even though she has never suggested it. The very thought of bringing up the subject makes Cyndi's insides queasy. Danny doesn't hit her – no – but he does something.

He keeps me under control, she thinks.

In her mother's room, Cyndi finds a bottom sticking out from under the bed. This position is familiar to Cyndi. Apart from allowing close-up cleaning, it protects her mother's face from fists and flying objects.

'Mum?'

The bottom wiggles out and reveals a beaming face.

'Cyndi!'

Her mother totters upright and gives Cyndi a massive hug.

The scent of Windex, washing powder and furniture polish wafts in Cyndi's nostrils.

'How are you, Mum?'

'Good, good, good.'

Her mother always was, and is, "good". She's lived her life believing it and, Cyndi supposes, it's too late for her to see the truth.

They talk of old times. But the old times are censored recollections. Never a hint of violence or unhappiness. Cyndi's father remains the hard-working man, the good provider, and the sadly missed husband.

Cyndi doesn't miss him at all. Sometimes her mother gets confused and thinks he's still alive. Her face clouds over and she looks frightened, like now.

'I'd better get back to cleaning under the bed,' she says. 'Your father won't be pleased if the place is untidy when he gets home.'

Cyndi nods. Trying to explain that he is dead, that he isn't ever coming home, only upsets her mother. Cyndi remembers how it was back then. How it really was.

Each afternoon at 5.30, the tension in their home would mount to an unbearable hum. The sort a vacuum cleaner might make when the bag is overly full. Her mother would dart about the house searching for something else to clean. Dinner was always ready and waiting, but it wasn't enough. Her father would find fault with something. Cyndi had often caught him hunting for something – anything – in the house that wasn't exactly right. Once he had fished a broken glass out of the bin to grumble about.

Her mother says something that jolts Cyndi from her memories.

'What did you say, Mum?'

'That man is a nasty piece of work,' her mother repeats, sticking her head back beneath the bed.

Cyndi can't believe it. She tugs at the hem of her mother's dress.

'Dad is a nasty piece of work?'

The head reappears frowning. 'Heaven's no. Your father's passed away, you know. I was speaking of that Daniel you married. Nasty, nasty, nasty. Don't know why you can't see it for yourself. It's as obvious as dirt.'

Cyndi stands in the lower level of Kmart, but it feels more like the lower regions of Dante's Hell.

'…And it has the features you asked about. Suction and blow.'

Cyndi smiles at the Godfrey's salesman. It's her best housewife smile, pilfered from her mother.

'Are you sure it's powerful?' Cyndi asks.

The salesman gives his best smile – she isn't sure where he got his from – a horror movie perhaps. He leans toward her like a conspirator, which he unknowingly is.

'Why, Madam,' he says (Cyndi hates being called "madam" marginally less than being called "high maintenance") 'you could perform an abortion with this sucker,' and he laughs.

Cyndi laughs, too. Her mouth feels stuffed full of cotton – or maybe it's dust devils. They seem to be everywhere.

That evening, Danny comes home to a house depleted of dirt, grime and spider webs. His expression is one of stark amazement.

Dreamily, he wanders into the bedroom where the dustless bedside table gleams in clear lamplight, linen washed, clothes folded away.

'Wow!' he says.

The kitchen sparkles like something out of a television commercial. Cyndi used a toothbrush to remove the built up grunge around the hotplates. She even cleaned in the crack between the oven and the bench, but Danny doesn't notice.

In the bathroom, the shower curtain has been washed with White King, the basin is scrubbed and the floor mopped. Her raw fingers have swollen to being fat, purple leeches. Danny doesn't notice her hands, either.

His satisfied and scowling expressions meet and merge into something new and, Cyndi thinks, ugly.

'I can't remember a time the house looked like this,' Danny says. He glances at her suspiciously, as if she may have emerged from a ruptured seedpod as the alien duplicates did in *The Body Snatchers*.

Cyndi's back aches, her arms feel weighted down with bags of wet cement, her ankles are bulbous slugs spilling out of the tops of her shoes.

'I bought a new vacuum cleaner,' she says, showing her teeth in what she hopes is a wide smile. 'Would you like to see it?'

Speechless, Danny wanders into the living room and collapses onto the clean, covered couch.

Cyndi leaves him in polished splendour and gets the new Volta vacuum cleaner.

She hauls it into the room and plugs it into a socket between him and the television set.

'Here it is,' she announces.

He gazes at it, then at her.

'Well,' he says. 'Well.'

Cyndi smiles smugly. Danny is at a loss for words, which is so unlike him. He has nothing to complain about. Nothing to put her down over. The poor thing. Look at him sitting there, with his mouth hanging open.

He clears his throat and wheezes. 'Now you need to do something about yourself.'

His satisfied expression resurfaces.

'Look at you,' he says. 'You're fat and your hair is a sight.'

Cyndi's smile dies. He'll always be the same. Just like her father.

From inside the Volta, she hears muffled voices.

'He is unkind.'

'Bosses you, he does.'

'Speaks down to you like…dirt.'

Cyndi bends over and removes the Volta's hose. She re-connects it to the "blow" outlet and flicks the switch.

The accumulated dirt of the days cleaning erupts forth in a fluffy grey cloud as she releases dust devils and bunnies alike.

Coughing, Danny grabs for his throat.

She directs the humming hose directly at him. 'You're nasty, nasty, nasty,' she says. 'Now SHUT UP!'

The grey cloud envelops his face. Danny slithers off the couch and lands on his knees. She switches off the machine and drops the nozzle. That shut him up wonderfully.

Danny gasps for breath. When the grey cloud settles, he's still kneeling, arms outstretched in a plea for compassion. Cyndi decides he looks like Al Johnson in the midst of a rendition "Mammy".

Cyndi walks to the kitchen and locates his Ventolin. When she returns, she tosses the inhaler at him. It bounces off his forehead, leaving a white dot, before it slips between the couch cushions and disappears.

'Now,' she says. 'I missed all my shows today because I was cleaning. But I've taped them.'

On the dusty couch, Cyndi sits and presses the remote control. Dust devils nestle on the pillows. Danny wheezes by her feet.

Tomorrow she'll call the hostel and tell them that her mother is coming to live with her. It should work out perfectly. Her mother loves to clean and won't she marvel at the new Volta vacuum cleaner? But Cyndi will have the house squeaky clean before her mother arrives. Dirt isn't a bad thing – unless it's evidence.

By the time Oprah finishes and Maury begins, Danny's wheezing has stopped. Without emotion, Cyndi realises he isn't breathing at all. Chronic asthmatics often die from their affliction.

Extraordinary things happen all the time.

2006

Mrs Wilcox's Milk Saucepan

Roxxy Bent

FIVE DAYS AFTER HER MOTHER'S BODY WAS TAKEN FROM NEXT DOOR, THERE she was, Alice MacKensie-Wilcox, on my doorstep with a form for me to sign. The hoo-ha hadn't yet died down. After all, her mother "Anita" (yes, the famous artist, but always "Mrs Wilcox Next Door" to me) had been found dead of a sleeping pill overdose. I was having difficulty coming to terms with Mrs Wilcox's suicide, but as the doctor attending said to the TV cameras outside on our street, 'It's becoming more common amongst the elderly.'

It must have been 20 years since I'd seen Mrs Wilcox's Alice. But in that second, after I'd opened the door wide and wiped my hands on my apron, I flashed back to more than double those years and saw Alice, a bespectacled four-year-old the week the Wilcoxes moved in.

She'd come to introduce herself and her memorably precocious speech was oft quoted in our house: 'I'm Alice Mackensie-Wilcox, I'm four years old and I've come to see if you've a child I can play with?'

We had, but none so articulate. My youngest, Anne, and Alice became fast friends and were inseparable until their early teens. It was then that Alice's passion for insects got between them.

That Alice has inherited her father's looks was more evident now that she was approaching 50. She had his short-sightedness, his stoop and, poor thing, a hefty dose of his awkwardness. There she stood, pen and paper in hand, writhing with embarrassment.

Mrs Wilcox's racy circle had been appalled that her daughter had inherited none of her mother's legendary beauty. I'd heard this said many a time and often in Alice's hearing. I thought her life a rotten one and did what I could to bolster her ego.

Alice wouldn't accept tea or coffee. Isn't it the devil when people won't? The paper turned out to be a form for her mother's superannuation. She needed someone who knew her mother, but wasn't related, to witness her signature. We signed and she got up to leave. I could tell she had something more to say but had no idea how start. I offered every possible opening but it wasn't until we were at the front door that she broke down. I made out the odd word while steering her back to the lounge, again offering tea, but she threw me off in a fit of frustration, said I must come next door, she had something to show me. She was distraught, eyes full of panic.

Walking up Mrs Wilcox's garden path I was aware of a strange mixture of excitement, sadness and dread. It was years since I'd been inside the house.

I hadn't been estranged from Mrs Wilcox but after our children were grown there wasn't much reason for us to have regular contact. After all, you couldn't get two people more different. I've never worked, I was married to the same man for 53 years until his death three years ago and, really, all I've done is be a mum and these days a keen gran. For her part, Mrs Wilcox was the hugely successful painter, "Anita", she'd had countless affairs, and was completely uninterested in being a wife, mother or homemaker. I live a quiet life; she was notoriously outspoken. Last year she caused a furore in the press over the plight of refugees. The only thing we had in common was age. We would both have turned 80 this year.

Over the years we'd developed our neighbourly habits. There's no way Mrs Wilcox would be twitching her curtains on neighbourhood watch duty, but even so I let her know when I'd be away and she did the same for me. Her trips abroad accompanying her work to exhibitions in Paris, New York, Milan, were exotic. Mine were to family. I still visit Anne and the children for a week twice a year and, up until last year, I was going to America every other year to visit Sarah, until my doctor ruled out international flights because of blood pressure. My youngest, Simon, visits regularly but seeing as he doesn't have children I don't bother with Brisbane (that awful humidity!)

For both of us, the trips had all but ceased. I can't remember the last time Mrs Wilcox was on my doorstep telling me where she was going and for how long. Even though for the last few years we'd rarely had occasion to see each other, we'd lived in gentle awareness of each other for fifty-one years.

As Alice and I headed along the hallway past the bedrooms, the house seemed smaller than I remembered. Memory plays strange tricks. It's still bigger than ours, of course, and much more grand. When we arrived at the back living area my heart did a sort of leap and I had to steady myself against the back of a chair and catch my breath. I was glad I'd tucked a hankie up my sleeve when I'd dressed that morning.

The room was so full of her. I expected to see her lying on one of the sofas, sketchbook upon her knees, charcoal flying.

The back of the house had been modernised 10 or so years ago. I know because of builders' noise. I'd not been invited in to a viewing because Mrs Wilcox would never have thought to suggest something as mundane as coming in to look at renovations, even though there was nothing I'd have liked more.

Despite its newness – the modern glass doors that replaced the wall and looked out to the lawn and her studio beyond – there was evidence of her everywhere in just the way it had always been. Her paintings, of course, friends' works on the walls, sculptures taking up every available space. Piles of books, magazines. Familiar, lively, rich mess.

I found myself way back in time, having popped over to collect Anne because she'd refused to respond to my 'Dinner's ready!' calls over the fence. Forced away from my organised, apron-wearing existence to confront whatever was happening at the Wilcoxes. Butterflies and dry mouth notwithstanding, I'd head through the always-open front door, run the gauntlet of the hallway, into the den of iniquity, which was how I always thought of this back area.

You'd never know what to expect. It could be as mild as a poetry reading; but more often than not there'd be a nude person – fruit in their lap with any luck – modelling for a charcoal drawing, and always people, people.

Once or twice I'd stayed, my protests waived. I'd find myself halfway through a glass of red wine, the afternoon softened, melting into evening.

Late on one such afternoon, Mrs Wilcox whispered to me, 'Stay', during a general leave-taking. My, 'But, the children's dinner...' was brushed aside and a surprisingly healthy feast of fruit and cheeses assembled for Alice and Anne. It was Clive's night at the Masons and the other two were out, so it didn't matter. She took me to her studio. I wouldn't take all my clothes off, but she said I was perfect in my underwear and made masses of drawings. She gave me the finished work a couple of weeks later. The oil paint was still so fresh it was intoxicating. Clive was appalled. What on Earth was I thinking? Was I drunk? (She'd painted me with the glass of red wine.) I put the painting away in the back of the wardrobe, where it's been ever since.

Surprisingly, Mrs Wilcox didn't drink, despite the fact that she was often in the midst of a party. She said it didn't mix with painting; she didn't have the discipline to work through a hangover. Like anything that got in the way of her work, husband included, alcohol got short shrift.

Alice hadn't stood a chance in the face of her mother's single mindedness. But she'd survived and by all accounts had become an extremely successful entomologist. On the form that I signed, she was a "Dr" but the scars were evident; her lack of social ease and the fact that she'd not formed a relationship (I won't add "never had children", for two of my own, the childless ones, tell me that this is no longer a criteria for success or happiness).

I got my breath back and took in the fact that Alice was standing staring at the kitchen sink. I followed her over there and was struck, immediately.

'Is this how they found it, or has someone…?'

'No!' Alice interrupted, 'This is how it was.'

'But,' I stopped myself, not wanting to embarrass Alice.

'Go on,' she implored.

'It's never ever been like this. Look!' I picked up the gleaming milk saucepan then dropped it back immediately.

'There are no finger prints, I made them check,' said Alice.

'I wonder,' I began, 'If I could be perfectly and completely honest and you not take offence?'

'If you're going to say that my mother kept a filthy, shambolic kitchen and her disgusting sticky, never washed milk saucepan was the talk of the street, then don't worry, I knew.'

I really didn't know what to say. Mrs Wilcox's housekeeping, or rather lack of it, had been legendary in our suburb. A view of her milk saucepan was regarded as a coup and would be the talk of the street. As a rule I didn't join in gossip, but I have to confess to being fascinated by her complete disregard for, or any attempt to, keep up appearances. There was something delicious about living next door to a woman who didn't give a hoot about convention generally, and housekeeping in particular.

Mrs Wilcox's milk saucepan became the symbol for this. It was unbelievably filthy. Thickly encrusted with ring after ring of stale milk, I never saw it clean. While her friends would often be imbibing large quantities of alcohol, she'd be heating up more milk for yet another of her rich, dark, hot chocolates. She said the chocolate stimulated her creativity and, if she wanted to stay up all night to keep going on a piece of work, that was what she used. She offered me one once and ridges of aged, yellowy milk popped into my mind and I almost gagged.

Alice and I sat on either end of the sofa where Mrs Wilcox had done so many of her drawings. We put the gleaming milk saucepan on the coffee table in front of us.

'I know it looks like suicide. An empty bottle of sleeping pills was on the draining board.' Alice swallowed tears. 'But… the kitchen, the milk saucepan, was as you see it.'

'You don't think, if she had decided to take her life, that she may have had one final clean up?'

As soon as I said it, I knew it was absurd. Mrs Wilcox had that rare talent, among women anyway, of not noticing mess. When I think of how many hours I've put into keeping house, cleaning, wiping, tidying for visitors! It probably adds up to years. Scratch the surface of every housewife and you may well find a talented painter, sculptor or writer, if only she had the time!

'The delivery girl who found her called the police. They were here when I arrived. When I explained to the detective how a clean-up was totally out of character, he laughed. 'Foul play suspected on account of a clean milk saucepan? Sorry love. The doctor had no hesitation in signing the death certificate.'

'But Alice, the alternative – it's just too awful to contemplate. It means…'

'Someone killed her,' Alice finished the sentence.

We were both absolutely stunned. Although I'd found the idea of Mrs Wilcox's taking her own life hard to swallow, I hadn't let myself think about what it meant if it wasn't suicide. I certainly hadn't let the word "murder" enter my consciousness. A prickle of fear crept up my neck.

'Can we be absolutely sure it wasn't suicide?' I asked.

'She didn't leave a note. She abhorred drugs. She wouldn't even take an Aspirin,' Alice continued. 'Where would she have got prescription sleeping pills? She didn't see doctors.'

'Alice, she did get some sleeping pills. She went to the doctor about two weeks ago.'

Alice's face was stricken.

'Two weeks ago,' I said gently, 'your mother told me she was having trouble sleeping. She asked if I had noticed any unusual noises at night. I wondered if it could it be a prowler and offered to call the police. She refused and when I telephoned next day, although she was edgy, she said everything was all right. She told me she'd been to the doctor who prescribed sleeping tablets.'

This timing struck a chord with Alice.

'Two weeks ago mother called my work, said she needed help. This was totally unprecedented. She never called me, nor asked for help. We had hardly any contact. We met so rarely, all we had were brief conversations about our work. Anyway, I was in South America picking up a colony of ants when I got the message. I called immediately and she said "You're no use to me on the phone". I tried to cut my trip short but there were no planes. As soon as we landed here, I settled the ants and dashed to her side. She said, "Problem solved". I pressed her, she refused to tell me, and we had a blazing row. That was the last time we spoke.'

Alice took off her glasses and sobbed. Deep, throaty moaning sobs. I found tissues, fetched a glass of water and patted her until she calmed down.

'You're not feeling responsible, are you Alice? When the police came next door and questioned me about her mental state,' I hesitated then said, 'I told them she'd been pretty fed up about her eyesight fading.'

'She wasn't depressed,' countered Alice. 'Worried, yes. The last time we spoke about her work she said, "I'm in my Monet phase". He struggled with blindness, you know. I know she didn't do it. I want an autopsy. I'm not having a funeral until I'm convinced that there was no foul play. I'm sorry to burden you, Mrs T. I couldn't think of anyone else to tell.'

'You're not to worry on my account,' I chastened Alice. 'I'm honoured to be in your confidence. But what can be done? If the police accept it's suicide?'

Alice looked defeated.

'Alice, I don't want you to worry anymore,' I said in my most positive voice. 'If the police won't do anything, we'll investigate it ourselves.'

Alice's smile broke through her tears. 'I knew I could rely on you.'

I must confess, lying in the dark, hours later, wound up like a clock and unable to keep still let alone sleep, I wondered if, given my high blood pressure and the fact that I'll be 80 next month, I hadn't taken on rather too much.

Alice and I speculated about Mrs Wilcox's worries and our case for the rest of the afternoon. Perhaps Mrs Wilcox had been worried about security? A few years ago Alice insisted her Mother upgrade all her locks. She'd refused an alarm system, but security screens had been fitted over all windows. Given that there's a great deal of valuable art in the house, this was an excellent idea. Many of Mrs Wilcox's paintings are in art galleries and private collections, but she'd held onto favourites. Add friends' work, many well-known, and you have a valuable stash. Maybe the "unusual noises" Mrs Wilcox heard were from someone trying to get in?

'There's something very odd in here,' said Alice and she took me into her mother's bedroom. The room, unlike any other in the house, was completely bare of art. However, there were distinctive marks on the wall that showed where paintings had been.

'There were 25,' said Alice. 'All of Beatrix. She said she'd never part with them. I know they were here before I left for South America.'

'Do you think they've been stolen?' I asked.

'No,' said Alice and showed me a book her Mother kept of who bought her paintings and where they were. Under "Beatrix x 25", it simply said, "Lent Out. Safe Place". It was clearly Mrs Wilcox's handwriting.

Other works were listed as in the state and national Art Galleries and with individuals. The Remingtons, of course, had the most substantial collection.

The Remingtons, Honey Remington specifically, had been Mrs Wilcox's patron. She'd recognised Mrs Wilcox's genius right from the beginning and it had been a mutually beneficial relationship. Mrs Wilcox's work was the instigation for the now famous Remington Gallery. The Remingtons' money had allowed Mrs Wilcox to flourish and not have to worry about teaching to make ends meet.

It hadn't been without its pressures, though. When Honey Remington decided to mount an exhibition, she'd be here on a daily basis making sure that Mrs Wilcox was applying herself and meeting her deadlines.

'Given that whatever happened is most likely related to your mother's work, our first investigative port of call should be Mrs Remington.'

But when Alice looked in her diary, she couldn't find a spot for us to meet with Mrs Remington until the middle of next week. Not only did Alice have her usual busy schedule, but she was on call to observe special activities in the South American ant colony. Just then, as if to prove how busy she was, her emergency beeper went off.

'You go, dear. I'll let you know what I find out,' I said.

Next morning, not early – I was acquainted with Mrs Remington's habits from years ago – I headed for the best street in town and knocked on her door.

I would have recognised Mrs Remington anywhere, although I hadn't seen her for more years than I cared to count. She was a tall woman, still very upright, and she cut a striking figure with her blonde hair (although that would be dyed these days) and piercing, blue eyes. She still favoured beautifully cut beige suits, understated jewellery and the glow that comes from being exceedingly pampered.

She didn't recognise me, which wasn't surprising. However, the length of time she took to register who I was reminded me how rude she was if she thought you not worth bothering with.

At first, walking past matching luggage in the hallway, I had a flash of amateur detective glory, thinking I'd come to the right place at the right time. I imagined apprehending a guilty Mrs Remington as she tried to escape the country.

She sat me down, ordered me tea and explained she'd just come back from a three-month cruise (so much for my citizen's arrest), then shed a few tears about Mrs Wilcox.

I asked her if she thought Mrs Wilcox had committed suicide.

'Anita would never take her own life! Her work may have taken a dive in popularity over the last two decades and prices dropped, but she was still working, healthy, positive! No!'

I ventured to suggest that if it hadn't been suicide, then foul play must have been involved. Mrs Remington was so horrified she all but pushed me out the door. On the way I did glean that she no longer had anything to do with the Remington Gallery. Her son Stewart had the reins. I also detected hostility. Stewart was always a difficult child, neglected, despite being surrounded by wealth. He'd performed oddly spiteful acts which Mrs Remington never believed him capable of.

On the doorstep, I asked about Miss Duke. She hesitated, then said, 'Beatrix is well looked after. She's at The Laurels.'

Then she closed the door.

There was only one "The Laurels" in the phone book. I rang, said who I was, that I was the neighbour of the recently deceased Mrs Wilcox, "Anita", and asked, did they have a Miss Beatrix Duke? I was informed that I wasn't on any of their inhabitants' visitor lists. Visits weren't encouraged as disruptions to routine caused distress. I asked, did The Laurels specialise in dementia? Although there was no absolute "yes" reply, there was enough hesitation to convince me that this was indeed the case.

That night as I was having my sandwiches, Alice called and said, 'Switch on the TV news.' When I did, there was Stewart Remington, grin barely concealed, standing outside the Remington Gallery, being interviewed alongside another man who looked just like him. Stewart said that even though only a few days had passed since her death, Anita's work was enjoying a massive upturn in demand and Remington Gallery was mounting an exhibition in response.

I was particularly alerted when he said that there was a glaring hole in his collection. The 'Beatrix' series, paintings Anita made of her muse, were missing. He made a plea that anyone holding them come forward, for they were essential for the retrospective and would command a high price.

Minutes later, Alice was on my doorstep in a flap. There was something she hadn't told me.

'Actually, until that news broadcast, I hadn't put it together,' Alice wouldn't sit but paced, hands clasping and unclasping. 'Did you notice the man standing next to Stewart?'

'Yes,' I replied. 'I noticed how alike they are.'

'That's Marcus. Marcus appeared at my gym.'

It was so difficult to imagine Alice at the gym, I must have made a face.

'I have to go because I get back pain. Hunching over at the lab, computer,' she justified.

'That's marvellous, Alice. Everyone recommends it.'

'Marcus said he'd been an aerobics instructor and wanted to help me. He thought the gym was lax with people who weren't sporty. He asked me out, took me shopping, to his hairdresser. Recommended contact lenses. He's 20 years younger and I was waiting for the catch. After a couple of months I abandoned caution and I asked him, begged, practically, to come to bed.

'Immediately afterwards, he started in about Mother. "Where were the Beatrix paintings?" I knew, or rather assumed, they were in Mother's bedroom, but said I didn't know. Next day he came to the gym and barged into the ladies' change-rooms. "Where are the paintings?" he shouted. I was naked, frightened. I said, "I don't know!" Suddenly he seemed to believe me. "You really don't, do you! You disgusting, old…" There was more. I left for South America that night. If only I'd told Mother!'

That evening Alice accepted tea and some of my home-baked biscuits before going next door to stay.

Early next morning Alice called, distressed. When I offered to come over she said no, she'd come to me, for my house had always been a haven.

Apparently Alice, wearing only her mother's nightie, had been going through some papers when Stewart rapped on the glass doors. Alice got quite a shock and she had the feeling that this was just the effect he'd wanted. He barged his way in and wanted to know, where were the missing 25 paintings?

She got rid of him, but she was very shaky.

Alice and I discussed everything we'd found out so far and decided to call the police. But when Alice recounted our story to the detective: that Mrs Wilcox had telephoned Alice in South America and called in on me; of Marcus's aggression; of both his and Stewart's obsession with the missing paintings; and, of course, the clean milk saucepan, I could tell she wasn't making much of an impression

Alice was very down when she got off the telephone.

I wanted to cheer her up and decided to show her my painting. I didn't say it was me and, given her reaction, I'm glad I didn't.

'Another person totally besotted by Anita,' she said.

'I beg your pardon?' I was thrown.

'Leaning forward, look of intense longing, parted lips, parted legs,' Alice spoke as if ticking items off on a list.

'You're reading too much into it,' I defended.

'Erect nipples?'

'She was cold.'

'There's a huge fire burning behind her.'

Not able to bear any more, I put the painting away.

After Alice left, a memory of sitting for the painting appeared, unsummoned. As if it were yesterday, I felt the touch of Mrs Wilcox's cool fingers as she adjusted my hair, the ripples of desire that flooded through me.

I first became aware of Mrs Wilcox's varied love life when Mrs Honey Remington, having commissioned an exhibition, was panicking about Mrs Wilcox not meeting her deadlines. She insisted I use my spare key to let her in next door.

There'd been a party at the Wilcox's for days, but the noise had died down overnight and I thought they'd all left for one of their mad camping trips.

Much against my better judgement I unlocked the studio and Mrs Remington barged past me. Bottles, glasses, full ashtrays were strewn everywhere and there, in beautiful morning light streaming down from the skylight, were Mrs Wilcox and Miss Duke naked on the rug (doing exactly what, I've never been able to fathom). Mrs Remington gave forth a stream of profanities and left. It took Mrs Wilcox weeks to forgive me and she never gave me the spare key again.

It was much later that night, when the memories began to fade and our present fix loomed large that I, unable to sleep, came up with my plan.

Strictly speaking, Remington's Gallery wasn't open while the huge exhibition of Mrs Wilcox's work was being mounted. The treacherous Marcus let me in when I told him I had one of the paintings they talked about on the television.

I was shown upstairs to Stewart's swanky office with its view of the park. Behind his desk in a neat kitchen, galley style, I think they call it, was Stewart, sporting rubber gloves, scrubbing away at a stainless steel percolator.

'How lovely to see a young man take such pride in his domestic duties,' I offered, my thoughts running to Mrs Wilcox's milk saucepan. I twittered on, old lady style, reminiscing about my knowing Stewart as a sweet boy (I had to make this up, obviously).

I told them nobody knew of my painting's existence! Laboured the point of how I live alone, how deaf I am. That, since Mrs Wilcox's death, I'd hung the painting in my front upstairs bedroom. They were practically salivating by the time I left.

My trap laid, all I had to do was wait.

I prepared for bed, then called Alice. As I'd thought, she was at the laboratory with the ants, who'd made an exciting break-away and were forming a new colony. She was up for the night.

So far, all was to plan. The lab was 12 minutes from my house at the most. Less, with no traffic.

'Just checking your number works, dear.' I said and settled down to watch from my bedroom window.

It wasn't in my plan to fall asleep! I thought I was far too nervous.

I wake to noises. They're already in the house! The clock glows 4am. I remember that was Mrs Wilcox's time of death.

I hear them moving around downstairs. I've lost precious minutes.

I find I'm absolutely frozen and they're getting closer. Finally, I manage to press "redial" to Alice. But before I'm able to say anything, they're in the room. A torch blinds me. I try "old lady asleep" but the phone in my hand gives me away. It's grabbed, the cord ripped out of the wall. The torch flashes until it settles on my picture. I hear grunts of satisfaction. I swing my feet down to the floor but am pushed onto the bed, a big arm pins my chest.

A pillow is over my face, my arms trapped. I struggle, get a kick to one of them. One throws his full body weight on me now.

Then there's blackness. Silence.

Alice is pressing a lavender-scented flannel to my forehead when I come to.

A policewoman grins to see me awake.

'You are one truly amazing woman,' smiles Alice. 'Anita would be so proud of you.'

I am so grateful she didn't tell me off, call me a silly old lady.

'Did they…?' I whisper, barely able to get the words out.

'Both caught; with the picture.'

'How did you…?' I strain.

'Your number came up on my mobile. I knew something was up. The police were here within 10 minutes. Luckily.' Her eyes fill with tears. Mine, too, I confess; I'm not ready to go.

I squeeze her hand. She grabs mine, puts it up to her mouth and kisses it with such affection I'm quite taken aback.

'If you can bear any more excitement, I've found out where the missing pictures are,' she says.

I try to sit up.

'Tomorrow. Shhhh.'

The Laurels, where Miss Beatrix Dukes is ending her days, is quite the nicest nursing home I've ever seen. Her rooms are an art gallery. As well as the 25 beautiful portraits of Beatrix in her youth, there is one of Anita and Beatrix together, naked on the rug underneath the skylight, entwined around each other. It's entitled, "Self-Portrait With Lover".

The nurse said that although none of them can make any sense out of Beatrix on a daily basis, she seems quite lucid when talking to that painting.

The autopsy showed Mrs Wilcox had bruises "commensurate with a struggle" and a well-hidden needle-mark puncture. Stewart Remington is being charged with murdering Mrs Wilcox with an overdose of morphine, with Marcus as his accessory.

After the forensics had their field day with the milk saucepan (there was no residue of sleeping pills, just aged milk and hot chocolate), Alice presented it to me mounted on a plinth, inscribed "Mrs T. Domestic Goddess".

I've put it on the hall table underneath my painting. That way no one can avoid noticing either trophy.

2007

KILL-DEAD-GARTEN

Aoiffe Clifford

LINDY DIDN'T DISCOVER THE BODY UNTIL WE'D BEEN AT THE KINDER FOR AT least ten minutes. I say body but I guess I should say Zarko because that's whose body it was; Zarko the Cleaner. That makes him sound like a professional wrestler or hitman but really he was the cleaner.

I was turning off the alarm and Rosa was making us all cups of tea in the kitchen for when we would sit down to discuss the children's curriculum needs for the term. This would turn into the usual whingeing about how little respect we preschool teachers get. It was a time-honoured tradition and we never failed to deliver. Or, to be correct, Rosa and I never failed to deliver.

Lindy, being a twenty-something Marxist socialist still living at home in Mum and Dad's McMansion, was more focused on ranting about the fascist male capitalist conspiracy which was oppressing the masses. She usually did this while flicking through high-end fashion magazines. She hadn't quite decided whether her destiny was to look after the sprogs of the proletariat or to design clothes for the bourgeoisie. Either way we figured she was destined to be sponging off her parents for a good while yet.

'I think you'd better come in here,' Lindy called out to us. 'On second thoughts, call an ambulance.' She hesitated slightly and then said, 'Perhaps just the police.'

This sounded more interesting than, 'someone's poured blue paint in the red paint bottle' which was the usual start to the day, so both Rosa and I walked down the hall. We passed the walls covered in stick figure paintings in primary colours, and posters advertising events masquerading as fun social nights out but which were actually designed to fleece the parents in a bid to keep the Kinder open. The hall opened into the playroom with its worn-out lino and lingering playdough smell. We walked to where Lindy was standing.

There in the home corner was Zarko. He hadn't been a good-looking man alive and fair to say he looked even worse dead, but then a large

THE SCARLET STILETTO

compass through the head was never a good look, sartorially speaking. It was a bit too cutting edge even for Lindy.

The three of us looked at each other and then back at Zarko.

'Gosh,' I stammered.

'Oh my,' murmured Rosa.

'Holy Fuck!' exclaimed Lindy.

Lindy had only been in the industry for six months and she often forgot the cardinal coffee rule. You might be looking as dark as a double espresso, you might be thinking thoughts murkier than the bottom of a Turkish coffee but you are not allowed to say anything stronger than babycino in the vicinity of the Kinder.

The only thing more sacred than the coffee rule was the no nuts policy. Sadly this was not designed to deny access to the occasional mad parent but was focused on what food could be brought into the centre. Even Lindy obeyed this one as she suffered from nut allergies herself.

After some silence and glaring at Lindy – we're not the types to let our standards drop even with a dead body in the room – Rosa asked, 'What's that poking out of the top of his head?'

'A giant compass,' I answered. 'I bought it to draw large chalk circles outside on the pavement for the four year olds. It's mostly wood and completely safe – except, I guess, for the rather large metal needle part that appears to have pierced his brain.'

'You don't think DHS will launch an investigation into this do you?' asked Lindy. She hadn't been here long but she had learned that a Department of Human Services investigation was something to be avoided at all costs; too much paperwork. We like to pass on our many years of experience to little grasshoppers like Lindy.

'No,' said Rosa. 'It isn't a kid. It's only likely to be the police.'

We all cheered up at that realisation.

'Is he definitely dead?' Rosa queried.

'Well he feels cold,' said Lindy, crouching down next to the body and fumbling around his neck area. As Zarko was a man who sweated large blotches through his clothes even in the dead of winter with the air conditioning on, this sounded like a clincher.

After some hesitation Lindy got up. 'I'll go and get Princess Anne – she's a nurse – she'll know about dead bodies,' she called as she walked back up the corridor.

Princess Anne was the nickname for Anne McKay, the Maternal Health Nurse who shared the building with us. She was middle-aged and jaded like the rest of us (except Lindy who was young and jaded) but did it with a nice manicure and blonde highlighted hair. Somehow she managed to stretch the pay cheque to look like she belonged to the ladies who lunched or had affairs with tennis coaches in between buying modern art and doing charity work. Mutton dressed as lamb I always thought but then, what's so attractive about dressing as mutton?

Lindy regularly recognised the designer clothes Anne wore and enjoyed shocking Rosa and me by informing us that the skirt or the shirt or the bag or, if it was a bad week, the haircut was worth more than our weekly wages combined. Lindy was torn between thinking this was evidence of the ills of the capitalist money-grubbing society we were forcing the children of tomorrow to conform to and wanting them for herself.

'I'll phone the police,' said Rosa, 'and then the Union.'

'The Union?' I questioned.

'If this doesn't get us danger money I don't know what will.' Rosa had been waging a one-woman war against our hourly rate. While no sane person would argue that the leafy-green, comfortable suburb we worked in was dangerous, similarly no sane person would work for the hourly rate we do, so I didn't stop her.

That left me alone with Zarko and to be honest he wasn't the greatest company. Zarko was a big man, at least six foot four. I hadn't talked to him much even though he cleaned the Centre six mornings a week – it's supposed to be six nights a week but often he was just finishing as we started work. We were on a good morning grunting arrangement – I'd say good morning and he would grunt in reply. So I can't say I was as upset at the death as I was at losing a perfectly good wooden compass.

Lindy came back looking pensive but without Princess Anne who, it seems, was sick today. Fifteen minutes later, Rosa came back with the police. As Zarko hadn't moved in the meantime, it was safe to say that we didn't need the ambulance.

Sergeant Michael Bakula looked like a tired middle-aged man because that was what he was. We all knew him well as he had three boys who'd all attended the preschool. George still attended, a regular expert at teaching the other four-year-olds about interrogation methods and kneecapping recalcitrant offenders.

Lindy looked at Mick in disgust and walked away muttering about the tools of a vicious authoritarian state. Clearly the Marxist was winning over the fashionista today. Rosa and I smiled at him. Mick took down the few details we knew about Zarko.

'Any idea who did this?' he asked hopefully.

'Nope' I said.

'Anyone who disliked him?'

'Well, outside the fact that he had virtually no education, learnt English from Sesame Street and still managed to get paid more than us with our four-year tertiary degrees, which I greatly resented, I can't think of anyone off hand,' retorted Rosa. She snorted to herself and walked away.

That left Mick and me looking at the body.

'Shit,' said Mick. I glared; the coffee rule applied to everyone. 'I'd better get this place cordoned off.'

'For how long? It's a curriculum day today but tomorrow we've got the four-year-olds for a full day.'

'I think classes will be cancelled for a few days at least,' said Mick and then as an afterthought swore again. 'George was supposed to be here tomorrow. I guess I'm going to have to chuck a sickie.'

In the end, the Kinder was closed for a week. But when we returned it all seemed surprisingly normal for a Kindergarten which had been emblazoned on the front cover of the Herald Sun under the banner headline of KILL-DEAD-GARTEN. A pedant might ask what other kinds of killing there are, but if such a pedant worked in a Kinder where the cleaner had been murdered, maybe they should just be grateful that the headline wasn't DUMB TEACHER BUYS KILLER COMPASS.

Once the police ruled out any underworld links to the murder, the media interest waned, though I guessed it would all be rekindled if it turned out to be the work of a psychopathic preschooler. I had finished a long session with the four-year-olds, which had included George Bakula explaining to the children about police procedure and not touching any toys for fear of disturbing the crime scene, when I walked into the kitchen where Rosa and Sue, the President of the Preschool Committee, were deep in conversation.

Sue was one of those people who didn't say much but got a lot of things done. The type of person who ran basketball comps, looked after elderly parents, sat on Parents' and Friends' Committees at schools and baked cakes for cake stalls – all without any whingeing. In my book, that made her a modern day saint or a complete lunatic. She didn't have much of a sense of humour, but then, not many saints were known for their humour – not so sure about lunatics. At the moment neither she nor Rosa looked too happy.

'Have you heard Mirabelle's latest idea?' Rosa asked me a little aggressively.

Now, most parents are all right, even those who are deluded enough to think that their little angel might be "gifted", which accounts for at least one third of the parents in any given year. However, there is always one who could try the patience of even a lunatic/modern day saint. This year it was Mirabelle, mother of Shalini.

Mirabelle believed in the purity of children, not setting boundaries around their wisdom, and allowing them to open our eyes to society's limitations. She had thought that Shalini should be home-schooled but had decided that Shalini was a gift that should be shared with the community. Shalini made all of us believe in home-schooling as well.

'Mirabelle thinks we should have a cleansing ceremony to banish the bad Feng Shui from Zarko's death. She is particularly concerned about how her delicate flower Shalini will cope with the negative vibrations of his restless spirit,' Sue said.

Rosa grimaced at the kettle and if I didn't know her better I would have thought that she was muttering some distinctly caffeinated comments under her breath.

'Shalini didn't seem too bothered today by the negative vibrations,' I said. 'I had to rescue little Sam Mikakos before she brained him with a piece of wood in order to recreate the crime scene.'

'If we don't have a ceremony, any chance Shalini might not be able to return to such a dangerous spiritual environment?' Rosa asked hopefully.

'No,' said Sue. 'And Mirabelle has been trying to gain support for the idea from other parents. We should just go along with it.'

'Fine,' answered Rosa in a tone that implied it was anything but, 'as long as I do not have to participate in any way.'

In the end we all went. Even Princess Anne attended (dressed in Prada, Lindy muttered) but looking like death warmed up. Must still have been getting over her 'flu. Rosa pretended to be there under protest but actually she wouldn't have wanted to miss the debacle it was likely to be. Debacle it was. Mirabelle hadn't managed to convince many parents to attend, only the handful who were too polite or too stupid to avoid her completely. Sue had dragooned the usual suspects, that is, everyone else on the Kinder Committee, and it was fair to say they looked pretty mutinous having to give up another Saturday for the Kinder.

Mirabelle, resplendent in a purple flowing mu-mu, started the ceremony with the lighting of incense, some chanting and the tapping of bells. Shalini was then invited, on behalf of the children of the school, none of whom were in attendance, to place a flower on the spot where the body was found and engage in a spot of liturgical dancing with scarves and a tambourine. Shalini, who thoroughly enjoyed the attention of the crowd, decided to change it into a dance of the seven veils and started shedding her clothes during the performance She also incorporated a few moves that made me think she had been avidly watching Saturday morning Video Hits even though I knew Mirabelle had previously claimed not to own a television.

After several minutes we discovered even Mirabelle had her limits as she tried to bring the performance to a close. Shalini was eventually dragged away kicking and yelling about respecting artistic differences. It led to an awkward silence as everyone noticed the cracks in the ceiling or the scuff marks on the floor. Finally, Sue stepped forward and thanked everyone for coming, at which there was a charge for the exit from people desperate to leave before Mirabelle returned to continue the ceremony. Princess Anne left the room looking red-eyed. She was the only one looking upset, as opposed to the rest of us who were a mixture of annoyed at having to come and relieved about getting out of there far more quickly than we'd expected. I stayed behind to put away the chairs and tidy up. Rosa came over to help.

'Anne looked a bit sad. Did she even know Zarko?' I queried.

'Yeah, he was her house cleaner.' Rosa answered. 'He used to clean for a few of the parents as well, like Mirabelle. All cash in hand kind of stuff. Nice if you've got the money.'

We grabbed the pint-sized chairs that everyone had been forced to sit on for the last twenty minutes as a kind of ritualistic torture and stacked them in the crafting corner.

'The police are no closer to working out who did murder Zarko,' I told Rosa. 'Mick was in picking up George yesterday and said that they are still waiting on forensics but really had nothing to go on. Mick says all of the resources are tied up with those underworld killings so it's going to be ages before they get any results.'

'Any word when we're getting our compass back?' asked Rosa.

'I don't think we are,' I replied.

'Darn – that looked like a good compass.' Rosa finished stacking her chairs and then started to move back some of the tables that had been shoved in the corner out of the way for the ceremony. She seemed to be a bit worried about something and finally blurted out: 'Look there's one thing that has been bothering me. It's about the alarm.'

The Centre, like every other centre these days, was well-alarmed against the occasional opportunistic burglary, though to be honest you'd think they would explore more fruitful opportunities, unless they specialised in the distribution of hot pots of Clag Glue.

'What are you talking about?' I asked her.

'When we came in on the day we found Zarko, you turned it off. That's right isn't it?'

'Yeah.'

'Well it should have been off already. Zarko would have turned it off when he came in to clean. He would only turn the alarm back on when he left.'

I pondered this for a while. 'So you are saying that the person who killed him turned on the alarm. Why?'

'No idea. But it narrows down who the killer might be.'

'Half the Kinder community has the alarm code,' I answered.

'Not any more they don't. Remember the break-in last year when the door was forced? After that, we changed the alarm codes so the only people with the codes are employees and Sue as President.'

I pondered this some more. Lindy walked over, having overheard the part of the discussion about the alarm.'

'And Mirabelle,' she said.

'How did Mirabelle get the code?' asked Rosa in exasperation.

'Remember when she wanted the Kinder to celebrate the pagan ritual of the Mother rather than Easter this year? She had to come in early to decorate and as none of us wanted to come in, I gave her the code.'

Rosa looked at Lindy in a double shot espresso kind of way. 'Well,' she said heavily, 'that leaves the employees, Sue and Mirabelle, unless everyone has given out the code willy-nilly.'

'I haven't given the code to anyone,' I answered, 'and Sue won't have.' Sue took official duties very seriously.

'I haven't either,' Rosa stated firmly, 'so that leaves a very small number of people who would have known what time Zarko actually cleaned and the alarm code to re-alarm the door.'

'Maybe they didn't know when Zarko cleaned, were surprised he was here and killed him?' I pondered aloud.

'Come on,' said Rosa. 'What else were they here to do – steal the precious artworks? Of course they must have been here to kill him.'

'You think it was deliberate?' asked Lindy a little shakily.

'He is six foot four and was found with a giant compass in the back of his head. I don't think he tripped.' Rosa's voice was dripping with sarcasm now.

Clearly I was no Miss Marple, as it didn't make much sense to me, but Lindy looked a bit dazed and sat down heavily on the last unstacked tiny chair.

'I think I know who did it then,' Lindy said.

'Yeah right,' said Rosa. 'OK, let me guess: Miss Scarlett in the home corner with the wooden compass.'

'No, I'm serious,' answered Lindy. 'I know who killed him, I just don't have the foggiest idea why.'

'Okay,' I said. 'Who is it?'

'If you don't tell us then you are bound to get shot by the stranger on the grassy knoll,' scoffed Rosa.

Lindy stood up. 'You wouldn't believe it if I told you anyway.' She quickly walked away, past Princess Anne who had just entered the room. She had reapplied her makeup and seemed to have pulled herself together.

'I'm off,' she said.

'You should have heard what Lindy was saying,' Rosa said. 'She reckons she knows who killed Zarko.'

Anne said nothing but began to look upset again.

'Oh well – I'm heading home.' I moved towards the hall. 'See you Monday.'

'Wait up,' said Rosa, 'I'll come with you.'

We walked out to our cars together. 'Let's go for a coffee,' suggested Rosa.

'What was up with Lindy?' I wondered. 'And what's up with you – you were a bit rough on her.'

'I probably was a bit. The Union got back to me yesterday; no go from the Department about the danger money.'

I laughed, 'It's only an extra thirteen cents an hour.'

'It's the principle,' answered Rosa huffily.

I could see she was pretty steamed. 'All right, coffee it is.'

Half an hour later we came back to the cars again. Before I got into mine, I looked back towards the Kinder and noted that the lights were still on.

'Hang on,' I called to Rosa. 'Lindy must have forgotten to turn off the lights.'

Rosa looked back and then checked around the street. 'No look, there's her car. She must still be in the Kinder.'

Sure enough there was Lindy's sporty little Holden Astra with the numberplates, Lindy 666. We liked to joke it was because Lindy could be a beast but I think it was some poorly judged attempt by her parents to celebrate her eighteenth.

'You should go in and say you're sorry,' I told Rosa.

'Oh well, I guess she needs to know the danger money is not going to come through,' Rosa said, just a little sheepishly.

We walked into the hall with its 30 little hooks, noticeboards welcoming new siblings for several of the pupils and other notes reminding parents to please pack a hat every day for Kinder, when we heard yelling. It sounded like Lindy.

'What was that?' asked Rosa, quietly for her.

'Where's it coming from?' I whispered. All of a sudden it felt a little creepy. We tiptoed down the hall towards the play room. We slowly looked around the corner. There was Lindy, tied with a skipping rope to one of the tiny chairs in the reading area with Anne standing over her – her back to us. Lindy looked scared but noticed us coming in and motioned with her head for us to stay where we were, just out of Anne's view.

'But what I don't understand is why you killed him, Anne,' she said in a clear voice. I noticed that Rosa suddenly grabbed her handbag and began to rummage around inside it.

'You wouldn't understand, would you, carrying on with that Marxist crap but letting Mummy and Daddy pick up all the bills. You think being a nurse working for a Council pays enough? It barely even covers the dry cleaning bill,' Anne ranted. She seemed demented.

'I wouldn't expect you to understand, Lindy. You barely look after yourself, let alone have to provide for a family. I had finally worked out the perfect scam. All those new parents suddenly relying on one income, barely able to cover the costs of their disposable nappies and formula while driving their 4 WDs and then suddenly realising that in three short years they will have to find the best Kinder and then school for their kids.

'Day after day I had to listen to the whingeing and the moaning until at last I couldn't take it anymore. As long as their address is within the permitted zone, they get into this excellent Council-funded Kinder and if they attend this Kinder then they are automatically entitled to apply for the excellent government primary school down the road. And I am the person who types the information into the computer when they make their first visit to me. So all I have to do is type the "right" address and they are in.'

'How much do you get out of it?' asked Lindy.

'Enough. I mean, they are going to save tens of thousands if they don't need to send their brats to all those high-falutin' private schools. So if they choose to be generous, who am I to knock it back?' Anne snarled. 'You should be applauding – I am doing my bit for the public school system. That should fit in with your pseudo-socialist ideals.'

'You are taking kickbacks and rorting the system,' said Lindy.

'The system that you want to tear down,' retorted Anne.

She did have a point.

'But what did Zarko have to do with it?' Lindy asked.

'I had deliberately chosen him as my cleaner at home. He can't read English. I got over-confident, started to be sloppy. One day I accidentally left out my bank statements. How was I to know he had his nephew moonlighting for him here and at my house? A nephew studying to be a computer analyst, what's more. He noticed the large payments on my statements from names that corresponded with names he had seen in the appointment book at the Centre.

'He told Zarko, who was no fool. He got his nephew to hack into the computer and realised that people he cleaned for had the wrong address on the system and that they were also the people who had paid me money. He worked it out and started blackmailing me. But then he started getting greedy, wanting more. Pretty soon I'd have had to start shopping at Savers like Rosa. That wasn't going to happen.'

I could feel Rosa bristling next to me.

'But how did you kill him? He's twice your size.'

'It was easy. I organised to make a payment to him that morning and while chatting to him pointed out some marks on the floor. He bent over to look and wham, I smacked the compass into his head. He underestimated me, Lindy; much like you've done.'

'And the alarm?' Lindy queried a little more nervously.

'Who are you, James Bond? Don't think you are getting out of this one. All right, so I stuffed up there. Being a nurse, you do everything by routine, so force of habit I suppose,' Anne answered. 'I was so used to putting it on every time I left here for the last five years I just did it.'

'What happens now?' asked Lindy 'You can't leave me tied up here with a skipping rope.'

'I don't intend to,' Anne replied nastily. 'You see, Mirabelle prepared a whole feast for the cleansing ceremony that no one bothered to eat. It's vegan, of course; but not nut free, I'm afraid. Typical Mirabelle, thinking that rules never apply to her. So it would be terrible if someone who suffered from anaphylaxis – someone like you, Lindy – accidentally ate one of these very nutritious but absolutely inedible nut patties that she has left behind. I, of course, will do my best and try to resuscitate you, but I have a feeling it will be too little, too late. So sorry that your last meal is likely to be one of the most tasteless.'

Anne started moving towards Lindy holding a nut patty in her hand.

That was too much for Rosa who, in one sudden movement, ran into the room, picked up one of the kids' painting easels and ran at Anne with it, screaming for all she was worth.

Anne turned around and copped the corner of the easel to the head. She fell to the floor, out cold.

'Jesus!' said Lindy. 'You haven't killed her have you, Rosa?'

Anne wasn't looking too good, with a trail of red trickling down the side of her head.

'Don't worry, I think it's paint,' Rosa panted.

'Untie me,' said Lindy. 'Did you hear what she said about killing Zarko?'

'Not only that,' boasted Rosa, looking very proud of herself, 'I recorded it all on my mobile phone.'

Mick Bakula was again the officer sent out to the Kinder. 'Christ, to think we leave our kids with you,' he said once he saw Anne hogtied with the same skipping rope.

'What I don't understand, Lindy,' I said, 'is how you knew it was Anne.'

'Well,' she explained, 'Rosa working out the bit about the alarm code confirmed what I had already been thinking. When I bent down to feel if Zarko had a pulse that morning, I noticed a torn piece of material just near the body. It was Scanlan & Theodore, last season. Now, only one person in our Centre, apart from me, would buy that.'

'True,' said Rosa, 'and now we know how she afforded it.'

'Why didn't you tell me?' asked Mick.

'I wanted to talk to Anne first, because I thought there must be some explanation, but she stayed away from work until today, when she returned for the cleansing ceremony,' answered Lindy and then, with a bit of the radical zeal returning to her face. 'Besides, I don't work with the servants of oppressive regimes.'

'But aren't you a servant of the same regime?' queried Mick, getting a little heated.

'I'm destroying it from the inside,' Lindy answered. Mick shook his head in disgust.

'Is the Kinder going to be closed again?' I asked Mick.

'Yeah,' he responded gloomily. 'Just when I ran out of sick leave, too.'

'Why are you looking so happy?' I asked Rosa, as she and I headed for the door. She was literally grinning from ear to ear. 'Do you see a future for yourself as a freelance crime fighter?'

'That's not it,' she answered triumphantly. 'We're bound to get that danger money now.'

2008

UNDECEIVE

Also won the Innovation Award

Evelyn Tsitas

Bad news

The kid is sick. Vomit.
Splashes, droplets on my office clothes.
'It's okay, darling, mummy's home'
Burning skin, the red face.
Feel so guilty.
But carefully spread my stilettos away
from the falling puke
Must get him into the bath,
change into track pants.
Phone rings, I ignore it.
But my husband runs in –
'Answer this!'

I shake my head – 'tell them to call back'.
Juggle plastic bucket,
cheerful red among the ruins.
'No!' he thrusts the receiver into my hand.
It is my mother.
Too preoccupied, I do not catch the sob.
Then silence.
A small voice.
'I have some bad news' she says.

All Alone

My sister. Charlotte.
A fragile bird on a broken branch.

We waited for this day
since the voices called.
She was full of promise – university, arts degree.
The doctors gave it a diagnosis.
Tablets, shock therapy.

Finally
we gathered her around,
safe, like a toddler in a playpen.
But she left.
'I need to live alone', she said.
And we grew old in her wandering.
Stories half written, books half read, she fled.

'They found her–'
My mother says.
The sounds in the bathroom swirl and cascade.
I am in a vortex of the fear
we would never name.
And all I can think of is that I haven't seen her in a week.
'Where?' I ask.
'On her bed.'

Three days dead

Three days it took to find her body.
Charlotte worked in an opportunity shop
down by the beach.
They rely on her to cost the books.
Sort the Joan Collins from the Peter Carey.
Realise the worth
of first edition Len Deighton
from the Reader's Digest collected edition.
On Monday morning
she didn't turn up.
Dot went with Maurice.
Charlotte's address carefully written
on the back of an envelope.
Lead pencil, copperplate.
Charlotte's doors were locked.
Blinds down. Papers on the doorstep.

The cat hungrily weaving through their ankles.
Did they notice then the padlocks?
The foil covering the gaps between the curtains?
Tape around the windows?
The police wouldn't break in until they pleaded.
A fragile bird on a broken branch.
Everyone expected the worst.

Kavanagh Street

I drove to Kavanagh Street,
Mum next to me
'It must be a mistake,' she says
'How do they know it's her?'
We didn't say what each was thinking.
Strangers found our Charlotte
in the early morning.
The police had knocked on Mum's door.
It took 36 hours to track her down.
Charlotte was good at hiding her traces.
We didn't know where she lived.
But Dot and Maurice did.

Before the city fully wakes,
we are far too awake.
I help mum from the car.
This part of Southbank is one I never wanted to see.
Forensic pathology.
Coronial services.
Identify the body.

'It can't be her; she's gone to Byron Bay again,'
Mum says. The building is warm and quiet.
People are kind and warm.
But we must go to a cold room.
'She would have let one of those strays in her home,
she always did,'
Says Mum. I agree.

My Other Half

Charlotte.

It is you.
Lying still.
As if sleep sat too deeply.
There is only the slightest mark on your unlined face.
A bruise perhaps.
Or is that your brush with death?
'That's my daughter,' Mum says.
It's a small voice and she has shrunk.
In five minutes age snatched away the grip she had,
pushed her body into the ground.
She's now bent double and wheezing,
an old woman.

I look for the small mole on Charlotte's earlobe.
She hated it.
Couldn't get her ears pierced properly.
It is there.
She is there.
Cold on the table.
My sister.

A crowded mind.
This ghost who now
inhabits my other half

The Photo

The policeman wants to know
'Was she married? A boyfriend?'
A laugh escapes me.
No one would ride the rocking horse of her mind.
Highs to fast, lows scrapping through broken glass,
drugs, despair.
'She was alone.'
He shook his head. 'There was a photo—'
He gives it to me.
'She was holding it when she died.'
I look at the face.
A bit like George Clooney. Strong, handsome,
square jaw and good teeth. Intelligent. Well dressed.
'I have no idea who it is,' I say

He tells me he checked the inside of the frame.
On the back the photo reads "Matthew".
It is in my sister's handwriting…
Who is Matthew?

Full Body Scan

The officials have told Mum
a full body scan will rule out
need for police investigation.
She signs a form.
Machines will tell us
where life went.
And why.

I want to know
did she make this trip down the River Styx alone?
Or was she helped?

Charlotte's House

We don't go home.
We go to Charlotte's house.
A place we have never been.
A drive across town.
'She always liked the beach' Mum says.
How can one city be so many different fragmented pieces?
It's a long way from Camberwell.
Rosebud. retirement homes, holiday houses
and welfare mums.
Low rent peninsula, seagulls and fish and chips.
And discount $2 shops.
'She was a private person' says Mum.
The doors are padlocked.
Windows taped.
It is her keep.
We look for clues.
Books, neatly stacked, fill the space.
The smell of time and careless neglect hangs
off the mildewed pages
But the choices are bold, eccentric.

The shards of a mind that could glow
when the pills wore off.
Michael Ondaatje, A.S Byatt, Kevin Rabalais,
Amanda Lowrey
Tama Janowitz, a slender book of poems by Miles Gibson,
The collected works of Zoe Fairbairns.
The copy of In the Cut I gave her
after we went to see Meg Ryan in Susanna Moore's book.
Charlotte loved the character.
'If I wasn't mad, I'd be her,' she said
'a caustic, sexy, literary academic'.

Instead, this is her legacy.
A place on the beach.
Taped windows.
Op shop books
and a cold body in Kavanagh Street.

Matthew's Book

'The kitchen is so clean,' says Mum, checking the fridge.
There are no signs of anything
except a small life,
lived even smaller
Food for one, a small carton of milk curdling,
Not even left overs.
I check the bathroom for evidence –
There is nothing.
Her tablets are lined up in the cabinet
suspiciously full.
But when I open the bedside table
I smile.
Condoms. A tube of lube.
A book by Matthew McKee.
I turn over the cover. His photo on the dust jacket.
I recognise him.
The last person my sister held,
even if it was his photo.

I sniff the glossy new pages.
An inscription reads:

'My darling Charlotte
To all the good times…'
Matt.

The Author's Trail
The private school run. Hawthorn at 8.15am.
I fight the throng of four wheel drives,
jostle for a space
along Barkers Road

Money is the perk of the job
that only asks for my soul

I book the kids into aftercare.
'But Mummy, I don't want to'
I tell them I have important things to do.
Someone to find.
A word to the teacher, watch Tommy – nightmares about
his aunt.
The older one tells me
'at least the cat was outside or it would have eaten her face'
So much for the
Discovery Channel.

Call in sick. Grief. They understand. For a day at least.
Catch sight of my puffy eyes in the rear vision.
I drive
to the other side of the river.

'We don't give out the details
of our authors' says the publisher's assistant.
I leave my card.

Brunswick Street
They don't do skinny lattes in Marios
I am told.
My Chanel bag
feels uncomfortable here.
I sip a long black
not sure what to do next.

This place reminds me
of university,
of youth,
of time before
partnership at the law firm.

I drop gold coins into the chipped mug
near the cash register
'Gee thanks!' glows the twenty-year-old
face covered with piercings.
Then I see it.
Matt's face.
A flyer pinned to the notice board as I leave.
I rip it from the wall.

Short Stories
Matthew McKee will be reading
from his new novel 'War is Kind'
at Readings in Carlton
Thursday 6.30 – 7.30 pm.
Book signing to follow.

Do I take my husband?
My hand on the phone, I text the babysitter.
I will go alone
and not be judged.

No time to make excuses anyway.
He flies to Sydney.
Another conference.
I am left to organise the funeral.
My mother calls.
'They have released the body,
there will be a viewing.'

The Coroner says Charlotte's heart
simply stopped.
It is common.
With schizophrenia comes
Arrhythmia

Anderson & Sons

At Anderson & Sons the chapel smells
of a scent to cover
decay.
Boxes of tissues
thoughtfully
on red velvet chairs.
Charlotte
in an open coffin.
'Like she is sleeping' says my mother.
But her hands are weird,
puffed and like sausages.
I look at them too long.
Her nail polish applied beautifully.

She always had chipped polish.
So who painted them?

She is wearing the dress Mum chose.
With little flowers.
Thirty winds back to thirteen.
My mother asks me to stroke my sister's face.
When we were little

we'd close our eyes,
feel the sameness.
Now I look at my death mask.
We are identical to the end.
Only life separates us now.
In the bathroom, I wash my hands thoroughly.
Soap thoughtfully provided.

Readings

I meant to get there early
but the babysitter is late.
I stand at the back
next to a man with a beard.

'Sorry' I mumble as I nudge past him.
I pick up a copy of Matt's book
for the signing.

The publicist speaks
glowingly.
Exults us with Matt's talent.
'Wunderkind, this young man will go far!'

The book is just released tonight.
In my hands the first copy.
I know this is not true,
I have read it already.
Charlotte's book
underlined in yellow highlighter

I watch Matt and wait to hear
his voice.
Confident.
Funny.
His dark hair tousled.
A wedding ring on his finger.
'I'd like to thank first my wife Rachel. It was she
Who introduced me to Melville.'

A woman older than me, face drawn, smiles.
I glance to her and back.
The older woman.
She must be fifty
if she is a day.
I stand too long next to
shelves of parenting books
waiting my turn.
The book signing
is lengthy.
Matt talks to all.

My turn and I hand his book to him.
'Make it to Charlotte's sister' I say.

He looks at me.
He drops his pen.
I have pulled my hair back so he can see

we were two peas in a pod
separated by birth and sanity.
Squint and she is me.
If I do not dress as a lawyer,
if I wear big earrings,
if I pull my hair back.

He sees a ghost.
He sees me.
'I am alone now,' I say.
'The first time in forty-two years.'

I realise he doesn't know.
Hasn't been waiting for her phone call.
He blinks.
He is white.
And then maybe I think he knows.
And has seen a ghost.

'Charlotte?' he asks.

I hand him my business card.

'Call me'.

Merton, Smyth & Grant

My secretary put the call through.
'Can we meet?'
Matthew chooses a hip bar
on Warburton Lane
I've never been to.
'It used to be a boxing ring,
they do Wagyu pizza'

I feel my age.
My Christian Louboutin patent red stilettos
trip me up down cobbled lane.
He orders sake.
I have mineral water.

'I knew your sister through the Rosebud Community Centre.
I was there on a writer in residence program.'

I thought of Charlotte's poems,
short and passionate.
The ones she wrote in her school exercise book.
Awards won,
a future juicy with promise.
Until the demons surfaced.

I pull his book from my bag,
the one Charlotte had when she died

'Did you love her?'

He laughs, swigs sake,
a droplet rolls
down a firm chin.

'I'm married.'

I point to the inscription.

'Look, she was sweet.
Her work was self indulgent and juvenile, but a lot better
than the peninsula pensioners I had to deal with.'
I pay the bill.
Back to glass and steel.
And litigation.
I spit on the cobble stones.
Bile and anger.

Eulogy

I work on the words to say.
My mother shakes her head.
'That's not how she was'.
And
'You can't say that, not now'.

So Charlotte becomes
private and complicated,
not paranoid or mad.

Will anyone know of whom we speak?

I turn to Matthew's book
to look for words
as he has
so many.

The book is on war
and the art of killing.
A young man looks at death
before it kindly stops for him.

I scan the index.
Interviews with soldiers.
During war they must be taught to kill.
It goes against the instinct
to plunge a bayonet,
release a bullet.
Good soldiers are fine killers.
Up close though
sorts the men from the boys
I read of a pressure point on the neck
that kills,
leaving only the slightest bruise

Mathew knows this
and now
I do as well.

Detective Martin Welsh

I drive to Rosebud to see him,
Detective Martin Welsh.
The country station,
cream brick fortress,
modern and imposing.

My office thinks I am having a spa treatment.
That's acceptable.
Not
chasing ghosts.

'Thanks for seeing me,' I say.
He looks me over.
Tailored suit, gold jewellery thick and expensive.
Outside, I see the ti-trees bend in a wind
that chases the white clouds
across the blue sky.

It doesn't feel like a holiday.

I show him the book.
The passage about the pressure point.

'You're upset,' the detective says.

'But this Matthew is a writer, not a killer.
Your sister
was a schizophrenic.
I've got the reports.
Her heart
just stopped.'

Rosebud Plaza

I need a coffee.
There's a Gloria Jeans at the Rosebud Plaza
before the drive to the city.

Young mums with toddlers
push strollers.
Chat.
I was never like that.
Rushed back to the firm.
A nanny took them to Gymbaroo.
I was never young either
it seemed.

My eulogy is stilted.
I read over my notebook.
A glob of cream falls off.
The mug
marks the keyboard.
I hear it in my head.
War is kind.

I see Mathew smirking,
'Your sister's stuff was better than most'.

I have a plan to
prove him wrong.
She was better than him.

No 3 Sandy Drive

It's a neat unit, wire cut brown brick.
The end of a sweeping court.
'It used to be a retirement home'
said a man in number 5.

He sees me go in and hurries to query.

When will the funeral be?
'Soon,' I say 'my mother needed to sit and grieve,
hold her daughter's hand,
day after day.'

A look of horror over a face
used to the Anglican way of death.
All disposed of quickly.

Inside Charlotte's house
we have not moved a thing.
Dust has yet to settle.
Even the imprint of her body
on the bed
fills the place with her presence.

Clocks do not need winding
anymore.
They tick on.
The fridge hums.
Life goes on
for the inanimate.

What am I looking for?
This time a clue.
I search drawers, the bookshelf.
Under the bed.
Not for tablets or photos.

I am looking for words.
Charlotte's words.

The Community Centre

The squat building features
a wide concrete ramp,
wheelchair access easy.

My phone rings.
'You're in court tomorrow'
says my assistant.
I text the nanny.
Instructions; make dinner, work on the school project.

I enter a parallel world.
Health posters on the wall.
Messages urging
updates for resuscitation certificates.
Mammograms.
Bowel cancer check-ups.
Special pensioner Christmas in July roast.
Gold coin donation.

Marge is in her office.
'We all miss Charlotte' and gives me a hug.
My broach snags her home knit cardigan.
'Oh, don't worry about that!'

I accept tea.
A high tide ring
shows others have been here before
and no one rinsed up.

I ask about Matthew.
'A nice young man,' she says.
I ask her about dates. I have my blackberry to log in the numbers.
And it doesn't add up,
it just doesn't.

Opportunity Knocks
They play Glen Campbell,
"Wichita Linesman",
and have the heater on.
The little bell above the door
ping ping.

I thought I'd be the only one
but the place is full.
Everyone is sifting through
racks of eighties clothes, old stuffed toys
unmatched floral tea cups and
knitting patterns.

At the front counter, a glass unit
keeps the treasures safe.
Some rhinestones and gold-plated broaches.

I ask to see Dot or Maurice.

His hearing aid lets out a soft whistle.

'So sad, so sad I lost my wife five years ago
to skin cancer. It was quite quick and
now I spend my time here
helping out.'

Dot pushes me into the back.
A vinyl TV chair for a seat and she puts down a mug of brown liquid.

International roast.
'You need a coffee, love.'

I sip and smile.
'Did Charlotte ever talk about her boyfriend?'
I ask
'I would like him to speak at the funeral.'

Dot smiles. 'Of course, her boyfriend the writer
– he would write a lovely poem.'

They met Matthew once.
He came to pick up Charlotte,
took her to the wineries around Red Hill.
Very romantic.

War is kind

Do not weep, babe, for war is kind
Herman Melville wrote.
Matthew McKee took his words.

He took my sister.
Did he take her words?

Pages covered the car
comparing her exercise book
with his impressive hard bound tome.
So many similarities.

In a court of law
I could defend her.
He took her words.

Did he take her life?

Chardonnay

I soak in the bath.
Free standing
shaped like an egg.

Architecture magazines
featured our bathroom
under "you wish"

My husband pours me a chardonnay.
Perches on the Eames chair.
A conceit in a wet room.
But this is our adult space
off our parental retreat.
The kid's bathroom is downstairs.

'Tommy made the school band,' he informs me
'and Mae read the word "surface".'

But in my mind
I am looking out to sea.
Watching the ships move across Port Phillip Bay
from where I sat on Red Hill.

'He killed my sister, that writer, I know he did.'

'Why?' my husband asks.
His tone is even
but I can tell
the professional edge.
He is a psychiatrist, after all.
To him, why means so many things.
A clinical diagnosis
to be precise.
I can see right through it.
Fifteen years is a long time.
You learn the shades of words.
I am a heat-seeking missile
when it comes to nuances.

Why?

'Because she was a better writer than him
and I have proof.'

'Your sister,' he says evenly
'Was a paranoid schizophrenic who periodically attempted
to take her life and
dangled you with guilt for your considerable success.'

He kissed my forehead tenderly.
'Charlotte died because her heart stopped.
You can't forgive yourself
for being the successful one.
But life is like that.
It isn't fair.'

When I get to bed, my husband gives me some tablets
for anxiety.

I pretend to take them.
I need this clarity,
this anger.

Tomorrow we bury my sister.

The Funeral

My mother chose a casket,
snub nosed, cushioned lined,
a sleek oak finish.
Almost like being buried
in a bookcase.

And it's bloody heavy.

A group of six men sway and stagger down the red carpet,
duck under the arch.
Even through tears I scan the crowd.
A surprisingly large group.
Charlotte gathered friends and lost souls.
She sang in choirs, joined community art classes,
theatre groups, writing groups.

Who would come to my funeral?
Work sent a large wreath.

They would be too busy
for my funeral.

I clutch the hands
of my children tighter.

How did I have the time and foresight
to schedule them into the world?

Charlotte wanted children.
The doctors said
the drugs would make them deformed
so she loved mine instead.

I bow my head at the grave site.
My fat tears fall on the rough quartz pebbles.

How can a heart just stop beating?
Her heart was too big
even if her mind was full of demons.

Litigation

The view from my office
sweeps across Melbourne.
Stand too close.

The window seems to float.

I could fall down to the soft green
park below.

I would rather, than listen
to a strategy to rescue
a heating company from bankruptcy.

I am not as clever
as I thought.
Two weeks have passed
and Mathew's wife has refused to call.

I tracked her down.
Told her about Charlotte.
She smiled
and said
'But I know your sister is dead.'

Walked away, not a second glance.
So to the victor go the spoils

Do not weep, for war is kind.

Followed

I decide to walk to lunch.
A business meeting
at The Latin.
I sensed him behind me
before I turned.

'Stay away from my wife' Matthew says.
Cold eyes slice.
He is so ugly now.
'I know where your kids live.'

Then he is gone
into the crowd.
A passing tram, I don't know.

That night
I lock the door

My sister's heart just stopped
I tell myself
as I tuck the children in.

Frank's Gym

My personal trainer
has a boutique gym. Hawthorn.
Me and the yummy mummies.
I warm up on the treadmill after a hard day's work.

Run a sweat.
Pump the heart.
Keep strong.
Keep thin.

Matthew's face on the TV screen
smiling
'War is kind –
it's from Melville's Shiloh, a Requiem he says.

'Every generation knows war and
this war on terror reaches out
through the media.
There is no distance
even in Australia.'

I stop. Shiloh.
How could I not remember?

Mrs Harrison
The advantages of wealth are many,
disadvantages few,
if any.
I laugh
to myself – I am a cliché after all –
as the BMW pulls up
outside Mrs Harrison's house.

This part of Glen Iris I remember
as Burwood West.
Times change.
Mrs Harrison's house hasn't.

Thank goodness she hadn't moved.
Teachers are not well paid
like Collins Street law firm partners.
Like me.

'I was so surprised by your call, Deborah,' she said.
Older than I remembered.
Of course.

How many years?
'It's such a shock about Charlotte and, of course,
the fact that you are twins.'

A comforting touch on my arm.
We played tricks on Mrs Harrison at school.
Pretended to be the other
but Charlotte's eyes gave us away.
They were on fire.
Bright Eager
Liquid in intensity.
Now there was only one of us.

Shiloh

'Shiloh,' I said. 'Was my message clear?'
She offered me tea
in china cups.
Her living room piled neatly with books.
She bit into a ginger nut biscuit and nodded.
'Melville. Year 12 English Literature:

Foeman at morn, but friends at eve –
Fame or country least their care:
(what like a bullet can undeceive!)
But now they lie low,
While over them the swallows skim,
And all is hushed at Shiloh.

'Charlotte won the Frances Grady Essay Prize with
her exploration of the effects of war and its irrelevance,'
I remember.

'The peace and despair after the great storm of War.
Charlotte had such promise.'

The word filled with more then.
Sadness.
and anger.
A quiet rage at the demons
no medication could erase
without the essence being dissolved.

For that's what happened.
Darkness lived with brilliance.
Equal measure.
The ying and yang of talent and insanity.
Without one
the other disappeared.
'I need to know – is this the essay she wrote?
You remember don't you?'
I am grasping
at anything.

Three years ago
Charlotte had burnt everything she owned.
All her poems, notebooks, music and sketch books
'I'll start again, clean.
Call me Phoenix'

Then she placed a plastic bag over her head.
Mum found her
before she turned blue.

Locked up again.
Next time I saw her there were no words.
The phoenix did not rise
for years.

Mrs Harrison held the exercise book.
She read and nodded.
'Of course – I could check with the school records
– did we even keep them beyond the winning title,
student and brief abstract – but yes,
this is her essay on Shiloh and war.'

Matthew's book taunted.
I asked
'What's the significance of Shiloh and modern war?'

Mrs Harrison eyed me.
Again I was the fat teenager.

The boring one, the clumsy one,
The one who didn't understand verse.
'You did law, not arts, right?'
My $500,000 a year salary and BMW diminished.
She explained:
'Shiloh was the bloodiest of battles.
A civil war bloodbath.
Two days when death snatched nearly a quarter
of all who fought.
Melville knew what would happen next
would be uglier. And it was.'

'Mother whose heart hung humble as a button
On the bright splendid shroud of your son.
Do not weep.
War is kind.'

The Literary Editor

Oh yes, Matthew had taken Charlotte's poems.
A clever twist.
She had seen
those twin towers.
She knew the truth of Melville's words:
that mothers would weep over shrouds coloured in the American flag
and wrapped in a Muslim burial.

War is kind to both sides of terror.

My secretary scanned Charlotte's exercise books.
My interview notes with
what amounted to witnesses.
I am not the jury.
I am the judge
and if no one will listen
then I will be a vigilante.

My sister's heart stopped
in the middle of life.
A brief shard of clarity.

Insight and words
we wait our lives for.

And Matthew took them
and turned them
in his greedy hands.
I sent the parcel to the Literary Editor of The Age.

Fraud Squad

I enjoyed his demise.
Public humiliation.
The media love a literary scandal.
Ern Mally,
Helen Demindeko, Norma Khouri,
James Frey.

Matthew can join the merit board.
I read Charlotte the stories
as I sit on her grave.

From the tree
a large crow lands,
black as an Edgar Allen Poe poem.

A literary magazine wants to publish her poems,
the ones written after the fire.
'But she was a private person' says my mother.
No

she was a poet.
And these are the words
that outran
the demons.

Words that left clues and tracer fire,
shadows to the truth.
Words to survive her.
A remembrance restored.
Attribution.

I will fight for those words.

They are all I have left
of my sister.
Except for my face
left to sag and decay alone.

PERSIA BLOOM

Amanda Wrangles

PERSIA BLOOM IS MY REAL NAME. SERIOUSLY. IT SAYS SO ON MY PASSPORT, birth certificate, everything. I love it. How many people can lay claim to a name like that?

Well, maybe my brother. His name is Cyrus J Bombay. No middle name, just J – and don't you dare forget it. Obviously our mother is very creative. Or a little nuts.

Cyrus and I are close, born only eleven months apart. He owns a very well-known jewellery studio just a few streets from my place. I see him as often as I can. He's a jeweller of the very arty, expensive kind. The kind that makes those weird pieces celebrities wear on the red carpet.

Me? I'm a hairdresser, or hairstylist as Cyrus would insist. He's flamboyant, a little out there, while I'm the quiet one, more reserved. He can also do hair almost as well as I can. But that's okay. My talents lay elsewhere.

Sure, I can cut and colour alongside the best of them, but I don't have any illusions about myself. That's not why I'm booked months in advance. It's not why my little suburban shopping centre salon is so successful. I'm not super-trendy or outrageously glamorous like many of my peers. In fact, I'm kind of mousy.

No, what makes me stand out from the crowd are my "People Skills".

As a hairdressing apprentice, you're required to spend a day a week at trade school. You'd be amazed at how much geometry is involved with a great haircut. It all comes down to angles. Then there's the chemistry of colours and perms. If your hairdresser doesn't know her disulphide bonds from her medulla, you're in trouble. This is what you learn at trade school. Along with design, some biology and "People Skills".

I was first introduced to the concept of People Skills on my third day of school. My fellow first-years and I hung up our spiky setting rollers and tail combs for a textbook and pen. The tiny room was stark, with a few outdated hair posters carelessly pinned to the walls. Laminated tables and plastic orange chairs formed a U-shape around a television trolley. The room was stuffy, the air-conditioning set too high. I began to yawn immediately and wondered how I was going to stay awake through a dull video on "People Skills".

We'd all scoffed at the idea of an entire subject devoted to something that was supposed to come naturally to hairdressers. What a waste of time.

Most of us had spent the last six months learning how to give the ultimate shampoo. That's the easy part. Not sending a torrent of water down someone's back to their underpants is the hard bit. Believe me, it happens to us all – hopefully only once. If you haven't got the People Skills to talk your way out of that one, you shouldn't be in the job.

Hint: You can never apologise too much.

Always accept the blame. There is no such thing as a neck that's too skinny or a spine too stiff to fit into a hard, plastic neck basin. Even if the client sits up unexpectedly, it is always your fault.

So you could say the opening sequence of the video took me by surprise. Actually, it was more of a WHACK! Ka POWEE! As in the old Batman television show.

The perfectly coiffed presenter explained with perfectly rounded vowels that we belonged to an elite group of professionals who touched other people. I don't mean sentimentally, I mean literally, as in the physical.

Doctor; dentist; physio; hairdresser. There's only a handful more. We allow, or by the very nature of these jobs, demand physical touch. Humans don't usually like our personal space being invaded, part of our animal instinct. The intimacy freaks us out.

It was the most startling thing I learnt in a four-year apprenticeship. It also explained a hell of a lot personally. Like my whole life.

As a kid, I didn't realise there was anything different about me. I thought everyone had weird and wacky names like mine. I also thought it was normal to feel other people's emotions.

I'm an Empath.

That much I'd figured out long ago. I'd read the New Age books, I'd trawled the internet, searching for a name, a definition to what I felt. What I didn't understand, until that day at trade school, was my trigger. From my research I'd learnt there are all kinds of Empaths, that is, people who feel the emotions of others. Some Empaths are extremely sensitive, hardly daring to venture out in public lest they take on the emotions of someone on a major downer. They might only have to walk past them in the street, or make eye contact on a crowded train and the poor Empath is drowning in contagious despair.

Others don't even realise there's anything unusual about themselves. They just naturally trust their instincts and how they feel about others. The whole "there's just something not right about him, but I can't put my finger on it" type of Empath.

Me, I'm somewhere in between.

Luckily, I don't take on other people's moods. I just feel them, physically, on my skin.

When I was little, I could only differentiate between three emotions: happy, sad, angry. They're probably the most obvious anyway – written all over the wearer's face.

No big deal, and no realisation back then that there was anything unusual in what I felt. I thought everyone experienced the gentle tickle of butterflies against their skin if they were with someone happy. Anger is not as nice, and gives me instant pins and needles in my feet and hands. I tend to stay rooted to the spot in the presence of anger, not moving to avoid the pain. Sadness is worse though. It's a cold, wet towel draping my shoulders, heavy as it clings. Sadness takes the longest to shake off, so to speak.

Adolescence and puberty brought a lot more than the usual hormonal issues with them. I began to recognise a whole tumult of new emotions. Imagine being able to actually feel when someone dislikes you. Prickles of little black ants run through my scalp to my neck. The intensity varies from uncomfortable for mild dislike to downright painful bull ant bites for hatred.

Hint: This is not very nice when you have no choice but to spend nearly all your time with nasty, hormonal teenage girls.

On the other hand, teenagers spend plenty of time in love. Feeling a warm, fluffy dressing gown, just out of the dryer, envelop your skin, magically sends the ants away.

All emotions are different and I learnt quickly which was which. Depression is like sadness, but so much heavier that my limbs ache. Sympathy is a tender hand stroking my arm. Guilt is a cold, metal object pressing against my chest.

What I couldn't figure out was why some days were like being bombarded in a game of dodgeball, and others were calm. Until that day in the People Skills class. Touch! It was such a simple answer.

I only felt it when I touched someone. I've got no idea why I hadn't been able to connect the dots until then. Maybe because, even when I do touch, I don't always catch the emotion. Sometimes people are too busy thinking to be feeling. Study, work, concentration; they all get in the way. Calmness and daydreams don't show up on my radar either. Unless, of course, the daydream evokes more than mental time-out.

So why did I choose a career that forced me to be hit with a new emotion time and time again on a daily basis?

That's easy. I like it. I like having a little insight into my client's true self. I like the game I play, figuring out how to make them happy. Every day I'm trying to beat my personal best. The sadder the client, the more I have to challenge myself to bring them out from under the towel. It's an eternal search for butterflies.

I also like the hairdressing, the creative play. It helps to make my own mind wander. But that always comes second. My strength is in my People Skills.

My clients often tell me how special they feel after an appointment with me. They always seem to get just what they wanted, even if they hadn't realised they wanted it.

Funny about that.

The secret to a successful salon lies just as much in getting to know exactly what your clients need as it does in technical skills. No-one would pay the most gifted hairdresser a penny if they were treated with hatred and contempt. Being treated like the most important person on the planet, even just for an hour, is priceless. There is also nothing like the satisfaction you get after lifting someone out of the doldrums and making them feel spectacular.

To be able to distract my client from the awfulness of their life is intoxicating. It's my drug of choice, my compulsion and need.

My success comes down to picking up the uncomfortable emotion, asking the right questions, then listening.

Hint: The best People Skill of all is to be a great listener.

You don't have to be an Empath to try it. Everyone likes to feel as though you are truly interested in their life, dreams and theories on climate change. The trick is in finding the key that gets them talking about themselves.

For example, trying to find a clue as to why the tender skin behind my knees is suddenly freezing with remorse is not easy. You have to build up to it. Imagine asking someone bluntly why there are fingers of grief wrapping around my neck, slowly suffocating me? Grief hurts, but you would be amazed how many people try to hide it.

You need to find the right questions. You have to make that someone trust you, know that they can tell you anything in confidence. You have to let them in, to know you in return. That's what you let them believe, anyway. I always give my clients just enough of the personal me for them to open up. Once their souls are bare, it's easy to find the happiness, however deep it's hidden.

These days, the system works well for everybody. My clients have a friend who truly cares about them, and they pay handsomely for the privilege. I get to travel overseas each year on the bounty of my caring, as well as pay the mortgage on my little apartment. I also get the ultimate high when I drag their hidden butterflies to the surface. Yes, the system works well for everybody – especially me. But it wasn't always like this.

Thursdays are my favourite day. My morning is crammed full with the same "mature" ladies each week. Every 40 minutes I visit with a different "best friend".

All older people carry the wet towel of sadness in some form or another. It's the degree of weight that varies.

Mrs Matthews, my 9am, only wears it lightly. She's in her eighties and still has her husband – and her marbles. Her light load of sadness comes from the inevitable loss of siblings and lifelong friends.

Nine-forty brings Marjorie Joan. She's a spinster in her sixties and positively gleeful. Her mood prepares me for the rest of the day. Glee is similar to excitement. They both send more than the gentle tickle of butterflies over my skin. There is nothing gentle about glee. It's short, sharp and astonishing. It's hundreds of beetles in flight, all beating their metallic wings against the roof of my mouth, the skin between my toes, every part of me. It is instant and frantic and very hard to hide my reaction. Glee makes me want to squeal with its infection.

My third client of the morning is Miss Clarissa Barnes, or Miss Lola, as she prefers to be called. Miss Lola is almost blank to me, other than an underlying whisper of butterflies that never fluctuates. I assume this is due to the Alzheimer's disease that has rampaged its way through her mind. I cherish the forty minutes I have with her, I can relax completely. She takes nothing of my own self with her, and leaves me refreshed and settled after playing with Marjorie Joan's glee. Unfortunately, I've only had the pleasure of Miss Lola's company for a year now. I wish she had walked through my door three years earlier – that way, I would never have met Nola Bruce.

I teased and pruned Nola Bruce's hair for three very long, painful years. It's not that I didn't like her personally. Quite the opposite in fact. She intrigued me. On the surface she was all bright and shiny like a new Japanese car. She was warm, kind and friendly with a saccharine smile you couldn't help returning. Her manners were impeccable. She knew all my staff by name, even Amy, my apprentice. She brought flowers on my birthday and good wine at Christmas.

But every Thursday morning, when I sat her down for a consultation and ran my fingers through her fine, 78-year-old hair, all I wanted to do was vomit. You see, Nola Bruce was what I call a show-bag. Like the sort you get at the Royal Melbourne. All fun and sparkles on the outside, but when you look inside – there's nothing but cheap, nasty crap.

Grief, guilt, remorse, depression, they were all there in spades. Along with a good dose of hatred, fear and, her strongest emotion of all, bitterness.

Bitterness is brutal. It hits my jaw like a white-hot cattle brand. Scorchingly acute, it almost brings me to my knees if I'm not expecting it. The simmering fury of bitterness moves swiftly from my jaw to my teeth. The cattle-brand morphs into claws: feral and unrelenting, they grasp and pull at my teeth. Striking first at my back molars, they spread with each flick of my fingers through her hair to the next tooth, a stampeding cancer in overdrive.

So why didn't I just palm Nola Bruce off to one of my staff, even an apprentice? Put simply, I couldn't. She wouldn't.

She had this weird attachment to me and refused (always politely) to let anyone else do her more-than-basic round-brush blow wave. If I was sick, she'd cancel. If I had holidays, she'd cancel. If I tried to make her appointment for another day or time, she would oblige. If I purposely ran late, she didn't complain and I would just bugger up my timing for the rest of the day. If I tried to make her booking with someone else, she just refused. Only I could do her hair properly. Talk about driving a girl to drink. Or drugs. Or both.

The physical pain I felt when I did Nola Bruce's hair was not what I dreaded the most. It was the total and complete absence of happiness. Everyone has a tiny increment of happiness – it's how I get my kicks, dragging that increment to the surface where I can touch it. Everyone, that is, except Nola Bruce. She was just so filled up with all the bad stuff, she'd forgotten about butterflies altogether.

I tried everything to find them. Every angle I knew. I put every People Skill I ever learnt to work, probing, prying, searching for the reason her happiness had taken permanent leave. She disturbed and fascinated me. She was my greatest challenge, my own private Everest. I'd do anything it took to get my hit from her.

Hint: They say love and hate are the most powerful emotions.

I beg to differ. Ask anyone in a 12-step program. Although not technically an emotion, addiction triumphs over all her competitors.

I began researching Nola Bruce in earnest after a year of living with this torture. I made notes at the end of each Thursday morning appointment, gathering together any information she offered. Never once did she blankly refuse to answer one of my incessant questions, but she didn't offer anything up without prompting either. This is what made her so different to anyone else I've ever touched. People like to talk about themselves. She did like to ask me questions in return though, kind of a quid-pro-quo sort of deal.

I knew she was a long-time widow. I knew she'd also lost her only son in early childhood. I knew she was highly educated, with two degrees to her name. I knew she lived alone and hadn't travelled outside Australia.

In turn, Nola Bruce knew Cyrus and I grew up with a slightly crazy mother, and an absentee father. She knew I hated the smell of fish, but loved a good meal of garlic prawns. She knew I didn't date although I never told her why. How do you explain that you can feel your blind date just isn't that into you? Even worse, that they are so consumed with lust my earlobes break out in a sweat – not to mention the other side effects lust has on me.

I gave Nola Bruce as much of my personal self as I dared. But she still didn't give me all of her. She didn't give me the opening or opportunity to ask the direct questions I needed to. Of course I knew that much of the sadness and bitterness would be from the loss of her family, but I didn't know any details of their deaths. I was sure this was where the secret to her misery lay. I just had to figure out how to unlock it.

I decided to try a different tack. Maybe if I couldn't catch a milligram of happiness from her, I could create it for her artificially. Even if there was a lone, solitary butterfly hiding within this damaged soul, I was going to find it. I knew that it would be the best I had ever encountered. I endured so much pain in searching it became my obsession.

I made sure the apprentices pampered her with extra-long scalp massages. I insisted she try out the latest conditioning treatments, free of charge. I surprised her with cupcakes and a few free highlights for her birthday. On the outside, she was so appreciative, so charming and grateful for the special attention. On the inside there was not a beat, nor a tickle. There was no happiness at all in Nola Bruce.

I became more and more obsessed. I knew it, was conscious of the fact that I was turning my search for her happiness into my personal quest. It was my Holy Grail, a seemingly unattainable crusade.

The happiness-hits I received from any other clients, my staff and brother became insignificant. Even Marjorie Joan's glee didn't seem to quite do it for me anymore. For three long years I endured weekly pain, both physical and mental.

The answer finally came easily and obviously one evening after a bottle of good white. Mulling over the information I had gathered on Nola Bruce, I realised I had not looked in the most obvious place of all, the internet.

I will never make a detective – surely that should have been the first step in my investigation?

There were exactly 23,104 results on Google for the name Nola Anne Bruce. My Nola Bruce. The fact that I had wasted three years for such a simple answer made me want to spit. But maybe that was the point? Maybe it had been the thrill of the challenge all along? I knew immediately what I needed to do. I could taste the syrup of victory already.

The morning after my revelation was a Wednesday. I woke happy and contented, if a little hungover. I'd slept better than I had for three years. Wednesday is my day off; it makes up for working late on Thursday nights and Saturday mornings. That particular Wednesday, I enjoyed a leisurely breakfast of crumpets, fruit and yoghurt. I took a long shower and then got out of my apartment for the day.

I had things to do and it was time I gave myself a treat. I bought a cute summer dress and ruby-red ballet flats. I dropped by Cyrus's studio to pick up some things and invite him out for lunch. We ate dim sims and chips on the Esplanade and laughed until our bellies ached. For the first time in so long, I made my own butterflies that day.

Thursday morning brought both excitement and trepidation. I was finally going to find Nola Bruce's happiness. The day was going to be warm, so I celebrated by wearing my new dress and flats.

Mrs Matthews was as lovely as ever, giving me a small brush of butterflies as she left, happy with her shampoo and blow wave.

Marjorie Joan's gleeful beetles were in full swing, and I was more than a little grateful for their energising jolt. I was in such a good mood that I made sure both she and Mrs Matthews were treated with our new luxury conditioning mask. Their 10-minute scalp massages sent the sweet scent of honey and almonds wafting through the entire salon.

By the time Nola Bruce arrived, I was skipping with nervous anticipation. I was a drug addict, about to get my best-ever hit.

I sat her down at my workstation by the staff room door, being extra careful not to brush against her accidentally. I didn't want to spoil the effect for later. I couldn't afford the slightest chance that her claws of bitterness would attack me before I was ready. I didn't want any distractions. Nola Bruce's happiness was all that mattered.

After our initial greetings, I sent her off to the basin with Amy for an extra long shampoo. She loved the new conditioning mask and massage that followed. I made one of her favourite flavoured lattes and popped in my special ingredient. I even served it on a paper doily with three pink sugared almonds off to the side.

Comb in hand, I braced for the hit of bitterness and despair that was thankfully muffled to more of an ache by the residue left behind by glee. I wound the setting rollers in record time and watched her take the first few sips of the slightly cool latte. Nola Bruce didn't like her coffee too hot. She liked to be able to drink it straight away.

Hint: An invaluable People Skill is remembering the small things about someone, such as how they take their coffee. It makes them feel special.

She finished her latte just as I lowered the overhead dryer. Her cheeks were a little flushed, so I asked Amy to make another cool coffee. I took my time rinsing and neutralising the first cup in hydrogen peroxide before accidentally smashing it to pieces on the cement tile floor.

It was while I was sweeping up the ceramic shards that the commotion began. Amy was calling me. It only took a few seconds to stuff the broken pieces of the cup under a pile of hair in the rubbish bin. But those few seconds were worth it.

By the time I reached Nola Bruce and flung back the overhead dryer, she was hyperventilating. I clasped her hands in mine, drinking in every ounce of fear, confusion and my old enemy, bitterness. I clenched down on my tongue and crunched my teeth together as the cattle brand attacked. I was determined not to let go. The morphing, burning claws were at odds with the freezing ice vest of terror that wrapped itself around my torso. Bull ants fought for running space over my scalp and a blanket of sopping wet sadness suddenly dropped me to my knees.

Nola Bruce was choking, ripping her hands from mine to grasp at her throat, then chest. She slipped from the chair as I frantically reached for her again, needing the physical contact to fully succeed. Her eyes bulged at me, condemning and hateful, realising exactly what I had done. She began to shake and then jerk like a landed fish. I held her tight, gasping in agony at the violence of the pins and needles stabbing my hands.

Then it just lifted.

Her accusing eyes softened as all the violence leached out, leaving only sadness behind. Her contorted mouth slipped into a twisted smile. I'm sure she whispered thank you through rose-coloured lips.

As Nola Bruce's life slipped away, so too did her sadness. The garment of soaking towels began to quiver and flicker. It rose from my skin and separated into tiny individual pieces. Fluttering gently at first, the butterflies finally took flight. They encompassed and surrounded me. They tickled and invaded. They flew through me, deep inside like none had ever done before. The butterflies I felt that day were stronger than any others, just as

I knew they would be. They were more than happy; they were euphoric, blissful, ecstatic.

They were gone.

It had only taken a few seconds for me to reach inside Nola Bruce and finally find her happiness. A few seconds for her to die. There was no question in the paramedics' minds when they eventually arrived: she was just another elderly lady whose heart had given out. Their tender hands of sympathy stroked my arm as they wheeled her body out the door.

It was then that I knew I was safe. They had no idea who Nola Bruce really was. She had gone by the name Nola Anne Longford-Bruce in her younger years. In those days she was an infamous killer, having poisoned both her husband and young son with potassium cyanide. She had claimed it was an accident, that her husband, a jeweller, must have left the cleaning product in the kitchen. She believed the fine white crystals to be sugar. The jury didn't believe her defence, that she hadn't noticed the pungent smell of bitter almonds as she sprinkled a little cyanide onto their porridge every morning.

She spent 22 years in jail.

The press at the time had branded her a cold-blooded murderer. I knew better. Nola Bruce was happy now, at peace with her long-gone family.

I love hairdressing. I love that I can sit someone in my chair and change their life forever. I love that I can always give them what they need, even if they didn't know it themselves.

My strength is in my People Skills.

2010

TALLOW

Ellie Marney

DEAR TUNNEY AND PETER,

I've been in such conundrums about this letter. I didn't know when to give it to you, or if I should give it to you at all. I considered enclosing it with my Will but finally decided that would be unfair. The posthumous surprise is the coward's way out, I believe. I didn't want you to feel like I was side-stepping the fallout from all this. I didn't want it to be that way.

So I've written this to be given to you both on the 25th anniversary of our aloneness. I should apologise before I begin – this is not a happy story, but I must tell it anyway. James pressed me not to do it; he thinks you will contact the police. Maybe you will. I will have to trust you both. Whatever happens, I will have to bear it.

A part of me wants to ask your pardon, beg your forgiveness, but another part of me stands resolutely beyond that. I did what I did for you both, and I have a dogged feeling about it: that things happened as they did, and I can't change them now in any case.

I don't have regrets; which isn't to say that I don't still have nightmares...

This is how you make a candle.

Cut your tallow into pieces, then place the pieces into a large double boiler, over water that is already gently bubbling. Stir the tallow until it reaches 71° Celsius, and is completely melted.

Add the colour chips or scent to the melted medium – this is really a matter of personal taste. Keep in mind that anything added will affect the way the candle burns. But raw tallow can have a meaty smell, and you might not fancy the amber greasy look; like yellowing teeth or tobacco-stained fingers.

Cut the wicks to the desired length of the candle, plus five inches, and

187

tie the wicks to the iron broach. Check that the temperature of the tallow is still 71°C, then dip the wicks in the tallow for a few seconds. Lift back out, and allow the candles to cool between dippings, about a minute or so. Once the weight of the tallow stiffens and straightens the wicks, things will get easier. Make sure the wet candles aren't touching each other.

Continue dipping and cooling. Repeat the process until the candles have reached the desired thickness, or forever, until your back and shoulders ache, and you wonder if this whole terrifying ghastly business will ever end.

Flora's cards are labelled Tallow, just the creamy square of 240gsm with the secretive dark script, her name and the contact for the shop, very much like an exclusive club, a health spa maybe. The products are exclusive, you know it's a good way to make something popular – people usually desire the things they think they'll never attain. Flora recognises that yearning, but she doesn't feel it any more. She has Douglas, and Tunney and Peter, to assuage it. She mines it only as a plank for the business now, working it into a recipe for commercial success. People desire, they desire candles and soap, even though candles and soap are really just fat and lye mixed together in the right proportions.

...standing there in your gown, smiling your Hellos and Thank Yous for Coming to My Wedding, when Bev Dingle comes up, clutching her Winnie Blues, already half-pissed before the reception has properly started. Heedless of Douglas' tall morning-suited bulk, she squeezes your arm. 'Oh Flo,' she sozzles out, 'Oh Flo yer mum would be so proud, I dunno how ya snagged him, but ya snagged a bewdy there Flo, ya lucky girl,' and then the press of the queue is pushing her down the reception line. You and Douglas exchange quick grins before you straighten, three more hours to go and you smile, stretch your face...

The soap is cut with a butcher's knife from immense pale-grained blocks. She only sells by weight.

The candles are not for the faint-hearted. They are big, bigger around than Flora's own thigh, and some as tall as herself. She likes the scale of them, an art form. She never uses colour, keeps the ice-white, or honey-gold, or brown-pear tones, as the focus. Natural is very in, like recycled wood panelling or free-range eggs.

...Dad only lived long enough to see the twins arrive, "the podling pair" he called them, and he never liked you talking with that Melbourne accent, but the twins, weren't they something, jus bewdiful, just what the doctor ordered, right before he had his stroke–

Tunney and Peter like to slide their fingers down the sides of wax mountains. Press their hands against a soap block, and then sniff the lavender on their skin. Flora likes to stand at the entrance to the shop and look at the graduating heights of the cold white pillars, the golden draped waterfall of dangling hand-dipped tapers, the massive chunks of soap, like something she's chipped off a glacier. The sense of personal accomplishment is fantastic. You can't buy that.

...but that was after Mum died. She was always into crafty things, making do, making soap, sewing her own clothes, the big Vacola jars labelled Peaches and Stewed Tomatoes, you can still remember the peaches, melting in your mouth after all these years...

The shop is entirely neat and pragmatic, much like Flora herself, a stylish amalgam that friends term "Quaker modern"; elderly gentrified industrial location and Flora's old-fashioned wares in combination with glass, white paint, pale wood. She revels in it.

It is like a present, a gift to herself, after years of dutiful marriage and the shepherding of her twin lambs through gestation and infancy and now school-readiness.

Actually, the shop is a present from Douglas, a reward or an apology. Compensation for all the business trips and late-night meetings and the isolation of solo parenting, all wrapped up in an old façade, rejuvenated by lime wash and varnished pine.

'I think it's more like a present from James,' Douglas says as he curls an arm around her. She leans into his embrace.

'Oh, James,' she says, rolling her eyes.

A year after Douglas had introduced him she finally nailed the accent. Since he talked about himself so little, she waited until Douglas was getting beers from the fridge.

'Afrikaner,' she said.

'What's that?'

'Your accent. It is, isn't it?'

He smiled, not looking at her. 'Most Australians wouldn't know an Afrikaans accent if it bit them on the rear,' he said.

She noticed he doesn't agree or deny.

'I remember. From my father's cricket Saturdays. The radio broadcasts.'

'Very clever,' he said approvingly.

Flora still doesn't know if it's the truth.

James Fisk is their accountant. Douglas has known James for years,

years before he knew Flora. That Douglas and James now work in the same firm is like a kind of inevitability. James comes for dinner, stays to talk business with Douglas. He's part of the furniture of their lives, ordering the nature of it to some extent.

Now's a good time to take a holiday, James says, before capital expenditure comes due. You should negative gear the rental property. You've been wanting that industrial tankage unit for the workshop, haven't you? James says. You should buy it.

Really? Flora smiles, sipping her wine.

Seriously.

You said yourself it'll make things easier, Douglas prompts with a grin. Increased productivity.

No, seriously, James says. And then I can claim on it for you in July.

The use of tallow or lard was the catalyst for the Indian Mutiny of 1857. To load the Enfield Rifle, the sepoys had to bite the cartridge open. It was believed that the paper cartridges were greased with lard, which was considered unclean by Muslims, or tallow, regarded as sacred to Hindus.

Later, Douglas finishes the last of the red while Flora tidies up.

'We should pay him a retainer, I think sometimes,' Flora says, wiping the benchtop.

Douglas frowns.

'Don't say that. He'd be insulted.'

'Do you think he's content?' she wonders absently.

'Do I think he's what?'

'I mean, he lives alone, he's obsessed with work, he's so…contained.' Flora has a sudden mental image of straw-haired James, loosening his tie by one degree as he sits, whiskey in hand. 'I wonder if it makes him happy…'

'I think James' interests are in other things,' Douglas confides.

'What, he's not interested in happiness? I know he's not gay, so maybe, I don't know, having a family, or at least a partner…'

'You sound like my Aunty Vi,' Douglas grins. 'Not everyone wants a family, Flo. James' loyalties lie elsewhere.'

'Elsewhere? What are his loyalties, then?'

'Pecuniary,' Douglas says. It rolls off his tongue, like he's tasting the word. 'Leave him be. He has his own code.'

Flora leans on the benchtop.

'It sounds a bit cold, I think. A bit mercenary.'

Douglas drains the glass, looks at the ceiling.

'Does it?'

The story of soap was first told in 1000B.C. Women rinsing clothes in the river, below the place where animal sacrifices were conducted, discovered that clothes became cleaner in contact with the soapy clay oozing there, where the rendered animal fat soaked through the wood ashes and into the river water.

…so my hand is shaking even as I write this.

It was Wednesday evening, I remember, because Wednesday and Thursday were the days I didn't open for business or do any preparation work. My mid-week weekend, Douglas used to say… He said he'd take the Sydney meetings from Wednesday to Friday. I wasn't expecting him back until Friday evening. He undoubtedly wasn't expecting me to enter the shop.

But we stopped there early on Wednesday evening because – oh Tunney – you had left Bear upstairs from the shop. Do you remember Thread Bear, dearest? We called him that because…

I'm stalling, I'm sorry. We entered the shop, and walked through the familiar dark colonnade, past the counter, toward the staircase. I remember wondering why I could see light under the workshop door, feeling that mixture of exasperation (it must've been me, I've left something on) and alarm (is anybody there?). When I slid the workshop door across, the rollers hissed, and you were both clinging to my pants legs, and I saw your father…

Douglas is standing near the centre of the workshop, in his business shirt and trousers. Flora's hands remember holding the iron over that shirt; now she is only holding her keys. Douglas is holding a small blowtorch, a kitchen one, like you use to glaze crème caramel, like the one Flora uses in the workshop. It is the one she uses in the workshop – she recognises this somehow. In his other hand, Douglas holds a short-bladed Bowie knife.

Tied to a wooden chair in front of him is a man in a singlet and a pair of dark trousers. He has bare feet. Flora can see only the back view – the man's sweaty black hair, his limp hands secured at the wrists, the bow of his shoulders.

The floor beneath the chair, beneath Douglas' feet, is covered in thick clear industrial plastic, and there are puddles of dark red ooze spattered onto it. To the right of the chair is a blue shopping bag filled with bundles of paper money: yellow, blue, grey, more cash than Flora has ever seen in its raw form.

The whole scene is aglow, stark and blueish, lit up from the side like a diorama in the halo of the workshop desk lamp. It looks staged, filmic somehow. It is unreal. It can't be real.

Rendering converts waste animal tissue into stable, value-added materials, and refers to any processing of animal by-products or, more narrowly, to the rendering of whole animal fatty tissue into purified fats (lard or tallow).

Rendering can be done on an industrial, farm, or kitchen scale…

Flora is arrested there in the doorway, her expression frozen. She stares at her husband, at the whole scene, all at once, as though her eyes have widened so much that she can see everything in panorama, there's no need for the eye to flit from detail to detail, her view is omniscient.

Douglas is not wearing his tie. His face is ruddy, a bit sweaty, energised – it is rather like the way his face looks after sex. This pulls Flora back: the way Douglas' expression and dishabille convey the sense of adultery, only this is not adultery. This is something else. Flora returns to her body in a rush, feels the press of the children's warmness against her leg. She blinks at her husband.

'Flora,' Douglas breathes out her name.

He is shocked, yes. Then his face changes, becomes paler, more still. His lips come together as he swallows. Flora recognises this: this is Douglas, composing himself. Possibly it is this tiny thing that tips her off, that clues her in. Douglas is composing his face for her. Only seconds after he says her name, he regains himself. He releases a switch on the blowtorch with his thumb. There is a zup as the blue flame goes out.

Flora feels realisation ignite as the blowtorch is extinguished. Perhaps it is the absurdity of it. How is it possible to put a composed face on this? But really, it is the speed of it, the rapidity of the transition in Douglas' face. This is not a singular act. This is something he does a lot. He can change his face, alter his expression at will, he can control his emotions quickly to cope with sudden changes in circumstance. This is not the reaction of an ordinary loving husband, devoted father, corporate businessman. This is not the reaction of an ordinary person.

Flora understands.

…but please believe me when I tell you it wasn't an easy thing to do. On any level. Physically, it went on and on, all night. Mentally and emotionally…I loved your father, loved him deeply.

What he did doesn't really take that away. And what I did…

I could say that I reacted on instinct. But in a way, he did too…

She takes her eyes off Douglas only long enough to glance down at the child nearest her right hand.

'Peter,' she says in a low voice, 'you and Tunney go upstairs and find Bear, please.'

Something, the frisson of energy in the scene they don't understand, communicates itself to the children, like when Flora and Douglas argue. The children don't complain or query. Peter takes Tunney's hand, and says 'Come on, Tun,' and they head for the staircase together. Tunney has her thumb in her mouth.

Flora does not let herself think that she is frightened. She takes the one step down into the workshop automatically, relying on reflex, with her eyes back on Douglas. She rolls the door closed behind her. She keeps her face very blank, as blank as can be.

The most significant problem when rendering fat for tallow is the smell. Chandlers and soap boilers were often relegated to the industrial section of townships, on account of noisome odours, an unavoidable by-product of large-scale boiling of animal carcasses.

Keeping her expression blank, getting the children out of the way – it's a miscalculation, she realises. It reveals something about her to Douglas; it reveals that she understands the situation. But what else could she do? When Douglas speaks again, she only starts because the tone of his voice is so familiar, so unnatural in this time and place.

'I wasn't expecting you,' Douglas says quietly.

It sounds so domestic.

And she should say something, she should say "clearly"; or something like that. She doesn't say anything.

Her breath is starting to come back in, short and tight. She mustn't hyperventilate. She mustn't scream, screaming is what you do when you have nothing left. She forces herself to just stand, hands at her sides.

Check the tankage unit at 10.15pm. She's wiping sweat off her lip as she watches James prepare the buckets. She wishes her hands would stop shaking.

Oh god I need a fag, I wish I had a fag she whispers, and she hasn't said "fag" for cigarette in about 15 years, but she's almost crying now she wants one so badly. It's like an ache in her chest, and James offers her a swig from his silver flask which helps some but…

With her omniscient eye, Flora observes the scene between the two players. The man in the chair is unmoving. She and Douglas are the players. The looks they direct at each other indicate that they have assessed each other correctly. All that remains is to act.

Douglas begins, he sets his face grimly and says 'Flora, I'm sorry you had to see this.'

Flora still can't trust herself to speak, so she just nods her head quickly, but before she's finished the action she's wondering what he means. When Douglas takes a brisk purposeful step towards her with the knife in his hand, she comprehends. He is apologising for what he's about to do.

He moves fast and she can't stumble back, there is nowhere to go. She makes a garbled cry, cringes as he swipes with the knife, she raises her hand automatically. She is still holding her keys. The knife clashes onto them with a sound like teeth clicking together – by some miracle none of her fingers are severed – and the force of the blow telescopes up her arm, sending her reeling off the step.

She bounces off the edge of the work table to her right, jarring her hip, twisting to see her husband. His face is unreachable, single-minded, and he has turned the knife to allow him to thrust down, make a clean plunge into her breast. She is half-sprawled over the table, pressed into the corner, and her left hand rakes the wall. She knows she is trapped completely and she feels her face, mouth stretched in horror, eyes gasping wide.

Flora's left hand hits something leaning in the corner, something hard, she grabs for it as Douglas steps in. She rams forward with the hard heavy broach-handle. The broach is made of cast-iron, and shaped like a broom. At the base, where the broom's bristled head should be, there are 12 five-inch metal tines.

The broach-handle slams into Douglas' face with a ghastly thud, blood explodes from his nose. For a moment his robotic expression is cross-eyed, confused, and Flora almost makes a hysterical laugh. She pulls on the handle; as it comes away she can see the impression it has made in Douglas' skin, in his skull. He stumbles back, raising a hand drunkenly to the indentation in his forehead. He looks alien and slow, so Flora almost lets her guard down. Then he lifts his eyes, and she only has time to swing the broach-base up – when he makes a lurching thrust forward, knife arcing high, she puts her whole weight into bracing, head hunkered down, shoulders hunched. The collision knocks her off the table, so by the time it's over she's semi-crouched over the handle of the broach, kneeling squeezed between table and wall, gasping, staring up into the ruined face of her impaled dead husband.

'Why did you call me?'

'Douglas always called you; in emergencies.' She exhales, feeling white and shocked.

'Yes, he did.'

'This is one. An emergency.'

'Yes, it is.' James still looks confused. 'And…you trust me?'

'I can do better than trust you,' she says. 'I can pay you.'

She stays like that for a minute, blowing hard, then the demands of gravity kick in. She sinks forward, lets the broach, with Douglas' body decorating the end, crumple to the floor. Douglas is half-on, half-off the step. His expression is one of total surprise. The tines of the broach have pierced him in four places across the heartline of his chest, and in one place on his right bicep, snagging the muscle there cruelly.

Flora's arms are sore and shaking but she uses them to climb her way up to the tabletop, then she uses the tabletop to support herself as she steps over the broach and the body, stumbling onto the clear floor area beside the man in the chair. She'd forgotten about him.

She stands, holding the table and shivering like she has hypothermia, then her knees give way and she sinks in a shambolic fashion onto her bottom. Her arms flop, her breath is blowing in and out, she feels something building up inside her, the scream she couldn't afford to let out before. But she can't let it out now either. She drags her hands up to her face, pushes them hard against her mouth, so that the only noise escaping is the "ung-ungh-ungh" sob of air, wheezing in and out of her nose.

She closes her eyes. Slowly her breathing comes under control until she's just going 'mmm…mmm', behind her hand. Then she can take her hand away, open her eyes, just sit for a moment. Her eyes move around: the scene, the bodies, the plastic she's puddled on. Minutes pass. Then something clicks inside her and she heaves to her feet, staggers over to Douglas. Roots in one trouser pocket before pulling on his hips to access the other. She pulls out the mobile phone. Hesitates. Her fingers shake so she almost drops the phone, but she's got it open, thumbing the speed dial clumsily. In the pause, she takes two deep levelling breaths, so when she speaks her voice hardly trembles at all.

'No. This is Flora,' she says, like her own name tastes odd in her mouth. 'That's all right. I'm at the shop. There's a, a bit of a mess here, James. Could you come over? Ten minutes. All right. Come in through the back. Thanks.'

She closes the phone carefully and puts it in her pants pocket. Then she looks down and pats herself over, like pressing down creases. She rakes at her hair, takes another deep breath, steps over Douglas' waist to get up onto the step, the door sliding, so she can go upstairs and put the children to bed.

> ...regarding the case of such absent (Missing/Lost) spouse, inasmuch as it has been satisfactorily established through evidence of circumstances approved by the court, that the "presumption of death" rule may be applied, thus allowing the State to grant probate and obtain an adjudication of the issue...

He enters through the backyard into the workshop; he must have parked around the corner. He seems very calm, hair sticking up like he's just showered, casual jeans, and he closes the door before turning around.

She sees the way he stands still, looks. He's not shocked. She doesn't find this surprising. His eyes move over everything, his face serious and without emotion, just assessing. She stands on the step holding one arm across her body with the other arm, her shoulders still throbbing.

The time she spent settling the children has made regular programming resume somewhat, and she feels a flare of panic. Suddenly she doesn't know what possessed her to call him, or what he's going to do.

Then he meets her gaze and holds it.

'Okay,' he says. He closes his eyes, opens them. 'Okay.'

'So if you're thinking four hours for the tankage unit, we'll...'

'Shut up for a minute, I'm trying to estimate poundage,' she snaps, and then she presses her lips. 'Sorry. Sorry, I'm...'

'It's all right.'

'It's not. I, I'm very sorry.'

'Flora,' he says.

She looks at the floor, rubs her fingers. He clears his throat.

'Pounds. So it's, what, the American unit?'

'Yes. That's right.'

'So you just halve the weight. Is that right?'

She blows out a breath. 'Yeah. Yes, I think it is.'

He starts moving immediately. Walks over and puts two fingers on the neck of chair-man, seems satisfied, goes through chair-man's pockets until he gets the phone, takes out his own phone, holds out his hand for Douglas'. She gives it to him.

He cracks them all open, takes out the SIM cards, pockets them, groups the phones on the workbench. He talks as he works.

'You walked in unexpectedly.'

'Yes.'

'The kids?'

'Yes. Upstairs. I've put them to bed.'

'Think they'll stay asleep?'

'Yes.'

'Okay,' he says. 'Do you have a baby monitor?'

'I've put it on.'

'Oh. Okay.'

He stands for a moment, considering her.

'You have very fast reflexes,' he says finally.

This is like a compliment, like telling her she was clever that time. She doesn't know what to say to this.

'I need garbage bags,' he says, 'gloves, buckets, bleach, cleaning gear. I need to get some things from my car.'

He is so efficient. He doesn't offer comfort, but this efficiency is comforting. She thinks of saying this, doesn't.

He rolls up his sleeves.

…only the steady grumming chew of the meat saw, which is really getting harder to bear every moment, second only to the noises when he finishes a section and then empties the full bucket of pieces into the tankage unit. Then plop and squelch. She goes all right for a while, keeps cleaning, but then on the last one she can't help it, rushes over to the rag bucket and retches, her stomach grinding painfully, her eyes scrunched shut…

His equipment and her supplies, gathered in a neat pile off the edge of the plastic, and he's already put the money in a garbage bag. She watches as he unties chair-man, tips him onto the floor, the body lying at an odd stiff angle.

'So, this is… What do we do now?' she asks, a little wild-eyed. 'To get rid of them. I mean, isn't that what we have to do?'

'Yes,' he says shortly. Then he volunteers, 'I can get rid of this one okay. It's Douglas we have to worry about.'

'Oh. Okay. So what, we, we burn off their fingerprints or something?'

James' face twists. 'Bloody hell, Flora, this isn't the movies,' he stops suddenly, looks at her. 'Hang on.'

…wanted you to remember the good things about him, too. The way he read to you both before bedtime, the hugs he gave you, the love. It was never just a lie, or a cover story, it was real; the love was real. You have his dark eyes, Peter; and Tunney, you have his dry deprecating humour. Something of him lives in both of you, and makes me love you even more each day, it's what got me through the...

They stop and sit together on the floor, backs to the workbench cupboards, sharing his hip flask. She feels washed out. She thinks they both look washed out, exhausted. There's hours to go.

'So are you going to tell me about it?'

'You mean Douglas?'

'Yes.'

'You want me to tell you about Douglas?'

'Yes,' she insists.

'Do I need to?' He passes her the flask. 'You're not an idiot, Flora.'

'How about I tell you what I think, and you just answer yes or no.'

'Just talk,' he sighs.

Flora nods, then begins.

'He'd been doing this for a long time.'

'Yes.'

'Longer than... No, forget that.'

James says nothing.

'And not as a...what-you-call-it, an official government...'

'No,' he shakes his head. 'Independent contractor.'

'Oh. And is that what you are too? An independent...'

'No.' He returns her stare. 'I mean, not any more, no. I'm just... I'm just an accountant, Flora.'

'Oh. So this...' She flicks a hand out, to the scene. 'This is normal? For an independent contractor?'

James shakes his head emphatically.

'No, this is horribly, horribly sloppy; unprofessional. Not at all what I would have expected from Douglas.'

'Sloppy,' she repeats. She sucks on her teeth.

'Yes. I'm sorry, you...'

'No,' Flora says. She closes her eyes. 'Don't apologise.'

'...reassure you, Mrs Ernst, that we're still looking into it. Your husband's disappearance is still important to us, whether it's six months or six years—'

'Thank you, Detective.'

'Thank you, for being so understanding,' he says, and looks around. 'It's good you've kept up with your business.'

'Well, it keeps me occupied. Would you like a candle, Detective, or maybe a block of soap? Here, these tapers are nice.'

'Oh, I couldn't .'

'No, please,' she says. 'I insist.'

It's 4.40am; she skims off the solid chilled fat from the aspic by just upending the buckets, like making sandcastles, and slicing the hard top white layer away from the jelly. James bags the aspic and takes it out to the car, with the other remains, for disposal.

Flora's hands are greasy, from stacking the blocks. She's anticipating a few hours' sleep beside her children until she has to get up and make them breakfast before kinder, before returning to the longer work of dipping the tapers and mixing the soap. James comes back for his gear as she's wiping her hands, closing the fridge.

'I've cleaned the U-bend in the sink, I'll do it again after you've finished,' he says. 'Remember to bag the rags, anything else touching...'

'I know,' she says tiredly. 'I will.'

'I'm going now,' he says, hesitates. 'Flora?'

She looks at him.

'Thank you, James,' she says. 'For everything.'

He moves, can't seem to decide whether to shake her hand or give her a kiss on the cheek, finally settles for squeezing her shoulder. His eyes seem slightly lost, hollow. Then he nods, and leaves.

...maybe asking too much, but I wanted you to know the whole story. All stories contain a spectrum from light to dark.

This one contains much darkness, but a candle emits 13 lumens of visible light, so I think of your father, and the love that produced you both, when I touch flame to wick.

That love still burns. It will see us through.

Forever,

your mother, Flora.

2011

THE TEARDROP TATTOOS

Angela Savage

YOU CRINGE WHEN YOU SEE MY TATTOOED TEARS. BUT DRIVEN BY THE SAME impulse that makes you slow when you pass a car crash, you look closer. One is transparent, a silhouette. The other, clear at the top and blue at the bottom, looks swollen, like it might roll down my cheek at any moment.

Who would do that to themselves?

I hear your mind ticking over, hear you whisper gang, murder, prison.

'Does it mean she killed somebody?' The boy is young and cocky, doesn't know to hold his tongue. His mother shushes him and steps up the pace. I want to yell out, 'Yeah, I did,' but his mother has dragged him away from the scary dyke and her dog. One of those dangerous breeds, she's thinking, the kind they train to fight.

I don't hate her. She's only doing her job. Protecting her boy.

People think I'm a lesbian because of the way I look, though I never had sex with a woman, not even in my mind. I haven't had sex with anyone at all in a long time, but not even the tattooed tears are enough to put some men off trying. Sully scares away the last of them.

Sully is a dangerous breed, an American pit bull. I got him through a contact I made in the rat house. I read up on dogs – had fuck all else to do – and concluded an American pit bull was the one for me. They've got a bad reputation. They look mean. People give them a wide berth. But get them when they're young and train them properly and you can't go wrong. Loyal, intelligent, protective, loving. My husband had none of these qualities. I could bloody well have them in a dog.

The guy I got him from said Sully was blue. But to me he's the colour of storm clouds with a streak of white on his chest I think of as his silver lining. He lies on his back as I run my fingers up and down his white streak, gives me a black-lipped grin and pounds the floor so hard with his tail I worry the neighbours in the flat below will complain.

But Sully isn't just a defence. He's my friend. A dog's affection is still more than I deserve, but Sully doesn't hold that against me. The flat where we live is in Brunswick, one of those inner city Melbourne suburbs where wogs and yuppies collide. Not my choice, but beggars can't be choosers. At least I got a place where pets are allowed. I would've preferred a car. Me and Sully could've slept in it, taken off whenever we wanted, made a home of the open road.

But you can't check in with your parole officer when you're on the road.

The-powers-that-be gave me a place three doors from a childcare centre. I can't hear the children if I keep the windows shut. Me and Sully try to stay out of sight at drop-off and pick-up times, though it means lying low for up to two hours at each end of the day, which isn't always possible.

It was winter when I moved in. The childcare centre opened at sparrow's fart and some kids were dropped off while it was still dark. Through the Venetian blind in my bedroom I watched mothers unbundle their babies from capsules and car seats, drawn faces illuminated by the interior lights of their SUVs. I watched them juggle their babies on one hip, close the car door with the other, stagger lopsidedly to the entrance and punch in the security code. When they reappeared minutes later, the women were light on their feet. I watched them dab at baby spew on lapels, slip into stilettos, touch up lipstick in rear-view mirrors.

I felt nothing for these women. Neutral as Switzerland, me.

When the childcare centre traffic died down, I'd take Sully to the park. Well, not so much a park as a grassy block surrounded by temporary fencing with a hole in it. It reeked of a failed development – like a builder had overcapitalised and didn't want to crystallise his losses by liquidating his assets. You surprised someone like me says things like overcapitalised and liquidate assets? Yeah, well, you would judge a book by its cover. Just so happens in a past life I was a girl from a nice family with a Diploma of Business and a promising career in insurance. Not that it matters now. No one's ever going to give me a job in insurance.

One day, Sully and me ran around the park long enough to work up a sweat, even though it was only September and the sun wasn't quite strong enough to knock the chill out of the air. While I squeezed out through the hole in the fence, Sully ran ahead of me towards the flat and nearly collided with a woman coming down the hill pushing a pram.

Apart from a purple scarf, the woman was dressed head to toe in black. Her hair was black with purple streaks. The pram – the fancy kind that costs as much as a car – was also black and purple. She slowed as I neared in that way of mothers who expect you to ooh and ah over their kid. I only glanced at it. Four or five months maybe, wearing a hand-knitted beanie. And fuck me if the beanie wasn't black and purple too.

The woman smiled. No one had fucking smiled at me since the night I killed my husband.

'Hello,' she said.

'Hello.'

I turned to make sure she could see my tattoos. 'Nice to see some sun.'

'Yeah.'

'Cute pup. What kind is it?'

'American pit bull.'

'Oh?'

She struggled to maintain her smile. But if looking like a murderous dyke wasn't enough to put her off, Sully was. I was enjoying my smug moment so much that I nearly let Sully scamper off the edge of the gutter and into the traffic. I scooped him up with my foot, dumped him on the footpath and smacked him hard across the face. American pit bulls have such a high pain threshold, I had to be forceful so he'd get the message not to run out on the street. Sully yelped in surprise and I saw the woman's smile take another hit as she added animal cruelty to the list of things she hated about me. She leaned into the pram and fussed over the kid's beanie.

'Well, me and Charlie better get going,' she said. 'See ya.'

She headed to the crèche at the bottom of the hill, trailing disapproval like a vapour in her wake.

When the letter came a week later, I knew who was behind it.

Council has received advice that you are in possession of a restricted breed dog, namely an American pit bull terrier, this being a breed whose importation into Australia is prohibited absolutely under the Commonwealth Customs (Prohibited Imports) Regulations 1956. As of 2 November 2005, the Domestic (Feral and Nuisance) Animals Act 1994 makes it an offence to acquire a restricted breed dog...

Shit, an offence would be a breach of my parole.

Council records show you have not registered your dog. All residents are required by law to register their dog by age three months. Persons applying to register their dog must make a declaration as to whether their dog is a restricted breed. A sizeable court penalty applies for a false declaration. Council cannot accept the registration of restricted breed dogs.

Fuck. I couldn't keep Sully without registering him, but if I tried to register him I'd get done for acquiring a restricted breed. So much for Sully's silver lining. Why the fuck couldn't that woman have left us alone? Why did she have to stop and talk to me? Couldn't she read the big neon sign over my head saying Fuck off? And why did I tell her what kind of dog he was? She'd wrong-footed me with her smile and her chitchat about the weather. Now losing Sully was the price I'd pay for being fucking polite.

I stood a moment in the galley kitchen of my flat, holding the Council letter, burning with rage. It was a slow burn, not a conflagration. I was in control. Then, a Eureka moment. It almost made me wish I could attend another session just to tell the group about it.

'Check it out,' I spoke aloud, as if they were there in the kitchenette with me. 'Anger therapy's worked. I'm controlling my impulses. I'm going to take my time, really plan my revenge to be sure to hurt this woman like she's hurt me.'

Sully, the sweet little mite, thought I was talking to him and drummed the floor with his tail.

That night I took him back where I got him. I didn't think I had enough heart left to break, but saying goodbye to Sully proved me wrong.

My first step was to find out where she lived. It's not easy to observe someone undetected when you weigh nearly ninety kilos and have tattoos on your face. You can't march into a childcare centre and ask to see the records for "Charlie". Shit, I didn't even know if Charlie was a boy or a girl. Could be either these days. I was at the local video store when the solution came to me. A DVD called Kiss Kiss, Bang Bang caught my eye. A Val Kilmer movie I hadn't seen, though I saw a lot of his movies in the rat house. My favourite was The Saint, where he had all the gadgets and disguises. That's when it struck me: I could disguise myself. I might not have Val Kilmer's budget, but I had a Savers down the road and a Vinnies around the corner. Stuff was cheap at Savers and if I played my cards right, the old dears at the Vinnies might give me what I needed for free. My spirits lifted for the first time since losing Sully. I grabbed Kiss Kiss, Bang Bang, found The Saint and took both DVDs to the counter.

The video store guy caught me smiling. Nearly scared the shit out of him.

I spun a story to the two old dears at the Vinnies about being single mum in hiding from a violent bastard who forcibly tattooed my face.

'I only want to buy my groceries –' I deliberately used the old-fashioned word '– without having to look over my shoulder.'

Well, fuck me if the old biddies didn't mobilise like a pair of retired army officers. One of them, Eunice, found me a couple of wigs: a grey curly one much like her own hair, and a long brown one with a thick fringe.

'We get them from cancer patients,' Eunice said. 'Survivors,' she added quickly, as if it mattered. 'They don't need the wigs once their hair grows back.'

While Eunice rifled through the racks, the other one, Carmela, put together an ensemble she called the Nonna look: black cardigan, shapeless black dress, black headscarf to go over the grey wig. She teamed this with some low-heeled, lace-up shoes and even found me an unopened packet of support stockings. Eunice reappeared with a blue tent dress, lambskin vest, beige boots and sunglasses with lenses the size of beer coasters.

I wasn't crazy about trying it all on but the old dears were keen and I wanted to keep them sweet. The Nonna-look was brilliant. My own mother wouldn't have recognised me. If she did, she would've crossed the street, but that's beside the point.

'Un momento,' Carmela murmured at my reflection in the change-room mirror. She ducked off and returned with a black handbag. 'I think the le vedove will try to speak italiano with you.'

'Vedovay?'

'The widows.'

She adjusted the lacy headscarf to hide the tattooed tears. 'Perfect.'

Eunice's hippy shit looked better than I'd imagined. It was years since I'd felt hair on my shoulders or worn a dress. I looked like one of those jovial plump women with an appetite for life, the type I normally did what I could to avoid. In the interest of authenticity, I let Eunice drape a string of beads over my head. But when she reached up to remove the sunglasses, I flinched.

'May I?'

A voice you'd use with a wounded animal.

I couldn't see what she was doing, felt something cool and damp press against my right cheekbone. She stepped back.

'Much better.'

I looked in the mirror. She had covered over my tears.

'Concealer.' She pressed a small cylinder into my hand. 'Hides a multitude of sins.'

I was too shocked to speak.

I used the Hippy Chick disguise to tail her. When she passed by my apartment window again, pushing her fancy pram, I gave her a twenty-second head-start, crossed the road and followed her up the hill.

Her house turned out to be a fifteen-minute walk in the direction of Sydney Road. If Brunswick was a body, Sydney Road was the spinal cord that held it all together and made it move. There's nothing suspicious about a hippy on Sydney Road, so I followed Pram Woman until she turned into the entrance of a sand-coloured weatherboard house opposite a small park.

At last, a lucky break. I slowed my pace and paused to rub an imaginary blister on my heel, used the park fence for balance. A row of spindly shrubs blocked my view of Pram Woman's house, but the front door was clearly visible through the gate in her picket fence. A tortoiseshell cat sprang out of the way as she pushed up onto the verandah. The number on her mailbox was 124.

Early next morning I walked down the same street in my Nonna disguise. A dark-green sedan I hadn't noticed the previous evening was parked out front. I headed for the park and chose the bench with the best view of the house. Someone had covered one arm of the park bench with a knitted sleeve. I'd seen fence railings, bicycle stands and signposts in the area clothed in random bits of knitting like this. Was it a joke? A message? Not knowing made me uneasy. I shuffled to the other end of the bench and took out a string of rosary beads I'd found in the Vinnies handbag. I'd long ago stopped believing in God, but I figured people would leave me alone if they thought I was praying.

Just before seven, a passing car projected a missile that hit the veranda of number 124 with the thud of paper on wood. The front door opened and the woman dashed out, snatched the newspaper, dashed back in again. Hair standing on end and wearing a too-tight black tracksuit, she made me think of a trapdoor spider.

Twenty minutes later a man in a suit appeared. Lean and polished, I could practically smell his aftershave from across the road. The green sedan beeped as he made for the driver's side, mobile phone against his ear before he'd even fastened his seatbelt. It was quiet for almost an hour after that. I sipped at a bottle of water and ignored the growling of my stomach.

A curly-haired woman with dark circles under her eyes entered the park behind a careening toddler. She sat on a swing and watched as the boy scooped up handfuls of tanbark and flung them into the breeze. I watched the boy too, accidentally made eye contact with the woman. She gave me a tired smile. I had my hand on the beads in case she came over but was saved by the arrival of a second mother-and-child duo. They all seemed to know each other. I returned to my surveillance.

Around eight-thirty my target re-emerged in her trademark black and purple and turned her pram in the direction of the childcare centre. This time the baby wore pink – a girl then. As soon as they were out of sight, I crossed the road at a pace appropriate to an overweight and elderly woman and paused out front of the house as if to catch my breath. I hadn't heard the tell-tale beep of a burglar alarm and there was no sticker in the front window, no blue light on the roof. The left side gate was covered in vines; the right was a recycled wooden door left ajar.

No alarm, no dog, ample cover and a gate left open. This was what the burg' merchants in the slammer would call a "dream job".

I took a tissue from my handbag, wiped my nose and leaned over the front fence to use the bin. The recycling bin was closest. Amid the empty wine bottles, newspapers, tins and plastic I found what I was looking for. An envelope addressed to Belinda Hyatt.

I spent a week of mornings in the park, getting a handle on the daily routine. Hubby worked full time; Belinda did three days from home, the days little Charlie went off to childcare. When she had the baby with her, Belinda usually went out. Once I followed her to a café on Sydney Road. It was jammed with prams. A sticker on the window said "Breastfeeding welcome here".

Sydney Road swarmed with old women in black. I'd barely noticed them before, but now that I was one of them I saw them everywhere. And I realised how much we had in common. Their public grief set them apart. My tattooed tears served the same purpose.

I learned to impersonate their rolling gait, a pace that allowed me to cruise past Belinda's house even when she was working. Through the shrubbery I watched her in the front room at her computer, the tortoiseshell cat lolling on her desk like an oversized paperweight.

I undertook evening surveillance in my hippy guise. You didn't see so many Nonnas out after dark, but as Hippy Chick I could always pretend to be going out or heading home, depending on the hour. Most evenings were quiet at Belinda's, the green sedan always home before seven. Lights shone from windows at the rear where the kitchen was located, moving later to the lounge room at the front. The place was dark by eleven.

I turned up one evening to find Belinda's husband in the front yard watering the garden. The baby was suspended against his chest in one of those carriers, arms and legs flapping like a pull-string puppet. The man was chatting to the baby but paused as I walked past to give me a straight-toothed smile that made my eyes water. I kept walking until I found myself outside a pub on Sydney Road.

The barman's pierced eyebrow made him look permanently surprised but he didn't blink when Hippy Chick ordered a pot. The smell was room deodoriser that reminded me of prison, so I headed out to the beer garden. It was like walking in on a summer camp. A pack of hairy men played ping-pong, exchanging banter with the young women at a nearby table who were drinking beer and knitting.

A guy at a table on his own was smoking rollies and reading a book. I thought next time I should bring a book, too, then laughed at myself for imagining there would be a next time. One of the hairy guys approached me. I almost told him to fuck off when I realised he was only after the ping-pong ball that had rolled under my table.

'Thanks.' He smiled. I smiled back. He went back to his ping-pong game. I wiped the sweat from my upper lip. A couple walked in, tattooed sleeves interlinked. On their heels was a Staffie, blue like Sully. I looked at the empty space at my feet. If it wasn't for Belinda, Sully would've been there too, making me smile with his goofy grin and thumping tail.

I drained my beer and left.

The following night it was after twelve when I ventured onto Belinda's property. It was dark apart from a dull glow in the second window on the right side – a night-light in the baby's room. I inspected the window: old wood, new lock, key dangling in it. Jemmying it open with a crowbar would be easy but noisy. I made my way to the back of the house.

The yard was organised into garden beds, a fig tree on one side, lemon on the other. A small deck held a trestle table and chairs. Security door, more key-locked windows... Belinda and her hubby weren't as slack about security as I thought.

A flash of light caught my eye. I took a closer look at what was on the table. Leadlight. A work in progress. Perhaps a feature window or a panel for the door. Leadlight was an activity we were offered in the rat house as an alternative to boredom, until the screws twigged that Traci "The Fox" Ferrigno was using the classes to conduct her own lessons in the art of glass cutting for B& E purposes.

I scanned the yard again, registered the shed in the corner. It was wide open. On a low shelf were Belinda's leadlight tools: pliers, rulers, brushes and glass cutters.

A square of light came on.

It beamed into the yard from the house. Someone was stirring. I crouched in the shadows by the shed, then hurried back the way I'd come.

Sounds from the baby's room. I squatted beneath the window and listened. Floorboards creaked rhythmically, a muted female voice accompanying the gentle drumming. I thought Belinda might be pacing the room, though I hadn't heard the baby cry. Then recognition hit me like a punch in the guts.

Belinda was in a rocking chair with Charlie at her breast. I just knew it. I slumped to the ground, my back pressed against the weatherboards, my tears like acid.

The right night presented itself a week later. New moon, north wind, wheelie bins out front. I wore black jeans, a long-sleeved T-shirt and sneakers; carried a Swiss Army knife in one pocket, WD40 in the other.

Not a night for disguises.

I reached number 124 at 4am, the quiet time between the baby's one o'clock feed and the man's six-thirty jog. I let myself around the back and took the glass cutters from the shed. The rusty wire screen on the window tore like tissue paper and the wind masked the sound as I carved a hole in the glass large enough to insert my hand and disengage the widow lock. A squirt of WD40 enabled me to ease the window open with barely a sound. I'd learned well from Traci The Fox.

My heart speeded up as I prepared to teach Belinda Hyatt how it felt to lose what she loved. I scooped up the warm body at the end of the cot, held closed her mouth and nose, hauled her back out through the window with me and slashed her throat with my knife.

The body jerked in spasms for a few moments then flopped in my arms, silent and still. I stood fixed to the spot, blood seeping into my clothes, the weight growing heavier in my arms. I expected to feel excited at this point, even elated. Instead, I was appalled, even as I felt compelled to see my ghastly plan through.

I retraced my steps to the front of the house and arranged the body on the door step where it would be seen when Belinda emerged to collect the newspaper. My hands were sticky with blood and even in the dim light I could see black liquid pooling on the doormat.

I stepped back, taking in the bloody tableau, trying to imagine Belinda's reaction. The horror in her face. The likelihood she would scream. But still I felt no satisfaction. Only disgust.

But I was a hardened criminal, for fuck's sake. I had the teardrop tattoos to prove it.

Then it was as if the characters I'd been playing had gotten under my skin: the tetchy old Nonna who commanded respect; the hippy chick with so few cares in the world that she probably knitted covers for street posts. I'd spent the past few weeks blending into a community. A door had opened that I'd believed was closed to me forever. Could I step through it? Or should I bolt it shut for good?

I returned my gaze to the mess on the doorstep. My Nonna thought about cleaning it up, burying the body in the park or disposing of it in a wheelie bin. Hippy Chick dreaded the thought of Belinda coming to the door with Charlie on her hip. But I reckoned the baby was too young to get upset at the sight of a dead cat.

Besides, I was only going through with this for Charlie's sake. Belinda needed to know her house was not secure. She needed to do more to protect little Charlie. The dead cat would be a wake-up call.

A wake-up call.

Would it have saved my baby if I'd called home from work that night? He might not have heard the phone through his drunken stupor. But perhaps the sound would have roused my son before he could suffocate in his sleep.

The transparent tear, that's for my lost baby. The other tear is for my husband, who put the baby to sleep on his stomach. My mistake was killing the bastard. I did it to punish him, but all it did was release him from the terrible pain I lived with every day. Grief so profound, so permanent, not even tattooed tears can do it justice.

I needed to put distance between me and the cat. I jogged back to my apartment, bagged my bloodied clothes, showered and dressed again to add the bag to the wheelie bin. When I turned to go back inside I spied something in my mailbox. Another letter from the Council. I ripped it open and read by the foyer light.

Council wishes to advise that we found no evidence to substantiate the claim that you are in possession of a restricted breed dog. Consequently, the childcare centre has now withdrawn its complaint on this matter and you are no longer under investigation.

I caught my reflection in the plate-glass door as it closed behind me. You see my teardrop tattoos?

Look closer.

SHADOWS

Josephine Pennicott

'My grief lies all within;
And these external manners of laments
Are merely shadows in the unseen grief
That dwells with silence in the tortured soul.'

William Shakespeare

This is how it begins. An ordinary Saturday morning; into the brilliant blue Sydney sky a plane traces "Eternal James", mysterious words of white-cloud skywriting. Familiar surroundings and routine cocoon you – but everything is about to shift, slice and fragment. Your taken-for-granted pleasant life is about to change irrevocably. It begins with a shadow; with swans gliding on a river; with sunshine, light, words, books – and your own careless, unseeing eyes.

You only have yourself to blame.

Katie is laughing, twirling, holding her arms up to the sky, turning her face to the sun. Her front teeth are missing, left to the Tooth Fairy in a satin pouch and exchanged for shiny dollar coins.

You photograph Katie's face alive with radiant mischief, joy, missing teeth and youth. You freeze the moment and she mouths, 'I love you, Mummy'. You should suspect at this point that you are dreaming. Katie always stubbornly refused to call you Mummy; from the moment she could articulate her independence she called you "Beatrice" and her father, "Steve". Both sets of grandparents were annoyed by this mannerism and cautioned against letting it continue – but Katie stubbornly maintained she should address you by your proper names.

So when she called you "Mummy" in her childish voice, with her large serious child's eyes gleaming and a face filled with sunshine, you should have realised…

And then you step to one side to photograph your shadow.

You wake crying and the pain is waiting like a black heavy web. You lie in your darkened bedroom, feeling the brilliant blue sky of the dream still breathing next to you. Loss engulfs you in its enormous, cold-grave mouth. Steve's side of the bed is long-empty. Somewhere across the city he wakes to a woman who was once your friend – but perhaps the same dream torments him too. Or does Katie only dance in sunlight for you?

You think I don't know about the dreams?

You hear the early-morning birds and the traffic on its peak-hour crawl to work. Down the hallway of your double-storey terrace is an empty child's room with fairy-pink walls containing seven years of sweetness, light and life. Shelves crammed with books: Babar, Miffy, Harry Potter, the Famous Five, fairytales. Baskets loaded with Little Angel magazines. Barbies, Lego, craft materials and photos of friends. You had delighted in decorating the pink princess room together. On days when the pain is tolerable you lie on her Strawberry Shortcake bed, closing your eyes, trying to feel her in the pinkness, smelling the sheets and pillowcase you will never wash to hold onto the faintest traces of your daughter.

One day you might pack up the room, but you couldn't face that now. It would be a betrayal of Katie. And you're not one to give up easily, are you, Beatrice? Sometimes you hope you'll enter to find her sitting on the bed, engrossed in a book or magazine. Even if the worst had transpired (but really, death is no longer the worst that can happen to Katie in your frightened heart, is it?) a ghost-child is preferable to no child. Ghosts at least carry memories and hope. There's pitiful consolation in silence and absence.

This morning is particularly hard on you. I understand, Beatrice, I really do. It's June 11, Katie's special day. It's been over a year since you photographed your shadow. The pain, shock, rage and grief doesn't lessen with the days, weeks and months – they worsen as the world revolves onwards. If there had been a body to mourn, it might have been different. But to contemplate the relief of your child's body being found – it's too terrible a thought for any mother to bear.

The sky outside the bedroom window turns a lighter shade of darkness.

Soon the phone will ring. Katie won't be forgotten on her special day. Both sets of grandparents with slightly faded voices, as if Katie's passing had diminished them. An entire generation had now faded quicker than an Instagram fake-retro photograph dissolving into time. Steve's parents had three other grandchildren but they had collapsed when they first received the news. Your parents were more forthright in their blame.

'Why did you want to photograph your shadow? How could you

take your eyes off her? Isn't it a bit weird to want to photograph a shadow?'

Over and over, as if you had done it on purpose. As if you were to blame, as if you should have had your eyes fastened on Katie the entire time. Their self-righteous position hadn't surprised you – you were used to them blaming you for all manner of things. Steve's parents had folded, but yours wanted instant answers, a solution, and a culprit. They demanded a detective-novel scenario with the predator sorted out tidily by the book's conclusion. Not the mangled Ferris wheel of police statements, intrusive journalists, well-meaning friends and horrified family. Real life is so much bleaker, bruised and pointless than in detective fiction. I should know, shouldn't I, Beatrice? I'm the mistress of bruised and bleeding. I've often toyed with writing crime fiction. I've had plenty of experience to offer an audience eager to escape into the suffering and deaths of others. But would I be able to provide a happy ending to satisfy them? Real life doesn't end so neatly for us. We're all hanging on grimly, waiting for our termination and the deaths of our loved ones. We want natural order when it comes to death; we just hope we die before our children. Sorry, Beatrice, I'm getting morbid and boring.

The morning birds must be sounding outside your window. Kookaburras with their jeering, triumphant call. I know what their cry is like as they echo inside my belly. I also feel triumphant and strong, for I've won. It's over a year, and I alone know the truth about Katie and her fate. I know exactly what you will do today, dear Beatrice. I know it even before you know. As if we're joined together in our separate beds, sharing the same nightmares. We are both threads of my sticky web, Beatrice. I know where you will go this morning, my juicy fly. You will walk to the park by the river near your lovely home as mist hangs over the city on this chilly day. You will wear the dark glasses you always wear now and you will stroll to the little park where you last saw your daughter playing over a year ago. You will recall the photographs you took of your laughing, beautiful girl. But I have much better photographs of dear Katie, Beatrice. I would enjoy sitting with you one day, perhaps in Novak's Café, which you often frequent. We could examine the photographs together. I believe they are rather artistic – immodest of me I know – although I did have an excellent subject.

I can already smell your movements, today, Beatrice. I know the direction your thoughts will travel because we're so connected without you realising; your thoughts have become mine. You'll remember the moment you stepped sideways to photograph your shadow a year ago. Yes, I read the entire account in the paper and magazine articles many times.

You're such an artistic, eloquent woman, Beatrice. A true Renaissance soul. I understand your need to photograph illusions, shadows, and spaces. I admire that need, Beatrice, even if your parents don't. Those fools who criticised you for not being more alert, the months-long debate the media whipped up about helicopter-parenting – it was all really shameful. This year as I've watched you navigate the "worst nightmare of any parent". (Not my quote by the way, the papers again. Don't you shudder at their clichés, Beatrice?) I know you'd create more entertaining taglines. You only have to see you to realise how intelligent, stylish and creative you are. Steve had no business taking off with that tart, did he? But I don't like to think about them, Beatrice. He should have stayed with you, but we both know he wasn't worthy.

I stored the coverage about Katie's abduction with my special clippings. Your account was so moving; how you took your eyes off her for only a second, snapped the photo of your shadow, and when you turned back she had vanished. You thought she was playing hide-and-seek in that tiny park. It was a few moments before true terror began to sprout its dark growth between your increasingly frenzied calls: 'Katie! Katie! Answer me. Where are you, Katie?'

You described terror so well. I experienced your panic as I re-lived how you approached strangers, begging them if they had seen a little girl. A man with his son playing with a soccer-ball thought he had seen her heading towards the road. I remember that soccer-ball meathead, and I wasn't surprised he'd given misleading information. He failed to notice me right behind him. The clod was all brawn; his soccer ball had more brain. And I still ruminate over that strange Indian chap you described running towards you, the one who held his arm out and smiled as you pleaded with him to say if he had seen your little girl.

'Not today, my dear, but it will come all-right another day,' was his cryptic reply. Now that was intriguing; I don't remember him at all. But I was rushing, pushing Katie along as we squealed together about the trick we were playing and how delighted you would be.

The Indian man brought me out in the sweats for weeks, thinking he would be an eyewitness against me. But nothing more was reported and I knew I was safe.

You described the young mother with the pram – I had long left by this stage – who hugged you and lent you her mobile to call the police. Not the best day to leave your phone at home, was it, Beatrice? Your oversight gave me extra time to escape. But the print reports couldn't equal the delight of seeing you and Steve making your appeals on television. I recorded them and memorised every word, every heartfelt plea. I knew you were speaking directly to me. It was so touching and significant to be close to you in that way. You've no idea of what it meant to me.

I'm rushing to get ready, to prepare myself, because this day I want to be close to you, Beatrice. I want to be as close to you as I was a year ago. I know it's dangerous, foolhardy and not the sort of risk I'm normally prepared to take. But it paid off for me last year, didn't it? I seized the moment in that impulsive action. In front of all those witnesses – if you could call the meathead and the enigmatic Indian chap witnesses. Men wouldn't notice what was right under their nose. Lucky for me. I'm proud of myself that I wasn't observed, though I realise there's a shadow-side to that truth. We always return to shadows, don't we, Beatrice? What is that William Shakespeare quote? You would know it by heart, but I shall have to look it up later. No time for improving my education on our special day. I want to look my best for you. Even through your grief, you're still the most beautiful woman in this area. I value good looks in others as I was never over-blessed in that department. At school they called me "the runt"; there's a hint of how others perceive me. Katie inherited good looks from you and Steve. But my father was a boar, Beatrice, and my mother a sow – so I inherited only snout, smell and fangs. I'm trying hard to be artistic and think metaphorically, like you, Beatrice. I do hope you appreciate that little touch. I follow all the advice on your photography website. I leave comments on it occasionally for you as "Anon". That name seems to suit me. You refused to add me to your Facebook page and so I needed to make some small connection with you. Silly, isn't it, when we live so near each other that I have to resort to the internet? What does that tell you about modern life, Beatrice? I'll tell you what it says to me: oink. Oink. Oink.

It's a beautiful winter's day. A day most Sydneysiders would call rubbish because the sun isn't blazing. I walk along the river and admire the black swans. Swans are such interesting birds. They mate for life and have incredible devotion. Steve could learn a lot from them, couldn't he, Beatrice? I know I keep going on about it, but he had no right to abandon you in the middle of your worst nightmare. Despite the swan's apparent gentleness and beauty, they are vicious killers at heart. Did you know that, Beatrice? You can learn a lot about humans from nature. Here are a couple of facts you might find of interest. I hope you don't think I'm showing off or being presumptuous, but I've learnt so much from you.

The male swan is the only known male bird to have a penis. Imagine that, Beatrice. He's a devoted father and husband. If he feels his family is threatened, he attacks using the "knucklebone" of his wing. The blow from his beautiful wing is powerful enough to break a man's arm.

Don't you find nature so inspiring, Beatrice? There violence and beauty coexist in such truthful harmony. In our so-called civilisation the foulest deeds are committed for such petty reasons, but there's a logical pattern in wildlife behaviour that mankind lacks.

The sky is silver steel-grey with some black clouds looming. The river is full because of all the recent rainfall: a record Sydney rainfall for this time of year. I wonder if you believe in climate change as I watch the rushing river, feeling soothed by the sound. There's an abundance of ducks, swans, pelicans, magpies and moorhens but only a few people. Just like this time last year, which suits my purpose.

And just like last year, I park my car in the library car park down the road. I had been at the library this morning last year and hadn't intended on taking a river stroll, but then I spotted you and Katie and changed my plans. You didn't see me; you were busy helping Katie select a book. There was quite a scene, if I remember. Katie wanted a teen book you didn't approve of and you were encouraging her to select something more age-appropriate. Katie won, but then she often did with the pair of you. She didn't with me, Beatrice. I set more boundaries than you ever did. I know it's not fashionable to say it, but spare the rod and spoil the child. You were wearing a beautiful skirt from the fashionable Japanese shop in High Street. I saved for months to buy a similar outfit. And you wore a black shirt with boots. But you always look so chic. Katie was wearing a black top, too, with a pretty floral skirt over black track pants. She had been swimming and her hair was still damp.

I had selected a few interesting books to read. I'm trying to improve my general knowledge. Not enough people care about that these days. It's unfashionable to say you're trying to improve yourself now all our celebrities boast about how dumb they are. You, of course, had a few architectural design books, a cookbook, a Swedish crime novel and an English mystery with a most lurid cover – The Body in the Library. That must have been for Steve; I couldn't imagine you being interested in that sort of thing. I saw you reading a book in Novak's once, Beatrice. Some old classic with a beautiful cover, a vintage-wallpaper design. After you left, I was brazen enough to ask the waitress what you'd been reading. She had no idea, and clearly thought I was a nut for asking. Luckily, her friend at the till recognised the novel, Someone at a Distance by Dorothy Whipple in a classic Persephone edition. I ordered all the Persephones I could afford after discovering you liked them. I feel so much joy and pride in my collection, Beatrice. I fondle their spines and elegantly decorated covers, thinking of you doing the same only a few houses away. The words connect our lives in shining threads; the sentences make some sort of meaning out of the nightmare we've been through. You don't know how it feels so orderly and right that we should share the same things. I bought so many books from the Folio Society – and also from our local bookshop Bookworm Lair, thanks to my snooping on your reading habits. Alas, you have expensive tastes and I'm not sure I can always keep up with you.

But in the library a year ago, I had no idea our collections were about to become so similar. And I don't just mean buying The Body in the Library and Swedish crime novels. That little girl scowling at me was about to become part of my other collection. Yes, unlike her mother, Katie noticed me in the library. Later she said she recognised me straight away. Children and swans are so much more observant. It's odd that not many people think to ask them the right questions.

I can hear my breath rattling, dislodging some foul odour inside me. It comes out at times and embarrasses me. As if the secrets and memories inside are contaminating my cells. That's a fanciful thought, but I've had these fears all my life; they've been like bruises within. I press them tenderly and dark and pus-filled ooze tries to soak my brain and make me think of things I don't want to remember.

A couple pass me. I tense, worrying it could be Steve and his new tart but it's just another pair holding hands and laughing. 'Good-morning,' they call. Yes, as you well know, it's that sort of friendly inner-city neighbourhood that everyone calls a village. 'Good-morning,' I reply and my voice must sound normal and not the pus-croak I expect, as the woman says naturally and easily, 'River's full this morning.'

They pass and I overhear the man say, 'I've often see her down here. Mr Reynolds said her daughter drowned in this river, poor lady.' They pass and I'm forgotten. That's not unusual, Beatrice. Most people forget me when they pass. I am Anon. I am memorable only for the death of a child. But nobody could ever forget you.

I watch the river, marvelling at the shadows within it. The tales and stories it could tell, and the one river story I can never forget. You see how similar we are? The river sings the same dark song to us. My husband left me too, Beatrice. I've never told you that before. He couldn't cope with Penny drowning. He blamed me because I wasn't paying attention at the time. I had the pram near the river, I was reading and it was a sunny day. When I woke, it was late afternoon and the pram had rolled. Someone must have released the brake, but he blamed me for it. As if I would forget the brake of my own child's pram! He accused me of always having my head in a book and not being interested in the real world. As if he knew what the real world was!

At this spot I've studied you doing exactly the same thing over the last year, Beatrice. I've thrilled as you've taken photographs of the same locations I've taken with my camera. I've learnt so much from you, Beatrice, and I've never had the chance to thank you. Bless you for noticing the shadows and hearing the river's dark tune.

They dragged this river last year. Most of the neighbourhood offered help but were waved away. It was distressing for everyone. It upset the wildlife terribly with the disruption to their nests. People have such little consideration for wildlife. We think we're the superior species, but really Beatrice – we're the main destroyer.

I was one of those friendly village people who offered to help search for Katie. A young policewoman waved me away; she looked more like an actress playing a cop. They never found Katie's body in the river as everyone had feared. It took me a long time and a lot of money to disguise and soundproof the cellar in my house. I can't remember when I first began the project. My fantasy was one day a child would live there. Of course it wasn't as luxurious as her strawberry-pink palace and didn't the little Madame let me know it! Don't fret, I don't put up with bad manners. I beat all the complaints out of her. And gradually I fixed the room to her satisfaction. I did the best I could with my meagre pay.

You were exactly where I expected you to be at the park near the river; but then I tensed at the unexpected sight of a young man with dark hair on the opposite bank. I hadn't seen him before. A well-built and intense-looking man. Unlike other people, I do notice things, and I watched with mounting apprehension as he spoke on his mobile. Anger was raging within me. I would hate to abandon my plan today on Katie's special day. I watched him warily, but he ignored me as he barked orders into his little machine. An Italian guy arguing with his lover, I surmised. He bored me already. I had long learnt to dismiss others before they rejected me.

I began walking along the bank, savouring the memory of this time last year and fingering the small gift I had for you in my pocket. This date is also the date of my daughter's drowning eight years ago. Quite a coincidence, isn't it, Beatrice? I realised it at once when I first met Katie and saw her admission record. Katie resembled how my Penny would have looked if the pram hadn't gone into the river. My girl would also have been eight today if I had only looked up from the page at the right time.

Today I'm carrying a copy of the book I had been reading that day. The book that engrossed me so much that my husband accused me of negligence. Luckily the jury was divided. It's The Collector by John Fowles, one of my main inspirations for capturing Katie. Books can transform our world, can't they, Beatrice? They can take us to better places and show us how life can be lived when we're merely shadows. Books reveal the truth of existence; they bring all our monsters gently into the light. They give flesh, form and substance to the shadows of our poor tragic theatre of life. With books, we are the audience, the writer and the book itself. We are no longer Anon; we are active in the play. Imagination is a wonderful thing.

I saw you and was taken aback for a second. You weren't wearing your usual dark glasses and Steve was with you. You wore a light trench coat and you were being assisted by Steve with his arm around you. He had the gall to touch you after all his rejection. After leaving you for that stupid girl. Why the hell was he touching you? Why would you let him touch you, Beatrice?

Steve had no call to be here on this important date. I could hear the sound of a father playing ball with his son in the park. I felt disorientated as if some strange dream was being replayed.

I moved towards you, which was idiotic, I admit, as Steve being there had ruined all my plans. I wouldn't be able to give you the book. Coming towards me was the Indian man you had described from a year before. He headed straight at me and seemed to have some sympathy in his face. He must know about the drowning, I thought. Too many people still remembered it. I went to move past him but he blocked my way and said gently, 'It will come right, today.'

Looking back, I must have imagined that because he continued walking quickly into the distance. I was drawn towards you as I had imagined a million times. I knew I should leave but I couldn't. I had to get you to see me.

I walked towards you and you turned and looked at me with eyes filled with anguish. You had lost so much weight, Beatrice; I hate to say this, but your year of mourning had taken your looks. I didn't have looks to lose in my years of grief, Beatrice. There is consolation in being plain. Although Katie has brought a beauty, peace and joy to my face with her innocence and light.

I held out the book, hoping you would understand the message inside. The coded words meant only for you and me; our private language. The sentences as meaningful and meaningless as the skywriting in the clouds this day last year. I had to be quick as Katie would need to be fed. Her favourite television show would be starting and we loved to watch it together. We love to do everything together now.

'Mrs Godfrey,' you said in a harsh voice. You did remember me! My elation made me more foolhardy. I had only been a junior teacher at Katie's preschool. I had no idea you would remember my name, which goes to show I did matter. I pushed the book into your hands. Steve was saying something but his words were white-noise behind your next shouted sentence. I still wake in agony that you could speak to me with such contempt.

'Where have you put her?'

You were holding onto me, screaming it repeatedly. Steve was restraining me and the young Italian man at the river bank was running towards us with the soccer father. Both were waving cards in the air. 'Police!' they called and, 'Hold her! '

It was all very dramatic and overblown like a silly American television show.

I knew then it was over. I had known it from the moment I saw the expression on the Indian man as he passed.

But I won't tell them where you are, Katie, and they still haven't worked it out. I've been interrogated for hours. Everyone is getting very angry and very panicky. Some of the psycho people speak very nicely and use all their tricks to try to connect me. They think they're expert in shadows but they just push me further where I need to be now. My mind has drifted to a river with its mumblings and gurgling. I'm always at peace when I meditate on the river. It took from me and gave to me. In the belly of terror there is always an eye of silence and peace if you can open your mind enough. I'm now following its blinking and its laneways because somewhere inside the river's stomach there is Penny, waiting patiently. I follow the river's ripples and tune when the police, social-workers and shadow experts ask their questions. I see a sodden baby's jacket and the face of my gorgeous Penny, surrounded by the black swans attacking her when they found her near their nest.

My lips stay sealed. My memory is filled with swans and the majestic flapping of their wings as they beat to death all who threaten their young. The harsh snapping of beaks and the call of the children as they play along the river bank, half-lost in shadows and trees, memories and dreams. Their soothing voices as they call to each and the sound of a pram rushing towards the river as I lie, drowsy and safe. The flapping pages of a book, flapping with the swan's wings, the knucklebone wing smashing the book's skull to pieces and the precious words spilling out like ants escaping to form the meaning of my life and ending my own Penny's life.

The shadow experts try to get me to remember that moment but all I see is the river. I look deep, deep into its depths. But I don't see my reflection. I only see you, Beatrice. I only ever see your beautiful face smiling up at me. In every mirror all I see is you.

One last admission before I press the delete button, written under my false Facebook profile on the laptop they have loaned me.

The answers are all in the book, if Beatrice only thinks to open it and read. Did she even take The Collector with her or is it too lowbrow for Ms Beatrice Smartypants? On the endpaper I've drawn the map, revealed Katie's room and where its entrance is concealed in the kitchen. The entire universe is hidden behind words, isn't it? If we have the curiosity and intelligence to care and follow their trail we get our answers to this shadow-play.

You must be getting very hungry, my darling Katie. And we've missed our favourite show. Hopefully they'll let me out of this cell soon.

Delete.

2013

Bunyip's Last Wish

Candice Graham

I hold onto a spindly ti-tree for support. I'm standing on a clump of dirt and dead grass that could easily give way if I shift my weight in the wrong direction. My dad often jokes that I inherited my swan-neck from my mum; I try to stretch it out as far as possible to see where Mandy was pointing, deep within the gully. 'Can you see it, Kelly?' she whispers. I scan the shadowy creek water. Immediately I know why she called us to a halt. My mum told me never to swear; she said that swearing is just a way out for people who have poor vocabularies. But I swear now. The ti-tree lets out a warning crack under my weight.

'I'm going down there,' I announce. Technically we shouldn't be here, taking a shortcut through my neighbour's land. I capture mixed words of protest before Mandy's voice is drowned out by my footsteps crunching dried leaves. The air cools as I descend. Mosquitoes and other small bugs float over the stagnant water, which sends a chill through my plastic gumboots. I hear Mandy moving about above me, occasionally sending down trails of dirt as she tries to find the easiest path. The number of flies increases as I get closer. Eventually Mandy appears beside me and pinches her nose shut.

The creature is roughly our size, maybe shorter if it were standing upright. Its long, thin arms and legs have oversized joints. The hands and feet are hidden deep within the mud. Its belly is massive and bulging, the skin slimy and pale grey with dark splodges. Its bulbous head is jutted forward, completely hiding the creature's neck. It has a snout that is half-covered in a tough nose, a bit like a koala's. The nostrils are just slits. The jaw is clenched shut but it looks large enough to be filled with rows of sharp teeth. Like a leaf on a stem, the ears start as tubes before flaring out widely. It has large silver eyes with frog-like pupils. While we gesture at its bizarre features, the eyes continue to stare vacantly at the opposite wall of the gully. It is unmistakably dead.

The reason is obvious to both of us. Two spears penetrate the creature, one in the belly and a fatal blow aimed at the top of its spine. Unlike the naturally falling branches, the spears are smooth and hand-crafted. Insects gravitate towards the carcass, eagerly picking at its wounds. This, coupled with the submerged body parts and the dark walls of the gully, create the impression that the earth is trying to reclaim the creature and conceal it from prying human eyes. 'Who did this?' I ask. I pull on the spear jabbed into its stomach. The creature jerks, sending the insects up in a furious wave and causing the release of an additional foul odour. The spear will not come loose. Mandy has had enough of the insects and the smell.

We climb back up and perch on a fallen ghost gum. 'It's a Bunyip,' Mandy declares.

'Bunyips aren't real,' I say, but the strange creature could be one for all I know…

'My uncle Jim reckons they're real. They're just good at hiding. He said you're cursed if you kill a Bunyip. But if you catch the killer, the Bunyip's spirit will grant you a wish.'

'Wishes? That's genies, not Bunyips.'

Mandy often embellishes stories but she looks adamant, 'Wouldn't it be great to get a wish?'

I do want to find the killer… We pinky swear to keep the Bunyip a secret until we get the wish. Our summer holidays have o□ered very little amusement, so Mandy is delighted by the prospect of this new game. 'We could wish for two ponies!' she exclaims as we start making our way across the empty paddocks. The long grass itches my bare legs. As I stop to scratch I notice something metal catch the light. Thinking it is a twenty cent piece, I pick up the silver disc. 'What is it?' Mandy calls.

'Our first clue.'

We take a shortcut along the back of a dairy farm, rich with the smell of manure. The drought means all of the mud has dried out and cracked, making it easy to walk over. I feel sad when we reach a rotting shed. Loads of tiny kittens live in the shed and they cry out for our attention. The first time I came to this dairy farm with my parents I ran excitedly towards the kittens, but the owner grabbed me by the wrist and got me to really look at them. They are diseased. All of the feral cats here pass diseases to their children so they never really stand a chance of growing up healthy.

'Something just went past me,' says Mandy and a kitten hisses before ducking back into the shed. As we stand still I hear a sharp thwack against the timber panels. Faint giggling comes from behind a stack of rusted tyre rims. 'Jessie Thomas,' I call, 'I will skin you and your brothers alive!' Three boys emerge from behind the tyres. They have scratched knees and their clothes are dirty and grass-stained. The youngest is blonde-haired Cody, who wipes snot from his nose onto his sleeve. In the middle, with mousy-coloured hair, is Dwayne. He looks like a ferret: the nasty kind that bites. The tallest and eldest is Jessie Thomas, who was firing the projectiles. He passes the slingshot to Dwayne and reaches into his pocket. 'Not if I skin you first,' he says, holding up a pocket knife.

These are the Barclay Boys. The brothers are well known pests in our town. I've seen Jessie Thomas kicking down fence posts, throwing stones at windows and stealing. Jessie is in the year above us at school, but I hear he often skips class to sleep on the roof. Dwayne is in the year below us and Cody has just finished prep. All three are known for starting fights with students and teachers. Over the years at least one of them tends to have broken bones in a cast. The holidays make matters worse; in boredom they get more destructive. Mandy grabs my arm and pulls me along, 'We don't have time to waste on you!'

Leaving the Barclay Boys far behind, we reach the town centre and enter the small public library. But the only paperback I can find on Bunyips is a little kid's picture book. Our only other clue is the silver disc I found yesterday in Tucker's paddock. One side of the disc is bare and there is a small hole at the top. The other side has a word etched onto the metal. Fido. It's a dog tag. Mr Tucker only has one dog and its name is Billy. It's old and smells bad. Most people in our town own dogs. But I have no idea who owns a dog named Fido or what it looks like.

We spend most of the day looking for as many dogs as we can find. Whilst old Phil sits reading his newspaper I stop to pat his Jack Russell but the name Fred is written on its collar. The grocer has a dog called Sam in the yard behind his shop. Mrs Magdany has two Pomeranians in her front yard but she calls them Princess and Precious; certainly not Fido. As we pass dog-owners Mandy takes a new approach to our lack of information about Bunyips. 'We're doing a school project,' she lies, 'Do you know anything about Bunyips?'

The answers we receive vary considerably... Phil suggests they are big and covered in scales, with yellow eyes and sharp teeth to eat fish. The grocer says they are like horses that can swim underwater and eat seaweed. Mrs Magdany replies they are furry, with big tusks and horns and love to howl at the moon. An older girl from our school says they're like birds, with a beak and feathers and chicken legs. 'Sucks you have homework, I don't remember having to do that project...' she adds. We are also told they look like a dog with webbed feet, a hippopotamus, or like a platypus. 'For a town with a Bunyip in it, nobody seems to know anything about them!' says Mandy irritably.

The General Store is blissfully air-conditioned; the sudden change in temperature causes my skin to get goose bumps. Mandy rummages for the cheapest icy poles at the bottom of the freezer while I bug Leslie with questions about who buys dog food. I know most of the names she mentions, but falter at "Melissa Kennedy".

'Don't you mean Melissa Barclay?' I ask when Leslie mentions the Barclay Boys' mother.

'No, she legally changed it,' says Leslie looking somewhat flustered discussing this topic with me. 'What about her sons?' I ask. Leslie shifts uncomfortably, presumably wrestling with how much to tell me. 'She said they could decide for themselves, when they're older.' But she also adds, 'Those boys will end up in prison too no doubt. They're always stealing from me.' Her face is slightly flushed now, but with my hopes raised I try for one more question. 'Do you know the name of their dog?'

'It's called Buckley. Stay away from their dog, Kelly. Mr Barclay use to kick it and throw stones at it. It's completely vicious.'

That night I dream that the Bunyip is angry and has decided to eat me. I must have been calling out in my sleep, because my dad nudges me awake. He gives me a hug and asks if I want to talk about it. 'No,' I say trying to forget the dream. But I don't want him to leave just yet either. So I show him the dog tag and ask if he knows anyone who owns a dog named Fido. 'Fido?' he asks, surprised. 'Yeah, I know a dog named Fido.'

'Who does it belong to?' I ask enthusiastically. I hate the name that comes as his response.

The sun is harsh once again. We find out he is drinking in the pub, but it takes a while for him to come outside to talk to us. Dan Barclay. He looks utterly confused by our presence. 'We found this,' I say giving him the dog tag, 'and just wanted to give it back to you. Dad said it belonged to your dog.'

'Huh. Didn't know it was missing,' he responds, 'I worked with ya dad the other day. I don't think he likes me much. He won't come out drinking with us, Kelly. You should tell him to be more sociable, eh?' I don't blame my dad for being unsociable; already I can feel myself becoming agitated in this man's presence. His lazy voice, his stench of booze and cigarettes, his ruffed up shirt and the stubble on his chin. The way his facial features resemble his incarcerated brother. Everything about Dan Barclay irritates me. He nods his thanks and turns back to the pub.

'Before you go, Mr Barclay, could you tell us anything about Bunyips?' I ask, watching him closely. The dog tag was right next to the scene of the crime; he has to know something. But he reacts like everybody else, 'Aren't they green monsters that live in billabongs?' Dan takes my disappointed face as a challenge. 'But stay away from Bunyips, Kelly. They're evil. They steal small children and drag them away to the water and drown them. They'll eat you up.' Dan seems to revel in Mandy's discomfort. 'Did you know there are cave drawings about the Bunyip?' he continues, 'at Dead Man's Peak. But you better not go there. A black panther escaped from a circus and has been living in the bush there ever since.' Dan laughs loudly, then causes us to flinch when he yells, 'Oi! You lads sulking back there! Get over here and say hello to your uncle!'

The Barclay Boys have been watching us, but they look reluctant to come closer. Dan is on them like a predator on prey. He brushes Mandy and I aside as he goes for Jessie and captures him with one muscular arm in a headlock. 'Don't!' I yell but instantly regret drawing Dan's attention. 'Oh go home and cry to your mother,' he spits. Mandy grabs my arm as tears swell in my eyes. Next Dan hisses in Jessie's ear, 'You don't visit me anymore. Haven't visited ya dad. Your mum lets you walk all over her, doesn't she? Now that your dad's not around to give you a firm hand.' As Jessie struggles the older Barclay laughs. 'You're so slow. No wonder you keep losing at fights,' he teases. Dan lets go and Jessie crumples onto the ground. Mandy and I leave a wide berth as Dan re-enters the pub and calls out for another beer. Jessie Thomas turns his dark eyes on me. He was completely humiliated in front of us. That means we are the ones he will take it out on. I really hate these Barclays.

I shove two water bottles and some muesli bars in my backpack. I find my old compass too, just in case. But really there are only two directions for Dead Man's Peak: up and down. The paddocks at the edge of town are wild and overgrown. Mandy and I have a hard time avoiding blackberry bushes. The bushland is a sprawling mixture of lightly shaded gums and smaller deep green trees. Pittosporums, I think, remembering the way my mum pronounced it. The pittosporums have bright orange seed capsules about the size of marbles. No doubt they make perfect sling shot material for the Barclay Boys. Snakes could easily hide under the thick layers of bark and leaf litter; we stomp our feet to keep them at bay. Finding makeshift paths becomes increasingly difficult, the boneseed bushes grow in big bunches that are too thick to climb through. I pull out some baby shoots of the noxious weed in protest but my efforts are disrupted when Mandy tightly grabs my shoulder in alarm.

'Kelly, I just saw something,' she whispers. I consider making a joke about the escaped panther. Then I hear the birdsong change around me. The Noisy Miners live up to their name as they set off a chorus of alarm calls. There must be a predator nearby. I look out towards the bush and fear sweeps through me. There is something running. Something big and black. I see the dark shadow bound upwards in a fluid motion. It's low to the ground and streamlined. As it ducks and weaves through the undergrowth I fail to capture a good look at it. I tell myself there is no way the legend about the escaped panther can be true. But a little voice in my head says: last week you didn't believe in Bunyips either; remember how that turned out? The Noisy Miners are beginning to calm down; the predator must have moved on. 'It was just a wallaby,' I lie to Mandy. If we turn back now we will never find answers.

Now every unusual noise makes me flinch. 'Look, I think that's it!' shrieks Mandy and I feel like telling her to keep her voice down. There are boulders and shrubs at the top and then a sharp cliff face perfect for long lost Aboriginal drawings. Mandy and I eagerly scan the rock. Nothing. I reach the last corner and the cliff forms a shallow cave. Just as I think our journey was pointless I look up towards the roof. There are drawings! 'We found it!' yells Mandy. The drawings show three stick figures standing from tallest to shortest, each holding a long spear. In the next scene, the stick figures are confronted by a monster with big teeth and claws. Two of the stick figures throw their spears and hit the creature. The drawings then show an excessive amount of blood gushing from the monster which slumps down, defeated. The stick figures cheer in success, the smallest one holding its spear in the air, the other two raising their arms high. Mandy is bouncing in excitement as she moves from scene to scene but I shake my head and touch the drawing, 'It's crayon.'

Laughter erupts from above us. Boy's laughter. 'You might as well come out now,' I call. Mandy looks up in surprise as the Barclay Boys emerge. Trailing behind them is a large black figure which I realise is no phantom panther but rather their muscular dog, Buckley. With a good amount of apprehension I see that the dog is unrestrained. Mandy steps behind me as Buckley lets out some ear-splitting barks. Jessie rests his hand on the dog's back as it growls at us. He has a victorious grin on his stupid face and his brothers are still chuckling.

'You like our artwork, do ya?' he asks gleefully. 'Worth the trip, wasn't it?' I sense that my face is turning red and I feel angry at myself. Of course they overheard us talking to their uncle… and how could they resist playing a little practical joke? Mandy and I had come all this way for nothing. Dan Barclay probably just lied about Dead Man's Peak for his own amusement.

I am overwhelmed with hatred for all the Barclays. I could punch Jessie Thomas in the head; maybe that would wipe away his ugly smirk. Instead I try to keep my voice controlled as I yell a warning at him, 'You keep that dog under control, Jessie Thomas, or else it will get put down.' Cody doesn't like that comment one bit; he nudges Jessie to take hold of Buckley's collar. 'Let's get out of here,' mutters Mandy. We start our way down the slope as the boys jeer at us with their best taunts.

Mandy and I trek back in silence. We are almost out of the bushland when Mandy shrieks in pain behind me. Thinking Buckley may have gotten loose and followed us I turn around in panic. Mandy is waving her hand about frantically and I realise she has been bitten by a bull ant.

I find a patch of bracken fern and rip off the tip of a young shoot. 'Here,' I say taking Mandy's hand in mine, 'The bracken fern sap will help reduce the stinging.' I put as much as I can over her swollen skin. Her tears start to ease up as she watches me.

'Who taught you that?' she asks gently.

'My mum.' I let go and Mandy withdraws her hand quietly. We look towards our home town as a gentle breeze lifts strands of our hair.

'Today really sucked,' says Mandy. I couldn't agree more.

The next day Mandy has given up. She pines for the lost wish, 'Imagine a lifetime supply of chocolate...' It is another scorching day and we both stink of sunscreen. We have no money to spend or clues to chase up, so we walk without purpose. 'I bet the adults would wish for an end to this drought,' she muses. My whole body is tense from another bad night's sleep. 'You never asked what I would wish for,' I mutter and she blushes. We part ways and I head towards home before abruptly changing direction. The rock drawings... The Barclay Boys heard we were looking for Bunyip drawings. But we never mentioned the spears!

Their weatherboard house is rotting on one side. The yard's overgrown and the fences are vandalised. I feel sick looking at this house. The Barclay Boys and their mum probably aren't home. But there he is, Buckley, slumbering in the shady front yard. A long chain trails from his neck to a metal post in the ground. In the drawings the smallest stick figure kept his spear. Cody probably didn't want his spear to get stuck like the others. It could be here somewhere. I slowly walk down the gravel driveway hoping the cicadas and birdsong mask the sound of my footsteps from Buckley. Their backyard is messy; the boys must collect odd bits of junk from the tip. Near the back steps there are wood shavings... There it is! The spear is resting against the wall on the patio. I can see the kitchen through the windows. Heart racing, I focus on the wish until finally my trembling hand grasps onto the spear. Then I let the panic overtake me and flee. Buckley wakes and strains against his chain, barking furiously as I run past. I keep on running until his barks are faint echoes in the distance.

If anyone saw me with a spear near the Bunyip they'd get the wrong idea, so I hide it behind the geraniums near our veranda before ducking under the fence into Tucker's paddock. When I reach the tallest hill, breathing heavily, I realise I'm not alone. Standing in the middle of the field is an enormous bull. In rushing to get to the Bunyip I had forgotten my usual caution. I knew Tucker owned a bull, but he always kept it in an isolated back paddock. This paddock was typically empty, though occasionally Tucker used it for his herd of female cattle. The bull had its horns removed as a calf. But that doesn't change the fact it could strike me with its massive head or trample me to death. Beneath his smooth dark grey and black coat the bull's thickset body is full of twitching muscles. My mind races for an escape route. The bull jabs the ground with his hoof and snorts. The roadside. That will mean he has to travel the furthest distance uphill whilst I run downhill. I bolt for it. I hear the bull call out behind me and its hooves thud against the earth. I'm sliding downhill as he gathers momentum. My legs are jelly as I falter at the fence line, trying to find a way over or through, dropping to the ground. It's metres away as I roll under the fence onto the dirt road. The bull tries to slow to a stop but hits into the fence with its shoulder. He snorts at me and calls out again. Rattling on the fence is a warning sign: 'Bull in Paddock – Keep Out.'

Over dinner dad mentions the bull was moved into the front paddock for easy transport after being sold. The new owners picked him up this afternoon. I ask to play outside but dad won't let me out after dark. Once the house is silent I get out of bed and secretly pull on a cardigan and my gumboots. The gully is dark and the smell is terrible. It is rotting. Insects, ravens and foxes have been enjoying a carrion feast, gradually returning the Bunyip to myth and legend. My chance at obtaining the wish has been disappearing… But I have the answer now.

'Spirit of the Bunyip. I want you to grant me a wish in exchange for naming the one that killed you.' The glossed-over eyes are giant silver orbs reflecting the moon. My heart thumps heavily against my chest. It was the tallest stick figure that pierced the Bunyip's neck and spine on the fabricated rock drawings. 'The one that killed you was Jessie Thomas Barclay.' A soft breeze passes over the still water and through the gully. I continue breathing slowly in and out, nauseated from the smell, aware of the mud clinging to my knees and the tainted water in my boots. The Bunyip is silent. 'It takes more than that, doesn't it?' I ask quietly. The Bunyip stares vacantly at me. 'I know what you need,' I whisper. I always suspected it would come to this. 'Revenge.'

I can do this. Before the Bunyip disappears, for that precious wish, I can do this. There is only one suitable way to enact revenge. Our house looks so dark without any of the lights on. I reach the veranda and start searching behind the geraniums when a male voice startles me. 'If you're looking for the spear, I took it.' Dad is standing on the porch. 'A spear is a weapon, Kelly. It's not a toy to play games with.'

'It's evidence!' I retort. Dad has to give me back that spear. I decide to break my pinky swear. 'Mandy and I found something on Tucker's land. A Bunyip in the creek. Only it was dead. It had been stabbed. It was Jessie Thomas. He and his brothers made spears and Jessie killed the Bunyip. That last spear is proof that he did it!' My dad lets out a heavy sigh and using a very adult tone he says, 'Kelly, Jessie Thomas didn't kill a Bunyip.'

His judgemental expression causes my chest to ache. 'Yes he did! I know it!'

'No you don't, Kelly, listen–'

'No you listen! I know it! I've always known it! HE'S A KILLER!' I hate the sound of my own voice; it breaks down into a shrill wail and I know I sound like a child. My father looks wounded. As he moves towards me I see some tears flow down the crevasses of his sun-worn face, like rain filling ravines after a long drought. He kneels before me in the dust and utters the words I dread to hear. 'Kelly, it's not a Bunyip.'

'Yes it is,' I breathe between heavy sobs, 'and Jessie Thomas killed it. I can show it to you.' He gently shakes his head, his right hand coming up to stoke my cheek. Everything melts away; all of my imagined maturity, my careful planning and my evidence gathering. I feel so out of place standing here in the backyard wearing my gumboots and pyjamas during the early hours of a Tuesday morning. 'One of Tucker's cows gave birth to a deformed calf last week. The mother nearly died in the creek. Tucker called on me and another few guys to help get her out and back to the herd.'

'Then Jessie killed the newborn,' I weep and he shakes his head.

'No Kelly, it was stillborn. It never lived.' I had been chasing a wish that never existed. It occurs to me that there was no sign of blood coming from the Bunyip's wounds. Because it never had a heartbeat. My body deflates in despair. I had always known it in my heart: I could never bring her back. My mind is flooded with images, sweeping hair that forms waves over slender shoulders, arms scooping me into a warm hug, her laughter and kind eyes. Every part of her is gone forever. I want it to stop here, but dad grips my shoulder. 'Kelly, you shouldn't hate Jessie Thomas. What happened wasn't his fault.'

I stubbornly wipe away my tears, 'Yes it was! It was Jessie's fault and Dwayne's fault and Cody's fault and Melissa's fault! It didn't have anything to do with her! Why did she have to… why did she have to die? They should have died!'

'You don't really believe that, Kelly. Melissa Kennedy didn't ask to be beaten by her husband. She couldn't watch him repeatedly raise his hand against her young sons. She had to get out and she knew your mum was a strong woman, the kind that helps those who need it. Your mother was trying to protect Melissa and her sons. Do you understand, Kelly? She never would have wanted you to hate those boys.' The tears come too fast, I can't wipe them back anymore. Dad hugs me for a very long time.

Dad tells me to apologise to Jessie, so the next day I spend hours waiting, sitting on the ledge of the gutter with my back towards their house. The building my mother died in. The boys are surprised to see me. Jessie calms Buckley as we walk down the drive together and ushers his suspicious brothers inside. But I can't walk into that kitchen. Instead Jessie and I sit on the back step. He listens as I confess that I was thinking of taking revenge. He seems unfazed by my story but slightly unnerved by my tears. After a long silence he begins talking about his dad and that night.

'We were loading up your mum's Jeep when he came home early from the pub. Dwayne and Cody were in the car already but I was too slow. He found me in the kitchen, saw mum helping me with my bags. When she screamed your mum came running in…' I realise he doesn't need to tell me this part. I know my mum. Just like dad said, she would try to protect Melissa and the boys, even if it meant putting herself in danger. I love and hate her for that. 'The whole time I didn't do anything,' Jessie continues, 'I just stood there… I hate myself.' But I don't hate him anymore.

'Can I come over again tomorrow?' I ask. Jessie looks uncomfortable. Maybe I am pushing too hard; I have been avoiding them for so long. But he nods his approval, 'Okay.' He walks me to the gate and Buckley barks again, baring his teeth and pulling on his chain. Jessie sees my nervous glance and approaches Buckley without fear. 'He's not a bad dog, really,' he says, putting his hand on the dog's head. 'He was just treated badly.'

I feel like crying again. Instead I smile, wave goodbye, and promise myself that I will make it into that kitchen before summer's end. School will be starting again soon and I'm sure the Barclay Boys will need a friend to keep them out of trouble.

Amy's Sandal

Judith Bridge

AMY'S STOUT BODY MOVES FORWARDS AT SPEED. HER BIG TOE, HOWEVER, makes friends with an obstacle in its dusty path and stops for a chat. Amy lands face-first in the wheat stubble, mouth open in surprise, inadvertently welcoming hot, crunchy dirt onto her teeth and tongue.

She looks at her toe, and her mouth widens into a black O of dismay. Half of her big toenail is sticking out at a scary angle. There'll be hell to pay when she gets home. She's not allowed to play in the paddocks wearing sandals; she's supposed to wear closed-in shoes. Dad says there are snakes. Amy lets loose a few sobs from the pain and anticipated scolding but remembers that big girls don't cry and hiccups to a stop, then tentatively flicks the skew toenail. Although it hurts, she can't resist doing it again, sucking the end of one brown plait as she teases the nail and winces.

The obstacle stands up proudly in the dull earth. Probably a bit of brick, Amy thinks, there are always lumps of brick in the paddocks. Leftovers from when giants built their castles in Carnakarra, which were then destroyed when the dinosaurs came.

She pulls the obstacle from its bed. It isn't a brick but a very small, partly gold-coloured, partly dirt-coloured sandal. Definitely a sandal, from the time when the Japanese invaded Australia during the Second Whirl War. A young Japanese girl lived in this paddock in a rice-paper house, which you could eat when you finished living in it. The girl's feet had been bound from when she was a baby, so she couldn't run away from her Dad, who beat her every day with one of those big brooms people use to smack the dirt out of carpets. She was forbidden to run around outside in her sandals, just like Amy, because of snakes and probably dragons, too.

Not that she could really run, with her tiny feet, so she more or less stumbled around. The Japanese girl's sandals were not made of rubber, but gold, because she was so small and light that she had to weigh herself down every day or she would float off into the sky.

One day, when the Japanese girl's Dad was away slicing peoples' heads off with his sword, she stumbled outside in her golden sandals and tried to run away from home. She became dehydrated and disorientated in the heat because she had forgotten to take a water bottle and wasn't wearing sunscreen or a hat and her kimono was two hundred layers thick, tied in a series of intricate knots that she couldn't untie by herself. Her heavy kimono dragged her into the loose dust and all the way down to China, where she bought a bamboo hat and stumbled around happily for the rest of her life.

Like Cinderella, the Japanese girl left behind one golden sandal that slipped off her foot as she hurtled eagerly towards China and away from Carnakarra and her horrible Dad.

When the girl's Dad returned from battle, his sword bloody, smiling from killing so many innocence he couldn't find his daughter anywhere. So he committed hari-krishna on himself in the stomach because he had to save his face.

Amy knows all about Japanese history from her best friend Miyu, who has a Japanese Dad and a Hopeless Mum. Miyu Watanabe lives on the farm next door, which is a twenty-five minute bike ride away. Dad says their farm's not good for growing anything except rocks and half-breed morons. Sometimes, during the school holidays, Amy helps Miyu sell melons from the Watanabes' roadside stall, which is her second favourite thing in the world. Dad says what kind of fool would grow melons in the driest place in the world?

But Amy knows that the Sahara Desert, in Africa, is drier than Carnakarra. In the Sahara Desert, you can't cry, even if you really want to, because the sun burns the tears up before they fall out of your eyes. Geography is her favourite thing in the world.

Amy turns the small, heavy sandal over in her hands. Dirt rubs off and more and more gold appears. The sandal is bumpy. Around the curve of the toe, there are a few sharp sticking-out bits, like the edge of a lid when you take it off the tin with a can-opener.

Hopping home on her good foot, she cradles the sandal carefully. Dad is out. With a sigh of relief, she hops the sandal over to the kitchen tap. The dirt washes away, and she holds the bright gold sandal up to the streaky window. The colour makes her shiver with happiness.

She hops to her bedroom, wraps the sandal in an old T-shirt and places it in her hidey hole. She's not allowed to keep secrets in her room, but there's one place Dad doesn't know about.

Dad says Amy's toenail will go black and drop off. Amy squirms with excitement. She can't wait to show Miyu her toe and the sandal. Miyu will be the only other person in the whole wide world who gets to see the sandal.

But Dad sees it too, a month later. When Amy returns home after her daily paddock exploration, he is waiting for her at the kitchen table, his face scrunched up with anger. The gold sandal stands pert and proud on the table, glowing softly into the amber dregs of the whisky bottle. Amy's heart thrums, her breathing becomes shallow and fast, her forehead burns hot. Dad has discovered her hidey hole.

She can't bear the unfairness of Dad anymore, not for another minute. Miyu's parents don't search her room or make her keep secrets. Snatching the sandal from the table, Amy roars in a deep voice that she didn't know she had. Dad lunges for her, but Amy is quicker today and slams him in the face with the sandal. One of the sharp bits slides into the soft space above Dad's eyebrow, and he slumps to the floor. Blood pools around his head.

Amy calls the police, as she has been taught to do in an emergency. Their number is on the fridge. Then she mixes up a big jug of lemon cordial with ice because the police will be thirsty in this heat.

Amy has to go to court and explain what happened. Miyu's Hopeless Mum makes her a new dress for her court appearance, yellow with blue flowers. She wants Amy to call her Denise, but Amy can't bring herself to call a grown-up by their first name, so they settle on Mrs W, short for Mrs Watanabe. Mrs W gives Amy's damp hand a squeeze before Amy takes the stand.

When asked questions, Amy explains to the judge that she isn't allowed to tell secrets, but the judge says that it's ok to tell now. The judge looks very sad when Amy reveals her secrets.

When it's all over, Mrs W takes Amy to the W's farm and tells the reporters outside the house 'no comment', but they write a story anyway.

ABUSED WOMAN MURDERS FATHER, GOES FREE

Amy Henderson, a forty-year-old woman with a mental age of seven, murdered her father last Friday. Judge Sally Morrison was moved to tears when Amy revealed the extent of physical and psychological abuse she had suffered at the hands of her father since early childhood. Following the special court session, Amy who has no living relatives was released into the custody of temporary guardians.

Judge Morrison said it would be inappropriate for Amy to be detained in either an adult prison or a juvenile detention centre. Amy will instead be monitored by a probation officer and a psychologist and is not considered to be a danger to society.

The sandal is removed from Dad's head, and the police return it to Amy at the W's house. She's told it's not actually a sandal but a gold nugget, and it's worth a lot of money. Mrs W takes Amy and Miyu to the library in town and shows them pictures of other gold nuggets, including a hand-shaped one called "The Hand of Faith". Miyu finds some photographs of nuggets which are named after the people who found them.

Mrs W signs the bottom of the library form as Amy's guardian, and the librarian gives her a membership card. Amy takes out books about far away countries. Miyu says if Amy's smile was any bigger, her face would split open. They crack up laughing.

Mr W explains to Amy that she can sell her nugget or keep it in a safe at the bank or put it in a museum so lots of people can enjoy it. The decision is hers. Amy and Miyu discuss the options for days. They decide on the museum option. The nugget needs a name, and Mrs W suggests "Amy's Sandal". Everyone likes that idea, so the museum makes up a plaque with the name (Amy's Sandal), where it was found (Carnakarra, Western Australia) and who found it (Henderson, Amy).

Life is very different at the W's and Amy feels good, yes siree. No-one goes into her room without permission. It's not her job to cook dinner every night and wash up afterwards. But she washes up anyway because she wants to. Miyu dries the dishes, and they mess around but not too much or they might drop something.

The Ws ask Amy if she'd like to look after the roadside stall while Miyu is at school and Amy says would I ever! She's in charge of stacking the melons in pyramids, which are in Egypt, and using the till. Mr W gives her a mobile phone so she can call the house if she needs help. Amy takes her library books to the stall and learns all about the world when she's not serving customers.

Mrs W sees Amy taking a pill and asks if she can see the packet. Amy gives it to her and when Mrs W realises what the pills are, tears well in her eyes. She tells Amy she doesn't need to take them anymore. But I have to stop the babies, Amy replies and Mrs W says there won't be any babies now. They throw the packet in the rubbish bin together. Amy's glad because it was hard to remember to take a pill every single day. Mrs W has a little cry after that. Amy tells her big girls don't cry, but Mrs W says sometimes they do, and Amy can cry any time she feels sad. But Amy doesn't ever feel sad with the W's because they have a happy farm.

After many, many months of paperwork, Amy inherits Dad's sad farm. Mr W explains to Amy that she can sell her farm or keep it. The decision is hers. Amy and Miyu discuss the options for days. They decide on the selling option. The farm fetches a huge amount of money, because prospective buyers think they will find another gold sandal in the dirt. Amy thinks this is funny because she knows that the Japanese girl from the Second Whirl War must have taken the other sandal with her in order to buy the bamboo hat and live happily ever after.

The money from the sale of the farm goes into Amy's newly created bank account, and she can withdraw money whenever she likes. She buys a world globe that spins so fast it makes her eyes go funny. Amy tells the Ws that she wants to pay for them all to go on holiday to the Sahara Desert so that they can try to cry, even if they're not sad. But maybe she'll wait until she's a bit older.

Mrs W says that Amy has made a very wise decision, and Amy's smile is so wide that Miyu says she can see the sun shining through her teeth.

Hard Knox

Also won Best Investigative Award

TJ Hamilton

Life, for me, was never meant to be easy. I wasn't born easy. Within twenty minutes of becoming part of this world, I was put into rehab because my mum was a junkie. My dad has been in prison since I was a baby, and my older brother died years ago during a botched armed hold-up. I have been a ward of the state longer than I belonged to someone, and I've had the added pleasure of growing up in a suburb called Redfern – hell on earth. Life, for me, was never meant to be easy.

As I stand, staring at the lifeless body of the mother who caused me all this grief, I know for certain that Lady Luck and I will never be friends – not even close.

I look to one end of the street and back to the other, hoping to find someone who can tell me what happened, but it's 2am. No sane person would be on the street at this hour.

I don't bother checking her pulse. I know she's dead. Her skin is a ruddy grey and the pool of thick, dark blood around her head is a fairly good indication that she's not about to spring up any time soon.

Sighing, I grab my phone from my pocket and look for the local police station's phone number. It's in my phone, and they know who I am. They always have done, for as long as I can remember.

Just when things were looking up, you have to go and die on me, mum.

'Redfern Police, this is Constable Harris,' the voice answers.

'Hi Danielle, it's Kaylee Knox…my mum's dead.' I might sound matter-of-fact, but saying those last three words makes me choke up.

Despite everything that's happened in my life, I loved my mum. She will always be my mum, even if she's a hopeless drug addicted prostitute – was a hopeless drug addicted prostitute.

'Where are you Kaylee? Have you called an ambulance?' Constable Danielle Harris asks, sounding a little hasty.

'Danielle, trust me, she's very dead. I'm just outside our apartment block. In the car park.' I look up to the top of the Housing Commission building. 'I think she may have come from the top…like she was pushed over the edge, or something.'

'Okay, just wait where you are and I'll have a car crew there immediately.'

Just as I hang up from the conversation, I hear the sirens in the distance. Looking at the top of the tower again, I try to picture my mum jumping. I just know she wouldn't have done it. Everything was starting to work out for us.

I had moved back home to care for her, and I had a good job at the local pub – for someone with the surname Knox, that's no easy feat. Mum was starting to look really good, too – she had just gone four months clean. We were saving all our money and were going to head off, out of this shithole of a city. We were heading north. Mum said she wanted to feel warmth in her marrow, the sun in her hair and breathe air that wasn't filled with the sadness of our life. I believed her, too. So she wouldn't have left me like this. Not now. Not after everything she promised.

Hearing a patrol car come screeching to a halt next to me, the headlights shine right on the wound at the back of my mum's head, I have to look away. The two male constables who came to do a licensing check on the pub earlier in the day get out of the car. I feel the pressure of tears on the back of my eyes, but I squeeze my lids shut for a moment to push them away. I haven't cried in years, and I'm not about to start. Life has thrown too much at me to lose it right now.

The larger of the two cops pulls a face when he sees my mother's crushed skull, and speaks into the radio piece on his shoulder. 'Redfern twenty, we have a confirmed deceased. Could you organise for the government contractors to attend our location.'

The other cop comes towards me. 'Did you see anything, Kaylee?'

I shake my head as he pulls his black notebook from his pocket. 'No. I just walked home from work, and found her like this. I haven't seen anyone around at all.'

The Constable scribes my words in his notebook as the other officer joins us. He taps me on the back twice, a gesture that I can only imagine is meant to be of comfort. 'Sorry about your mum, Kaylee. I thought she had been doing well lately.'

My chin quivers as I speak. 'That's the thing, this doesn't make any sense. She wouldn't have jumped without being forced to. We had plans. We were getting out of here. She promis–' I can't finish the sentence.

The officers trade glances, and the round "back-slapping" cop, who I remember is named Tom, shrugs. 'Sorry to say, but there are always suicides around here.'

I shake my head again. No! She didn't jump! I know it.

The police hold up a big white sheet as strange men in black suits pack my mum into a body bag. The sight is all too common in these parts of town. A small group of the locals gather near the stairwell to the apartment block. News travels fast.

They all know who it is. Some of them cry. Mum's best friend, Bessie, comes over and wraps her arms, tight around me. She stinks of booze.

'Oh, sweetie. I'm so sorry, baby girl. Your mum was a really good person, you know. This shouldn't have happened to her. She was a beautiful soul. She was so proud of you,' she wails into me.

Most of that was a lie. My mum wasn't a good person, but she was proud of me. I'm proud of me. I'm the only member of my family who isn't dead or incarcerated, because of crime. I even managed to complete school, and get a job. Four things my entire family failed to achieve.

Watching the flashing lights as they leave, the white unassuming van carries my mum's body behind them. It dawns on me – none of the police bothered to take photographs of the scene, or follow their usual investigation procedures. I'm sure they think my mum was just another junkie whore who suicided.

But I know my mum didn't die by her own will.

The pub's owner, old Mick, is kind enough to give me the day off work.

'Go and get some rest, love', he'd said on the phone.

The problem is, I can't rest. I need to find out why the police aren't investigating my mum's death. I mean, I get why they couldn't be bothered, but what happened last night is just ridiculous.

Walking into the police station, a young cop immediately comes up to the front counter when he sees me. I don't know him, but I'm sure he knows who I am. I can tell. I hate that they all know me. At least they have always been nice to me, so I can't really complain. Unlike my family, I've never given them a reason to treat me otherwise.

His soft eyes and downcast face scream of sympathy, and it's already making me sick. I get that I've had a rough start to life, but I just wish they'd stop reminding me of it every time they look at me with such pity.

'Hi, Kaylee. Sorry about your mum. Can I help you with something?'

See, sorry. They're all sorry.

'I want to speak to the boss, please.' I throw in pleasantries for effect.

'Sure, I'll just see if he's available. Why don't you take a seat in the private room?' He points to the room on the right.

After waiting for ten minutes in the stark waiting room, the man who sometimes steps in as boss of the station opens the door. I don't like this guy. I never have. He's never been mean, but he's never been nice either. He's just cold.

I look at his badge when he sits across from me and read the name GLENN SCOTT.

That's right, Glenn the asshole.

'It's sad news about your mum. If there's anything we can do for you, Kaylee, you just ask, okay?'

I doubt you're sad.

'Yeah, there is something you can do for me. You can tell me why you're not investigating how my mum died.'

'There is a Coroner's Report being finalised. It's standard procedure for suicides. Once that's completed, your mum's body will be released to you.' He looks so smug with himself as he leans back in the chair and folds his arms across his chest.

Shit! I hadn't even thought about burying mum. How am I going to afford that? I have just over two thousand dollars saved for mum and I to move north. I don't even think that's enough to bury her.

'How do you know it was a suicide? My mum wouldn't have jumped. Did you know she was clean? Had been for months. Test her. She'll come up clean.' I can feel the tears threatening to spill.

He nods slowly – sympathetically. 'Toxicology reports will arrive in a few weeks' time. I'm sure you're right about her being clean. I'd heard she was doing better than she ever had. I'm sorry, but it's quite common for users to have psychotic episodes when they come off of years from a serious drug dependency.'

I try to bite back the snarl in my top lip, but he's making it difficult. 'MY MUM DIDN'T JUMP!' I scream.

Launching from my chair, I storm out of the police foyer. I have to get out of here. I don't want them to see me cry – see me vulnerable.

Racing out of the police station, I walk as quickly as possible back to our apartment, four blocks away. The first tear slips down my cheek when I walk through Redfern Park. It bites against my skin with its icy wetness. That hurt more than I cared for. I have to sit. My vision is blurred from the tears that stain my eyes.

Taking a seat on the bench near the road, I feel like there isn't enough air filling my lungs, and my cheeks burn with a prickly heat. This is all too much. My mum is dead, I have no money to bury her, the cops have it wrong and her death will be as insignificant as her life was.

'Hey, Kaylee,' I hear a soft voice next to me.

Looking up, my watering eyes meet the young cop who was just at the front counter. I frown. 'What now?'

Holding his hands out in non-threatening pose, he speaks again. 'I'm not here to harass you, I promise. I just wanted to tell you that I believe you. I don't think your mum suicided.'

Why is he saying this? What does he want?

'Why? How?' I wipe at my tears with the back of my hand.

'There was someone who we heard was hanging around. A really bad guy. We have been trying to get to this guy for a while, but you know how those towers work. No one wants to talk to police. They all protect him. If he is around, I can guarantee he was involved. This is right up his ally. Your mum is the ideal type of victim for him. Vulnerable, desperate and weak.' He winces at me when he says those words. 'Sorry, Kaylee. I didn't mean for it to sound like that. Your mum was getting stronger by the day. Do you know if she was seeing anyone?'

I hate the way he described my mum. Vulnerable, desperate, weak. The problem is, he's right.

I shake my head. 'No, she wasn't seeing anyone. At all. She shut herself away from everyone because they were all bad influences. She was serious about getting out of here.'

He nods. 'Yeah, I know. I used to chat to her when I'd see her walking back from the supermarket. I'd never seen her so bright and alert.'

'What about all that stuff the boss just said, about recovering junkies going psycho?' I still don't know whether to believe this cop or not.

'He's an asshole. Don't listen to him. You know your mum best.'

Nodding, I agree with what he's saying. I did know her best. She had no one else left but me. My dad will die in prison with his life sentence, so I'm all alone – again.

'So what am I supposed to do from here?'

'People will talk to you. Find out everything you can and give me names. I will do what I can to get the investigation rolling if I know there's some substance to my theories. I know you want to clear your mum's name. You've always been one of the good ones, Kaylee. Here's my card.' He pulls out a small white card from his top pocket. 'Call me as soon as you hear anything.' He offers a smile, but I pay little attention to it. Instead, I take the business card from him, get up and start walking without saying goodbye.

I need to sort my head out. I'm going to the place where my mum spent the last moments of her life.

The stairwell door to the rooftop hangs on its broken hinges. My skin prickles at the thought of whether the person who dragged mum up here did that or not.

Stepping through the gap where the door hangs, I almost lose my footing on the stones that scatter randomly on the rooftop. They're dangerously slippery.

The breeze blows heavily from this height – forty stories up. It's the perfect place to bring someone if you wanted to throw them off the edge. Nothing survives forty stories.

I hear whimpering and catch sight of Bessie, crouched in the corner near the brick wall barrier, a cask of wine by her side.

'What are you doing up here?' I ask on approach.

She springs to her feet, shocked, and sways. She's drunk already and it's not quite ten o'clock.

When she sees that it's me, Bessie relaxes a little. 'Oh, Kaylee. You scared me. I was just having a drink for your mum. We used to come up here for a drink every now and then, you know. Just to have a moment to ourselves. I didn't…' She doesn't finish.

Snot dribbles from her left nostril. She wipes her sleeve along her nose and tears splutter again. Slumping back to the ground, Bessie clutches the cask of wine, as if it's her only friend. It probably is her only friend.

'I was hoping to find some closure by coming up here,' I lie. 'Hey…did my mum have someone new in her life? I thought we were re-building our relationship finally, and we felt close, but there just seems to be something missing. I just know she didn't kill herself.'

Bessie's bloodshot eyes shoot quickly to me, and rest back down on the ground in front of her. Bessie breathes heavy between sobs. Her head turns to the side in thought. 'You know…she did mention this new bloke in town… Jacob Mitchelton. He's from out Bourke way. A bit of a womaniser. I don't like him. I told your mum that. But she was knocking about with him a bit, you know.'

I shake my head. 'No, I didn't know.'

'He's staying with his cousin, Johnny, down on level fourteen. You know Johnny Mitchelton?'

Nodding, I take a deep breath. Yes, I do know the Mitcheltons. They're all bad, all four generations of them. My brother was with a Mitchelton when he died. Johnny is the worst of them. I know he touches kids. I've heard things, and my mum always told me to stay away from him. He tried it on me once, but my family carry a surname that's more troublesome than theirs, and my old man would've had a hit out on him the moment he caught wind of anything happening to me.

That thought reminds me to get in contact with my dad. He should know about what's happened. Even though he and mum didn't talk much anymore, he deserves to know mum's gone.

Wandering slowly around the rooftop, I scan along the edge to see if there's something I can catch sight of – a clue, anything. There's got to be something.

Nothing.

With my eyes scanning along the railing, I circle back around to where Bessie is. Just above her there is a dent in the flimsy boxed metal that sits above the brickwork.

Is that where mum went over?

I replay the possible sequence of events in my mind. Did she step up onto the ledge there? Was she fighting someone off and they pushed her into it?

With a name to take back to the cop who wants to help, I leave the rooftop. I can still hear Bessie sobbing as I step back through the broken door.

'Are you looking for Jacob Mitchelton?' I say over the phone to Constable Matt Sells – as the name reads on the business card.

'Bingo. Good work. That was quicker than expected.'

He was right about one thing; the towers are a hive of information. It's always been that way. Everyone knows everyone's business, because no one has a job. Gossiping and boozing are their only outlets, and the two easily go hand in hand with one another.

'So you think this guy had something to do with my mum's death?'

I hear a sigh. 'It's not the first time he's done something like this. The problem is, we can't catch him. He's a slippery piece of shit.'

Why is he telling me this? Does he really want to help me, or is he running his own agenda?

'What can I do to help?'

'Where is he staying, do you know? I need you to come in and give me a positive ID on him. Then I can set up a search warrant to catch and arrest him. Can you get eyes on him at all?'

I nod first before speaking. 'Yes, I'll try to find him first. I've been told he's staying with his cousin, Johnny.'

'We thought so, but so far no one has been able to positively identify him to us. You are doing the right thing, Kaylee.'

'There was one other thing.' I think about the dent in the metal railing on the rooftop. 'There was a dent near where my mum fell.'

'Once we get this guy, I'll follow up your mum's death, okay?'

'Okay,' I reluctantly reply.

Ending the conversation with Matt, I rush out of the apartment that mum and I shared and take the stairs to level fourteen, a few floors down from us. My mind races to come up with an idea of what I'm going to say when I get to Johnny's door.

Maybe I can just wait around on his floor and hopefully I'll see him that way?

As I get to the door of level fourteen, an idea comes to me. My heart pounds in my ears as I approach 14C – Johnny's door.

Three light taps on the door and I hear yelling from inside. 'Who the fuck is it?' I don't recognise the voice.

'It's Kaylee Knox.'

'Knox? What the hell do you want?' The door swings open to a tall, solid man with a ginger beard and tattoos covering the left side of his neck. Two teardrop tattoos sit on the outside of his right eye.

It's him. It's Jacob Mitchelton. I can tell already by the dark eyes that seem to be a distinctive trait in the Mitchelton family.

A ball feels lodged in my throat as I try to speak. 'I…I was just doing a door knock around, collecting coins, cash, anything to help me pay for my mum's funeral.'

He sniggers, baring his yellowed teeth. 'Who would want to help out a dirty, filthy whore like your mother?' Running his fingers through his beard, he tilts his head to the side and looks me up and down. 'But if you wanted to come in, I'm sure I can let you work for the money.'

My emotions are teetering dangerously between wild stabbing rage and utterly disgusted nausea. 'Not a chance. Forget about it.'

I turn to leave, but he catches my arm. 'How about you get that father of yours to help you out, and tell him that Jacob's coming for him one day.'

Pulling from his grip, I snarl back at him. 'How about you go fuck yourself.'

Walking as fast as I can down the corridor, I hear him call out. 'Come back anytime you want to earn yourself some cash, girly. I promise to be gentle with you. Nothing like I was with your old whore of a mother.'

The fury feels like it's burning a hole straight through my chest.

He's really got it coming for him now.

Making my way into the police station again, my palms feel slippery with perspiration. I hate being on the side of the cops, but what choice do I have? I need them to help me just as much as they need my help. Plus, with someone like Jacob Mitchelton as their target, swapping teams doesn't feel so bad.

I give Matt's name to the female constable at the counter, and take a seat in the foyer. Within a matter of minutes Matt bursts through the side door and smiles wide. There's something endearing about his smile that makes me feel comfortable.

'Let's go upstairs. I'll take a statement from you up there.' He holds the door open for me and waves me through.

Looking behind my shoulder, I make sure there's no one around to recognise me. Luckily the station's empty of anyone except for cops that work here.

I take a seat opposite Matt at a desk with nothing but a computer on it. He taps on the keyboard and the computer comes to life.

After typing all my words about the conversation I had with Jacob Mitchelton, and the way he looked, Matt looks up at me and smiles.

'You've done really well, Kaylee. You've described him with fine detail. We're initiating Strikeforce Fortis, effective immediately. The rapid response team are set to go now. So that we can storm the building without too much disruption to the rest of the residents, I would prefer you to come with us and let us in. We don't want him to get away this time. You deserve this moment. What do you say?'

Nodding, I consider his invitation. After what Jacob said about my mum, and knowing that he no doubt killed her, I agree that I probably do deserve this. My mum deserves this, too.

I hesitate for a second, before replying, 'Okay.'

Matt smiles again. His optimism creates a flicker of hope inside me – things may just work out for me, after all.

Where Jacob Mitchelton is going, my dad will finish the job from prison. Once my father hears that he's mum's killer, the job is as good as done. If Jacob Mitchelton's reputation is bad, my dad's worse. Dad has nine counts of murder charges on his life sentence – he's not someone you want to threaten.

The thought makes me smile.

'Ready to go then?' Matt asks.

I nod again. 'Let's take this asshole down.'

Standing in front of 14C for the second time today, I take a deep breath and hold it. However, I don't feel nervous this time. How can I when I have a dozen cops standing behind me, all dressed in black and carrying enough weaponry to start a civil war?

Glancing to the left of me, I catch Matt and he nods – encouraging me to knock.

With three taps, I hear Jacob yelling again. 'Who the fuck is it this time?'

'Just me again, Kaylee Knox.'

'Aaaaah…taking me up on the offer, hey?' he says as he swings the door open. 'FUCK!' He yells when his eyes catch the wrath of fierce black force, surrounding me.

Everything is a blur. I'm shoved harshly aside and plucked from the centre of the craze. There's yelling. It's so loud that it's all just a solid wall of intimidating sound. There's a flash of light and some loud bangs that make me scream and cower into the warm surrounds of the arms around me.

It all happens so quickly that I can hardly register a thing. I turn to whatever's holding onto me and see Matt. Jacob is bellowing out. He's not giving up easily. Shrieking pierces the air. He's pleading with them to stop whatever they're doing to him.

Within seconds, four cops carry a bloodied Jacob Mitchelton into the hallway. His eyes catch mine, and the hairs on the back of my neck stand on end.

'You fucking little bitch. You will have it coming. I am coming for you!' Blood spits from his mouth as he yells.

One of the big cops looks down at him and drives his fist down onto his face. 'Shut the fuck up,' he says as his fist connects with Jacob. Jacob's head droops as they leave down the stairwell.

The fear on my face must be noticeable, because Matt holds his arms a little tighter. 'It's over now. Where he's going, there's no way of getting out. Ever. He's been our number one fugitive for five years. There's enough charges against him to keep him away for the rest of his life.' He loosens his grip around me. 'There's also one other thing.'

His eyes smile before his lips do. 'What?' My eyes widen in fear again.

I don't think I can do any more. I've helped the police enough. I can't take it. I just want to run away – far away.

'There was a reward out for his arrest and capture.' Matt's grin is infectious.

'Pardon?' I don't believe what I'm hearing.

'The reward for the arrest and capture for Jacob Mitchelton was the biggest in our country…and now it's all yours.'

Heart thumping in my ears, I answer. 'How much is it?'

'A quarter of a million dollars.'

'Pard–' The world around me slips away, everything fades to black. The last thing I feel is Matt catching me as I fall.

As I pack the last of my belongings in the back of my new car, Bessie comes staggering out of the tower. She's drunk, as usual.

'Kaylee, your mum's service was really something. She would be so proud of you, and everything you've done. That Jacob got everything he had coming to him. He killed kids and all.' She pauses uncomfortably long between breaths. 'Look…there's something I need to get off me chest. About the night your mum died.' Tears slip down her cheeks as she continues. 'We had a bit of an argument, me and your mum…and something happened. I haven't been able to live with me-self.'

Staring at her, I feel the knot in my chest tighten. I can feel what she's about to tell me.

'She hated me drinking. She wanted me to stop. She was stronger than me though. She got through it…I never could. When she found me on the roof that night, she tried to take the drink from my hand, that's how angry she was with me. She slipped, or something and landed against the edge…I tried to help. She just went over. I don't even know how she got there, you know. I was too drunk.'

The tears fall freely down my own cheeks as Bessie recounts the night my mum died.

'She held on as long as she could, but I just couldn't…I tried. I promise, I tried. Then she just–'

I raise my hand up to stop her finishing the sentence.

Taking in the gravity of Bessie's words, we stand in silence – Bessie swaying.

If she told the truth from the start, I wouldn't have helped the police get Jacob. Without them capturing that bastard, I wouldn't have got the reward. Without the reward, I couldn't bury mum and life would've been as dismal as before she died.

Sighing, I take out some money from my wallet – three hundred dollars. I grab hold of Bessie's hand and slap the money into her palm. 'You don't need to tell anyone else that story, okay. You've told me, so your conscience is now clear.'

With the police's investigation leading towards Jacob Mitchelton murdering my mother, this is the last thing I need. I don't want to be stuck here any longer, for more police questioning.

Bessie looks at the fifty-dollar notes in her hands and nods, vigorously. Three hundred dollars isn't much, but to someone like Bessie, it's about a month's worth of grog. She will drink to forget, and eventually she will do just that – forget everything.

For me, I'll never forget where I came from, but I can't stay here and dwell on the sadness of it all. Through her death, my mum has given me the opportunity she always wanted me to have. Her life and death is now worth something.

I get into my little car and drive away from the towers and the life, as I have known it. I don't look in the rear vision mirror – I don't need to. It's finally over.

No longer will I live the hard knock life.

2016

STONE COLD

Ruth Wykes

NIKITA BLINKED. IT WASN'T THE FIRST TIME THIS DAY I HAD THOUGHT OF A goanna when I looked into her eyes; reptilian, indifferent, predatory.

'I asked you a question. Where is Max Newstead?'

'Dunno.'

'Nikita, you were seen on CCTV walking away from the primary school with Max. Where did you go?'

'I already told you a hundred times. He walked to the corner with me, 'cause that's where his mum was picking him up.'

'We both know that's not true.'

'Are you calling my kid a liar?' Nikita's mother, whose name I couldn't remember, was a ball of belligerence. 'We've been here three hours and she's been nothing but cooperative.' As cooperative as a cat being walked on a leash.

'Why didn't you go to school yesterday?'

'I fell off my bike and hurt my hand. Mum let me stay home.'

'What were you doing hanging around the primary school?'

'I just walked past it. I was on my way to visit Chloe.'

'Who's Chloe?'

She shrugged a shoulder. 'Friend.'

'So you walked to the corner with Max. Where did he go next?'

'Dunno. Didn't see him after that.'

'And did you go straight to Chloe's?'

'She wasn't home.'

'What time did you get to her house?'

'Dunno.'

I gritted my teeth so hard my jaw ached. Seven-year-old Max Newstead had been missing for 26 hours, it was winter in East Jindabyne and there'd been a blizzard on the Alps overnight. If Max was out there somewhere it was imperative we find him today. It would be -4° C in the town tonight.

'Mrs Jones, at this stage Nikita isn't in trouble. She was the last person who saw Max, and I need her to tell us what she knows.'

'Probably some paedo picked him up. It happens all the time, you know.' Mrs Jones folded her arms across a concave chest and nodded. Her daughter shuffled in her seat and smirked.

'Yeah, a paedo.'

Just as my fantasy about poking her eyes out with my ballpoint was becoming technicolour a sharp rap on the door interrupted it. It was my partner, Bull Reynolds. Ginger hair, a dangerous red stain on his cheeks, he looked ready to implode.

'Kate, can I see you for a sec?'

The squad room was almost empty save for Bull and me. Everyone else, other than the desk sergeant, was out looking for Max.

'Here, don't say I don't do anything for you.' Bull stunk of sweat as he handed me a cup of something muddy. I knew him well enough to see how tightly coiled he was.

'What's up?'

'We've got a witness who saw Raynes' ute near the primary school yesterday afternoon. We need to go and have another little talk with the bastard.'

Mitchell bloody Raynes, the local sex pest. Fair enough, he'd been caught with nasty photos when he'd stupidly taken his computer into Logans to get fixed last year, but it was a long leap from downloading images to abducting a child in broad daylight.

Bull and I had talked to Raynes last night along with every other known sex offender in the district – all three of them. Two of their alibis were solid, but Mitchell Raynes we weren't so sure of. He'd told us he was home, tiling the bathroom, all day.

The place he called home was an old fisherman's cottage on the edge of Lake Jindabyne. A muddied HiLux ute told us Raynes wasn't far away.

'Was that kayak there yesterday?' Bull nodded towards the lake's edge. In the distance I spotted the orange uniforms of the SES who were doing a perimeter search of the lake.

I hadn't seen a kayak, or anything else for that matter and I muttered a curse when my imagination took me to the middle of the lake, in a kayak, with a restrained child helplessly…

I strode over to the verandah and banged on the door.

'Mitchell. Detective Madden. Open the door.' As if he wouldn't have heard us pull up.

When there was no reply I looked in through the lounge room window. Oh shit.

'Bull, get over here.'

I flew to the door and kicked hard at it with my size sevens. Flimsy, it opened on the second kick.

As I ran into the lounge room I had two impressions: he was an immaculate housekeeper, and a lonely man. He lay slumped on a leather recliner and blood ran in rivulets down his wrists.

Raynes was semi-conscious and I fought to fit latex gloves on slippery fingers as I called for an ambulance. I pressed down on his wounds, trying to staunch the flow of blood.

'Mitchell, where's Max? Come on, mate. It'll go better for you if you tell us.'

I was surprised that when he opened his eyes they were brimming with tears.

'Fuck off,' he whispered.

With Raynes tucked up in bed at Jindabyne District Hospital and assurances from the doctor that he would survive his suicide attempt, Bull and I headed to the Newsteads.

'I told you it was him, Kate.' Bull drew hard on his cigarette and blew smoke out the window of our government-issued no-smoking car.

'We don't know that yet.'

'Pfft! No better statement of guilt in my book than trying to top yourself.'

'No better copper in the business than one with a closed mind, mate.'

'Whatever. Anyway, Stacey has finished searching the lake's edge. They're gonna bring divers in tomorrow and search near his house.' Stacey Rimer was captain of the local SES. In her day job she was a self-employed plumber.

I didn't want to hear him talk like this. I wasn't ready to accept that we were talking about recovery instead of rescue. Max Newstead is a child and I was not about to give up on him.

'When did you talk to Stace?'

Bull laughed. 'Are you fishing, detective? She told me you two aren't speaking. Lover's tiff?'

'Just the usual. She wants babies, and I want…'

'Don't fuck this one up, Katie. She's good for you.'

Fortunately we pulled into the Newstead's just as the conversation threatened to go somewhere I was trying to avoid.

Elena and Jason Newstead lived in a three-bedroom house near the edge of town. They'd moved there eight years ago and their three kids had been born there. Max was the eldest. I knew the family a little, as you do in a small town, and often ran into them at the RSL Club or at the sports oval. They were middle Australia in the flesh but when Elena Newstead opened the door to us I barely recognised her.

She searched past my shoulder then panic flickered in her eyes. 'Have you found him?'

'No, not yet.'

If someone could deflate like a pin-pricked balloon, Elena did in that moment. She stared through me, hope and defeat waging war in her heart.

From the hallway a voice boomed. Gravelled, rubbed raw by too much grief, too little sleep.

'It's that fucking rock spider. If you can't get him to tell you where Max is, I'm gonna go over to the hospital and beat it out of him. What the hell are you doing here? Get out there and find him.'

Jason Newstead had been drinking. For hours, by the look and the smell of him.

'Mate,' Bull moved to steady him, 'we just came to give you an update.'

'How's that gonna help Max? You haven't found him. My son is out there in the freezing frigging cold and the sun's about to go down. You've gotta find him tonight. He's little, Bull. He won't last another night out there.'

'Out there' was wilderness, an eerie lake and the imposing mountain that claimed bragging rights as our country's biggest. How were we going to find one small child?

There is something unique to small country towns. Throw a crisis at them and they band together; a strange foster family of misfits. So I shouldn't have been surprised when Bull and I got back to the station at 10.30pm to discover that Marie Collins had dropped off a casserole, and her friend Mary had made us blueberry muffins. I was more surprised that sitting in my chair in the most disgusting muddied overalls was Stacey, almost inhaling a plate of spicy beef.

'Hey, babe.' I feigned cool as I ladled food onto a paper plate.

'You look knackered. Are you OK?'

'I might be if we could find Max. It's dark and it's freezing and I don't know what to do.' I sounded pathetic, even to my own ears.

The most beautiful woman in the world reached up and stroked my face. 'You eat, darlin'. That's what you do.'

I chewed as I flipped through a daunting pile of phone messages and tips: check out this bloke, I saw him peering through my neighbour's window; you might want to know the publican hits his wife; someone's been mutilating rabbits and leaving them near the cemetery; someone else is cheating on his wife.

'OK, where haven't we searched?'

'The lake,' Bull yawned. 'But that'll get done in the morning.'

'And what if it's not Raynes? What if we're looking in all the wrong places?'

'Well who else would it be? He's a paedo; he's got no alibi, and he tried to top himself when the kitchen got too hot.'

'I don't know that he fits for me.'

'Oh come on, Kate. You saw his house; normal blokes don't live like that. And where's his computer? You can't tell me that someone like him suddenly doesn't have a computer. He's hidden it, just like he's hidden Max. We should be over at that hospital now putting pressure on that prick to tell us where the kid is.'

'They've been at him all afternoon. Sarge was over there; the FLO had a crack; even the bloody Uniting Church minister tried to get him to talk.'

'Oi, you two. Stop.' Stacey wedged herself between us. 'I don't know about you, Bull, but Kate hasn't slept for nearly two days. You're both going home to bed.'

The doors to Accident and Emergency slid open and I walked into the chaos of a typical winter's day. East Jindabyne was Base Camp for skiers and their cronies whose dreams of conquering Thredbo often ended up in splints and crutches. I dodged a gurney where a teenager sucked on a green whistle. The glistening bone that jutted from his ankle almost made me feel sicker than he was.

Mitchell Rayne's room was stark relief. I don't know what it is about hospital beds but they always make people look smaller, more vulnerable than they probably are.

'Can't you people leave me alone?' He tossed aside the newspaper he was reading.

'I brought you a coffee, a decent one.' I scraped a chair towards his bed.

'I got nothing, detective. Nothing to tell you.'

'I'm not here to ask you anything. I'm here to give you an update.'

He smirked at me.

'We searched your house yesterday, and your ute. Divers are going into the lake today. Are we going to find Max?'

He shrugged, struggled to make eye contact with me, and failed.

'Mate, help me understand. Why did you have those photos on your computer?'

'They weren't mine. My brother put them there.'

'Mitchell, look at me. I'm not judging you. I just want to understand.'

'Really? More like you've come here to play good cop and get me to confess to something I didn't do.'

'Didn't you? Then help me. Did you see Max at school the other day?'

He flared. 'You bastards couldn't find a beer in brewery. Didn't you even look at the photos on my computer? It's girls I love, not boys. You fucking blame me for everything that farts in this town just because you're too small minded to understand that what I feel for these girls is love. And I would never hurt them.'

'Girls like Nikita Jones?'

'She's too old.'

'She's 13.'

'Like I said, she's too old.'

He was rigid with anger.

'Alright, mate. Calm down. Have you ever acted on this love?'

'No, but there's a couple of girls here in town. And I know by the way they look at me they want it as bad as I do.'

Fire ants crawled under my skin and it was a massive effort to appear neutral.

'Is that why you were at the primary school?'

'I told you I wasn't there.'

'Yeah you were, mate. Mitchell, how old are you?'

'I'll be 23 next week.'

'Have you ever acted on your fantasies?'

'None of your business.'

The sexual exploitation of children most certainly was my business, but I let it go.

'It's not a crime to think, or even to fantasise. But there's a line, and you can never ever cross it. I think you saw Max from a distance, and you thought he was a girl. And I think that by the time you realised you'd made a mistake it was too late. Where is he, mate?'

I saw in his eyes that he wanted to hit me. I was still grappling with my next question when my phone rang. It was the duty sergeant.

'Kate, they've found him.'

I held my breath, not yet wanting the answer to the only question in my head. As the sarge filled me in I started to run.

I don't care how tough you are, or how thick a skin you wear there are moments in this job that rip your heart out of your chest. The lifeless body of Max Newstead protruded from an abandoned dog kennel at the back of a garden shed. Bloodied, matted hair was all we could see and we needed to leave it that way until crime scene got here from Cooma.

It was a big yard, at least half an acre, backing onto the primary school's sports oval. I sidestepped a puddle of vomit as I walked back to the verandah. On the way I called the station and barked to the sarge that he needed to send someone over to the Newsteads. Now.

Ross Howard reminded me of every Mullumbimby dropout I have ever met. A 50-something hippie, he looked spaced-out.

'I thought I smelt something yesterday afternoon when I was working in the shed, but I put it down to a dead animal.'

'Were you home on Tuesday?'

'What? Ah, no. I was at work. I think.' Shock seemed to have stolen his faculties, and I understood that. But my own coping skills were threatening to fray. I had to focus.

'You think? Where do you work?'

'Got a ski-hire business on the main street.'

'Did you see or hear anything unusual when you got home?' I peppered him with questions as the hive of the crime scene began to get busy.

A while later the forensic pathologist called me and Bull back to the shed. 'I've had them take the roof off the dog kennel. Do you want to see him while he's in situ?'

I did. And I didn't.

Nothing prepares you. I don't care what anyone says, nothing does. He was curled tightly into himself as though his last living instinct had been to crawl back inside his mother's womb. His little face was battered, one eye hung from its socket. His nostrils were caked with soil and mucus, and his front teeth were broken and bloodied. His nails were splintered; he'd fought.

'He's fully dressed. I don't think I was expecting that.'

'The fucker probably put his clothes back on him.' Bull's face was a dangerous beetroot.

'I'm fairly certain he was attacked here.' Even the forensic pathologist sounded angry. 'And it took him a while to die.'

A donkey kicked me in the guts as I absorbed what he said.

Bull bowed his head and for a minute I thought he was going to say a prayer or something. Until a sob caught in his throat.

The next few hours passed in a blur of busyness. As the jungle drums beat through the town a crowd gathered in the street. Flowers, teddy bears and toy trucks formed an unruly shrine against Ross Howard's fence.

We knocked on neighbours' doors, organised the SES to search the school grounds, and consulted with the crime scene crew. It was almost 3pm when I heard the sharp whistle of an SES searcher and a few minutes later Stacey called out to me and Bull. They'd struck gold.

Normally I would push her away if Stacey touched me while I was at work. But this day I let her hold my hand while we watched a crime scene officer unwrap a bloodied towel that revealed a hunting knife, and a brick that had been smashed to pieces.

'Reminds me of when we went out to the cemetery. The dead rabbits.'

I turned towards the voice and saw one of the uniformed constables gawking.

'What's fucking wrong with you, you insensitive flog?' Bull glared.

'Settle down, Bull. I'm just saying the bricks are the same.'

Bull rolled his eyes and turned his back.

'C'mere.' Stacey nudged me away from the huddle.

'What's up?'

'Just checking in. I won't insult you by asking if you're OK. Do you need anything?'

I rested my head on her shoulder, as if everything that was safe and familiar in my world could fix this terrible day.

My phone vibrated and I fished it out of my pocket.

'Kate, I need you and Bull over at the hospital now. Mitchell Raynes is dead.'

Jason Newstead answered the door: drunk, defiant and covered in Mitchell Raynes' blood.

'Saved you bastards a job, didn't I? And I saved the taxpayers a shitload of money.' He wobbled a finger in the air.

'Mate,' said Bull, moving in, 'we need you to come with us.'

'What for?'

'Come on, let's talk down at the station.'

'Nah, El needs me. I ain't going anywhere.'

'Come on, Jason,' I tried. 'Let's do this the easy way, mate.'

'Piss off, bitch.' He bunched a fist and connected just below my eye socket.

Shit that hurt.

Does it feel good to wrestle a man to the ground on the worst day of his life and slap handcuffs on him? Or to drag him away from his family at the moment they needed him the most? No, it feels like the shittiest thing I have ever done. It didn't help that my face was throbbing, or that I had seen his son, and what had been done to him.

As soon as this was over and we had him locked up I was going home. To Stacey. I was going to get blind, motherless, falling-down drunk.

And I did.

The weekend came and went, and I didn't go into work for three days. Word in the office was that Jason Newstead would be released on bail after a court appearance today, and I didn't mind that. He would eventually serve time in prison but a half-decent lawyer would win him a greatly reduced sentence, given the circumstances.

Three days and two bottles of Johnny Walker later I still couldn't get the image of Max Newstead out of my head.

'Nice shiner, Katie.'

'Piss off, Bull. You OK, big fella?'

His chair cushion exhaled as he eased himself into it. 'I'm still a bit rough.'

My phone jangled.

'Detective Madden, this is Mick Delaway from Forensic Services. We've got a problem.'

Of course we do.

'What's up, Mick?

'First of all, something surprising, we discovered at autopsy there was no evidence of any sexual assault.'

'Really? None?' Small mercies. At least the poor little bugger had been spared something.

'Nope. But that's not the big news. We've had a preliminary report on the DNA that was scraped from under the little fella's fingernails.'

'OK, that was quick. Why is that a problem?'

'It's female.'

I couldn't speak.

My hands trembled as I hung up the phone. Head bowed I thought about a young man whose body lay in a morgue, his family too ashamed to claim him. And a father who sat in jail, about to face the terrible truth that he'd killed an innocent man. I thought about a little boy, lying bludgeoned in a dog kennel. But this new truth; my brain couldn't grasp it, couldn't make it make sense.

'Nikita, do you want to tell me your version of what happened?'

Reptilian eyes blinked under the harsh fluorescent light. The smirk seemed to be a permanent fixture.

'Nothing happened.'

I wondered, not for the first time this night, if Nikita Jones was evil. On the surface she was attractive, sassy even, but I couldn't see that in her right now. She was flanked by her mother and the family lawyer.

'Let me clue you in to what we know. We know you stole your neighbour's pet rabbits for practise. We know you planned this for weeks.'

'What. Ever.'

'And we know you didn't really fall off your bike. We know that bandage was to cover up the scratches and the bite marks, wasn't it.'

'You can't prove anything.'

'See that's where you're wrong. We've got your DNA under Max's fingernails, and in his teeth, and on the knife.'

For the first time those soulless eyes became curious.

'So you're going to lock me up, then?'

'I am. Tell me something. Why did you do it?'

'I've always wanted to know what it's like.'

'What what was like?'

'Killing someone.'

'And what was it like?' I am not having this conversation.

'It was great. It's the best feeling in the world.' The smile she gave me chilled me to my marrow.

'You should have seen his eyes bulge–'

'Enough!' I slammed my hand on the table.

'What's the matter, Detective? Squeamish?'

The gun, snug against my hip, became an itch I desperately wanted to scratch. In that moment I saw her future. She would be out of juvenile detention and on the streets by the time she turned 18. The bleeding hearts would protect her, scream that she was fixed, deserved a second chance.

I knew better.

This child wasn't broken.

She was a monster.

2017

Locked Out, Locked In, Locked Up

Rowena Harding-Smith

I'M AT THE FRONT DOOR TURNING THE HANDLE, PUSHING ON THE BRASS plate, expecting it to swing open so I can go back inside. The door doesn't move. It's locked. I bang the lion's head knocker and the thuds echo down the hall as if the house is deserted. It isn't. The rest of the family is in there; the kids are in their bedrooms, sleeping, which is what I want to be doing. Jason is in there – God knows what he's doing. I'm tired, hot, sticky, and so over today. I only remembered it was garbage night while trying to squeeze more rubbish into the kitchen tidy. I called out to Jason but, naturally, he didn't reply. We missed the collection last week so there was no option but for me to trudge out to the street with the overflowing bin. While I was outside, Jason closed the door and locked it. Now I feel stupid because I should have been prepared. This is, exactly, Jason's idea of fun. And when I'm caught out, like tonight, it proves I'm not as smart as he is. I press my ear to the glass panel and hear water gurgling. He's taking a shower so he can pretend not to hear me knocking.

I plod around to the back door, pushing past the drooping hydrangeas. They would be panting if they had tongues but the air is musty and heavy with rain so they won't be drooping for long. I turn the handle. No luck. I could wriggle in a window but even if it looks open it has a dead bolt half way up the frame, so I might not be able to fit. I don't always push the pins in, though. Especially in the laundry. I need a breeze when the drier is pumping. I hate the dead bolts. They make me feel trapped. I only use them because Jason will blame me if there is another robbery. When we bought this house I initially refused to install them. A week later we had a break-in and then it became all my fault even though I was the only one to lose anything. The thief climbed through a window and stole my jewellery: rings, bracelets, and the cameo his mother gave me to wear on my wedding dress. Jason was as angry as if I had tossed them onto the road.

If the laundry window is open I can stand on the outdoor table and clamber in over the soaking school uniforms. It will be messy but better than being stuck in the garden.

He is still in the shower. He will be pink and wrinkled as a prune when he gets out.

The laundry is closed and pinned, as are all the other windows. How could Jason have locked everything so quickly? I have only been out here for a few minutes, putting the garbage bins on the curb. But, of course, I also sorted the recycling. And I stood for a few minutes in the carport looking at the clouds, breathing. I've probably been out here longer than I thought.

Still, securing the house is not a quick process. Every morning it takes me nine minutes and thirty seconds to bolt all the windows and doors. That's nine minutes and thirty seconds of my life I'll never get back, but I'll do anything for a quiet life. Some days I work from home just so I don't have to lock the house.

A fat drop of rain splashes on my head. Looks like I'll be showering outside while he showers inside, the bastard. He must be laughing.

I return to the carport. The harbour looks beautiful from here. There is no moon tonight so the Iron Cove Bridge is a white streak across the inky water. The reflections waver and undulate with the shadow of a boat, running dark.

I can hear a mechanical drone – probably his hair drier – so I sprint up the path and begin pressing the bell incessantly. The light turns off in the bathroom and on in the bedroom. I wait, huddled under the eaves. He always complains that I never give him the benefit of the doubt; maybe locking me out was an accident. If he really doesn't know I'm outside he will at least notice I am not in bed. The light switches off in the bedroom and my heart sinks. He's going to leave me out here. I hammer on the etched panels with my fists willing the glass to smash. I pick up a piece of sandstone edging. It's heavy and rough but if I put it through the door I will have to stay behind tomorrow to wait for the glazier. And clean up the mess of broken glass. And Band-Aid the kids' feet after they walk through it. I toss the rock back into the garden.

My options now are to wake one of the children or go next door and use their phone to ring Jason. But they'd be curious and I'm too angry to make excuses for him. 'He must not have realised I was outside.' Yeah, right.

259

The rain is coming down in sheets and I suddenly remember hiding a spare key under a rock near the carport. Hopefully any redbacks or funnel webs will be sheltering from the rain and not lurking in the garden.

In the front yard, I turn over stones but it's hard to see. My hair is dripping in my eyes. I take shelter in the carport. As I lean against Jason's Jag the door moves behind me and my body goes soft with relief. The car is unlocked – the door wasn't even closed. I sink into the driver's seat. If necessary, I can sleep here. Or I can blast the horn – stuff the neighbours. Or I can continually slam the boot. He'll hear the heavy thudding, even through the noise of the rain, and be worried. He loves his Jag but for someone so obsessed with security he's surprisingly careless with it.

As I am waiting for the storm to ease, Sophie stumbles barefoot down the path.

'Mum?' she mumbles, peering in the window, her breath fogging the glass.

I climb out of the car. 'I left my key inside.'

She nods and we dash up the path to the house.

'Thanks.' I kiss the top of her head and brush the rain from her curls.

The bedroom is dark. He pretends to sleep even when I switch on the light and tell him in my most controlled voice that he shut me outside. I am trying not to shout and frighten Sophie. His eyes stay closed.

'You locked me out!' I shriek in his ear.

He rolls over and stares at me then turns away.

It's pointless trying to discuss anything with him; I drop my wet clothes on the floor and climb into bed. He is lying with his back to me. I check the time.

It's eleven-twenty so there's no risk of him wanting sex. He's only interested in sex at three minutes past eleven, not a minute before or after. And it always lasts exactly twenty minutes.

I fall asleep quickly because it's better than thinking.

In the morning I wake as he tosses his trousers across the bed and the heavy belt buckle cracks against my shins. I bite my lip to stop crying out. I'll have bruises today because I slept in. If I had woken earlier I would have made sure my legs were hanging over the side of the bed, safe. It's my fault if the buckle hits me. I know it's coming.

'You locked me out last night,' I say, massaging my legs.

He stares at me in the mirror while adjusting his tie. 'No I didn't,' he says, calmly.

'You did. Sophie let me back in.'

He saunters out of the room without answering.

In the kitchen I repeat, 'You locked me out.'

'I didn't,' he says, reading the news on his phone. He snaps the cover shut and picks up his lunchbox. 'Time for me to save some lives,' he states, smiling. It is twenty-five minutes past seven. This is when he leaves every morning even when his shift at the hospital starts at ten.

I am folding the washing when I find it. The cameo. At the back of his underwear drawer. I was late doing the washing this week so most of his undies were dirty and the drawer was nearly empty. As I stacked his t-shirts at the back of the drawer I felt the rigid edge of something inside a sock. Curious, I shook it. It rattled. I turned it out and jewellery fell across the bed – my rings, my bracelets. The cameo. I held it up to the light – it was translucent, beautiful, the profile serene and contemplative. I choked on bile. I shoved it all back and slammed the drawer.

That evening, I deliberately leave my keys on the kitchen bench while I take the bottles outside to the recycling bin, and put his bulky wallet of car and house keys in my pocket. I spend a few minutes in the garden bed between the hydrangeas watching Jason hurry through the house locking the doors and pinning the windows. I hadn't realised before how unimaginative he is.

At the end of our road is a public boat ramp leading to the harbour. It is a poorly lit place favoured by lovers and drug dealers. I hear a motorboat rev. I see a dark shape accelerate away from the ramp towards Iron Cove Bridge. The wash foams at my feet as I step through the shallows. I have timed my arrival perfectly.

I walk to a car parked in the shadows, under a tree, facing the road ready for a quick get-away. One dealer has his head in the boot sorting parcels wrapped in white paper, the other one lounges against the open car door. He gives a signal as I arrive and the boot slams shut. They both stare at me. I stare back and hand them money. The smaller of the men counts it and nods as it goes into his pocket. 'Ten past eleven, tonight,' he confirms.

I jog back through the carport and click open the Jag. Serve him right if someone steals his car. The entry door is locked again but I don't bother pretending I can't get in. I slam it behind me. Jason is in the study checking bank balances on his computer. He ignores me. My keys are not on the kitchen bench where I left them so I place his where mine were and go to bed. I will find them in the morning. They will be at the bottom of the washing basket or behind the frozen peas in the freezer or in some other unlikely spot.

I am in bed, dozing, when Jason switches on the light.

'What's this?' he shouts, jabbing at an item on our joint-account bank statement, waving the paper in my face.

'I don't know.' I rub my eyes, trying to focus through the white glare.

'You don't know,' he says, voice dripping. 'You've forgotten what you've bought? Maybe you've got early-onset Alzheimer's?'

'Some internet companies have weird names,' I mutter, glancing at the bedside clock. Eleven pm, right on time.

Jason pulls down the sheet and drops into bed. 'You can make it up to me,' he says, squeezing my breast.

Twenty-three minutes later Jason slides off me and begins to snore. Twenty minutes of noisy, distracting sex. I should be grateful, and I am, but not for the reasons he would imagine.

In the morning I lift my legs just in time to avoid the trousers thudding across the bed. I don't need any more bruises. I have enough. I prepare the kids for school. Jason eats and then drives to work.

After he leaves, I use the new, prepaid mobile I bought from the internet company with the weird name to make a call, then I look for my keys. I check all the usual places without luck. Jason has taken them to work. The windows are still bolted from his efforts the night before so we are locked in. It's better than I could have hoped.

I tell the kids they have the day off school. They celebrate by challenging each other to a computer game. They enjoy these locked-in days. In the past when he did this – by accident, I used to think – I begged him to send the keys home with a courier but the only courier that ever arrived was Jason at seven pm with my keys still in his pocket. I had some spares cut. The kids don't know I have a spare, nor do I want them to know in case they accidentally tell him.

While they are engrossed in their game I slip out and toss the new mobile phone off the cliff into the harbour. I watch the sun glint on its silver case as it sinks into the green water. It's already hot. I go home and force myself to change into shorts and a singlet. It's been years since I wore anything other than pants and long-sleeved shirts. In the mirror my legs are ridged crimson with green and yellow blotches. I don't look at my arms.

Jason rings me two hours later, on the landline, but I am logged-on to work and let the call go to voicemail. He keeps calling, his messages becoming increasingly hysterical. An hour later, I answer.

'I've been arrested,' he shouts over my greeting. 'Come to the police station now with your debit card. I need bail. The police found cocaine in my boot.'

I am silent.

'It was a tip-off.' His voice falters. 'They're saying I offered cocaine to a patient. I would never do that. You must believe me.'

I do believe him. But I tell him I can't come to the police station. My keys are missing, and I am locked inside the house with the children. Perhaps he could check his pockets and send a courier? Or maybe he can ask the police to come around and let us out?

Darkness in the Port

Philomena Horsley

I cradle Mickey's child-body with my bloody hands, trying to press back the coil of guts spilling from his belly. His eyes flash at me, shocked, bewildered, then fading. I lay him gently on the icy concrete floor then bolt for the exit.

I roam the back streets of St Kilda. I drift across to the Port 3207 zone when I need to get away from others. It's not that the people in Port are fewer, but they are the beautiful people. Well off, well fed, well dressed in that wealthy, downbeat way. They don't see me. What's to see? Small and stringy. Eleven maybe? Fifteen? I can look younger or older, depending on what clothes I snatch from the op shops. I go young when I want to hang out in a library. It seems safer. I don't get so many concerned or distrusting looks from staff. Why would a kid that young be on the streets? I need those books, crave them. It's not that hard convincing local kids to sell me their library card. Terrible how little they care about books. Idiots.

At night I hang with Sacha a bit. She worked for a time in the licensed brothels but she says the streets give her more freedom. Yeah, and more bruises. She pays me a bit to be a look out for her. I'm good with faces, number plates. Really good. I mean, I never forget them. Photographic, Sacha says. So I can warn her, warn the others, when the creeps drive up. The Ugly Mugs. The ones who always want to do weird things, the ones who squeeze the women's throats too hard, or rip them off. Sometimes I've had to suck a bit of cock to get by. Like Mickey. But I don't put myself out there much. Mostly I hang in the shadows, looking out for scum, warning the working girls. I have good instincts too; I can really sense the bad in some people. And the real goodness too. The women say I have a gift.

That's how I knew Shelley was safe. She used to visit the libraries a lot, that's how we met. And sometimes I would carry her books home for her. But it's got too hard for her. She's too stiff, too creaky, she tells me. So now I take her card and go to Port's library and choose her books. She likes romance, crime, any of those grand stories from English history. Best if they are in big print though. Of course, I can remember everything she's read so I don't get the same ones. I expect the staff think I'm her family. I deliver the books to Shelley and have a wash up, all my clothes, and she makes me a meal. Then we sit together on the couch and read. I can stay and sleep on the couch if I want to. I know she knows I'm on my own, and she won't tell. But this will all end soon. Her family's started coming around now. Not because they care, no, not that. They just want to move her into a home so they can take her home. She's got no hope against that lot.

Anyway, I'll have to find another option soon. Maybe Alice? She's a really good person, I just feel it. She works in one of the libraries I visit. I think she has me sussed. She was cautious and friendly when we first started chatting, not in my face. I think she knows I'll scram from that place, not to be seen again, if she mentions "help", "people who can help", "services" or whatever. We talk books mostly, safe stuff, but I know I impress her with my ideas. I can relax a bit with her, though I try not to. I can tell she likes me. She's curious but careful, like me.

I know where she lives. I've followed her home, carefully, so I know she lives alone. It's off Graham Street, a worn out looking house, one of those places with an old laundry and toilet still outside. I've used that space a few times to wash up, being really careful to leave it as I found it, nothing out of place. Sometimes I have a look inside. Alice's house is full of books – piles on the kitchen table, on the floors, by her bed. I can't see their titles through her windows, but those ragged stacks of stories warm me every time.·

At times I've been tempted to climb inside and borrow a few. But I respect Alice, and I just don't steal from people. Except from Op shops. They're supposed to be there to help people like me anyway. And from stupid rich people who leave their stuff in their cars, practically giving it away.

I'm hanging out with Sacha and some of the others. It's pretty early still, but it's gloomy. Winter feels harder, colder, when you're near the sea. The wind blows dark, mean, painful. Business is slow. Maybe on a night like this even the regulars want to be on the warm couch with their boring old wives. Sharp headlights suddenly swing through the corner, lighting up our grim street pocket.

'Run', I yell. 'Cops'.

Most of us scatter, except for a few girls too new to know the drill, too new to know they should trust my warning. Handbags swing and high heels pump around me as we sprint to the corner towards lights and shops and, hopefully, obscurity. Sacha and I dash into the MacDonald's and plonk ourselves in a booth. Tingling from the sudden warmth on cold, bare skin. Laughing like hyenas.

'How do you do that?' she gasps.

I shrug, roll my eyes.

'Don't know really. Something about the way that car slunk around the corner set me off. Just a vibe. I saw the plate number as we ran. Cops from the Prahran shop, not sure what they're doing here.'

'Well, I owe you a burger kiddo! Hey, do you wanna crash at my place tonight after? I think I'm done for the evening.'

I nod gratefully. Sacha heads to the counter to order. Her tiny sixth floor flat can be a great option. But I know, after most nights with those scummy men, she usually likes to go home alone, clean up, drop a few tabs and visit her blissful private dreams. And honestly, I feel pressed against the walls by that tiny space – too high up, nowhere to run, to get away. But tonight feels right.

The doors swing open and two men enter, showering me with chilly air in every way. I glance outside. There's the car, parked illegally near the verge. It's the same one we fled. One of the guys ambles over, pouchy, pock-faced. I can tell he's bored, looking to warm up his night with a bit of hassling.

'What are you doing out so late on your own kid? What's your story?'

Just then Sacha is back at the table, tray in hand.

'Why Officer, sir, Jazz is with me. We are just feeding up after a wonderful night at the opera!'

He looks at her quizzically, sees what he sees, but knows it's a public place and he can't do much, and anyway, it's too much bother.

'Well, make sure you're in bed by midnight' he commands, faking a caring tone. 'Both of you!' he adds, giving Sacha a knowing look. We leap on the burgers, sauce oozing from our smirking mouths.

Mickey and I have nestled into a sandy niche between the grassy mounds at Lagoon Pier. We've climbed over the barbed wire fence, off limits to all but us and the squawking gulls. We can lie here unseen. Back of us there's the familiar traffic hum, the growl of big trucks changing gear. If we lift our heads to the sea we can follow the slow progress of the bulky freight ships, cartoon cut-outs on the horizon. Close by, gentle waves lap the shallow shoreline, rhythmic but erratic. This is one of my favourite places. From the pier you can see the sentry line of palm trees curve all the way around the bay to St Kilda.

At night the standing lights along the pier hang their heads and cast a magical glow over the boards.

Mickey and I lie together, eyes closed, slightly warmed by the winter sun on our faces. It's a thing we like to do when we catch up. The breeze sends the faint chlorine tang of fresh spunk my way from Mickey's clothes; his opportunistic session with a mug is the reason we're feeling well fed. I'm worried about Mickey. I know he's feeling down and he's getting reckless on the streets. Mickey has been spat out too many times by the system. A few years ago, after he had his twelve-year-old arsehole drilled by his last foster dad's big dick, Mickey decided the streets were a lot friendlier, and safer. Sure, survival came with a lot more dick, but at least it paid. Which meant he could get the stuff he needed to numb himself, or lift himself, keep himself bright for the blokes. But Mickey's ageing too fast, more man than boy now. And the rich gents want them young. I've started to feel Mickey slowly untethering from life.

He rolls over slowly and squints at me. The afternoon sun gives his skin a healthy glow it doesn't deserve.

'You heading out with Sash and the others tonight? Around Grey Street?'

'Yeah, maybe. Why?'

'Thought I might tag along. There's a spot nearby where I've got lucky a few times in the past. Simple stuff, blokes on heat, any dick sucker will do.'

'OK, I'll hang with you for a while, see that you don't get into any trouble.'

I tried throwing a cheeky grin at Mickey but even I knew it was pretty empty. He reached over and touched my cheek, just a light feather down my cheek to the corner of my mouth.

'I really love you, Jazz, you know', he whispers. 'You are so tough. You're stronger than me, so much smarter, smarter than anyone.'

'Yeah, that's what you get from too much reading,' I joke, trying to lighten the mood.

'Yeah well I can't wait to see you out of this shit, set up in the world proper. But hey, don't forget this ignorant fuck-up when you make it'. He throws this at me fiercely. So of course I punch him. Looking back, I wish we'd lingered a little longer in the snuggle of that sand.

Mickey turns up very late. He is wearing his favourite black puffer jacket, black pipe jeans showcasing his sparrow legs. He's doped on something. Sacha takes one look at him, rolls her eyes, and shoves him down the street a way. She won't work fucked up, says she'd rather enjoy the benefits of that stuff in the comfort of her own home. I wander down behind him, anxious.

'Not a great way to go, Mickey', I mutter to him. He ignores me. Fair enough.

A sleek, sporty, silver car turns the corner. It idles on the other side of the road, fifty metres down, bugs hazing in its lights. The driver sits quietly in the dark, waiting, watching. It doesn't feel right. There's a pain in my chest bone, a deep jab. Mickey starts to amble down to the car. I grab at him but he shakes me off.

'I'm just checking it out, be cool,' he flicks at me. He leans on the bonnet of the car, chatting with the driver. Then he moves over to the passenger side to get in.

My chest gets fierce, explodes in shrapnel.

'Mickey, NO!' I scream, jagged, hoarse. He looks up briefly, stares at me. Defiant, puffed up in his black jacket, then he shoots me a sad grin and pops a thumb. He bends into the car and it squeals a U-turn before I can even move.

I start to chase. I can run, I'm a runner. I love it. Sand, bitumen, grass – I love it all. The spring in my legs, the gasp of my lungs, ears zinging with heat, the sense of flow that comes with distance. But not this running. This is desperate, jagged, gut-busting stuff. I hurl myself into the night. I hit the corner and spill right into Beaconsfield Parade, panicked, desperate to find that car. Nothing. A few lazy headlights rolling my way. But not that silver glint. It's late, it's winter, nothing much about. I think hard: where would Mickey go if a guy wanted more than a suck? I start pounding down the bike path towards Middle Park.

The car is starkly framed beneath the toilet block lights. No-one around. I stagger to the entrance. Three kilometres is not a long run for me. But I ran this route hard, with concrete in my chest.

I step into the dim light. 'Mickey.' Suddenly I'm slammed hard against the wall, then dropped onto my back. The man stands over me, grinning. He licks his fleshy lips slowly, eyes glinting, taking me in. My vision drops, catching the dark smudges on his shirt. As I do he kicks me in the guts hard and leaves. I push myself up the wall and lurch into the change room. There's the knife, here's Mickey. Oh Mickey.

I crouch under Lagoon Pier, behind the mossy round stumps. Shaking, heaving into the damp sand. Blood coats my shirt, stinking me up, seeping into my pants. They'll be looking for me because I yelled, pointed to the Block's entrance. But then I ran. I have to get somewhere safe, clean up. Alice. I figure the route in my head, the back way. Soon I'm creeping into her backyard. She never locks the laundry. Once inside I slump for a while on the cold concrete floor, almost too tired to stand. Then I heave myself up to the big sink, turn on the taps and strip. Suddenly the light flicks on and she's standing there. Alice, wide eyed, bewildered. I clutch the bloody shirt to my chest.

We sit in the warmth at her kitchen table. The stink has been washed off my body, Alice knows now it isn't mine. Some clean scruffy clothes are found and folded to fit me. My fingers grasp a cup of tea, hot, lotta sugar. It's quiet at the table. Alice hasn't thrown any questions at me but I can see them throbbing in her temple.

I'm just so tired. But I'm wired. I pick up the top book from her stack. It's Invisible Man.

'Did you like this one?' I query. I tried to read it last year, even though it was so old. That guy was so different to me but I think I got some of it. Even though it was another country, another time, it's still intense – there's a lot of nightmare in that book.

She ignores me for a moment, then opens to her mouth to speak.

'I haven't done anything wrong', I gasp out. 'Honestly. I tried to help someone who got hurt. But I couldn't help them. So I ran. I had to run. They wouldn't believe me.'

I'm spent. I put my head down on the table. Alice rests her warm hand on the back of my neck.

Finally, Alice speaks, suggesting we head to bed as it's nearly morning, and we can talk then. She pulls out some blankets and a pillow and rolls her couch flat and I slither underneath all that and wait for being awake to end.

I'm holding Mickey and he's screaming at me, 'Drop the knife, drop the knife.' And I'm trying to let it go but my hand has frozen, and the knife is waving about, streaming blood on me. Then a hand grips my shoulder and I punch out wildly. I punch hard, just like I've learned to do on the streets. And I hear a cry. So I punch again, harder, and it's Invisible Me hitting that person, and I turn the knife 'cos I'm going to slit their throat, just like Invisible Man wants to.

Then I hear a moan, and I wake up. Alice is lying on the floor, face bleeding and I feel shock, then such awful, drenching shame. And I run.

Sacha tells me they are looking for me. Suddenly everyone wants to see me now, corner me, catch me. Apparently I dropped a library card by Mickey's body. It's not me, of course, but they've tracked me to the library lending. I'm too regular for people not to notice, too loyal to my books.

Sacha will go to Alice's library and pass on my note. To pass on to the police. The make and model of the car, the number plate. The police have to catch that dark man. I know he won't stop doing this stuff. I've seen those eyes, that grin.

Sacha goes back to the library again a few days later. This time Alice is ready for her. Sacha says Alice's bruises are fading, and she stands steady when Sacha approaches.

'She says to tell you the police told her that the owner of the car says it wasn't him. Someone took his car that night and then left it in the next block. She says they told her the owner is a hot shot lawyer, important, respectable. They believe him. Alice says, 'Please, if you saw the killer's face you could help the police if you can describe him'. Alice says, 'Please come and see me at home'.

I walk up the path to Alice's front door. I sit on the bottom step; I don't want to scare her. I'm really not that person from that night. She comes out and sits on the top step, but she smiles a little as she does it. We're waiting for the Detective. He comes alone which is good. Alice says he's a "good man". I wouldn't know, I've never met any myself. He sits on the middle step to chat, which is funny. It's so not the three bears here.

We go inside and Tony – that's the cop's name – shows me some pictures. It's the dark man, there, plain as day. Probably a photo off a website. He's got a confident, serene smile, but I know different. Tony asks me if I'll go to court and say that it was him. I can, but what would happen to me if I say yes? I'm not going into the system, into care or worse.

Alice says she could give me a room at her place, no strings. She and Tony talk hard. School gets mentioned. Yeah, as if. Tony says I could be a protected witness. As they try to sort it I just think of Mickey, his big wrong choice. After Tony leaves I go back to Sacha's place. She tells me to trust my gut on all this.

I sit outside Court Three waiting to be called. I've grown, but not that much. I've read a lot of books since that night. I still ferret out the good ones, classics, but I loafed through some Reacher books because Alice said it's good to let some light stuff in. Now I'm trying to remember all the information the lawyer told me, how court works for real, not like TV.

The door opens and I'm in court. There he is, the dark man. He's aged a bit but he still looks handsome, well fed, well bred. He sits, looking slightly perplexed, like he shouldn't even be here in this room, it's some big mistake. I'm also dressed well, Alice made sure of that.

The prosecutor takes me slowly, step by step, through that night. I'm stiff in my responses. I recount it fact by fact, image by image. I keep a steady voice; I know it's down to me. I'm asked to point out the culprit and I do. I look at him, really look at him. He tries to stare me down but I won't bend my gaze to him.

The defence lawyer stands. My gut grips tight. I try to breathe slow and even just like Alice said. The lawyer starts with my life on the streets. Of course he would. I've read Helen Garner, so I know how knotty these blokes can get with witnesses. How they can act like they really believe the people they are defending are innocent, how outraged they are that these poor, ordinary blokes are caught up in such a bad luck story.

Yes, I've hung out on streets with sex workers, yes, I've sucked cock for money – but we don't use those exact words in this court room. He's trying to make me small, dirty, and disrespect my friends with his contempt, but I absorb it all. This is not about me, it's about Mickey. The lawyer's getting to his high point now, preening to the jury.

'So Jazz, despite this sordid, chaotic life you've lived, you claim to have excellent recall? On a dark winter's night? All this time later?'

I eye him off, his slinky suit and all. He's not so clever, just full of himself.

I smile, as innocently as I can, 'Yes, absolutely.'

'And why should we believe you?'

'Well, people have told me I have this photographic memory sort of thing because I can remember things so well.'

He turns to the jury. 'Well that kind of thing has been debunked by science, as we know.'

I sit and wait patiently 'cos I know he has to actually ask a question. He seems a bit annoyed and changes tack.

'So, Jazz. Do you do drugs? Have you ever done drugs?'

'Nope.'

'What, never?' Mock surprise.

'Nope, they fuck your brain, and I really like mine. What about you?' I hold his gaze. 'I've heard a lot about lawyers' parties.' The jury chuckles. They're sure they know all about how Australian lawyers work from watching all those American shows.

Mr Shiny Suit pauses a moment, and I jump into the gap.

'I could never forget the night that Mickey was killed. We were special friends, we helped each other. We looked out for each other. He was not a piece of trash. But this man –' and I pointed '– this man carved him up like he was nobody, nothing. And then he just drove away. In a silver sports car, rego HER061.'

My shoulders lift as Shiny Suit turns back to me, and I steam on.

'And you came here yesterday in a pale blue shirt and green and red tie. You were dropped off outside by a blonde woman in her twenties driving a dark blue Merc. But on Monday you turned up in a white shirt with a blue and yellow tie. And you were dropped off by a dark haired woman in her thirties, white BMW.'

The court goes silent except for a muffled moan in the pews. Probably the blonde woman from yesterday, but I don't look.

I sit with Sacha in her tiny flat. We're sharing some Thai takeaway while talking about books. I've finally got her reading something. She's baulked at Michael Connelly. I get that. Harry Bosch lives such a grim life, battling corruption on every side. It never ends well, and he never bloody learns. On the other hand she likes the Lee Child books. That Reacher, he just gets the job done: all the bad guys die, or at least walk away with serious nose damage. No agonising, bloody justice for all, then he moves on. As I will soon.

We're at the start of another hot summer and the beautiful people of the seaside and their pricey dogs, are out marking their territory. The sea now feels too dark for me, too haunted. Dark man is in gaol. But Mickey's still in the ground, and I miss him. I sometimes lie quietly in a nook at Lagoon Pier, fingers trailing in the warm sand, feeling for Mickey. But mostly I just want to run.

AT LENGTH I WOULD BE AVENGED

Also won the Body in the Library Award

Blanche Clark

I AM THE BODY IN THE LIBRARY. I HAVE BEEN HERE, UNDER THE FLOORBOARDS, for two years now, enduring the scuttling and squeaking of rodents, the same ones that ate my flesh and left maggots to clean my bones. The students and bibliophiles who energised this room for more than 150 years are long gone.

Water leaks from the roof. Mould clings to the crumbling plasterwork. Exposed electrical cables twist around the rafters like wild vines.

The council decided people needed more space, light and warmth. Children needed to learn coding. Coding? The word library comes from the Latin word Liber for book. It does not mean software, applications and websites. It does not mean "snugs" where parents lounge around on beanbags with their pre-genius children reading picture books with as much grace as a garrulity of galahs.

The new library is a monstrosity. A monument to this vitiated world. The wooden beams, the so-called "ribs that protect the beating heart of the community" were probably plundered from an old growth forest.

I imagine my former assistant Mercedes is now running that show. I naively employed her, not realising her ambition was more ruthless than my own. Was she my killer? I always thought of her as the figurative backstabber rather than a crowbar-wielding criminal. I have no memory of the repeated blows that smashed my skull or even how my body was dumped in this storage room among forgotten maps and catalogues.

When my spirit disassociated from my corpse, I rose in time to see a balaclava-clad person unblocking the old fireplace, shoving the murder weapon up the chimney and replacing the cladding. They were deceptively bulked up with extra clothing and their hood made it hard to tell their height. This person may have assumed this condemned building would be demolished, but I had one posthumous win.

All the letters I wrote and the protests I made prior to my death persuaded someone in the Department of Environment to apply a Heritage Overlay, thwarting Mayor Gillian Sparrow's plans to let that bovine bully Frank Oberlin replace this 19th century treasure with a 300 metre luxury apartment tower.

I heard about my triumph when two building inspectors came to inspect the prematurely condemned library, as I lay half decomposed about two metres beneath their feet. They gagged and complained about the stench, but they did not ask themselves why a decaying building and a few wet books would smell so foul. They hastily walked around my precious space, criticised the heritage ruling, made wild estimations about how much it would cost to stabilise and waterproof the roof, and promptly left.

Perhaps it was Gillian who killed me? But surely I would have recognised her? We were lovers once, if you must know. She stayed with me when it was her ex-husband's turn to look after their son. She was the one who knew about my trespassing, my retreats here after hellish days in the new library showing retirees how to use computers and processing email bookings for children's robotics workshops. My key to the old service entrance still worked and I would walk up the two flights of stairs to my haven, sit on my old chair and reimagine my life while listening to Erik Satie's Gymnopédie No.1.

Or was it Frank Oberlin who ordered my demise that night? He would have employed someone else to do his dirty work, no doubt, someone agile and strong who could move quickly and wield a crowbar with killer force. Agile and strong. I could be describing Gillian, who would leave me in the mornings to run with her personal trainer, while I read the newspaper and enjoyed a strong cup of English Breakfast with a dash of milk.

I knew about Gillian's kickbacks. She wanted the money for a beach house and for a time I was complicit. What were a couple of extra skyscrapers in the city if I were 140km away happily ensconced in a beach-hut reading a book? But then it became personal when Oberlin's proposal to demolish the library and build the luxury apartment building was approved by the council.

'Over my dead body.' Those were my very words. Now look at me. I put all of Gillian's detritus out on my front veranda and refused to speak to her again. She came to the library a couple of times with other council officials but I made Mercedes deal with them. Did I imagine that affectionate glance between Gillian and Mercedes the week before I was killed?

Do you know that prickling feeling you get in cemeteries and old houses, that shiver associated with the phrase "someone just walked over my grave"? I've discovered ghosts experience a similar sensation when a living creature is near. Like now. Do you hear it, that noise? Bigger than a rat. Here she comes, seeking shelter from the rain.

They come and go these homeless youths, these Orphan Annies and Oliver Twists. This one is about 15 or 16. She's wearing filthy grey tracksuit pants and a black windcheater with a dragon logo plastered across the front. She's somehow loosened one of the boards that cover the windows. That's quite a feat. Smashed the glass too and, of course, cut her hand. That's all I need, blood dripping across the floor, interfering with any forensic evidence the police might find, if they ever deign to search this place.

She crawls over to my old desk, curls up on the floor next to a pile of mulched romances and slips into a drug-induced slumber. I watch to make sure she keeps breathing. Not that I can do anything if she dies, but it wouldn't be fair if the police investigated her death rather than my own. I find myself reciting one of my favourite short stories, Edgar Allan Poe's The Cask of Amontillado. I begin: 'The thousand injuries of Fortunato I had borne as I best could.' But I got no further than: 'At length I would be avenged.' Such plans I have should my killer ever return to this place.

The girl wakes hours later, cold and, no doubt, nauseated.

She uses her phone torch to illuminate the room and doesn't bother to stand up, instead crawling over to the desk. Another homeless person has already pulled the drawers out of the cabinets. She picks over the pens, paper clips, rubber bands and clumps of damp paper.

'You won't find anything of value to sell,' I say. 'The desk is bolted to the floor and the chair isn't ergonomic.'

She freezes, then flashes her torch around.

'Who the fuck?'

Now I'm the one who is surprised. She can hear me, and I'm sure she's no longer high, either.

'Someone who can help you.'

She stands up and pulls a knife out of her pocket and backs slowly until she reaches the wall where the large print books were once housed.

'Don't youse mess with me. You hear what I'm sayin', you cunt?'

Such language offends my phantom mind, but I persevere.

'Listen,' I say. 'No weapon in the world can kill me. I'm already dead.'

I find it comic the way her knife darts around trying to make contact with an invisible assailant.

I continue: 'What is it, five hours since you last injected the heroin or whatever chemical it is you've bought off some ruthless drug dealer? You'll be experiencing withdrawal soon. You'll need money to buy more drugs. I don't condone your behaviour, but I can give you money if you do a couple of things for me.'

'What do I look like, your fuckin' slave? I don't give a fuck about you, ya hear me, ya fuckin' cunt?'

She brushes her long fringe back from her face and I recognise her. There's still enough of the child in her for me to see the long black plaits and the big brown eyes peeping over an open book. I laugh, such is my relief that this foul-mouthed feral child is a reader. There is hope in the world.

She used to come to the library when she was at primary school, but I remember now those visits suddenly stopped. She must be in Year 9 or 10 now, surely.

'I remember you loved the Friday Barnes series,' I say.

'You nos nothin' about me, cunt'

'You used to sit in the corner and read books, but you never took any books home.'

'My brudda used to piss on library books,' she says.

'You were always alone. I would ask you where your mother was, and you'd say she was in the toilet.'

'Yeah, well, that's cos my brudda was fucked, like, used to do fucked-up things when me Mum was at work. I come 'ere until she got home.'

She says that and I feel a sharp intake of breath at the horror of her situation. A phantom breath. I can't explain these residual sensations. How is it even possible that a spirit could have a nervous system? But this is sentimental gibberish.

'I'll give you $ 50 if you help me.'

'Help ya? In what fuckin' way? I don't do pussy.'

'Oh, for heaven's sake, unless you want to suck bones, I'm in no state to warrant physical contact. Do you know where the new library is located?'

'Might.'

'I'll take that as a yes. I want you to go to the information desk and say you wanted to say hello to Mary Bennet, who used to help you in the library when you were a child.'

'Ya never use-ta help me,' the little Goth says. 'You were a bitch. It was always, 'Shhh. Shhh. Keep the noise down. People are trying to re–''

'Do you want the money or not?'

'What's fifty dollars gunna get me? A couple of pills.'

'There's more money if you help me. But first, do this simple thing. I want you to use your phone to record everything the person at the desk says about me. If they don't know what happened to me, ask for Mercedes

Rodriguez and we'll see what she has to say. And come back and let me hear everything you've recorded.'

I direct her to the false drawer, which is under the desktop, a drawer undetected by those who ransacked the library in the first few months after its closure. It's where I kept the kitty. She counts out the $5 notes and change.

'$53.55 cents.'

'At least you can still count. I'm assuming you haven't been at school for a while. Do you have any clean clothes you can put on? Perhaps you could find something at Vinnies on the corner?'

'I'll shower at the swimming pool and nick some stuff out of their charity bin.'

'Ingenious. A thief as well as a drug addict.'

'Like you've never done nothing dishonest in ya life.'

'I...I...' I start to protest and then I remember my complicity with Gillian.

'Lis'in,' she says, as though she has some authority. 'I can fuck off like any time and youse be stuck here. I'll find out ya shit for ya, but only cos I want to. But there bedda be more fuckin' money.'

I can't help but admire her feistiness. I want to ask her what happened, how she came to be on the streets, but all in good time.

'You'll find some keys in one of those drawers, that way you can come in the old service entrance instead of through the window. What's your name?' I say.

'Traceey,' she says. 'Two "e"s and a "y".'

I nearly say, 'How uncouth.' But I stop myself. This young woman isn't responsible for the bastardisation of the English language. I remember my manners.

'Thank you, Traceey.' I say.

Will she come back? I'm on tenterhooks. How is it you can suddenly feel more alive when you're dead? Now every second feels like a minute, although I have no real sense of time. There are no clocks and with the windows boarded up, it's dark even during the day, although slits of light cut through when it's sunny. I'm about to give up on her, when she returns in an addled state. I have to wait for the effects of whatever drug she has taken to subside. I was never this tolerant in life, but my options are greatly reduced.

Eventually she sobers up and plays the recording for me. I didn't expect Mercedes' voice to affect me so much. I feel weighed down and teary, earthly feelings I can't explain.

'Miss Bennet,' Mercedes says. 'She's not here anymore, I'm afraid. She retired. I think she lives in Italy now. A small town. I can't remember the name. Sangi. San Gimignano, that's it.'

'What treachery. What travesty.' I splutter.

'That's why the police haven't been here. No one even knows I'm dead. How is that possible? How the hell could they create that illusion? To what end? Mercedes has my job. She could have acquired that without killing me. What is her motive for making it seem as though I am alive?'

'I need more cash,' Traceey says. I admire her single-mindedness.

'If they think I'm alive, then nothing will have been done with the house. I need you to go to my house and find out if someone is living there. You have the key, it's on the key ring. You can take anything from the house to sell. I don't care.'

'What if they've, like, fuckin' pulled down the house or, like, changed the lock?' Traceey asks.

'They won't have pulled the house down. It's a Victorian terrace, heritage listed. You can enter through the laneway at the back, that way no one will see you.'

'No fuckin' way. I'll get done for breakin' in. Just give me cash.'

'I can give you jewellery, but you'll have to come down here and get it.'

'Fine.'

I direct her to the trapdoor. She lifts it up and climbs down the ladder into the basement. She shines her phone torch and squeals like a child when she sees my skeleton and splintered skull. My spine and legs are twisted from my fall.

'Jesus, fuckin', Christ.' She shudders and thumps back up the ladder. 'Not fuckin' touchin' that thing.'

'The diamond ring, that was my mother's. It's probably worth $ 5000 or so. The pearl necklace could be worth $ 5000 too, I have no idea. You'll have to take them to a pawnbroker. Say they belonged to your grandmother. Obviously my killer wasn't a robber.'

Traceey slowly climbs back down. She stands beside my skeleton for a long time.

'First time I've seen a skeleton. It's creepy. Different from a dead body.'

She bends down and prises the ring off my finger bone. I can see there's a hint of deformity in the bone, though arthritis is obviously the least of my worries.

'What dead body?' I ask.

'Brudda. Necked himself cos he knew he'd get banged up in jail. Fuckin' pedo. I'm glad he's dead.' She sniffs and adds: 'This'll do for now. I'll come back 'n' get the beads.'

'Is that why you ran away?'

'What would you like fuckin' know? My brudda was a prick. But Rick, he's a dirty arsed cunt. Guess what, I don't give a fuck now.'

'Who is Rick?'

'Just another dirty arsed cunt. I told im he could shove his fuckin' cock like in a blender. Mum wos screamin' and carryin' on, taking his side. Fuck her, too, she can go to hell.'

'I'm sorry to hear you were treated that way.'

'Like youse would know.'

'Well, of course, I don't know. But I know you like books. I think that's why you came back here. Books will never hurt you, books–'

'Whatever gets you off, Mary. What's the address?'

Her absence this time is agonising. I need to know what is happening. All the anger and frustration that keeps me here, keeps me tethered to this building, feels like it is loosening. I'm floating, rising above my body. I no longer recognise the skeleton as my own. I have no sense of time. Traceey comes back but curls up into a foetal position and I can't get any sense out of her. I have to wait until she is clear-headed again.

She has letters from the letterbox. They are addressed to me. The world thinks I'm still alive. But who is orchestrating this?

'I got a pic of the guy living in ya house,' she says. She shows me the photo on her phone. There is something familiar about his face, but I can't place him.

'He could be any number of people who came to the library', I say.

'What if he's like the killa, not the fuckwits you keep bangin' on about?' Traceey suggests.

'I can't think of anyone else who would benefit from my death. All my money was going to this library, specifically to this building.'

'Maybe we should let the cops sort it out,' Traceey says.

'No! Your fingerprints are everywhere, your DNA, you'll get all mixed up in it. No, I want my killer to come here. I want the chance to confront them. There will be no justice any other way. In the words of Edgar Allan Poe: At length I would be avenged'.

'Poe, schmoe. We should see if this S.O.B is using your social media accounts.'

'I didn't have any social media accounts.'

Traceey rolls her eyes.

'Don't roll your eyes at me. I wasn't a complete Luddite. What about my email? We could see if he is using that?'

'We can create an account, like use a fake name, and send an email pretendin' to be, like, an old friend,' Traceey says.

'Jane Hall. She was a friend at primary school. Use her name.'

Traceey sets up an account on her phone and we send an email saying Jane is going to be in town next week and would love to catch up.

Two hours later we get a reply.

Traceey reads it out in a tone that proves she had an education at some stage in her life: 'Dear Jane, How lovely to hear from you. I'm afraid I'll be out of town next week attending a library conference in Vancouver. I travel a lot these days and never seem to get time to catch up with anyone. Do tell me everything you've been up to. At least we can stay in contact via email. Kind regards, Mary.'

'What on earth is going on? Why would anyone pretend to be me? Show me that photo again.'

Traceey magnifies the photo on her phone, and I stare at the man but to no avail. I don't know who he is.

'There's only one other thing I can think to do. The murder weapon was a crowbar. It's hidden in the old chimney.'

'What's the fuckin' deal with the chimney?'

'It was used in the 19th century to heat the building. It was blocked off long before I started here as head librarian. Let me think. Over in one of the drawers on the floor you should be able to find some old white gloves, the ones we used for handling old books.'

Traceey picks up a damp pair of grey gloves.

'Fuckin' gross,' she says.

'Stop fussing. You slept on mouldy books for weeks, before you dragged that old mattress up here.'

'I need a fix.'

'Just do this for me first. Please. Pretty please, with sugar on top.'

'I don't like suga', you bony bitch.'

'Good for you. Your teeth are rotten enough as it is. See those old boards in front of the chimney. They're easy enough to pull off. I know you're good at doing that.'

'Oh, ha ha. You're fuckin' lucky I'm even here.'

Traceey gives a few tugs but the boards don't give. She looks around for something to act as a lever and finds an old divider from one of the metal bookshelves. She manages to prise a couple of nails loose and then she gets enough traction to pull one board off. She finds the crowbar wrapped in a towel.

'Wow.' She swings the crowbar. 'It's fuckin' heavy. Someone really wanted you dead.'

'And I want to know why. Take a photo of it and send it to that email address and let's see what happens.'

'It's too fuckin' dark in here. I'll do it outside.'

She gets to the service door and turns back.

'I might be gone a bit.'

She's disappeared before I can protest. Now I don't even know if she's going to send the photo. Bloody junkies. What am I doing? I've become complicit again, like I was with Gillian.

It's night-time when I hear noises, the sounds of a board being prised off one of the windows and someone overexerting themselves. It feels like I'm going to pop, that all the energy that defines me is expanding and filling the room. She's wearing black clothing, runners and a beanie. She's put on weight since I last held her body close to mine.

I watch her go over to the chimney, feel around for the crowbar. When she doesn't find it, she goes over to the trapdoor and lifts it up, shines a torch down into the cavity and illuminates my bones.

'Why did you do it?' Traceey's voice is loud and steady. I didn't realise how much I loved this child until this moment.

'What the hell? Who are you?' Gillian asks.

'I sent ya the fuckin' email. Mary wants to know why ya did it, bitch. She can hear ya; ya know.'

'I don't know what game you think you're playing, but you're in way over your head', Gillian says.

'Ask her if she knows the person living in my house,' I shout.

'Who's the guy living in Mary's house?' Traceey relays.

Gillian laughs.

'Well, you obviously don't know everything. That is my son, Aidan. He's looking after the house for Mary.'

'Bullshit,' I shout. 'Your son is a teenager. That's a man in that photo.'

'Mary sez that guy's too old to be ya son,' Traceey tells her.

'Aidan is 22 years old.'

'Twenty-two? How can that be? He was what, 14? How have eight years gone by?'

'Mary, if you really can hear me, then I'll tell you why,' Gillian says. 'Do you think I don't know who tipped off the press about the kickbacks. You fucked everything up. So, let's call it karma, shall we? I wasn't going to let your money go to this old library. It was easy to hack into your accounts. You use the same password for everything: Proust1871.'

'Ask her if Mercedes and Frank were in on it.' Traceey relays the question.

'Fuck no,' Gillian says. 'They were as gullible as everyone else. As far as they know you're still alive and living in Italy. You might have saved this building, but it's as unloved and as dead as you. Nobody liked you and nobody has missed you.'

'That's where ya wrong,' Traceey says. She runs at Gillian and shoves her in the back. Gillian falls into the cavity and lands on my bones. One last embrace.

Traceey closes the trapdoor and turns the lock.

'Youse are so fuckin' wrong. Like someone did like Mary. I've got all your bullshit on my phone, cunt, and I'm going to the cops.' She pauses, then addresses me: 'Promise me ya won't like, you know, kill her, Mary.'

I sigh. 'At length I would be avenged,' I whisper, and then loudly: 'Only if you promise me you'll get clean and go back to school, do something with your life, write about this, become a bestselling crime wri–'

'Sure, Mary, like whatever turns you on. As long as you fuck off to the afterlife and let us all rest in peace.'

Death in the Skies

Also won the Mystery with History Award

Jessica Southern Reid

The day was perfect. The sky was clear, the air was still, and the plane was magnificent. Evelyn held the control column with one finger, marvelling at the way the machine responded to the lightest touch. She was used to ferrying damaged planes for the Air Transport Auxiliary. Not this time. This plane was brand new and she had fought hard for the right to be the first in the cockpit. There had been some ruffled feathers amongst the RAF boys, but she hadn't cared, and now she was zooming above the world, in the best plane she had flown since the start of the war.

She soared over the patchwork fields of Southern England, keeping an eye out for barrage balloons. To her left was the distant glimmer of the Channel. A shudder ran through the engine and she frowned. The aircraft lost altitude before righting itself. Evelyn didn't panic. She checked all of her controls, and found the dials all where they were supposed to be. Once more, a shudder ran through the engine, stalling it.

'Bugger,' she muttered, still determinedly not panicking. She had read her pilot's manual so many times that she could practically recite the passage on "mid-flight engine restarting" blindfold. She confidently pushed the nose of the plane down towards earth and sent it into a dive.

'If in doubt, point the whirly bit towards the ground and hope you have enough space to get going again,' Evelyn told herself, remembering what her instructor had said years before. The engine remained stubbornly silent, refusing to be restarted.

'And if all else fails, look for a road or a smooth looking field, extend and lock wheels, and say a little prayer,' she added, working the landing gear lever as she spoke. According to her instruments, the plane was still perfect, aside from the fact that the engine wouldn't start.

The ground rushed up to meet her, but Evelyn held the plane steady. She flew low over roads and fields and readied herself for landing. At the last moment, she took her eyes off the ground and reached for the photograph she carried in her breast pocket. Two small boys witnessed the crash and hurried over on their bicycles. They leapt the hedgerow and sprinted to the downed plane. It had come to rest in the far corner of the field, leaving a trail of destruction behind it. The pilot had misjudged her landing. Had it been the middle of summer, she likely would have pulled it off, but the autumn had been long and wet and the field was sodden. She had hit the ground too hard, her landing gear getting caught in the November mud.

The boys pulled the cracked cockpit cover back to reveal the pilot.

'Hey, it's a girl,' exclaimed one.

'And she's dead,' added the other excitedly.

'Poor wee lass,' the farmer muttered, shaking his head. A man in an official looking uniform stood beside him, agreeing somewhat absentmindedly. He arranged for the aircraft to be towed to the nearby aerodrome where he could examine it properly, in a hangar, and where his feet were less likely to get wet.

Evelyn's funeral was a week later. Her fellow ATA pilots wore their uniforms, pressed blue jackets and pleated skirts. The local vicar spoke of her virtues, though he'd never met her. At the back, Mabel sobbed. Tears flowed fast and freely down her cheeks and dripped off her chin. Ruth stood on one side of her, Florence the other, ready to catch her should she sway.

'I want to see the plane,' Florence announced when they got back to the room they all shared.

'Why?' Ruth asked sardonically.

'Don't you think it's a bit strange?' Florence asked.

'We've been over this already,' Ruth replied. 'Yes, we do think it's strange but what can we do about it? She's dead. Seeing the plane won't bring her back.'

None of the girls could believe that Evelyn, who was by far the best pilot amongst them, had managed to crash a brand-new plane. They flew damaged aircraft all the time, but this one had been perfect. Until it had ploughed into a turnip field and taken their squadron leader with it, that was.

'I know it won't bring her back but I just don't understand why it happened. I want to see the plane,' Florence repeated. Ruth looked as though she was about to mount an argument but Mabel interrupted.

'I'd like to see it too,' she said quietly.

It was settled. There was to be no arguing with Mabel, not on the day of Evelyn's funeral, so they went. The downed plane had been dragged to the hangar to await expert examination.

The aerodrome was abuzz with activity as final preparations were done for the nightly bombing raids. Nobody paid the slightest bit of attention to the three ATA pilots.

'Is it here?' Mabel asked as they reached the hangar. 'I'm scared to look.'

Ruth switched on her flashlight. The plane looked terrifying in the darkness, like some kind of broken monster. The hangar was full of spare parts and aerodrome debris. Shadows danced on the walls and the flashlight glinted off Evelyn's cracked cockpit cover.

'Mabel, you don't have to do this,' Ruth said carefully.

'I think I do.'

'Right, well, best get on with it,' Florence said, her mechanic's brain ticking almost audibly. She ran her hands along the wing struts and the ripped fuselage, examining it all. She climbed up onto the wing and pulled back the cockpit cover.

'It all looks perfect, she exclaimed, puzzled. She reached in and pulled out a scrap of paper before jumping down and landing catlike beside them. She popped open the fuel cap and stuck the flashlight in. Barely a moment had passed before she pulled it out with a gasp. She plunged her arm in, up to the elbow. Withdrawing it, she held something tightly between her thumb and forefinger.

'What is it?' Mabel asked warily.

Florence held the flashlight close, examining her fingers. She stuck her tongue out and licked her finger.

'It's sugar!' she gasped. 'Someone's laced the Avgas with sugar.'

'You can't be serious,' Ruth said, and grabbed the flashlight from Florence to check for herself.

'You're right. Bloody hell – how did that get in there?'

'Well, it certainly wasn't by accident,' said Florence. 'Someone must have sabotaged her.'

'Who would do something like that? And why?' Ruth asked.

A sudden noise from outside caused the girls to freeze. Ruth switched off the flashlight and they were plunged into darkness. All three dropped to the ground and they crawled behind the wing of a Hurricane. Another flashlight beam lit the room and they huddled down, out of sight.

'Let's get this done quickly,' a voice instructed. The girls heard a strange combination of noises. Somebody was climbing on the wrecked plane, and there was an odd sucking noise, like a plug being pulled from a drain. Finally, a sound they all knew. The sound of a fuel tank being filled from a jerry can.

'Her funeral was today,' a second voice said.

'Who cares? One less demented bint in the sky if you ask me,' said the first voice, full of malice. Ruth reached out in the darkness and found Mabel's hand, squeezing it tight.

'I didn't know she'd die,' the second voice said.

'It's a war, Humphries, people die. Do you feel bad for every German bastard you blow out of the sky? Besides, it's not our fault she couldn't land properly.'

The girls stayed rooted to the spot long after the two men had left the hangar. When the silence was finally broken, Ruth's voice was icy.

'They killed her. They killed her because they didn't want her in the sky.'

'I found this,' Florence said, offering Mabel the piece of paper from the cockpit.

Illuminated in the beam of the flashlight, they could see what it was. A photograph. It was slightly damp and the glossy surface was marred with flecks of blood, much like the interior of the cockpit. In the photograph, two girls sat close together. Evelyn, her thousand-watt smile in full force, beamed at the camera. Her arm was around Mabel's shoulder, drawing her closer as Mabel placed a kiss on Evelyn's cheek. Mabel glanced quickly at it and stuffed it into her breast pocket. She didn't need to look, she had her own copy of the photograph, tucked safely between the pages of her aeronautics manual.

'Oh, Mabel,' Florence said, 'I'm so sorry.'

The three girls snuck out of the hangar and crossed the darkened runway to the Nissan huts they called home.

'You don't think that they did it because she was, you know, a Tom?' Ruth asked, throwing an apologetic glance to Mabel.

'I doubt they even knew. Anyhow, the way that brute was talking, it sounded as though he sabotaged her because she's a woman, not because she loved women,' Florence reasoned.

'And now they're destroying the evidence, cleaning out the fuel tank. The investigation's going to say it was pilot error.'

'We can't let that happen. We have to report them,' Mabel said, looking utterly distraught.

'There's something else I need to tell you both, but I swore I'd never say, so this has to stay between us,' Florence whispered conspiratorially. 'Remember Emily Granger? Well she came to me after her crash and asked me to have a look at the Lancaster she'd been flying. She thought there might have been something wrong with it.'

'She left the ATA after the crash, didn't she?' Ruth asked.

'Yes. But not before she came to see me. We took the engine apart. Nobody cared much, it was an old plane. They hadn't even taken it out of the field she'd crashed into.'

'Flo, get to the point,' Ruth urged.

'Rags,' Florence answered, 'the engine was full of rags. Wrapped around everything. It was obvious she'd been sabotaged.'

'What did you do?'

'We reported it, of course. We went to the Air Commodore but he didn't want to hear what we had to say. I was told to keep mum about the whole thing or risk my wings, and Emily was booted out – dishonourably discharged.'

'How horrible,' Mabel said. 'I think we need to speak to her.'

Ruth pushed open the heavy door of the pub, squinting as she led the way from the bright sunlight to the gloomy, low-lit interior of the Rose & Crown.

'It's so good to see you all again,' Emily said, rising as they approached and hugging them each in turn. 'I'm so sorry about Ev,' she said to Mabel, whose eyes filled with tears. They'd been doing that on a regular basis ever since the crash. She blinked furiously and hurried off to the bar.

'The thing is, Emily, this is not just a social catch-up. Flo told us about your plane and what they did to you. And we think they did the same to Evelyn, only she didn't make it out alive.'

Emily gave Florence a horrified look. 'What if they find out you've told someone? They practically threatened to court-martial us if we said so much as one word!'

'I'm sorry,' Florence said. 'But I had to. See, the thing is, Ev was just like you, maybe even a better flyer. And she was in a brand-new plane. There's no way she caused the crash, but that's what they're saying. So we snuck a look at her plane. We found sugar in her fuel tank! But we don't have any proof because they've already drained it to get rid of the evidence.'

'We just thought,' Ruth said, 'that you might have some idea of who it was that sabotaged your plane.'

Emily drummed her fingertips on the table slowly.

'You know some of the men think we're taking their jobs, so I just assumed it was one of them. But like you, I've got no proof.'

A sudden burst of swearing came from near the bar and the girls turned. A large blond man in uniform was swaying drunkenly. Next to him, dwarfed by his height, stood Mabel, clutching four half pints.

'Wash where you're going little girl!' slurred the man. 'Bloody women, you ferry a few planes and you think you're as good as us. Get out of the way.'

Mabel looked like she was about to burst into tears again but, regaining her composure, pulled herself up to her full height of 5'3" and stomped hard on his foot, before escaping under his raised arm. The man staggered in the other direction, mumbling obscenities, the most discernible of which was "fuckin' demented bint".

'That man,' Florence said quickly, 'what did he just call you?'

'It's nothing, forget it,' Mabel said, keen to move on.

'No, he called you "a demented bint". Isn't that what the man in the hangar said?'

'It could be, he was certainly rude enough.'

'It was the same voice, I'm sure of it,' Florence insisted. The others didn't seem as convinced.

'That's William Farrier, his father's the Marshall of the RAF. He's a brute and a bully. I flew in a Hurricane with him once and he kept making passes at me in the cockpit. I made a complaint to the Commodore but he told me that I was best to forget it, Farrier's untouchable,' Emily told them, lips pursed.

'But do you really think he could sabotage a plane?' Ruth asked.

'Well, he hates female pilots and he knows his way around an engine. But even if it is him, how do we prove it?' Emily asked.

Ruth had a gleam in her eye that bespoke bad things for Farrier. 'I've got an idea, but you're not going to like it,' she said, grinning at Florence.

'Unbutton your blouse a bit and go make friends with him. It might help if you mention how much you hate women pilots.'

'Why've I got to do it?' Florence asked.

'Easy, he's seen Emily and Mabel, and my drink is full,' Ruth reasoned.

'Hi there, flyboy.' Florence batted her lashes. 'I was told this was where I might find myself a real pilot.'

'You've got that right, girlie.' Farrier raked Florence up and down with his eyes, unabashedly pausing on her chest. She felt a wave of revulsion run through her but fought it off with a smile.

'You boys are so brave,' Florence gushed. 'I can't believe I'm actually here talking to a Captain.' Florence knew full well from his uniform that Farrier was only a second officer, but he failed to correct her. 'You must fly so many dangerous missions.'

Farrier visibly swelled with pride. 'Yeah I do, really dangerous ones.' He reached out to grope Florence's bottom, but she deftly sidestepped.

'I can't believe the government is employing girls to fly those planes when they have men like you. I mean, surely they can't be as good.'

'Disgrashful. Should be baking cakes and making babies,' he trailed off.

'And I don't understand why any girl would want to fly a plane when she could be at home cooking and cleaning for her very own hero,' Florence said, wondering if she was laying it on a bit thick.

'Not right in the head, none of them. But don't worry, I fixed 'em.'

'Oh really?' Florence tried to keep her tone admiring.

'How about I tell you all about it,' he said, hiccupping, 'over dinner. Lesh say seven, tomorrow, here?'

'That dress is perfect,' Emily said. They were cosily ensconced in their room for a war council, helping Florence to get ready for her date. 'He's going to tell you everything and more.'

'What am I supposed to do if he gets all handsy?' Florence asked, conscious of the low cut of the dress and the low morals of her date.

'I have something for that,' Emily said, pulling a little vial of pills from her purse.

'What are those?' Florence asked; examining the pills.

'I nicked them from Dad, he uses them to get to sleep. Thought it might come in handy if you needed him to be a bit dazed, you know, to make him confess.'

'Em, you're an evil genius.'

'Now remember,' Ruth cut in, 'you need to make him talk. Get him to tell you how he did it without anybody noticing, that kind of thing.'

'Ruth, I am so unbelievably well-briefed on this mission, I think I could do it in my sleep,' Florence said reassuringly.

'Right, well, off you go then, it's nearly seven,' Mabel said.

Florence put on her coat and took a slug from a little silver hip flask before tucking it into her handbag. 'Liquid courage,' she explained. She kissed them all goodbye and went out into the cold, not feeling nearly as brave as she had pretended to be.

Farrier was waiting for her outside the bar, looking significantly cleaner and more sober than the previous night. He led her inside and they found a table. He was attentive and sweet and nothing like the drunken buffoon the girls had encountered the night before. Florence could almost feel his charm working on her but reminded herself that he was likely the one who sabotaged Evelyn's Spitfire.

'Tell me about your missions, Captain,' Florence flattered, 'it must be awfully dangerous.'

'Of course, but when you're up there in the sky, all you need to do is think of the beautiful girls waiting for you when you land,' Farrier replied with a winning smile. 'If I knew I had a girl like you waiting for me back on the ground, I'd never have to worry about a thing.' She giggled, inwardly cringing.

Florence had been concerned with her ability to tell a lie if he asked her anything personal but she needn't have worried. William Farrier didn't ask her a single question about herself.

'What kind of planes do you fly?'

'Me? Spitfires. Yep. I'm a fighter pilot. And a damned good one, if I do say so,' he said cockily.

'I read in the papers that there was a Spitfire crashed not far from here, only last week. Did you know the pilot?' Florence asked, fighting to keep her tone light.

'Ah, that. Bloody waste of a plane, that was. But, like I always say, that's what you get when you put girls in the cockpit. It's the air, you see,' he explained, 'it's thinner up there, and women, it affects their brains differently. They lose their senses.'

'You don't think there should be any women in the planes?'

'Absolutely not. It's nothing personal. Like I said, the thin air affects their brains. It's simple biology.'

'Oh well, I suppose there's not much you can do about it. At least they don't let women go on missions and fire guns,' Florence said, steering the conversation.

'You might be surprised. There are some of us who see it as our duty to get these girls out of our planes. Ah, but I shouldn't say—'

'Oh go on, tell me,' Florence teased, taking his hand and smiling coquettishly.

'Let's just say that lass, the one who crashed the Spitfire, she might have had some help.'

Florence leaned forward in her seat, willing him to continue. A yell came from the other side of the room and Farrier's attention was stolen.

'Ah, Humphries, you old dog,' he yelled jovially to a man who had just entered the pub. The name clicked with Florence and she wondered if she was about to meet the other man from the hangar.

'Humphries, may I introduce you to the lovely Florence?' Farrier gestured to her as though she was a prize he'd won. Humphries took her hand and Florence fought the urge to rip her fingers from his clammy grip.

'Where were we?' he asked, shooing Humphries away.

'The Spitfire. You didn't, you know, do something to it, did you?' she asked, forcing herself to giggle as though it was the naughtiest thing she had ever said.

'I might have done,' he whispered conspiratorially, 'but that's nothing, you should hear about what we've got planned next.'

Florence's blood ran cold. She swallowed and made herself smile up at him as though there wasn't a thought between her pretty ears.

'Actually, you know what?' he said. 'I can show you, if you'd like. Shall we get out of here?'

She stood and slipped back into her coat, hoping he got the message. She didn't trust herself to speak, worried that her voice might come out shaking.

'Humphries,' he called, 'we're off. Florence wants me to show her Hangar Two. Perhaps she'll let you join us later on.' He winked at his friend and turned back to Florence. 'Don't worry about him. He can never get the girls for himself so sometimes he likes to watch.'

Florence gave him a vapid smile and fought the urge to vomit into her handbag. She allowed herself to be led back down the road and to Hangar Two. It was the biggest hangar at RAF Maidenhead but was mostly empty due to the night-time raids happening all over occupied Europe.

'Two days from now,' he told her, 'four planes are being ferried to RAF Hamble. I've had a few of the lads make complaints about the girls who'll be flying them. They're incompetent, they come to work drunk, that sort of thing. Now when the whole squadron fails to arrive at Hamble, they'll have to look into the complaints, won't they,' he explained, tapping his nose genially.

'Why won't they arrive at Hamble?'

'It's simple, really. Bit of sugar in the fuel tank. It clogs the filter and stalls the engine in mid-air.'

'How can you be sure it'll work?' she asked, barely keeping her voice steady.

'It already has. That lass in the Spitfire? That was us. Bit of a bungle, that one. Brand spanking new plane, so there's an investigation. We had to do a bit of a switch of the fuel before they could check it.'

Florence's mouth fell open at the readiness of his confession. Farrier interpreted this as a sign of how impressed she was.

'Don't worry, they'll never catch us. We're cleverer by far than those idiot girls,' he reassured, wrapping his arm around her waist and pulling her close.

'Erm, it's getting late,' she said, attempting to disentangle herself.

'Where do you think you're going, missy? I bought you dinner, remember?' She realised he had no intention of letting her leave.

'D-do you fancy a drink?' She stuttered, pulling the hip flask from her handbag. He grinned at her and moved to grab it.

'Wait, can we have a bit more light? I w-want to be able to see you.'

'Of course you do,' he laughed. 'I'll be right back, don't you move.'

He crossed the hangar to the little office in the corner, in search of some candles. The second his back was turned Florence scrabbled through her handbag for the tiny vial of pills. She popped a handful into the flask and secured the lid, shaking it surreptitiously.

Farrier returned with a kerosene lamp and a pilot's greatcoat, which he spread on the floor, next to an open-bellied Lysander. He sat on the coat and motioned for her to join him. She did, putting the flask to her lips, keeping them tightly shut. She passed it back to him and he gulped back several mouthfuls.

'Where were we?' he said, in what he obviously thought was a seductive tone. He reached up and took her cheek in his hand, leaning in, eyes closed, lips puckered. Florence recoiled and he fell forward. She jumped up, ready to fight him off but he slumped down and his face hit the floor. Florence breathed a sigh of relief that was cut short when a voice rang out through the hangar.

'Oi, Farrier, is that you?' called Humphries.

Florence slipped into the shadows behind the Lysander and armed herself with a wrench.

The girls played cards by the light of a single candle, none of them paying much attention to the game, all waiting for Florence's return. She opened the door and practically fell through it. She was shaking from head to toe and there was a look of utter terror in her eyes.

'What happened?' Mabel asked, wrapping the trembling Florence in a tight hug.

'I did something bad,' she stuttered. 'Help, please.'

She broke free of Mabel's hug and fled the room. The three girls, astounded, followed her. They ran the whole way to Hangar Two. There in the middle of the hangar, next to a Lysander, were two prone figures, illuminated by a kerosene lantern.

'Flo, what did you do?' asked Ruth, aghast.

'I gave him some of the pills. He was trying it on and I didn't know how to get away,' Florence explained. 'And him,' she added, pointing to Humphries, 'he saw Farrier on the ground, and I didn't know what to do, so I hit him with a w-wrench,' she sobbed.

'How many pills did you give him?' Emily asked, picking up Farrier's arm and dropping it on his own face.

'I don't know, maybe five?'

'Five?' Dad takes two and he's out for the night. Wonder what this'll do to him?'

'I don't like the way blood's coming out of his ear,' Ruth said, turning Humphries' head to the side.

'Did you make sure it was them before you tried to commit murder?' Mabel asked.

'It was them. And, I learned that they're planning another sabotage, for two days' time. There are four planes being ferried to Hamble, and he said they're going to bring them all down. He told me all about it. Gosh, he was so stupid. All I had to do was bat my eyelashes and pretend to hate female pilots and he told me everything. Pride of the RAF, these two,' she said disdainfully.

'Four?' Emily squawked, 'they're going to sabotage four planes?'

'Unless we stop them,' Mabel said.

'I'm not sure this fellow will be up to much sabotage,' Ruth said, gesturing to Humphries.

'Ladies, we have a more pressing matter on our hands,' Emily interrupted. 'What are we supposed to do with these two?'

'I might actually have an idea,' Florence said slowly. 'I was thinking about it while I was hiding from the one I hit with a wrench.'

'Well, go on,' Emily urged. 'We're going to need a plane.'

Mabel waved to the ground crew as she climbed into the cockpit of the Avro Anson. Luck had been on their side when the girls had examined the roster for the next day's flights. Had it been a smaller plane, they wouldn't have all fit. She took her seat and increased the revolutions to the engine. The plane gained speed and tore off down the runway, soaring over the hedge that marked the end of the aerodrome.

In the back, one of the men was stirring. They were both tied to stretchers, requisitioned from the air ambulance storeroom. The girls had loaded the two unconscious pilots into the bomb bay of the Anson as the sun was beginning to rise and it was an utter miracle that they'd not been seen. Emily had farewelled them with a kiss for luck, just before dawn.

Hamble was south-west of Maidenhead but Mabel swung the plane out to the east until they could see the sparkling blue of the Channel below them.

'He's waking up,' Ruth yelled. 'What do I do?'

'Leave him, there's not much he can do from there.'

Farrier's eyes opened and he made a quick mental assessment of the situation before screaming bloody murder.

'Bit pathetic, isn't he,' Ruth said.

'Girls, I'm going to have to start heading back soon, otherwise we run the risk of running into actual enemy planes out here,' Mabel shouted.

Florence and Ruth nodded to each other. Ruth pulled the lever to open the bomb bay door and suddenly the aircraft was filled with wind and the noise of the engines.

'Out you go,' Ruth said unkindly, and heaved the stretcher Humphries was tied to. He didn't stir as he went over the edge.

'You know, I think he might have already been dead,' she said lightly, as though she was commenting on the weather.

'You're next, big boy,' Florence said with a coy smile.

'No, what are you, you can't do this! My father, he'll–' Farrier screamed, looking from one to the other in terror.

'Your father won't do a bloody thing. You'll just join the thousands of other brave pilots who died over the Channel,' Ruth said.

'Why are you doing this? I can pay you!' His desperate shouts fell on deaf ears.

'You killed our friend. You sabotaged Emily's plane. You planned to hurt others. Or maybe we've just gone a bit loopy. The air up here, it's very thin, you see, and our little female brains just can't cope,' Florence replied, deadpan.

'Goodbye flyboy,' Ruth said as she heaved his stretcher out into the open air. His scream was gone in a second, taken by the November winds.

Florence banged her fist against the cockpit. 'Mabel, let's go home.'

Mabel heard all that happened behind her cockpit and looked down to see if she could spot the falling stretchers but they were gone, lost forever. She smiled as she pulled the photograph from her breast pocket. She pressed her lips to the photo, still flecked with Evelyn's blood, and turned the plane for home.

MONSTER HUNTERS

Also won the Great Film Idea Award

Hayley Young

JUSTICE MOVED SLOWLY IN THE SMALL OUTBACK TOWN OF STILLER ROCK. Though a far cry from her fast-paced beat in the city, Superintendent Rose "Sprig" Collings had a deep love for the town she grew up in and, in the five years since returning, enjoyed the quiet responsibility of keeping Stiller Rock's peace. Admittedly, peace was easily kept when the job was largely traffic infringements and minor possession charges, though lately the latter was gaining traction.

Some thirty years earlier, Stiller Rock gained notoriety for all the wrong reasons. A spree of crime resulted from an influx of drugs in the region and a cop turned up dead. The superintendent at the time, Sprig's own father, had shut the whole sorry circus down within the year. He uncovered the dead cop's involvement in the drug ring, and a prominent local businessman was arrested for the murder, though he committed suicide before it went to trial.

Her Dad was a hero for his remaining years and the town had known relative harmony since. Though it was history, thanks to a recent movie based on the events, the past resisted burial; and any time Sprig got wind drug use was on the rise, she became nervous. She remembered the intense pressure on her Dad.

The combination of the town's infamous past and Sprig's stellar reputation at the city station, meant a number of young police found their way to Stiller Rock. Most didn't last the year, driven mad by boredom and transferring back to the city. But still they came. Sprig made a double shot coffee, knowing the newest recruit was starting today. She wondered if the others had started bets on how long this one would last before turning tail.

'Superintendent Collings!' The young man all but flew out of the chair out front of the station, glasses slipping down his nose.

'It's an absolute honour, ma'am.'

'No need for such formalities here, mate, you can call me Sprig.'

'Uh, Sprig,' he began tentatively. 'You're a legend in the city–'

'I hope you had other reasons for preferencing this station,' Sprig said cheerily as she led him inside. The young man stood nervously. Sprig sighed. Like many before him, he probably thought this would be an action-packed town.

'What's your name, Senior Constable?'

'Ernest Tickle.'

Sprig stared. Pam at the desk dropped her teaspoon.

'You get this far unscathed, name like that?' Sprig finally asked.

'Not exactly,' Tickle pushed his glasses up his nose sheepishly.

Sprig hid a smile. There were different types of grit. Perhaps there was more to this kid than met the eye.

'This is Pam, local legend. Works the desk these days but she'll still have you on the floor if you step out of line. The two in the back pretending to work are Smithy and Kel; excellent cops, even though they think I can't see them playing five-draw.'

Ernest Tickle shook hands and turned back to Sprig with a face so full of enthusiasm it warmed her practiced smile, though she figured the kid was in for a boring year, if he stuck it out.

'Welcome to the monster hunters,' Sprig said drily.

'Morning, Sesame Street.'

'Not the worst I've been called,' Tickle responded brightly to Smithy as the station door clanged shut behind him. He handed Sprig a coffee, before carrying a cardboard tray around the room to the others. She looked down appreciatively. The kid might be a kiss-ass but at least he was the kind that got her coffee order right.

'Best not let Sesame Street stick, boss,' Pam observed, sorting filing as a waft of cappuccino steam danced in front of her.

'Reckon you're right, Pam. What's a suitable alternative?'

'Well, I had a good think,' Pam said thoughtfully, rapping her papers on the desk. 'Settled on Tick, like the insect. Implies he'll be subtle but dangerous.'

Sprig looked at Tickle.

'Nicknames are a rite of passage in this place, Senior Constable. But, if it makes you uncomfortable, let me know.' The last thing she needed was a bullying complaint landing on her desk.

'Nah, I like it,' he admitted, a grin breaking onto his face. Sprig matched his smile; she suspected her first instinct was right, this kid was tougher than he looked.

'Alright Tick, you're with me. First stop of the day is to check on Mad Annie.'

'Something to say, Tick?' Sprig asked. They were driving in silence, but Sprig observed him fidgeting in his chair.

'It's not really politically correct to call someone mad, is it?' He fiddled with a thread on his shirt.

'You're 600k's west of politically correct, mate. You can't expect Stiller to be like the city.'

'They had organic almond milk at the café,' Tick offered hopefully.

'I assure you, they did not.'

'Oh,' Tick raised a hand to his hair. 'That explains why the coffee was so good.'

Sprig snorted. 'Look, it's archaic to call her Mad Annie but that's what she calls herself. She's been here as long as I can remember, relatively harmless, except for a couple of instances of marijuana possession. She forgets to look after herself, so we do a weekly welfare check. She's not known for hygiene but she's part of the town, so she deserves a bit of dignity. Ready?'

Sprig switched off the ignition and emerged from the car. It wasn't even 8am but the heat hit immediately. The cicadas were already deafening and Sprig pulled at her collar as she eyed the trees, letting the faint breeze brush her neck.

'Mad Annie, it's Sprig. Got a new friend for you to meet.' Sprig gestured to the backseat, and Tick retrieved the shopping bag of water and food.

A small, old woman emerged from the bushes, eyes darting between Sprig and Tick. She scratched her matted grey hair and held out her hand. Sprig nodded and Tick gently handed her the bag.

'You take care now, Mad Annie.' Sprig lowered herself into the driver's seat.

'It's happening again,' Mad Annie said, staring at Sprig. 'Like when you were a girl.'

'What's happening?'

'Monsters.' Sprig was interrupted from replying by a buzzing in her pocket.

'Boss, it's Pam. There's been a break-in at the pharmacy.'

Sprig stepped carefully over the broken glass of the pharmacy shopfront,

Tick in tow. She knew Smithy and Kel were going door-to-door to source security camera footage, though that was likely a dead-end. Most shops only had cameras for show. She spied the pharmacist, Millie, and the local doctor, Dr Webber, trying to placate a disgruntled customer.

'I've got nothing at the moment,' Millie pleaded, 'but the doctor and I will have a chat and sort something out this afternoon.'

After a few choice words the man turned to leave, reddening when he saw Sprig. Sprig recognised him. She reckoned Lou was about the meanest old bugger in history. Sprig walked to the back of the shop.

'Millie, Webb, everything okay?'

'I don't get paid enough for these pleasantries,' Millie sighed, rubbing her forehead.

'I assume they've taken the usual goodies?'

'Cleared me out of everything with high street value.'

Sprig's eyes narrowed. There were murmurings of more drugs around the local towns, but she assumed it was coming from the city. If the situation was getting desperate enough to rob the local pharmacy, it meant the problem was becoming endemic.

Dr Webber shook his head. 'I have patients who genuinely need this stuff, it's not like they can easily go elsewhere.'

'Lou among your patients, Webb?' Sprig asked.

'He knows I won't be bullied into prescribing painkillers. He sees someone a postcode over,' Dr Webber said wryly.

Sprig smiled at Millie and put a hand on her arm.

'We'll find who did this. Anything I can do in the meantime?'

Millie shook her head. 'Insurance will cover it, it's just the inconvenience, and the violation.'

Sprig nodded her understanding and Millie talked her through the damage in between serving customers as best she could. Dr Webber stayed on hand with his prescription pad, the two of them coming up with makeshift pain management plans.

After a long day of interviews and forensic procedures, Sprig stretched her aching back in front of the pharmacy. Neighbouring shopkeepers had finished helping board up the window, and Millie waved dejectedly as she got in her car.

'Long day,' said Dr Webber, mirroring Sprig's stretch. 'Don't suppose I could prescribe a drink at my place to decompress?'

Sprig laughed. It wouldn't have been the first time she spent the night, though it had been a while between sleepovers.

'Not tonight, Webb. Still plenty to do.'

'Never-ending paperwork,' Webb grinned. 'You're worse than me.'

Their first stop the following day was an interview with Lou. Sprig spent the drive to his farm explaining him to Tick, though nothing could really prepare you for Lou. Although she'd never been able to pin anything illegal on him, he was well known for cruelty. Yelling at kids, hurling racial slurs, shooting any dog that had the misfortune to step on his property – just about everyone in town hated him. Sprig grimaced as they walked the dry dirt to his verandah, eyeing the rifle rack that sat next to Lou.

'Who's the new pig?' Lou sneered.

'Senior Constable Tick,' Sprig said, the old man's attitude grating. He called them pigs, but he was the animal.

Her questioning of Lou went about as well as she expected, though she noted his constricted pupils with interest. He wasn't about to let them in his house without a warrant but it was clear Lou was getting his pain relief pills somewhere.

Back at the station they ran through their information. As Sprig expected, there was no security footage. While they were waiting on forensics, all they had to go on was instinct. Lou was an obvious suspect, and from their long interview with Millie, Sprig suggested that whoever had broken in was familiar with the pharmacy; they knew where to look, and hadn't taken any cash.

'What about the pharmacist?' Tick suggested. 'She said she didn't get paid enough to deal with Lou, maybe there's money trouble? If she could sell those drugs for their street price plus claim insurance, she'd be sitting pretty.'

'Good observation,' Sprig said. She hated to think badly of Millie but objectivity was key until they had more information.

Information, however, proved scarce in the following weeks as forensics turned up nothing and interviews went round in circles. Sprig heard of a similar break-in in a neighbouring town and scheduled a meeting with police there to compare notes. The night before the meeting, her sleep was rudely interrupted.

Sprig grumbled as she rolled over, mobile buzzing persistently. The police phone diverted to her after-hours but she was surprised to see it wasn't a work call.

'Webb? It's 3am.'

'Sorry, I know the cop-shop diverts to you anyway so I thought I'd save a minute. The alarm at the practice went off, there's been a break-in.'

Sprig and Kel were there in fifteen minutes. Sprig was surprised to see Millie there, too. Millie looked at her sheepishly.

'I set up a camera at the pharmacy. I'm not sleeping well these days and saw lights flashing from the practice alarm. Thought I'd check it out.'

Sprig knew that story was about as likely as her getting more sleep tonight but let it slide. Who Webb chose to spend his nights with was no longer her concern.

'Any idea what they took?'

'Just my doctor's bag, far as I can tell,' Webb said, gesturing to a blue asthma inhaler discarded a few metres down the road. 'Not much in there to keep them happy for long, though.'

Sprig sighed. 'Looks like they're getting desperate. Alright Kel, let's get to it.'

'You two look like shit,' Tick chirped.

'Wow, Tick, run it up the flagpole,' Sprig muttered, sinking into her chair.

'We're running off three hours sleep,' Kel yawned as he distributed the morning coffees, double shots for himself and Sprig.

'What's the plan, boss?'

'I've got that meeting with the other area cops this arvo, in the meantime I reckon we pay Lou another visit.'

Lou proved predictably unhelpful during their second conversation, though Sprig observed enough to consider the visit worthwhile. Not only was he off his face, she spied the strap of a black bag in his overflowing trash heap, buried by empty packets of Winnie Blues. She couldn't get close enough to confirm but it looked an awful lot like a doctor's bag. She feigned defeat as they finished their chat.

'Worried you're losing control, Sprig?' Lou smirked as they returned to the car.

'Control isn't real,' Sprig smiled charmingly. 'Can't lose something you never had.'

'You believe control isn't real?' Tick asked curiously as they drove back to town.

'You'll be a better cop when you learn to let go of the illusion you're in control. Maintaining order is different to wielding power, it's only our job to do the former.'

Tick nodded thoughtfully but his reply was interrupted as a red car flew by them. Sprig sighed and turned their car around, turning on lights and siren. The red car pulled over without any fuss and Sprig walked to the driver's window. Her heart sank when she saw the car full of teenage boys and recognised the driver. They scurried to hide boxes of cigarettes and a half empty bottle of bourbon.

'What the hell, Tom?'

'Sun was in me eyes.'

'Uh-huh, is that why they're bloodshot? There's sun in your eyes, Tommo, and there's reckless driving. Tell me boys, how small does your toolkit have to be to drive that fast?'

The passengers sniggered. Sprig lowered her sunglasses and stared at the guilty-looking Tom.

'I catch you going this speed again, I book you – if you're lucky. If you're unlucky, I'll be scraping your teeth off the road.'

'Why didn't you book him?' Tick asked as Sprig returned.

'I knew Tom's parents. Mum died of cancer a few years back, Dad drank himself to death after. Tom mucks about but he works three casual jobs to look after his little brother. That kid's had a worse go than most, I'm just glad he didn't hurt himself and his mates.' She bit her lip as she wondered at the destination of Tom's car. The only thing in that direction was Lou's farm.

Sprig's afternoon meeting with the neighbouring town's police left her anxious. Immediately prior to her arrival, those police received reports of a body under a bridge. It was a teenager, and it was a drug overdose. Kids didn't know what they were doing with these serious painkillers. They were playing a game where no-one explained the rules. She worried it was only a matter of time before kids started dying in Stiller.

The following week, another death was reported in a nearby town, another teenager. Sprig's anxiety was through the roof, though she tried to keep the station running as normally as possible.

'Righto team, who wants to check on Mad Annie this week?'

'Really, Sprig, with everything that's going on?' Kel asked gently. 'Mad Annie will be okay without us for one week, she's been here forever, long before you even arrived in Stiller as a kid.'

Sprig smirked, knowing that was not the case, but you couldn't argue town history.

'People in town say she did something to her kid, years ago. They say she talks about her dead baby.' Tick said, nervously.

'Well, whatever people think, there's never been any evidence and I reckon she's punished herself enough for imaginary sins. As long as she's on the right side of the law we don't antagonise her,' Sprig said firmly. 'We've always looked after her. Smithy, Tick, take her some water.'

Two hours later, Smithy burst through the door.

'Sprig, it's Mad Annie, we had to take her to hospital. She's okay, Tick's with her.' Sprig jumped out of her chair.

'What happened, heat get to her?'

'I wish,' Smithy shook his head. 'She was unresponsive when we got there. Found this next to her.' Smithy held up a small wrapper Sprig recognised from the pharmacy, a strong narcotic patch.

'Shit,' Sprig whistled, sinking back into her chair.

'Yep,' Smithy agreed. 'Mad Annie's part of this now.'

Sprig's heart froze when she received the phone call she so desperately hoped would never come. A body in the park, a teenager. As she dipped under the police tape, her frozen heart shattered.

'No,' she whispered. 'Please, no.'

Tom was unmistakably dead, his lips as blue as his eyes had been in life. Sprig didn't bother fighting the tears that formed in her eyes. The others were sniffling too, Smithy put an arm around Sprig's shoulder.

'Boss, we've got to get these bastards.'

Sprig's eyes narrowed as she looked at the small collection of Tom's belongings. She knew he bought cigarettes underage, she'd issued countless warnings. She also knew she'd never sprung him with a pack of Winnie Blues, so what was one doing here?

'Morning Kel.'

'I know it's your day off boss, but you're going to want to come in. I'm at Lou's farm, someone's blown his face half off.'

Sprig stared at Lou's body, still fascinated how quickly the heat got to them.

'Jesus, Sprig,' Webb buried his nose in his sleeve. 'Why'd they bother calling me? He's beyond medical help, he's moved to Nick Cave inspiration.'

'Sorry Webb, standard procedure,' Sprig apologised, covering her surprise he had been called. 'As you see, we don't need you here.'

'Agreed, he's dead as disco mate. I walked through the house. Sorry, didn't know where he was. Hope that doesn't stuff up forensics.'

'Shouldn't do,' Sprig said, 'he was killed outside.'

She was annoyed, though not surprised, that Webb hadn't thought not to traipse through a crime scene. The team remained at Lou's for the rest of the morning, the heat making the already grim task almost unbearable. Sprig was finally able to dig the doctor's bag out of Lou's trash heap and shook her head as they bagged it for evidence.

'It's not over, is it?' Tick asked as they buckled their seatbelts. Sprig couldn't tell if his tone was fearful or hopeful.

'Not by a long shot. Someone decided Lou outlived his purpose. He may have been dealing but there's no way he was the head of the operation. Didn't have the HR skills, or brains.'

Tick smirked at the mention of brains.

'At least supply will be interrupted. He must have been the Stiller-based dealer. All the surrounding towns have problems too, it's unlikely the big fish is here, right?'

'I'm not sure,' Sprig frowned.

Sprig undid her seatbelt, noticing Tick made no move to do the same.

'You aren't coming in?'

'Can I not?' Tick asked, looking at his hands. 'I asked Millie out last week, it didn't go well. I think I'll make her awkward.'

'Okay,' Sprig conceded. She entered the pharmacy and walked to the back. Millie gave Sprig the routine update and Sprig made to leave after ten uneventful minutes.

'Sprig,' Millie hesitated. 'The night of the practice break-in, I lied. I was at Webb's. He left before me. Guess I slept through his phone but he rang me to meet him there.'

'Thanks for telling me. Any reason you wanted to share this now?'

Millie shuffled.

'Thought I might get in trouble for lying. Plus, I respect you Sprig, I know you and Webb were involved. It was just one time. I find him narcissistic, to be honest.'

Sprig laughed. Webb was narcissistic, which is why they had never gone past casual.

'I appreciate it Millie, but there's no bad blood there. On that note, I believe my colleague is avoiding you?'

Millie frowned. 'He came on a little strong, got defensive when I said no. Plus, don't you think it's odd this drug stuff started up the day Tick arrived?'

'Whole world is odd, Millie,' Sprig waved as she left, though she tucked the thought away for later.

'Millie says you didn't take no gracefully.'

Sprig looked directly at Tick when she got in the car. Tick's ears reddened.

'If it had just been no, I would have taken it like sugar,' he muttered. 'It was no, plus a few snide insults. Millie isn't as kind as she first appears.'

Sprig paused, having never heard of Millie being unkind.

'Just words, Tick. You can't kill someone with words.'

'I disagree, Sprig. Words kill us all in the end.'

Sprig noted the darkness in Tick's expression, before turning her eyes to reverse the car. She had seen that look before. The look of someone who experienced a lifetime of rejection, someone who had the potential to snap.

Sprig's phone buzzed as they arrived at the station.

'Set up the whiteboard, Tick. We're making headway on this tonight, before anyone else dies. I'll be in soon.'

Tick nodded.

'A little busy, Webb,' Sprig said into her phone.

'Of course, I know. Just wanted to remind you the offer of a drink stands. You're doing good work, Sprig. People who live ordinarily can't imagine extraordinary pressure.'

Tick had not only set up the whiteboard, he'd also made tea and started a mind map. Sprig couldn't help but chuckle, happy he kept his head after a confronting day.

'Let's run through suspects,' Sprig said.

'Millie,' Tick began bitterly. 'She could make a profit from the break-in, plus it directs attention away from her being involved.'

'Agreed, though not sure you're objective,' Kel chimed in. 'I know you'll hate it Sprig, but we can't discount Mad Annie.'

Sprig sighed. 'I know, though I highly doubt she's a ringleader. It's safe to say Lou was heavily involved, probably became a liability when they realised he was using more than dealing.'

'I think we should consider Dr Webber,' Tick said, looking apprehensively at Sprig. Sprig raised an eyebrow. It had crossed her mind, too, but she wanted to hear Tick's suspicions.

'Go on.'

'He was at the pharmacy before us, was also first on scene at his Practice. He was at Lou's when he shouldn't have been, and walked through the house for no reason I can see.'

'All good points,' Smithy agreed, 'but characteristic of Webb, he's arrogant; no offence, Sprig.'

'None taken, but I agree we should consider him. Let's keep going.'

They wrapped up several hours and cups of tea later.

'See you tomorrow,' Tick waved as he shut the door behind him.

'Boss, there's one more suspect we have to talk about,' Pam said gently.

'I agree,' Sprig said. 'It did all start with the arrival of Tick, and his enthusiasm borders on macabre.'

'He's also the first person I've ever heard say a bad word about Millie, since she turned him down,' Kel said. 'The kid's obviously been at the wrong end of some extreme bullying. That affects a person.'

Sprig nodded, and the four of them stayed another hour, discussing their suspect list. As Sprig drove away from the station, she had absolutely no doubt who the mastermind was and she didn't like the truth one bit. She sighed, thinking she did need a strong drink.

Sprig stared at Webb's back. His head was resting on one outstretched arm and his legs curled away from her. It had been months since she had spent the night and, though it was always fun, this was the last time. She glanced at her watch, knowing she had to get moving if she was to be on time for the visit she had to make.

Sprig found herself lost in a memory as she drove, one that took place just before they moved to Stiller Rock. There had been a police murder in that first town, too, and she remembered her Dad talking to her about leaving. It was a very grown-up conversation, given she was only eight.

'What about Mum?'

'I've got a choice Sprig, between Mum, or you and me. It has to be you and me kiddo but we'll look after Mum, always.'

'We'll take her with us?'

'Of course. She's not well, I won't leave her. You know she won't stay under the same roof as us but we can at least look after her if she's in the same town.'

'I promise I'll look after her, and I promise I'll keep all the secrets.'

'Brought you some food, Mum.'

'Monster,' Mad Annie snarled, rocking back and forth.

'No Mum, monster hunter, remember?'

'Should have killed you before you were born,' Mad Annie snivelled, wiping her nose. Then she started sobbing. 'Sorry Rosie, my baby.'

'It's okay, Mum, there now,' Sprig patted her back gently. Her Mum had never been the same, not since she walked in on her husband killing his colleague. It broke Annie's mind, that dead young cop on the kitchen floor.

Sprig remembered that too, though she was just a kid. She was her father's daughter, and she understood when he explained it to her. That dead police officer was a bad man, he was involved with drugs, he caused deaths. Her Dad would do anything to keep his town safe and you couldn't always wait for the courts; more kids would die if you waited. He told Sprig it was a big responsibility, protecting the town, and you had to be very careful. You must only kill if it was absolutely necessary and you must be smart about it. Sprig knew beyond doubt the dirty cop and local businessman who died thirty years ago at Stiller Rock met their end at the hands of her father and now the responsibility had fallen on her.

She had made her difference, protected those kids. Her job was to keep Stiller Rock safe.

Sprig had known Lou couldn't possibly have the brains to pull off such a sophisticated drug operation. He played his part though, had handed Tom a loaded gun, so to speak, so it was only a matter of time before he ran into trouble with his own. The death of Tom was unforgivable, and though Sprig hated to admit it, shooting Lou had been easy.

Killing Webb had been devastating. Webb was supposed to be one of the good guys and Sprig's heart sank further with every piece of the puzzle that painted his picture until, in the end, it was inescapable. It was all Webb; this path to hell for lost local kids. It was his pride that gave him away in the end, as Sprig realised he was dangling himself in front of her, clearly enjoying the fact she remained clueless for so long. She had confirmed it last night, of course, found the drugs in his house while he showered.

Sprig knew Webb was smart enough, rich enough, to have contingencies in place. There was a chance he would get away with everything he had done. There was no such chance for Tom or the other two dead teenagers, or any of the kids that now faced the dark road of addiction. They didn't have the foresight to understand the endless torture those drugs had in store for them but Webb did, and he condemned them in his greed.

Sprig couldn't erase her memories with Webb, though, couldn't forget his hands in her hair, so she gave him the benefit of a painless death while she stayed by his side. Drugs mixed in Scotch, a taste of his own medicine. She could excuse herself that mercy; forensics would expect traces of her, given their relationship; and Webb would be given no kindness once his deeds became public. His memory would be mud for the anguish he inflicted. He would also be blamed for Lou's murder, then branded a coward for a death that would certainly be ruled a guilty man's suicide.

'Are the monster's gone?' Mad Annie asked, hiccoughing as her tears stopped.

'Yes, Mum. We're safe again.'

Sprig entered the police station to universal stares of pity.

'Darling, it's Webb,' Pam started, tearfully. 'His cleaner found him this morning. We've already been around. It looks like he killed himself and there were lots of drugs in his house. I'm sorry, Sprig, I know you were close.'

Sprig dropped into her chair. She didn't have to feign grief and disappointment; they were overwhelmingly real.

'It's almost unbelievable. He was supposed to help people, keep them safe.'

The sound of a throat clearing at the door interrupted them. Two teenage boys were standing there, Sprig recognised them as Tom's friends.

'Is it true the doctor is dead?' one asked uneasily. Sprig sighed, good news travelled fast.

'It's true, love,' Pam said, opening the door. 'Why don't you come in?'

The two boys shuffled in nervously. The one who spoke earlier raised his eyes.

'It was Lou the first time but then it was the doctor sold us the drugs. He said he'd kill us if we told anyone, but...' his voice caught. 'He's dead now, and we want to tell the truth, for Tom.'

'Tick,' Sprig said seriously after the boys left. 'You did a great job here. Congratulations, mate, you have great instinct.'

Tick blushed.

'You'd already figured it out, hadn't you?'

'I had my suspicions, but you organised the information for us. We couldn't have done this without you.'

Tick's blush deepened. 'I hope you guys at least discussed me as a suspect, otherwise you're terrible cops.'

Sprig laughed and clapped Tick on the back.

'Your name may have come up.'

'There's still a lot to do, plus the mess at the doc's house,' Kel winced, 'but I reckon we've earned ourselves a team coffee in the sun before we tackle it.'

Sprig turned to Tick and smiled. 'I've said it before, but I think I can say it sincerely now,' she held out her hand. 'Welcome to the monster hunters.'

2022

Tuesday Jocks

Fin J Ross

THE MISSING TUESDAY JOCKS BUGGED ME. ACCORDING TO HIS WIFE, BRIAN Sheridan was anal retentive about his wardrobe – so much so that he compelled her to place his day-labelled jocks in order in his bedside drawer, Monday to Sunday. He'd been missing since Monday night, yet Tuesday's jocks weren't in the drawer. Julie Sheridan was as perplexed as I was when Sergeant Dave Dryden and I had searched the couple's bedroom two days earlier. I'd noticed the neatly layered undies and wondered why anyone needed prompting to change them every day. Or were the K-Mart bestsellers designed to remind men what day it was every time they peed? Julie could only speculate that Brian had planned ahead by taking clean jocks to change into after soccer practice. He hadn't been seen since he'd been left to lock up the Kershaw Soccer Club around 9.30pm.

Why was I pondering about a man's smalls while wading thigh-deep in a muddy dam? The mud oozed between my toes and sucked up my legs, immobilising me. And I'd thought quicksand was the stuff of B-grade movies or long-forgotten Tarzan episodes.

Dryden stood on the bank, arms akimbo, supercilious face. Obviously, he was relishing the fact that I'd drawn the short straw to wade in and retrieve the bloated, floating body. Two weeks into my posting here and I was acutely aware of the gender bias of Kershaw Police.

Even Joe Green, who'd reported the floater in his dam an hour earlier, sat in his Ranger, 20 metres away, reluctant to assist. But then, he was pushing 80.

Where were the search and rescue heavies when you needed them? 'Don't s'pose you'd care to help?' Dryden shrugged.

'Nah. You're doing fine. You're nearly there Cunst.'

'Easy for you to say. And don't call me Cunst.'

Sheridan, face down and clad in a striped polo shirt and jeans, was still three or four metres away, but the effort to get to him sapped every muscle. So, he had showered and changed after practice. With Amazonian effort,

I finally reached out and wedged my fingers under Sheridan's super-tight waistband and pulled him towards me. The thud as his body bumped into me would have knocked me over had I not been stuck fast. My first objective was to peel his waistband down to reveal the elastic band of his jocks. Huh? Thursday. Not Monday, or Tuesday. Thursday.

Now I was truly perplexed. This wasn't the fastidious man his wife had described. So, where were his Monday and Tuesday undies? In his missing sports bag? We'd searched his car, still parked at the soccer ground, along with the clubhouse on Tuesday morning and found no sports bag. Where was it?

'Oh', I groaned. Probably at the bottom of the damn dam. This was one of many questions swimming in my head. Like how did he end up in a dam seven kilometres from the clubhouse? Was he suicidal? What didn't his wife know about him? Was he in financial strife? Was he having an affair? We'd asked Julie and all his team-mates these questions on Tuesday but had unearthed nothing untoward. On the surface, Sheridan was an honest, likeable, stand-up guy. A real team player. A respected club captain. Also, did Joe Green know more than he was saying? Or was it, as he'd said, mere coincidence that he'd inspected his dam this morning?

I started the sludgy haul back to the bank, thankful that a floating body doesn't weigh much. Then, as my left foot sank into the mud, it met resistance an inch or two down. Something hard and smooth. A tree root? The sports bag? No avoiding getting completely sodden now to save me venturing in to find it again. I locked one end of my handcuffs around Sheridan's hand and the other around my belt to stop him floating away. Then I plunged my arm into the opaque brown water and felt around my foot. I clutched the object, about the diameter of my closed hand, and levered it up and down to break the suction of the mud. I pulled hard and when my hand emerged with it, I gasped. A femur. A distinctly human-looking femur.

I brandished the bone at Dryden. 'Well, looky what I found.'

He looked unimpressed. 'Probably a cow.'

'Looks human to me.'

I looked across to Green, who appeared to be contemplating his navel. Or asleep.

'Think we might have some questions for old Joe.'

'Think we should wait for the Homicide guys to arrive.'

'Have you called them?'

'Not yet.'

'Well, hello. Isn't that your responsibility?'

'Don't need you to tell me how to suck eggs Cunst.'

Arrgh.

'Chances are there's a whole lot more bones down here. I mean, somebody would surely miss their femur, don't you think?'

Dryden pulled out his phone and dialled, while I continued to tow Sheridan to the edge.

'They reckon it'll be six to eight hours until they can get anyone here, possibly longer for the coroner. Double shooting in Melbourne.'

'Guess that's more important than a probable murder and equally probable cold case in Hicksville,' I said as I hauled Sheridan up the bank. I undid the handcuff and plopped onto my bum beside him to recover. I drummed the 40 -centimetre bone on my hand. With a few good breaths on board, I asked Dryden to help me flip the body over. That was when I saw the deep gash in his forehead; so deep it appeared his skull was fractured.

'Well, I'm not thinking suicide,' Dryden observed.

'I didn't from the start. If he were going to come here to drown himself, surely he'd have driven, not walked.'

'True.'

I put my socks and shoes back on. 'I'm going to ask Joe if he heard anything Monday night.'

'Good luck. He's deaf as a post.'

I was halfway across to Joe's car when the glint of sun off the windscreen of a vehicle approaching across the paddock almost blinded me. Finchley Crime Scene Investigation unit. Hallelujah to that. I jogged to steer them clear of the unexamined tyre marks over to the right; no doubt the vehicle in which Sheridan was transported, dead or alive, to his watery grave.

'Hi, I'm Jordan Mulcahy. You guys might have your work cut out for you,' I said as the van pulled up.

They introduced themselves as Matt and Shannon, no formalities. I explained that, aside from the floater, we had another suspicious find on our hands.

'I'm just going to ask the property owner if he has a pump. We'll have to drain the dam. Dryden'll give you the heads-up.'

I knocked on Joe's window and motioned for him to wind it down. As he did, country music blared from his car radio, drowning out any prospect of discussion.

'Could you turn that down please?'

'What?'

'The radio,' I yelled, 'turn it down please.'

'Oh, didn't know it was on.'

'Do you have a pump? We need to drain the dam.'

'Why?'

'We need to investigate further.'

'Yeah. Pump's up at the house.'

Not being a forensic expert, I had no idea how old the femur might be, but I suspected it had been there a very long time.

'How long have you lived here, Mr Green?'

'Twenty years. Yeah, 2002   we bought the place.'

'We? That's you and your wife?'

'Yeah.'

'What's your wife's name? Is she at home?'

'Sheila. Nah. Gone to bingo. Thursday's bingo arvo. And Saturday. And Tuesday night.'

'Who owned the property before you?'

'The Helliers. John and Denise.'

'Are they still around?'

'Well, John is. Lives in town but he'd know that,' Joe said, pointing towards Dryden. 'And you should know. I mean, their son's your boss. Never met her. They were separated or divorced or whatever.'

I'd heard the name Sean Hellier mentioned around the station, but evidently Joe didn't know he'd retired a year earlier.

'Thank you. Now, if you wouldn't mind getting the pump.'

I headed back to the dam and found Matt examining Sheridan's body and Shannon snapping off pictures.

'Where's Joe gone?' Dryden asked.

'To get a pump so we can drain the water.'

'Oh, good thought.'

'You didn't tell me this place was originally Hellier's folks.'

'Didn't think it was important.'

'Think it is now. I guess one of us needs to notify Julie Sheridan.'

'You go. We can sort this. Might pay to clean yourself up first. I can get a ride back with these guys.'

'Or if I'm not too long, I'll come back.'

'Whatever.'

As I exited the driveway, I sniggered at the sign, Shady Grove, a complete misnomer for a treeless, Weetbix-coloured acreage. I dashed home, showered, dumped my muddy clothes in the washing machine and donned a fresh uniform before driving the three blocks to Julie Sheridan's home.

She was distraught at the news, though I suspected she'd expected a fatal outcome. I made her a cuppa and waited for her to collect herself enough to speak. It wasn't just that Brian was dead – he'd been murdered.

'God, how am I going to tell the kids?'

I couldn't offer much advice there, aside from saying I could be on hand when they arrived home from school if she wanted.

'How the hell did he end up in a dam seven ks away?'

'We're still trying to figure that out. Can you think of anyone who might have done this? I'm doubtful it was a random attack.'

Julie shook her head. 'Everyone loved Brian. He was really popular.'

'You're sure he wasn't having an affair, or perhaps owed someone money?'

'I can't see how he could have had an affair. He always came straight home from work, he was only out on Monday nights for soccer, and aside from his Saturday morning matches, he'd be here all weekend.'

'What time did he usually get home from soccer training?'

'Around 10.30, sometimes 11.'

'The other players said they all usually left by 9.30. Why was Brian always later?'

'He'd stay back to do paperwork, you know, team selections and stuff.'

'You're only what, half a block from the soccer ground. Why would he drive?'

'He usually goes straight from work.'

'Did he usually shower and change before he came home?'

'Sometimes. Not always.'

'It appears he did. He was wearing casual clothes, but there's one mystery.'

'What?'

'Thursday jocks.'

Julie shook her head. 'No. Not likely. Really weird, at least.'

'That's what I thought. Can we check his drawer again?'

Julie led me to the bedroom. We looked at each other quizzically upon discovering Brian's Thursday jocks.

'Did he only have the one set?'

'Yes.'

'Tell me, do you know the Helliers? They originally owned the property where we found Brian.'

'Actually, John lives just down the street, number 43 I think, but I don't really know him. I think he must be old or sick because I occasionally see the district nurse's car there. I never met her. I gather she left him about 25 years ago. Word was she took off to Queensland with another bloke.'

'What about their son?'

'You mean Sergeant Hellier?'

I nodded.

'Only time I ever met him was when he pulled me over for speeding in Main Road a few years ago. He seemed like a reasonable guy.'

'I'm new here; haven't actually met him.'

'Have you found Brian's sports bag?'

'Not yet. We're about to drain the dam. Now, is there someone you can ring for support?'

Julie said she'd get her neighbour to come in, so I told her I'd be back in touch if we needed more information.

What was it with men? It seemed the older they got, the grumpier and more recalcitrant they became, and John Hellier was no exception. I was greeted – no, harrumphed – at the door by a weedy, wheezy man with what I suspected was a perpetual scowl.

'Whaddya want?' No courtesy to my uniform.

'I have some questions. May I come in?'

He rolled his eyes, backed up and gestured into a dark, musty living room. 'What's this all about?'

'You may, or may not, be aware that a man went missing on Monday. His body has been found in the dam of your former property this morning.'

'What's it got to do with me? Haven't lived there for nigh on 20 years.'

I nodded. 'Yes, I realise that. Can I ask why you sold the farm?'

'Had a heart turn. Couldn't manage the place on my own after that. Those bloody Greens screwed me on the price, then switched from cattle to sheep which was bloody daft. You'd wanna talk to Joe and that bitch of a wife.'

'What about your wife. Did she help on the farm?'

'Yeah, up to a point. Till she had the bloody accident. After that, she was friggin' useless.'

'The accident?'

'Yeah. Got squashed against a fence by a bull. Lost her leg.'

'Oh. That's terrible. Where is she now?'

'Blowed if I know. Bitch took off with someone. Haven't heard boo from her since.'

'When was that?'

'Geez. You want to know the ins and outs of a duck's bum, don't you? Around 24 years ago.'

'And you've no idea where she went?'

'Nope. Why are you asking about her anyway? She's ancient history.'

I'd decided not to mention my find yet. Setting a trap was sometimes more productive.

'What about your son? Has he had any contact with her?'

'Nope.'

'He never tried to find her? Why? He'd have had the means. As a police officer, I mean.'

'Dunno. Ask him.'

'I will. What's his address please? Oh, and is he married?'

'Not anymore. Murray Street, number 19, but he won't be home. He'll be at bloody golf.'

'Thank you for your time.'

I was about to leave when I had a thought. 'Sorry, one more thing, does Sean play soccer?'

'Not anymore.'

I'd bet my bottom dollar that Hellier Senior was on the phone to Hellier Junior before I'd even crossed the threshold to let him know that some bitch of a policewoman was on his path. Though something about dad's tone gave me the impression he and his son weren't best buds. Why? I was itching to get back to Shady Grove to see what was transpiring. After stopping at a milk bar to grab some Cokes and a salad sandwich (minus beetroot because I didn't want to risk messing another shirt), I headed back out to Willow Road.

I'd thought that today was going to be one of those nothing happened days. Now I was confronted with two dead bodies. Were they connected? How? Was the Shady Grove waterhole the local dumping place for inconvenient corpses? Were there more bodies? Sure, this was all the domain of the Homicide squad, but given they were conspicuous in their absence, I figured I could demonstrate my detective skills. Detective training, with a later view to Homicide were both on my forward agenda.

Despite knowing that Sheila Green wouldn't be there, something prompted me to drive up to the house instead of turning into the paddock. One or other of the Greens was obviously a keen gardener judging by the neatly trimmed roses, flowering shrubs and well-maintained pots in the house yard. I parked and got out to survey the place. A beeping drew me onto the back verandah. I peered into the first window; a green light flashed on a washing machine indicating the cycle was finished. In the garden flanking the porch below the potted geraniums and hanging baskets of fuchsias and vivid zygos, a string of hearts spilled from an unusual planter – a deep, pink plastic cup-shaped thingy attached to a metal post. I'd seen something like this before; the stainless-steel button on the shaft a dead giveaway. Interesting.

Must be one hell of a water pump, I thought, as I parked by what was now a mud bowl.

Matt and Shannon were knee-deep in the quagmire, while Dryden stood, barefoot, at the edge, laying more bones onto a tarp as they were handed to him. A skull, a seemingly entire, though broken, ribcage, two scapulas, a pelvic bone, several spinal knuckles, almost enough arm bones, and a jumbled collection of phalanges formed an almost entire skeleton. Beside that, a tarp-covered Brian Sheridan was baking in the sun.

Dryden grunted at me. 'You're back then.'

'Any sign of the sports bag?'

'No.'

Matt was moving his forearm back and forth in the mud, evidently trying to locate something particular.

'If you're looking for another leg, I suspect you won't find it,' I called out to him.

He looked up at me. 'Why?'

'Because I suspect that's Denise Hellier, and she only had one leg.'

'Oh. That explains a lot.'

'I thought you'd have figured that out Dryden. You must have known about Denise.'

'Jesus, Cunst, I was, what? seven, when she took off. Far as I know, she was never reported as missing, so why would I suspect... anything? Who have you been talking to, anyway?'

'John Hellier.'

'Yeah? What'd he say?'

'Told me Denise left him for another man 24 years ago.'

'That's as much as I knew.'

'Well, I've just found her prosthetic leg in the Greens' garden. You'd think she might've needed that if she were going away for good.'

I held up the Cokes. 'You guys want a break?'

Matt and Shannon slogged out of the dam and sat, grateful for the respite and refreshment.

I walked further along the dam bank and spotted two parallel scores in the dirt running from the rim to the waterline.

'Hey Shannon, you might want to photograph these. Might be where Brian was dragged in.'

She came over and snapped off some pictures.

'Still have to take casts of those tyre prints.'

I headed back to the others. 'Tell me Dryden, what was Sean Hellier like as a boss?'

'Okay. Why?'

'Just wondered. His dad's a grumpy sort, I thought Sean might have followed suit.'

'Had his moments, but he did everything by the book.'

'Any idea what he's doing with himself now?'

'Keeps himself busy. You know, Rotary, golf, fishing, the Men's Shed I think. Why?'

'Hello, we're going to need to talk to him.' I pointed to Denise Hellier's remains.

'Yeah. Nah. I'd leave that to the Homicide guys.'

'That mightn't be until tomorrow. He'll have got a whiff of this from his father by then.'

'Are you suggesting–?'

'That's exactly what I'm suggesting. I also want to find out what he knows about Brian here.'

'Doubt there's any connection.'

'I don't know, but it's highly sus to me.'

'Leave it. You're not on overtime you know. Time to call it.'

An order, not a suggestion. I said bye to the others and headed home. What would I do with the rest of the day? Sit at home twiddling my thumbs? No. I detoured to the soccer ground. Parked a few metres from where Brian's car had been parked. We'd scoured the whole car park for evidence on Tuesday and had found nothing. No blood, no churned gravel. Nothing at all to suggest that a murder might have happened there. But something told me Brian hadn't left there alive. If he had, who did he go with? Dryden had started his car; nothing wrong with it.

I checked my notepad, found Nathan Foster's number and dialled. Apart from Brian, he'd been the last player to leave the club on Monday night. When he answered, I asked whether he could recall if Brian had showered.

'Don't think he does usually. Pretty sure he was still in his soccer gear when I left.'

I'd just figured there wasn't anything more to be gleaned here, when I heard footsteps in the gravel. I turned to see a woman, led by a beefy black Labrador, emerge from the trees. I waved to her and she walked over.

'Something I can help you with?' she said.

I introduced myself, asked her name and whether she walked the dog here often.

'I'm Simone Blake. Oh, and this is Rufus. Every day, if I can. I live across there.' She pointed across the soccer ground.

'At the same time?'

'No, depends on my shift. I'm a nurse at the hospital. Why?'

'You haven't heard that a man went missing from here on Monday night?'

'No. All I seem to do these days is work, eat, walk the dog and sleep. Don't even watch TV.'

'What time did you walk Rufus on Monday?'

Simone thought for a moment. 'Would have been around 10 .30 maybe.'

'In the morning?'

'No. Night.'

'Do you recall seeing any cars here then?'

'Yes. There was a ute thing, like a tradies' ute parked there. Couldn't tell you what colour it was, because that car park light wasn't on.'

'Did you see anyone?'

'No.'

'Were the clubhouse lights on?'

'No, I don't think so.'

'Any other cars?'

'Yes, but not in this car park. It was round the other side of the clubhouse.'

'Can you describe it?'

'Pale colour, maybe white. Think it was one of those old Toyota things with a fibreglass canopy, but I really didn't pay much attention to it. Didn't see the number plate. I can show you where it was though.'

I followed Simone around the back of the clubhouse to a grassy area we hadn't searched.

'It was parked about here,' she said.

'Nose in or nose out?'

'It was backed in.'

'Thanks for your help.' I noted Simone's phone number in case I needed to speak to her again and patted Rufus on the head. When they'd gone, I trod carefully through the grass looking for any clues. It took a while to spot it. A spray of dried blood stuck to a capeweed leaf. I stuck my pen into the ground beside it and called Dryden.

'When you're done there, might pay to take Matt and Shannon back to the soccer club. Check out the grass around the back. I've stuck a pen in the ground to mark the spot.'

'What are you doing there? I thought you'd gone home.'

'I just spoke to a woman who saw another car here late Monday night.'

'Oh. Okay. Now, go home woman.'

No. I didn't go home. I didn't know when Sean Hellier would arrive home from golf, but I intended to be there when he did. Nobody else was doing much actual questioning, so why not me? I sat in the divvy van outside Hellier's 70 s-era brick-veneer house drumming my fingers on the steering wheel. I hoped he wasn't one of those golfers who spent hours after the game at the 19th hole.

Something didn't make sense. More than one thing actually. I was pretty sure that either Sean or his dad, or both, knew that Denise was in the dam

– and how she got there. But did Sean have some connection with Brian Sheridan? Was it his Toyota? I'd checked his details and he did have a Hilux registered. Nobody mentioned him being at the soccer club. Did he come later? What for? Did he murder Brian? Why? Did Brian know something about Denise? And if Sean killed Brian, why would he toss him in the dam and risk his mother being found? Maybe he didn't know she was there. Nothing made sense. What the hell happened? Simone said two cars were there at 10.30, yet no lights were on. Strange. So many questions.

Then I remembered. Not so strange. The blackout. Power went out 20 minutes in to The Closer. Yeah, I like it because I reckon I can learn from Brenda Leigh Johnson's interviewing technique – minus the twangy accent. But I didn't see the rest of it. Power was off for a good 40 minutes so I gave up and went to bed around 10.40. How could Sean have been doing paperwork in the dark? Why didn't he leave? Was he in the shower? Was he alone?

Oh. I'd no sooner had that thought when I looked up to see a white Toyota ute indicating to turn into the driveway. That answered one question. I had no way of knowing whether his father had warned him about my likely appearance.

I got out of the van and followed him into the short driveway. I could see his golf clubs and buggy in the back through the ute window, along with something lumpy under a checked blanket. A swarthy, sweatless, impeccably dressed Sean Hellier got out and spoke before I had a chance to.

Guess you're the new girl. To what do I owe the pleasure?' He seemed affable. Or was it deflection?

'Yes Sergeant, ah Mister Hellier. Constable Jordan Mulcahy.'

'Everyone still calls me Sarge.'

'Good game?'

'Yeah. Good day for it.'

Enough small talk. 'I have some questions if that's okay.'

'Sure. What about?' Was his calmness rehearsed, or was I barking up the wrong tree? 'Do you want to come in?'

'Here's fine, for the time being. Do you know Brian Sheridan?'

'Of course. I was his soccer coach. Have you found him yet?'

'We have.' I divulged no more than that. Hellier remained disconcertingly deadpan.

'When did you last see him?'

'Pfft. I don't know. Maybe a month ago at the hardware store. I was stunned when I heard he was missing.'

'Yes, I'm sure you were. So, you weren't at the soccer club on Monday night?'

'No. Hardly go there anymore.'

'This is your vehicle, yes?'

'Sure is.'

'It was seen parked behind the soccer clubrooms on Monday night.'

'Not likely. I was home all night.'

'Ah huh. Can anyone verify that?'

'Really don't think my neighbours keep tabs on me.'

The bombshell question to catch him off guard. 'Are you homosexual?'

'Huh? You've no right to ask me that, you little upstart.' Good. I was rattling him.

'I believe I do. I believe that you and Brian had a regular little Monday night tryst. Perhaps you liked to shower together. A bit of rumpy-pumpy.'

'Rubbish. You know, you ought to not overstep your rank with foolish suppositions. What are you, straight out of the academy?'

Yeah, be condescending. That'll shut me up.

'I suppose then, that if I inspected your underwear drawer or clothes basket I wouldn't find two pairs of Monday jocks and no Thursday jocks.'

'What the hell are you on about?'

'I'll tell you. Sometime during your shower, the power went off, which would explain why you were wearing each other's jocks. You couldn't see whose were whose in the dark. But what happened then? Did you argue about something? Something serious enough to kill him for? Or … or did you rape him and then murder him?'

Hellier rolled his eyes. 'Oh, do go on. This little scenario of yours is just fascinating.'

I hoped to God I was right about my next suppositions.

'So, I suppose that if I checked under the blanket in the ute I wouldn't find Brian Sheridan's sports bag, or that if I checked your phone, I wouldn't find a call or message from your father earlier. A warning message?'

'You got a warrant? Bet you don't.'

'You could make my job easier if you just agreed to let me look. You know, give a girl a break.'

I pulled out my phone and texted Dryden.

Get a warrant to search Sean Hellier's car for sports bag, and house for evidence, including undies, and meet me there.

He replied instantly. You're kidding. What gives?

Not kidding.

Hellier handed me his phone. I checked it. No messages from dad. That surprised me.

'I suspect you already know that we found Brian's body in the Shady Grove dam.'

Hellier feigned surprise. 'How could I know that? I'm out of the loop now, you know.'

'And I suspect you put it there.'

Hellier opened his mouth to speak, but I cut him off. 'What I can't figure out is why you chose there. Was it to be certain your mother would also be found after all these years? Did you murder your mother too?'

'No, I didn't bloody murder my mother and nor did I murder Brian.'

'But you knew about your mother, didn't you? Do you get along with your father?' Hellier shrugged. Then it dawned on me. Senior hadn't warned Junior, ergo, they weren't on friendly terms. What was their secret?

'Your father killed your mother then. And you knew. Either you covered his tracks, or … you suspected she was in the dam. Which was it? Either way, you're an accomplice.'

I expected Hellier to chuck a wobbly. He didn't. He denied nothing. Nor did he admit. Yet his shoulders sagged in defeat.

'Look, I get that you'd cover for your dad. But I don't get Brian. Why did you kill him?'

'I didn't kill him, alright. I loved Brian.' Hellier wiped his eyes. No charade.

'Dad did. He'd found out about me and Brian and, well, he's an absolute homophobe. We didn't know he was waiting outside the clubhouse with a crowbar. Didn't see him in the dark. Also wouldn't have thought he'd have the strength to clobber anyone so violently. I could've killed him, but–'

'But he's your dad.'

'That, and I'm no murderer.'

'So, let me guess. You put Brian in the dam so we'd be sure to find your mother.'

'Yes. Only way I could think to get back at the bastard. I'm sick of covering for him. He bludgeoned Mum to death and now he's killed Brian. And you're right. Until you mentioned it, I could not figure out how I ended up with two pairs of Monday jocks. You're very astute, you know. Ever thought of detective training?'

'I have, actually. We'll have to charge you, you know.'

Brian nodded resignedly.

I rang Dryden. 'Charge John Hellier with the murders of Denise Hellier and Brian Sheridan.'

SKIN AND BONE

Also won Art & Crime category

Romany Rzechowicz

I WAS BESOTTED FROM THE MOMENT SHE WALKED THROUGH MY SQUEAKING garden gate, all tattooed limbs hanging out of a dinosaur sundress, dusted by long snake earrings and glossy black braids. My sleek little bob, jeans and crocs felt prudishly conservative – especially given the unexpectedly inappropriate desire that crashed through me at exactly that moment.

'That gate is just adorable,' she said after we'd dispensed with the awkward, overenthusiastic first-time meeting greetings and I was getting a hold of my heart rate. 'Where on earth did you get it?'

I regarded the silhouetted children with their kites, strings creating the vertical bars, a dog leaping for a beribboned tail. Smiled like it held a pleasant memory, and lied: 'My parents commissioned it when I was young – I'm the girl on the left. Next to the daffodils.'

'They're your siblings?'

'Uh-huh.' Her intoxicating scent fogged up the entryway and my synapses, making words vanish and leaving only sounds. Only formless grunts and an increasingly magnetic obsession–

No.

Back on track.

'You're wanting to make a book, right? Come out back to the studio.'

I gestured along the hallway which, in a terrible Feng Shui decision, ran the length of the house straight to the back door. She clomped past me in purple doc martens. It was all I could do not to stroke her multicoloured skin as it moved in front of my nose. So close. So tantalising... I dropped my gesturing arm a little too soon, collecting a delicious stroke of her forearm on a backward swing.

Yes.

I would have her. I would touch that skin–

But not yet.

Her wake smelled like frangipanis – too tropical for this corner of the world – with an earthiness, an undertone of dirt. Something organic and elemental.

She spotted the books and detoured into the sitting room before I could correct her course to the back door. Of course, that's what she was here for, so it was completely understandable. It was only natural, I was beginning to feel, that she should be as drawn to the books – my books – as I was.

My hands knew them so intimately they ached as she caressed each spine. I'd bound many of them; folded, sliced, stitched, wrapped and glued. I could remember the feeling of battling to stitch the thick pages in the one her strong fingers currently touched. And the brittleness of the faux leather I'd tried with the one she held now – I'd had to redo that one into real, buttery vellum. She smiled indulgently at each of them as if she were holding a child. Watching from the door, my fingers curved into my palm as I fought to keep them to myself.

'Did you make all of these?'

'Yes.' Another lie. There were dozens more books in my library than I had made in my twenty years of bookbinding. Thirty years if you included the "books" of folded, stapled paper and coloured cardboard that I'd make for my classmates in primary school. In high school my friends had the fanciest notebooks of any fifteen-year-olds anywhere in the country. Until Vanessa not only etched her boyfriend's surname alongside hers, but tried to hack it out two weeks later after seeing him behind the tennis court with Mandy Sutton. The ending was quick and, well, mostly clean.

My visitor caressed the covers as lovingly as I did and it made me shiver with delight to watch. She even took care to slide them back in the shelf gently, parting the neighbouring tomes with one hand and gently easing them home into their rightful place, skin resting against skin. So delicious. Such anticipation.

'I should take you to the studio,' I said abruptly as her mouth also opened to speak – there was no gentle way to shake myself out of such a meandering mind.

She turned her head to me, then her body followed, braids and dress eddying around her slim figure. I wanted to feed her up a little, to be honest. There should be more of her. Slowly and carefully, mind you. There'd be no call for stretch marks or warped tattoos. No. Slow, steady and perfect.

'That's why you came, isn't it?'

'Yes, it is.' She galumphed back into the hallway. Inhaling deeply, I managed to keep my hands to myself this time as she passed me.

'Are you hiding something in there?'

'Where?'

'In your library.' She paused and I nearly – accidentally on purpose – ran into her, but pulled up just in time. 'It sounded urgent that we get out.'

'A body in the library? In my library?'

'Hey, I dunno. If you didn't like me touching your books you could have just said.'

I couldn't tell her how much I had adored her touching my books. That I could feel her stroking their covers, caressing their skins. That it had been almost like she was touching me.

'There are bodies in my library, actually.'

Her eyes widened, body tensed. She glanced over my shoulder to the front door. Dammit – don't scare her just yet.

I smiled. As non-threateningly as I could.

'My parents are in a box on the mantelpiece. I was worried you might bump it.'

'Oh,' she exhaled. Laughed nervously. Glanced at the door again. 'Ok. I was worried things were getting weird.'

Oh, sweetheart, they will, I promise. Just not quite yet.

'I always fancied putting them into something beautiful. Keeping them together forever.' Another lie. But I'd figured out the earthy smell that moved with her, and why her fingers looked so rough yet touched so delicately. I couldn't wait to feel them against my own skin.

'I could make you an urn for them if you like? Something custom?'

Jackpot.

'Is that what you do? Pottery?'

She nodded and restarted her journey to the studio, hidden amongst the depths of my charmingly overgrown backyard. Honestly, it probably needed a gardener. But equally honestly I didn't need a hairy hulking dude getting all up in my business. All that hair tended to clog my drains.

She had studio etiquette, I had to admit. She tucked her hands in neatly hidden pockets as she roamed the studio; inspecting my paper, cover boards, threads, the press that was currently unoccupied. I'd been gluing yesterday, and the sticky scent hung in the air. It didn't seem to bother her, and she breathed deeply as if evaluating the ambience.

'You do it all?'

'When I can.' I rested a finger on a recently-completed project. Just one finger. Just one fingernail. Just the very tip of one fingernail, lest the visceral urge to feel it, full contact, overcame me and I made a fool of myself.

'Will you do it all for me?' she cocked her head, snakes peeking through her braids, a Sailor Jerry bluebird on her shoulder sharing her expression.

Of course I would do it all for you. Everything for you. In a heartbeat. I–

Don't give yourself away. Not yet.

'Depends on the project,' I said, as if hedging my bets.

She didn't answer at once, but came closer. Lay her hand flat on the recent project, next to my tenuous fingernail. I think I closed my eyes, although I kept seeing her rough fingers within a hair's breadth of mine. So close. I definitely shuddered a little.

'What if we trade?' she suggested. 'I do your parents and you do mine?'

'I–'

'Not that mine are dead, though. Not yet, anyway.' She chuckled.

I had bound romances, research, memoirs, love letters, and none of the words on their pages came to my rescue. Not one.

'Sorry, that was insensitive.' She picked her hand up and tucked it back in her pocket. I exhaled as if forcing out every secret I'd ever kept, every lie, pushing my fingernail deeper into the soft leather cover. If I did that to her, she'd probably recoil. Maybe even hit me – the prospect of contact, even in violence, filled me with even more desire. The crescent mark of my nail in her flesh would be red and fresh. And then it would fade. Unlike the one I was leaving now in the cover. A living, breathing creature had given its life so the book could be born, and now here I was, marking it. Disrespecting it. And thinking only about the marks I would make on her skin, punctuation marks amongst the images permanently embedded there…

Back on track.

'I still don't know what you want.'

'Oh, right. Yeah. It's kind of a family history. Dad wrote it, Mum drew the illustrations, and I'm on publication duties. It's not long, but I thought it'd make a nice Christmas present.'

'Very nice.' I lifted my fingernail from the book. I would wait. Fatten her up. Stretch it out. The delicious anticipation would make it even nicer.

She returned the following week with a sample of her work: a sculptural vase, all odd shapes and unexpected divots that my daffodils sought out and settled into. I envied the daffodils: surely they could feel how a memory of her caresses oozed from the fine grain. The material was almost translucent. Like the soft, pale patches of skin – inside elbows, thighs – that provide windows to the transit of blood through our bodies. The patches that tear easily.

I stroked it curiously.

'Bone china,' she said. 'It's more common in mass-produced tableware, but I've been experimenting with my own blends and I think I could make something really special out of your parents.' She frowned charmingly, tried to correct herself. 'For your parents? For you, I guess.'

It was for me, truth be told. My parents weren't really on the mantelpiece. Although, they were in my library. She'd have to make do with the remains of Gerty, their loyal greyhound.

I made us a cuppa using my Mikasa bone china teapot in honour of her vase. Not as fancy as her sculptural vase, but quite pretty, really, with a similarly mystical milky appearance. All-in-all, I felt proud of my self control today. I'd practiced being distant all morning, steering clear of my books or anything else with skin that would make me want to touch. To reach out… the things that made me lose control of my fingers, and let them roam free.

I handed her a teacup.

She reached for the saucer.

I saw it.

A blackberry bramble had grown around her wrist and up her forearm. Delicious little black bubbles ripe enough to pop between your teeth. I couldn't help myself. I reached out…out…

And she let me touch it, holding her tea awkwardly in mid-air as I grazed across the surface, sticky with ointment.

'I got it last week. The day after I saw you.' She transferred the tea to her other hand and slowly rotated her now free arm for me to see it better. 'I used to go blackberrying with my parents, so it's got good memories.'

'It's exquisite,' She let her arm rest in my hand and I felt the weight of her for the first time. Her quick pulse under my fingers. The smoothness of the old skin, the stickiness of the new.

'Isn't it? I was thinking it might be a cool motif to put on our book.'

Our book. Yes. Of course it would be. I was slicing it in my brain already, figuring out how to transfer what was wrapped around her arm to a flatter, squarer medium.

But not yet. It was too soon.

'How long until it heals?'

'It should be healed over in another week or so, but it won't really be part of my body for almost six months.' She drew it back and looked at the artwork lovingly. 'I love the two month mark probably best, though. The ink's still sitting kind of high and the skin heals over the top and it gets this silvery, shimmery, 3D kind of vibe. It almost looks like it's been embroidered onto my skin.'

My mouth watered at the thought. My stomach roiled at the extended waiting time. And then I remember that the tea was not the tea she should be drinking today.

'We should pick your materials.'

'Now?'

'Yes.' Leaving my own undrunk tea on the bench, I led the way to the studio. The freesias started coming out yesterday, and the scent followed us inside, battling against the glue. Her nose wrinkled.

'What would you like for the pages? Paper? Parchment? Thick? Thin? White? Cream?'

Hands firmly in pockets – if only I could keep mine tucked away from temptation like that – she perused my shelves.

'Something off-white, perhaps? And thin. Like an encyclopedia that just knows everything. Dad would like that.'

'Ok.' I should have at least made a show of taking notes, but I'd rather watch her invade my studio, let her imprint on everything I can touch later in memory of her. 'Endpapers?'

'What're they?'

I pulled open a previous commission – the one with a crescent-shaped imprint marring the smooth cover – and flipped it open. The endpapers were marbled in smoky greys. A book carved from stone, fit to last for eons. I pulled another from the shelf and showed her a detailed art deco print I'd found at an antique shop.

'Do you even make those too?'

I nodded. It was only a little lie.

'Hmm, I guess it'll depend on the colour of the cover, won't it?'

I nodded again. I could see blackberry brambles tumbling across the endpapers, perhaps skimming the tops of the pages, flowing down the spine of this marvellous, beautiful book. This beautiful person. I wondered what flowed down her spine: suspected it's something beautiful too. If only I could lift her hair, lower the zip…

I kept that to myself.

'Ok. Cover?'

'Leather, I guess?'

Of course, animal membrane is the only real wrapper for a good story. And hers – her book, will – well… our book, she called it. Ugh, words were so evasive in her presence. Action was needed.

Behind my workbench, what looked like a cupboard door at first glance opened into a pitch black room. I pondered the shadows for a moment: I hadn't really thought this through. She brought out impulses in me that were unexpected, thrilling and terrifyingly out of my control.

As long as they didn't scare her, though.

I flicked the switch.

She gasped, then (thankfully) stepped forward to see more clearly.

Pulled tight with strings and stones, the paper-thin skin still vaguely resembled the piglet it had once been.

My skin prickled as she came to rest in the doorway next to me. I breathed her earthy scent. Good, good girl.

'It can be hard to get one's hand on real vellum these days, so I sometimes make my own.'

'You kill animals?'

'I have some farming connections, wildlife carers who tell me about intact roadkill – I've been doing it a while.' The bone scraper was on the cabinet by my hand, so I picked it up to scrape at the skin. I only started preparing it the day after she visited, so it was nowhere near ready, but I could already see it – feel it – taking shape, and the stories it would contain.

Already contains.

She peered closer.

Ahh, she saw them.

'Are those tattoos?'

'They are. It was a practice pig for apprentices.' I scraped more vigorously, keeping my hands and my eyes busy. She was too close now, and it wasn't time yet.

'I think I should go.'

I continued scraping as she headed back to the garden, falling into the rhythm.

She was right about the silver skin thing. When we next met, the brambles were no longer gooey with ointment. Instead they were vibrant and slightly unreal. She let me touch them I thrilled at the contact, feeling the leaves and berries still raised, like embossing on her skin. Definitely not ready yet. Something I also discovered with the pigskin. The fresh tattoos had made the skin unpredictable when I stretched and scraped it.

We met at hers this time, so she could show me her studio. Although all I noticed was her skin covered in flecks of porcelain clay, dusty white confusing the busy pictures and creating patterns where there were none. And her heady, earthy scent washing over me; caressing my nostrils, settling on my own skin. Maybe later I could bury my head in my cardigan and smell her in my clothes.

She moved easily around her workspace; plain crockery drying on shelves against the wall, a spinning wheel, bags of white powders, a large mortar and pestle. Gerty's box by the window. Gerty'd like that, actually; that great big yard out there with all the bones drying in the sunshine.

Of course – she worked with bone china. The bone part had to come from somewhere.

'Will the book be ready for Christmas, do you think?' she asked, turning so that bluebird peeked cheekily between her braids.

I hesitated. I'd brought out the larger stretching rack in the back room in preparation, but she seemed to be getting even skinnier despite the cake I tried to feed her and the chocolates I'd brought this time. And clearly her new ink needed more healing.

'If it's not, that's ok. I'll just get them something else.'

'Maybe as a backup. That's probably a good idea.'

She picked up her gin – apparently she didn't keep tea in her studio – and wandered into the garden, drawing her hand across the rough exterior of the cold kiln.

'Could I come back and browse your library?'

'Anytime.' She was always meant to be part of that room, part of my library. The heart and soul of it, in fact. It was just a matter of patience.

'How about my parents?' It was the first time I'd asked her about the tribute to "my parents". I waved a hand at the window where Gerty's box basked in the sunshine. 'How are you going with them?'

She nodded multiple times as if hearing a beat in her head. Maybe her pulse, or her heartbeat. I was so sure I could feel them too. Feeling closer, more connected to her with every visit.

'Slowly. There's something I want to try with the clay, and I don't want to stuff it up.'

Part of me wanted to tell her it was just a dog and she could toss poor Gerty out the window if she wanted. As long as she came back to me once her tattoo healed, I didn't care about her pottery. Her fine china with bones in it. She would be memorialised as so much more than that; I had been lying awake at night thinking about a picture book. Those brambles on the spine, Sailor Jerry bird cheekily winking on the back cover. I was saving the front cover for something magnificent hidden on the tender parts of her body that wouldn't be revealed until I had undressed her. It was hard to plan a publication when you didn't have all the content.

'It's the heart in it that matters, though, isn't it?' I offered carefully.

Like a spy with the script, she responded 'It's the love and consideration – not the perfection.'

I nodded in agreement. We were of one mind, moving slowly around the garden, stroking leaves and proudly regarding blooms. 'There's always a bit of the client in everything I make.'

'Me too,' she said. Although, of course, I knew she didn't mean it like I did. Not literally.

There was so little of Mother by the end, that her book came out pocket-sized. Father on the other hand; his excesses were such I had to split him over two racks and could have turned him into an encyclopedia. I didn't, though, I made him into a street directory. He would have hated it – a fact which brought me great joy.

I tipped the rest of the gin down my throat and followed in her wake, feeling the delicate petals under my fingers, squeezing just enough that they'd be brown by sunset. Her garden was quite idyllic. I wondered if she had more flowers hidden around her body. I wondered how I could fatten her up in time for Christmas publication.

Then I saw the grass. It was much closer than I'd anticipated, and coming closer.

The garden embraced me and I found myself swimming through a camellia bush.

'Oh, about time,' she said, threading a fine arm under mine before I ate dirt. Despite my condition I felt her touch in every molecule of my being. And I could almost see a delicate cat's ear peeking from underneath her bra strap and the warm fuzzy anticipation feelings made my legs even less cooperative. 'Let's get you inside while you can still walk.'

I hadn't remembered the two steps on the way out of her house, but they were exceptionally tricky on the way back in. As was the hallway. And the bathroom door. My one-too-many arms may have knocked a pot over somewhere along the way.

She settled me in the bath, then turned on the taps. Held my hand. Then my head.

A bit of my client in everything I make.

We were on the same wavelength.

A bit of my client…

…a bit.

About the Authors

Judith Bridge

Jude was most recently published in the anthology *Deceased Estates and other foul stories*. She was shortlisted in the Rachel Funari Prize 2023. Her flash fiction will appear in the 2024 Spineless Wonders anthology *Remnant*. She works at Curtin University Library and is still a hobbit.

Blanche Clark

Blanche dabbles in writing fiction while working full-time as a production editor. She is slowly completing her Bachelor of Media and Communications, with a major in Creative Writing.

Roxxy Bent

Roxxy is a founder of South Australia's Vitalstatistix Theatre Company. She has written wrote award winning plays for Vitals and other SA companies. A number of her plays have been published. She has also written for TV, worked as an actor and as a writer on community arts projects. Winning two Scarlet Stilettos, for best short crime fiction in 2002 & 2006, inspired her to take a Masters in Creative Writing. She has continued with the long-form, earning a Varuna Scholarship and a Text Publishing Fellowship for her novel, *The Pear Tree*.

Aoife Clifford

Aoife is the author of *All These Perfect Strangers*, which was long-listed for both the Australian Industry General Fiction Book of the Year and the Voss Literary Prize; *Second Sight*, a Publishers Weekly (starred review), PW Pick for Book of the Week and was Highly Commended at the Davitt Awards; and *When We Fall*, which was shortlisted for the Davitt Awards and the Ned Kelly Award for Best Crime Fiction.
Aoife's short stories have been published in Australia, United Kingdom and the United States, winning premier prizes such as the Scarlet Stiletto and the S.D. Harvey Award.

Liz Filleul

Liz is a writer and editor. Her short stories have appeared in *The People's Friend* in the UK, Woman's World in the USA, and in various anthologies in Australia, the UK and the USA. She won the Scarlet Stiletto Award in

2004, was runner-up in 2007, 2011 and 2016, and has also won the Cross-Genre and Mystery with History category prizes. She was a finalist in the 2023 Derringer Award – run by the Short Mystery Fiction Society in the USA – with 'Dead Men Tell No Tales', a short crime story set in 1830s Van Diemen's Land, originally published by *The People's Friend*. She also writes serials and features.

Candice Graham

In 2013, Candice Graham was studying her Masters in Clinical Neuropsychology when she won the Scarlet Stiletto Award. One year prior, she'd won the Catherine Leppert Best Environmental Theme Award with her first ever Scarlet Stiletto entry. Since then, Candice has spent many rewarding years working as a psychologist, primarily with children and young adults. She believes the time feels right, however, to start writing the multitude of novels brimming in her mind.

TJ Hamilton

TJ is a retired police officer, a criminologist, a published author, and now TV screenwriter. With a deep understanding of the crime genre, TJ is one of Australia's most sought-after technical consultants and story producers.

Winning the shoe in 2015 was a huge turning point in her career. Shortly after, she began studying screenwriting at AFTRS. Meeting actor Danielle Cormack, who presented the 2015 awards, proved to be a fruitful pathway into writers' rooms when she introduced TJ to other screenwriters. In the eight years since, she's worked in script departments for a variety of Australian dramas, including *Home and Away* during the Covid pandemic. In 2023, Hollywood came knocking, and she now on the development team in Los Angeles for a new TV show with one of Australia's most successful industry exports. She says none of this would have happened if she hadn't taken the plunge and entered the Scarlet Stiletto competition.

Rowena Harding-Smith

Rowena is a cross-genre writer with a preference for writing crime. She has been publishing and winning awards for her short stories, creative non-fiction and articles since 1994. In 2017 she won six awards, of which the most thrilling was the Scarlet Stiletto. Since then, she's continued to write and sell short stories but she's also written two (unpublished) thrillers and has embarked on a third. Her work has been featured on the ABC Radio National's Book Show, Earshot and most recently on Radio Melbourne.

Philomena Horsley

Philomena is a long-time member of Sisters in Crime and Facilitator of the Judges Panel for its Davitt Awards. She won the Scarlett Stiletto in 2018 and was runner up in 2019, while other entries have received Special Commendations. She is looking forward to publishing her first novel, an excerpt of which was long listed in the 2023 Geelong Writers Prize.

In her professional life, Philomena has authored an extensive and diverse range of health and community publications for the general public. She is a Medical Anthropologist who loves talking about autopsies and the joys of life in the Otways bush.

Jacqui Horwood

Jacqui is a librarian who lives in regional Victoria. She was an emerging writer working at Victoria Police and scratching away at short stories when she won the 2003 Scarlet Stiletto. In 2016, when she won the Silver Stiletto, she was an emerging writer who had two draft manuscripts and a number of published short stories under her belt. She was highly commended in the 2019 awards. The shoes have boosted her confidence and remind her that she can do it. She is still an emerging writer. She loves her crime hardboiled and her eggs sunny side up.

Cate Kennedy

Cate cut her short story writing teeth on the Scarlet Stiletto Awards in the early '90s, and has gone on to publish two collections of stories, a novel, three collections of poetry and a travel memoir. Short story is still her first love and she is an avid reader of crime fiction (she doesn't have a 'book problem', she has a 'shelving problem') and has taught creative writing and story structure in all its forms for many years.

She gained her PhD in Creative Writing in 2021 and currently mentors fiction students in the MFA program at Pacific University in Portland, Oregon. She has an unfinished and endlessly morphing crime novel in the works.

Christina Lee

Christina won the Scarlet Stiletto First Prize twice, much to her surprise, in 1992 and 1994, with an Honourable Mention or Third Place or something in between. They stopped letting her enter the competition after that, and she's have been on the Scarlet Stiletto judging panel every year since then. She still thinks this is a wonderful experience.

Christina has been writing a long time. Decades ago, she co-authored two crime novels, set in a Melbourne tertiary institution: Unable By Reason of Death, 1989; Not In Single Spies, 1992 (Penguin Australia). Both sold and reviewed well. The first was an ABC book reading (1990) and optioned for screen. After that, an all-encompassing thirty-year academic career seriously got in the way of writing for about thirty years, but she's an Emeritus Professor now and says she's back.

Ellie Marney

Ellie is a *New York Times* bestselling and multi-award-winning author of crime thrillers. Her eleven titles include smash hit *None Shall Sleep* and its Kirkus-starred sequel *Some Shall Break*, as well as *The Killing Code*, the 'Every' series, and *White Night*. She's spent a lifetime researching in mortuaries, interviewing autopsy specialists and law enforcement officers, and asking former spies how to make explosives from household items, and now she lives quite sedately north of Melbourne, Australia, with her family.

On the night she won the Scarlet Stiletto, she'd walked out of her flooded house (leaving aunt-supervised crying children, and a plumber investigating how a rat had had chewed through a pipe) and into the ceremony, hoping her outfit looked ironed. Her win for 'Tallow' win catapulted Ellie into a publishing contract, a debut novel, and what has turned into a long-term career. She couldn't be more grateful.

Siobhan Mullany

Siobhan is a Sydney based writer and a co-convenor of Sisters in Crime New South Wales. For over twenty years she worked as a criminal defence lawyer representing people charged with murder and terrorism offences. Her non-fiction has been published in legal journals and her short stories published by Sisters in Crime. She conducts writing workshops and is a lecturer in law.

Josephine Pennicott

Eleven years elapsed between Josephine's first Scarlet Stiletto shoe for 'Birthing the Demons' in 2001, and her second shoe for 'Shadows' in 2012. This taught her a lot about tenacity and belief in self. She'd already won Second Prize in 2000 for 'Bait'.

In between the two First Prize winning stories, she won the Kerry Greenwood Malice Domestic Award and Third Prize in 2003; the Malice Domestic Prize again in 2004; and Third Prize in 2005'. She also received

Special Commendations for four other stories in 2002, 2006 and 2009. As soon as she won her second Scarlet Stiletto First Prize trophy – like the other two-shoe winners before and after – she became a judge.

Winning the Scarlet Stiletto gained her attention from a major publishing company, which led to her securing a literary agent. Since then, she's had five books – *Currawong Manor, A Fire In The Shell, Bride Of The Stone*, and *Circle Of Nine* – published both in Australia and internationally. Her mystery novel *Poet's Cottage* was a Spiegel bestseller in Germany.

Fin J. Ross

Fin is a repeat offender, winning nine category prizes between 2014 and 2021, including setting the record of four category wins in one year. Those prizes were one Third Prize, two Environmental Crime, one Body in the Library (plus the runner-up in this category), one Forensic Linguistics, and one Cross Genre. Oh, and one commendation.

She finally kidnapped the coveted Scarlet Stiletto trophy at the 2022 awards with her entry, 'Tuesday Jocks'. Fin has two published novels – *A.K.A. Fudgepuddle* and *Billings Better Bookstore and Brasserie* – and several short stories in various anthologies. She's co-written three true crime anthologies with her sister, Lindy Cameron. She's also a mosaic artist, and teaches both writing and mosaics in her Paynesville studio.

Romany Rzechowicz

By day, Romany helps organisations share their true stories; by night, she writes not-quite-so-true stories that have been published in places like *The Canberra Times* and the Newcastle Short Story Award, as well as winning Furious Fiction. Winner of the 2023 Scarlet Stiletto, Romany lives on the land of the Ngunnawal and Ngambri people.

Angela Savage

Angela's debut novel, *Behind the Night Bazaar*, won the 2004 Victorian Premier's Literary Award for Unpublished Manuscript. She has won the Scarlet Stiletto Award for short fiction and was thrice shortlisted for Ned Kelly awards, with *The Dying Beach* also shortlisted for a Davitt Award. She is a contributor to the anthology, Deadlier: 100 Of The Best Crime Stories Written By Women, among others.

Angela holds a PhD in Creative Writing, giving her the Bond villain-like name of Doctor Savage. She currently works as CEO of Public Libraries Victoria. Her most recent novel is *Mother of Pearl*.

Jessica Southern-Reid

At the time of this publication, Jessica was putting fingers to keyboard on her latest manuscript while sitting on the cannon deck of a replica 18th century tall ship in the midst of a North Atlantic storm. What started as a distraction from real life led to falling in love with the sea and a series of novels set on the ship. She now knows what it is like to look down from the top of a 47m mainmast onto the heaving ocean below. She now knows what it is to have her whole world reduced to the size of a ship. And she now knows that there is nothing better in the world for writer's block. That and the complete lack of internet access, of course.

Jessica travelled the world for several years before covid clipped her wings, but once home in Australia she took her first flying lesson. This led to 'Death in the Skies', her 2020 award winning entry, which she has since expanded into a novel.

Janis Spehr

Janis lives in northern Victoria. She has published five story collections and a novel with Ginninderra Press. She is currently writing her second novel, *The Blue Door*. Her writing journey has taken her away from crime fiction but she retains fond memories of the Scarlet Stiletto. She won first prize two years on a trot, 1999 and 2000.

Evelyn Tsitas

Evelyn is writer and curator whose research in the Gothic, body horror and the visual arts informs her writing, and vice versa. Her published and performed works range across fiction, nonfiction, stage and journalism. She curated the exhibitions Future U (2021), Pleasure (2019) and My Monster: The Human Animal Hybrid (2018) at RMIT Gallery.

Julie Waight

Back in 2005, Julie entered the Sisters in Crime Short Story Competition for the first time and astonishingly, according to her, that story Dust Devils won first place.

She was the first Australian writer to win the Science Fiction Writers' of Earth Science Fiction and Fantasy Award in 2002 for a short story titled, The Overcoat. Another short story was accepted for inclusion in the Celapene Press anthology *Short and Twisted*. She has written a fantasy novel, *Kindred*, a crime novel, *A Stab in the Dark,* four other novels and over fifty short stories.

Amanda Wrangles

Back in 2009, when Amanda won the shoe with her story 'Persia Bloom', the ex-hairdresser/ex-dive-master was busy being Mum to three young boys. Winning the award on her first attempt gave Amanda the courage to continue writing, going on to be short-listed for the Scarlet Stiletto a further three times, to participate on the judging panel for two years, and co-write a novel with Kylie Fox – published by Clan Destine Press; and a number of other short stories in various anthologies over the years.

These days, Amanda's sons are grown young men, and she loves her work at a local primary school and taking on art commissions. However, her hairdressing alter-ego Persia Bloom is still knocking around, nagging to become a fully-fledged novel.

Ruth Wykes

Ruth is an author and editor who lives on the Mornington Peninsula. Ruth has co-authored two true crime books: *Women Who Kill* with Lindy Cameron and *Invisible Women* with Kylie Fox. Ruth works as an independent editor and is currently writing fiction. In her previous life in Perth, Ruth owned a monthly lesbian magazine, *Women Out West*, which she published for almost a decade.

In 2023 Ruth was on the judging panel for the Davitt Awards, became a national convenor of Sisters in Crime Australia.

Hayley Young

Hayley lives in Canberra with her family and enjoys writing across multiple genres. In 2021, she was at work (sneaking a snack) when she returned a missed call to learn she had won the 28th Sisters in Crime Scarlet Stiletto Award, and the Scriptworks Award for a Great Film Idea. Winning inspired further dedication to her love of writing, and in 2022 her success was followed by Second Prize as well as the Best Thriller Award in the 29th Scarlet Stiletto Awards. She was also the winner of the inaugural ACWA Louie Award 2022, and Audio Arcadia and MNC Writers' Centre short story competitions in 2021.

She has been published in multiple Australian and international works, including four anthologies by Stringybark Publishing, and two shortlisted entries in the Hammond House International Literary Competition (UK). She is currently working on three novels.

2016

The Silver Stiletto

Cate Kennedy won the the inaugural Scarlet Stiletto Award in 1994. When she won First Prize again in 1995 – and Third Prize for another story – the judges were amazed and thrilled for her. And then thought, '*Uh-oh* we've discovered a talent, created a monster; is this going to be the annual Cate Kennedy competition?'

To stop that possibility in its tracks, Sisters in Crime "banned" her from entering again, and asked her to be a judge of the Scarlet Stilettos instead. She took up the challenge.

Remember, the stories are read blind. The judges have no idea who has written what.

Over the next couple of decades the improbable and wonderful happened another four times. The other entrants, who became known as the "two-shoe winners", were also banned and invited to judge.

Those double trophy winners are: Janis Spehr, Roxxy Bent, Josephine Pennicot and Christina Lee.

In 2016, to celebrate *SheKilda 3* – the third weekend crime convention run by Sisters in Crime – they offered a special prize category only open to First Prize shoe winners, which meant for one year only the five recidivists – and the other first prize trophy winners – could compete against each other for a Silver Stiletto.

The honour that year went to a single-shoe winner, Jacqui Horwood, for her story 'Diving for Pearls'.

DIVING FOR PEARLS

Jacqui Horwood

I TIGHTENED THE BELT AROUND MY COAT AGAINST THE ICY WIND AND MARCHED down Collins Street. Plastic bags of new clothes banged against my legs. For the first time in ages, I was feeling positive. I just had to nail my job interview on Monday and I'd finally be starting a new life after a decade of dead-end jobs.

Two weeks ago I'd woken up on the morning of my 30th birthday and realised I was technically homeless and my bank account was so red, it practically glowed. A giant kick up the bum that had made me vow I would break out of my comfort zone and embrace fearlessness.

I turned into Spencer Street, finally escaping the wind tunnel, and headed towards the station. Above me, heavy grey clouds gathered to discuss their party plans. I burrowed my head into my collar and kept walking.

A nearby door swung open and I caught a snippet of music and chatter. A small bar sat snugly between a 7-Eleven and an abandoned Thai-massage shop. I couldn't remember ever seeing it before. I glanced through the window at the inviting burgundy walls and dark wood panelling. Maybe I could have a quick drink to celebrate my new beginnings. That was something a bold career woman would do.

I walked through the door just as another person was heading in. The guy was tall and broad shouldered. His dark hair curled over his ears and his cheeks needed a shave. He had a big black duffle bag slung over one shoulder. The guy gave me the once-over. I glared at him and let him walk ahead of me.

The new arrival headed for the bar. He turned to me.

'What can I get you?'

I shook my head. 'I'm fine, thanks.'

'Come on, one drink,' he said and then he gave me a slow smile. 'I don't bite.'

I bristled at the idea that he scared me and thrust out my chin.

'Fine. I'll have a chardonnay.'

'A pot and a chardonnay,' he said to the girl behind the bar.

Drinks in hand, we sat at a nearby empty table. The guy pushed his bag under his seat with his foot.

'Dale,' he said. He smiled that smile again.

'Natalie,' I replied, raising a glass. We took sips. I glanced down at the duffle bag covered with tags and nudged it with my foot.

'You travelling?' I asked. He edged the bag further under his chair.

'Yeah, just down from Sydney,' he said. 'Supposed to be meeting a mate here.'

'How long are you in Melbourne for?'

'Couple of days, maybe. I'm just passing through.' He took a sip of beer. 'How about you, Natalie? What's your story?'

I shrugged. 'Not much to tell. I'm sort of between jobs at the moment. How about you? What do you do?'

'This and that. Bit of security. Odd jobs.'

This and that. Security. Odd jobs. What was that supposed to mean? I lapsed into silence and sipped my wine. Dale checked his watch.

'My mate's meant to be coming now. He's late.' He slugged the last of his beer. 'Want another one?'

'No thanks, I'll just have the one.'

'Come on, Natalie. I don't want to drink alone,' Dale said. He tilted his head at me and I couldn't help noticing his chocolate brown eyes.

'Okay, just one more.'

I watched Dale at the bar. Admired his shoulders. He was probably as shifty as hell but I wasn't planning on going home with him. He sat down and I smiled at him over my glass.

'Thanks.'

I asked him about his travels and the conversation started to flow. Dale had a dry sense of humour and, under the dishevelled exterior, there was a sharp mind. As we spoke, though, he had a habit of scanning the room. Not like he was checking out other women. Like he was making sure of who was around him. As new people arrived, Dale would duck his head until they walked past. It unsettled me and a niggling little voice suggested it might be better if I called it a night. Before I could wind things up, Dale leapt to his feet and ordered more drinks. He kept me talking and before I knew it, hours and beers had passed. There was no sign of Dale's mate.

'What's happened to your friend?' I asked. Dale shrugged.

'Looks like I've been stood up,' he said. 'You hungry?'

'Yeah, I am a bit.'

'How about we go to your place and order pizza?' he suggested, one eyebrow raised. The sense of disquiet from earlier in the evening hadn't completely left me and I shook my head.

'How about we find somewhere in town?' I said. Dale gave me a slow smile that warmed me all over.

'Come on, Natalie. One pizza and I'll be gone,' he said. I bit my bottom lip. Maybe this was what being fearless was about. Taking chances. Dale was gorgeous. Why shouldn't I take him home? It would only be for a quick dinner.

'Okay, my house isn't far from here.'

Dale picked up his bag. 'Sounds good. Let's go.'

We grabbed a taxi and headed to my place in Kensington. My place. Listen to me, will you? The house was someone else's and I was housesitting. In a few days Olivia the owner would be home from swanning around provincial France and I'd move from being technically homeless to being actually homeless. All the more reason for me to start my new life.

I opened the door to the little red-brick house and ushered in Dale. In a fit of short-lived energy, I had thankfully spent that afternoon cleaning up. I pointed to an open door in the hallway.

'That's my room. You can put your bag in there.' Dale stepped in and swung his bag under my bed.

In the lounge room, I cleared a place to sit amongst the patchwork cushions, Olivia's cats and a pile of old newspapers.

'Beer?'

'Sounds good,' he said, following me into the kitchen. He leaned his hips on the sink as I fossicked in the fridge and the cupboards.

'Nice place,' commented Dale. 'What's out there?' I turned and found him peering out the back window into the inky darkness.

'A little courtyard. Gate to the laneway out the back.' Dale grunted and nodded. I found a packet of chips and a couple of Coronas.

'Sorry, no lime slices,' I said as I handed him a bottle. I shook the chips into a plastic bowl and we headed back to the lounge.

Dale dropped onto the couch and tilted his beer at me. 'Cheers.' I settled at a safe distance beside him and clinked my bottle on his. Silence settled as we drank.

'So, what are you planning to do in Melbourne?' I asked.

'No plans,' answered Dale with a shrug. 'Just keep a low profile and enjoy what this place has to offer.'

'There must be something you want to do?' I asked. He put his bottle down on the coffee table and moved closer.

'Actually there is something I'd like to do.' He pressed his lips against mine and I stiffened but, as he kissed me, I felt my body soften into his. I breathed in the scent of skin and beer and cotton, and returned his kiss. His hands ran over my hips and thighs. My fingertips stroked his cheeks. I hadn't known this guy for very long and wasn't even sure whether I trusted him. I closed my eyes and let his lips run down my neck.

I flipped myself onto my back and stretched out my arm, expecting to find a warm, willing body. Instead my fingers fell on cold sheets. I opened my eyes. The bed was empty.

'Dale?' I rolled onto my side and listened. The house was silent. I wrapped a ratty terry towelling dressing gown around me and wandered down to the kitchen. I hoped I'd find Dale making tea and toast, and not rifling through my belongings with an intent to steal. I found neither.

Back in my room, I checked under my bed. Nothing there but little dust bunnies. I scanned the bedside tables for a note. Nothing. Dale had gone and he'd left without a word.

'Bastard.' Was this how one night stands usually ended? With abandonment? I could feel the creep of disappointment so I picked myself up and got moving. Fearless women didn't dwell. Time for a shower and my weekly trip to the market.

The doorbell rang just as I was pulling on my runners. On the other side of the security screen door was a tall, skinny man with greasy hair. He sniffed and jiggled on the spot.

'Yes?' I asked cautiously. I could smell grime and the jitters on him.

'Huggo there?' he asked, trying to peer through the flywire screen. A wave of rancid breath nearly knocked me off my feet.

'Huggo? I don't know any Huggo,' I said, getting ready to close the door. The guy made a strange gurgling sound and it took me a beat to realise he was laughing.

'The guy you were shagging last night,' he said.

'Dale?'

'Yeah, Dale or whoever he says he is.'

A tide of nausea tickled my throat. I didn't like where this was going. Who the hell was Dale and how had the guy at my front door known Dale had been at the house?

'He's not here. He left this morning,' I said loudly, trying to mask my panic with bravado.

'What?' said the man, his eyes wide. 'Bastard.' The guy flexed his hands, itching for something to pummel.

'Tell that little shit-for-brains that Razor wants to see him. Tell him that Razor knows everything that goes on in Melbourne.'

'Razor?' I said, my stomach churning. 'Why Razor? Is that, like, your weapon of choice?'

Razor frowned at me as if I was nuts. 'Nah, that's my surname.'

'Well, I don't know if I'll see Dale again but I'll pass on the message if I do,' I said and closed the door. I leaned my forehead against the cool wood, listening to my heart hammer against my ribs. What had I walked into? I'd guessed that Dale was shady but this was ridiculous. This was the first and last time I'd ever pick up a guy at a bar.

I pulled open my bedroom curtain. Razor had crossed the road and jumped into a gleaming silver Cortina circa 1972. Razor may not have been into personal hygiene but he certainly looked after his wheels. He sat in the front seat and crossed his arms. It looked as if he was settling in to wait for Dale. I contemplated calling the police but wasn't sure if that would be asking for more unwanted attention. One thing was for sure, I had to get out of the house. I was starting to feel trapped but there was no way I was going to leave via the front door and advertise to Razor the house was empty. He'd be inside before I turned the corner at the end of the street. It'd be better if I used the rear access. Small drops of rain splattered against the window. Heavy grey clouds rolled overheard.

'Bugger.' I'd have to wear my boots. I closed the blinds on the front windows so Razor couldn't see my movements.

I rummaged under my bed for my boots but came up empty handed. I couldn't remember when I'd last seen them. I pulled open the cupboard door and dived into its black-hole-like depths to see what I could find. Shoes, dirty socks, T-shirts I'd thrown aside. My fingers brushed against something more solid. I pushed my jackets aside to see what it was.

Dale's rucksack. I frowned. When had he put his bag into the cupboard? Did this mean he was coming back? I pulled out the bag and dragged it into the middle of the bedroom. It was black and soiled like it had been on a million trips. His name tag was tied to one of the handles. I crouched down and flicked it over. Damien Hugginson. Great. I ran a finger up the zipper. What the hell was going on?

Stuff him. I unzipped the bag and peered in.

'Shit.' I fell back onto my bum. The bag was filled with smelly clothes and money. Bundles and bundles of money. I scrambled backwards on my hands and feet before standing and walking a couple of figure eights around the room. This explained why Razor was sitting outside the house.

What was I going to do? I licked my lips and considered my options. In front of me was a bag of undoubtedly ill-gotten cash. Outside was one angry crim and somewhere nearby was Dale. My well-honed risk-averse side argued that I should push the bag back into the cupboard and play dumb. Let Dale come back and retrieve it, and wave him good-bye. My new fearless side yelled at me. Loudly. It told me the bag represented a new start. The opportunity to get out of Melbourne and try my luck elsewhere. This voice told me to take my chances. I stood rooted to the spot, immobilised by indecision and doubt.

When I was little and showed any sign of timidity, my grannie used to say, 'You don't find pearls on the beach, love. You gotta go dive for them.'

Apparently it was a Chinese proverb. Goodness knows where she got it from. Probably read it in one of her Reader's Digests.

Do it, screamed my new voice. Dive for pearls.

If I was going to do that, I was going to have to act fast.

I peeked out of the curtains. Razor still hadn't moved. A newspaper was spread out over the Cortina's steering wheel. He wasn't going anywhere in a hurry.

Right, how was I going to go about this? Bags, I needed bags. I scavenged in the cupboard for my backpack. Fortunately I didn't have too many personal items to worry about. I threw all my clothes, shoes, books and toiletries into a bonfire pyre at the end of the bed. I considered the two bags and decided to swap them over. With shaking hands, I took the bundles of money out of Dale's bag and put them into my backpack. The bundles were mainly orange and yellow. There were thousands of dollars in my sweaty palms. I put a jacket, and my purse and mobile phone on top of the stash. The rest of my stuff went into the roomy confines of Dale's duffle bag, and his stuff was pushed into the nether regions of the cupboard.

I did a quick tidy of the bedroom and made my bed. I emptied all of the dry cat food into one of the cats' dishes and filled the other with water. After a quick rummage through Olivia's desk, I found a pen and paper and scrawled a message, claiming that the ill health of my mother had sent me home prematurely. One more scan of the house and I was out the back door and into the courtyard.

I opened the back gate in a slow arc, poked my head out and looked right. The alleyway was quiet, the bluestones slick with rain and bordered by ruffles of autumn leaves. I stepped out and turned left. A blue Commodore was blocking the laneway, its boot and driver's car door were open and the motor running. I shook my head. The place was full of idiots. I wriggled my shoulders, adjusting the weight of the backpack, and tightened my grip on Dale's duffle bag.

The soft whisper of shoes across the bluestones stopped me and I hesitated, the hairs on the back of my neck stiffening.

'Going somewhere?'

My heart froze. I turned to find Dale with a gun in his hand. The gun was levelled at me. I sucked in a mouthful of air and almost choked. I wanted to look for an escape route but I was too scared to take my eyes off Dale.

'Where have you been?' I asked without really wanting to know the answer.

'Out stealing a car,' he said. 'I can see what you've been up to.'

He moved towards me, his gun hand rock steady. His chocolate brown eyes now just looked as hard as flint, and the sexy smile was nowhere to be seen. My lower body turned to water and I almost buckled over.

'Who are you?' I said, stalling for time. I listened out for signs of other people. Surely there was someone nearby. The only person who could help me out of this was sitting in a silver Cortina in the next street.

'Never you mind,' said Dale. He flicked the gun towards the car and I flinched. 'Throw the bag in the boot.'

I did as he ordered and then backed away. Hopefully he'd get in the car and drive off.

'Where do you think you're going?' he said. 'In the boot you go.'

My vision flashed black and red. This was no good. If I got in that boot, I was as good as dead.

Behind me, the engine of the Commodore was still grumbling. My fearless little voice told me I had to take my chances or die in a car boot. I lunged at the open car door. My backpack was still clamped to my body and I felt like a turtle as I sat down and ripped off the hand brake. Dale screamed my name as I floored the brakes and hurtled towards the end of the alley, the car boot flapping like a bird's wing before slamming shut.

I could see Dale in the rear view mirror, running and trying to level his gun at the car. I wasn't interested in driving anywhere. I just wanted to hand Dale over to Razor. I turned left into Macaulay Road, narrowly missing oncoming traffic and then turned left again into my street. I pulled up, leapt out of the car and ran towards the Cortina.

'Razor,' I screamed. 'Razor.'

Razor looked up from the paper. He squinted through the front window, trying to work out who the hell was calling his name. I pointed behind me.

'It's Huggo,' I yelled. 'He's here.'

Dale must have rounded the corner because Razor's face lit up. He threw aside the paper and started up the car engine. I stopped running and whizzed around. Dale recognised the car and scrambled to get into the Commodore. He was pulling a U-turn just as Razor screamed past me. The Commodore tore into Macaulay Road with the silver streak in hot pursuit.

I stumbled off the road and leaned against a fence with my eyes closed for a moment. I waited until my legs stopped trembling. My forehead was damp with sweat. I couldn't believe what I'd just done. Was taking chances always going to be this hazardous? I had to get moving. Razor and Dale weren't going to be happy when they discovered the duffle bag was full of my dirty undies. I began running on unsteady legs to Kensington station.

I jumped on the first train into the city. I had no real plans, only the desire to get out of Victoria and go somewhere warm. Somewhere with a beach.

And maybe pearls.

ALSO FROM CLAN DESTINE PRESS

Clan Destine also publishes the eBooks of the winning category stories from 1994 to... forever and a day.

A selection of stories from 1994 to 2010 appeared in *Scarlet Stiletto the First Cut* and *Scarlet Stiletto the Second Cut*, then all category winners were eBook-published annually.

The Fifteenth Cut of all the 2023 winners coincides with the 30th anniversary paperback of thirty years of First Prize stories.

www.ingramcontent.com/pod-product-compliance
Lightning Source LLC
Chambersburg PA
CBHW022207010726
47493CB00002B/448